THE ROGUE RETRIEVAL

DAN KOBOLDT

HARPER
VOYAGER
IMPULSE

An Imprint of HarperCollins *Publishers*

EPub Edition JANUARY 2016 ISBN: 9780062451903

Print Edition ISBN: 9780062451910

10 9 8 7 6 5 4 3

To Betty Dietrich (Nanny), the first true believer.

> **"I never leave home without three things. A deck of cards, a pair of shades, and an eye for easy marks."**
>
> —ART OF ILLUSION, AUGUST 19

CHAPTER 1

DISAPPEARANCE

On the night of his strange job offer, Quinn Bradley was making things disappear. He worked nights at an off-Strip theater in Las Vegas, where show magicians came in two classes. One was the quick-fingered hack, the kind that copied everyone's tricks to use on drunken tourists. The second class, the true illusionist, ran less common. Illusionists were magic's elite, masters of distraction and misdirection. The Strip drew both classes from all over the world, just as its game tables and bright lights drew ill-fated gamblers.

It was Saturday night—show night in Vegas—and the club was packed. Word about Quinn's new trick must have gotten around. The crowd was a typical Vegas mix: mostly marks, most of them drunk. Half a dozen of the more persistent copycats. And talent scouts from three major casinos, easily picked out as the sober guys wearing two-thousand-dollar suits.

Quinn surveyed the audience from a hidden alcove backstage. *About damn time the casinos started scouting me.*

He'd been a second act off the Strip for nearly two years. Countless hours of practice and training and equipment design. They'd ignored him as long as they could, because he was from here. Recruiting him wouldn't bring the fanfare of nabbing a performer from New York or London.

But they can't ignore me any longer.

"Quinn Bradley?"

A man in a dark suit stood behind him. He was tall, and wore the suit well. Light hair, delicate features, and that youthful clean-shaven look of Nordic ancestry.

"You shouldn't be back here," Quinn said. Backstage was off-limits to everyone. The last thing he wanted was some wannabe poking around his props and equipment.

"We need to talk." He had a faint accent, definitely European, but Quinn couldn't place it.

"I don't know you."

"I'm Lars Thorisson." He offered his hand.

Quinn ignored it. He wasn't about to let a stranger touch his hand two minutes before a performance. "Did you say Thor's son?"

"Thorisson. It's Swedish."

And I'm probably not interested. The last thing he needed was a distraction. "I'm about to go on."

"You're going to get a job offer tonight."

"I certainly hope so."

"You shouldn't take it."

"Why not?"

"The company behind the offer . . .". Thorisson began. He glanced behind him, lowered his voice. "Let's just say you don't want to get in bed with them."

Quinn could have smiled. He knew what this was. "Oh, but I suppose your employer can make a better offer."

"I'm not here to make an offer."

"Then I'm not sure why we're talking."

"I'm doing you a favor, Mr. Bradley. Here." Thorisson snapped his fingers once. A playing card appeared in his fingers. Jack of spades. Decent sleight of hand, for an amateur. He held it out.

"Not bad," Quinn said. He took the card, and knew right away it wasn't a normal. Too heavy, and not enough flex. "What is this?"

"A way to get in touch. When you realize you're in over your head, push down on the jack's face," Thorisson said.

"I'll think about it." Quinn made as if to tuck the card behind his ear, palmed it into his sleeve.

If Thorisson was impressed, he didn't show it. "You'll regret taking their offer," he said. "Trust me."

Quinn chuckled. "I grew up in Vegas. I don't trust anyone."

The noise in the theater picked up. Quinn looked out, saw that the emcee was ready for him. When he turned back, the man in the suit was gone. The emcee's voice boomed an introduction.

"Here he is, folks. Quinn Thomas!"

Quinn Thomas wasn't much different from Quinn Bradley, but in Vegas, you never gave away anything for free.

He smoothed the jacket of his tuxedo one more time, and took the stage. He felt all of their eyes on him. The energy in the room was palpable; even the drunks were quiet. His breathing was too quick, and he was sweating. Damn that guy in the suit. He couldn't afford to screw this up. Not with the scouts watching how he handled himself, how he engaged the crowd. A bad performance in Vegas could kill your career. Quinn had no family, no job prospects, no dreams. The career was all he had. But he couldn't show that.

It was all part of the illusion.

The drab theater had one redeeming feature: a massive bay window that looked out over the desert to the lights of the Vegas Strip. The marks seemed to enjoy a view of why they'd come to the city of sin. For Quinn, it was a constant reminder of what he wanted. What he worked for. They were all there, framed in the glass: The Mirage, Treasure Island, Mandalay Bay. Glowing in the night, waiting.

"Ladies and gentlemen, I have an announcement," Quinn said. He spread his arms wide, as if in apology.

"You're not on the Vegas Strip." Light laughter from the crowd. Maybe a few looks of genuine surprise.

"Don't worry!" Quinn said. "You made the right decision, coming here." He flashed a grin. "Who'd like to see a magic trick?"

The audience cheered. He got it started with some parlor tricks. Humor and sleight of hand, for the most part. He pulled a watermelon out of a top hat; the audience always loved that one. It wasn't exactly groundbreaking, but ten minutes of small stuff got them warmed up for the main event.

He doubted they were ready for *this*.

Stagehands delivered Quinn's only prop, a brass candelabra with eight unlit candles. Quinn held up both of his hands, palms out, to show that they were empty. This part was all about building the audience's trust; in the business, it was called "the prove." He lowered them over the candles, clapped once, and spread them wide. Eight wicks burst into flame. Simple sleight of hand, but the audience ate it up.

"My favorite thing about magic is that it's completely unbiased," Quinn said. "It goes wherever the magician goes." He gestured to the window. "You didn't go to the Strip tonight for your entertainment. You came here instead."

That was his cue for the stagehands; they dimmed the lights. The audience could only see the candles, Quinn, and the window behind him.

"And the magic did, too," he said.

He raised a hand over the left-most candle. "It's not at The Venetian." He snapped once; the flame went out. And behind him, The Venetian's elegant columns, unmistakable on the Vegas Strip, winked out of view. A few members of the audience gasped, tugged at their neighbors, pointing.

"Nor at Treasure Island," Quinn continued. Another snap, and the sprawling pirate-themed casino fell into darkness. The audience was buzzing now. One by one the candles went out, and with each, a landmark casino disappeared as well. Caesar's Palace. The Bellagio. MGM Grand. When Quinn extinguished the last candle, most of the Las Vegas Strip was dark.

There was no keeping people in their seats. They crowded the stage, pressing forward to the window. Velvet ropes kept them back just enough. Quinn stole a glance at the casino scouts. They were trying to keep the excitement from their faces and failing badly at it. One of them took out a phone and dialed, probably to check on his home casino.

Stagehands guided the audience back to their seats. The emcee announced Quinn's name again; he bowed. At that moment, all of the casinos on the Strip popped back into view. The applause was thunderous. He'd always loved that sound. He let out the last half-breath he'd been holding. He'd done it.

The theater owner waited for him offstage. Rudolph "Rudy" Fortelli was fifty pounds overweight and perpetually sweating over a bad spray tan. He'd grown infamous in Vegas for a vicious self-inflicted business cycle. Step one, buy an old theater and fix it up enough to attract a good show. Step two, marry the show's starlet. Step three, lose both in a nasty divorce. Rudy had backed a new horse in Quinn, but a good one. Club profits had more than doubled.

Good thing I'm not the marrying kind.

"Incredible, Quinn. Just incredible!" the man gushed. They shook hands.

"Aw," Quinn said. He waved off the compliment. "You put together a great audience."

"We're having a good night. The bar's doing well." Rudy wiped his hands on his sports jacket, suddenly nervous. "I—I think I spotted some scouts in the audience," he said.

"Were there?" Quinn asked. He couldn't hide his smile.

Rudy's face fell. "You wouldn't leave me, would you?"

"I don't know what I'm going to do yet," Quinn said. It depended on what the scouts said, what offers they made.

Rudy's eyes had the sheen of desperation. "I'll double your pay. Triple it!"

"It's not about the money," Quinn said, and it was true. He'd worked for years to have this shot. To see his name in the neon lights.

Rudy buried his face in his hands. "Oh, God! It's— it's happening again!"

He seemed a little bit pitiful, and Quinn felt for him. Rudy had given him a gig when the casinos wouldn't even talk to him. He put an arm around the sweaty man, steering him back toward his office. "You'll be just fine. I've got my replacement lined up already."

"No, no. Won't be the same," Rudy moaned.

"It'll be better," Quinn promised. "She's the real deal. I wouldn't leave you with anything less."

Rudy looked up. "Did you say 'she'?"

Quinn laughed. "Don't even think about it! Now, change your shirt and let's go bask in the crowd."

He was going to enjoy himself a little bit, for once. It felt like the first deep breath he'd taken since his parents had died. He could still see the disappointment on their faces when they asked if he'd made it yet. If he'd done something with his life. Finally, he'd be able to say that he had, even if it was far too late to tell them.

The audience gradually cleared out, filing like automatons to the bar or to the slot machines. Quinn signed a few autographs, shook hands, and made nice with those who came up. All the while, he kept his eyes on the three casino scouts. They were on their phones, which he took for a good sign.

Near the back of the theater, a man and a woman were also sticking around. They weren't regulars; Quinn could tell that right away—you learn to size up marks in an instant if you're going to get anywhere in this racket. He noticed the suits weren't flashy enough for anyone in the entertainment business. Good posture on both of them, though. Beyond that, they were a mismatched pair. The black guy looked like a linebacker, right down to the military buzz cut. He cased the room constantly, but was casual about it. The woman was tiny by comparison, but more business-like. And watching Quinn like a bird of prey.

The scouts got up and started working their way to the front. He felt a thrill in his stomach. Three of them coming to talk to him at the same time. He was going to have a bidding war on his hands. He only hoped Rudy got back in time to savor the moment.

Still, the couple at the back kept distracting him. She had something metallic in her hand. Bigger than a phone, smaller than a tablet. She hadn't recorded him with it; he'd have noticed. She seemed to tap out a brief message before putting it away.

Almost simultaneously, three phones rang in the pockets of three expensive suits. The casino scouts halted in their casual circling and answered.

That can't be good.

He watched each of their faces flicker from puzzle-ment to acquiescence. They turned in their tracks and made for the door.

"What the hell?" Quinn muttered. Damn it, they'd been on their way up to him! He thought about going after them, but there was no time. They were already out the door.

Had someone burned his trick? No, that wasn't pos-sible. In his early years, he'd fumbled an illusion or two. He knew the way the audience changed, when they figured it out. That hadn't happened tonight. If anything, it was the best show he'd ever given.

He felt like he'd been punched in the gut. There went the bidding war and the competing offers. His promising future. Poof. Gone. As quick and inexplicably as one of his own tricks.

He sat in a chair at the front of the theater, waiting for Rudy. Replaying the whole performance in his head. The audience reactions, the applause. Everything had been perfect. But the scouts were gone. A shadow fell over him and he looked up. "Rudy—"

But it wasn't the owner. It was the big guy from the back of the theater. He was over six feet, and had to weigh at least two-fifty. All of it muscle.

"Good show, Mr. Bradley," he said.

"Do I know you?" Quinn asked. That the guy knew his name, his real name, put him off. Then it dawned on him that the Swedish guy had known it, too.

What the hell's going on tonight?

"My name's Logan. My boss would like a word."

Quinn stood up, and tried to balance the glimmer of hope with caution. "Absolutely. Let me grab the theater owner, and—"

"No need for that," Logan said. He put a massive hand on Quinn's shoulder and steered him down the aisle. "Let's just have a quick chat."

Damn. He'd really hoped to have Rudy around, to help drive up the price. To make them work for it a little. *A little turnabout is only fair.*

As he walked, Quinn sized up the man next to him a bit more. Logan was a little older than he'd thought at first glance. Maybe mid-thirties. His suit was tailored, too. More expensive than it looked. Quinn glimpsed something in the inside pocket, some kind of metal case. A chance to get one ahead, where any decent magician wanted to be. So he stumbled and half fell against him. "Oh, sorry."

Logan put him back on his feet and kept moving, as if nothing had even happened. "That vanishing act was impressive. What was it? A mirror? A plate of glass?"

"Come on, man." Quinn couldn't help but grin; this was something he understood. "You know better than to ask that."

"High-def video, looped back to the audience."

He shook his head. "I'm not going to tell you."

"Maybe you'll write about it on Art of Illusion."

His blog about magic. He wrote it under a pseudonym, and he'd been careful about not linking it to his real-world identity. He gave Logan a side-eyed look. "Now it's my turn to be impressed."

Logan looked as if he couldn't care less.

They approached the woman who had remained seated in her chair. She watched him the whole time, but kept her poker face on. She seemed a bit older than Logan, maybe forty. There was something brusque about her, though. Maybe it was the stiff-backed way she sat there. Her look was a cold one.

Not a lot of magic in her life, that was for damn sure.

So what the hell does she want with me?

This had better not be another waste of his time. Everything was going sideways tonight. There's nothing a magician hates more than being one behind.

"My name is Kiara," she said. "Is there somewhere we could speak in private?"

She was far too direct for someone in the business, and it threw Quinn off a little. His heart sank, too. Anyone from the Strip would know how to play the game. "Well . . . I suppose there's Rudy's office," he said.

"The theater owner."

"Yes. It's backstage."

She made eye contact with Logan and gave a little tilt of the head. He pressed Quinn down into a seat and went backstage. Quick on his feet, for a guy his size.

"Are you with one of the casinos?" Quinn asked. Even though he knew the answer already.

"Not exactly."

Logan reappeared and gave her some kind of signal. She brushed past without looking at him. "Come along, Mr. Bradley."

His name again. This whole thing was starting to worry him. He followed her backstage, where they found the office empty. Rudy's sweaty shirt lay haphazardly across the cluttered desk; it looked like he'd left in a hurry. Kiara settled into his worn leather chair. Quinn slid past the desk, and took the chair facing hers. Logan seemed content to stand in the doorway and just sort of loom there. He made the tiny office seem even smaller than it was.

"I feel like I'm in some kind of trouble," Quinn said. He watched Kiara's face for any hint of confirmation. Nothing.

"Just the opposite," Kiara said. "We're here to offer you a job."

Thank God.

A job offer. As long as it wasn't the one he'd been warned about. Although at this point, he wasn't sure he was in a position to be picky. They didn't need to know that, though. "I already have one."

Kiara swept a few empty soda cans into the overflowing trash can. She wrinkled her nose, the first hint of expression he'd seen from her. "From what we just saw, I think you can do better."

"It's for triple what I'm making right now." That was sort of true.

"Money is not a problem."

That got his attention. Sure, he wanted the Strip more than anything. But if three casinos walked out tonight, it just might not be his time.

A lot of money could take the sting out of that. "All right," Quinn said. "What's the job?"

"A six-month engagement."

He frowned a little. That was shorter than he wanted, and awfully vague. "Where?"

"I'm not currently at liberty to say," Kiara said. "It's nowhere that you've been before. A completely new audience."

Outside of Vegas, then. His disappointment warred with curiosity. "I'm going to need more than that."

"Five hundred thousand."

Quinn blinked, not sure he'd heard it right. "I'm sorry?"

"Five hundred thousand, for six months. Plus we'll cover the expenses of any equipment you require for your *performance*."

She hit the last word hard. Gave it a special meaning, though he couldn't guess why. But sweet Jesus, that was a lot of money. Too much, maybe.

"That's quite an offer," he said. And he waited. There had to be a catch.

"There are certain conditions, of course," Kiara said.

Quinn smiled. "Of course."

"The first and most important is a nondisclosure agreement."

"That's no problem. I sign those all the time."

"Not this kind of NDA. You won't be able to tell anyone about the work you do for us. And you'll be completely incommunicado during the engagement."

"*What?*"

That was ridiculous. A performance without any credit wouldn't help him at all. He remembered the foreign guy again. The one who'd given him the odd warning before the show.

"That's a little unusual," he said. *It's insane*, he wanted to say.

"So is the money we're talking about."

"You could buy out any magician in Vegas for that much," he said. "Why me?"

She glanced at Logan, and seemed to think it over. "You're not very well known, for starters."

"Thanks a lot."

"And you build your own equipment, correct?"

"Yes." That was no small thing, either. It saved money but it took a lot of time. Which is part of why he'd spent five years getting this far.

"Not to mention the fact that you're one of only a handful of magicians who passed the background check," Logan added.

Quinn hadn't seen that one coming. "You ran a background check on me?"

"Of course," Kiara said. She didn't sound apologetic about it, either. "That's how we know your real name. And that you're half-Lebanese."

He curled his lip in half a snarl. "No, I'm not."

"Your mother wasn't from Beirut?"

Jesus, they *had* been thorough. He kept that little part of the family legacy under wraps. Not even Rudy knew about it. "I was born here. I'm as American as you are."

"Well, we checked everyone, if that makes you feel better."

It didn't, but Quinn figured he'd save the full speech for the next time he was "randomly" searched by airport security. He supposed a background check wasn't too surprising, given how freely available that information was. He'd run a few himself.

Besides, they *probably* wouldn't have found anything.

"I'll need a couple days to think it over," he said.

Logan chuckled. Kiara looked at him flatly. "You have five minutes."

"Then my answer will be no," Quinn said. He felt a thrill just saying it. God, what a feeling! This was just the first offer. He wasn't about to let them push him around. "After tonight I'll probably have a few offers to mull over."

"I doubt it."

The certainty in her voice was chilling. "What the hell does that mean?"

"My employer's not interested in a bidding war with the casinos. So we've taken out an option on you with every major theater in Vegas."

He couldn't believe what he was hearing. "For how long?"

"Six months."

"You—you can't do that!" he said.

It messed up everything. The planned negotiations, the offers and counteroffers. Five years of trying to show that he was good enough to be one of their headliners.

"It's done."

"*We're* done," he said. "And you'll be hearing from my lawyer."

"Lawsuits take time, Mr. Bradley. And they take more than the two hundred dollars you have in your checking account."

So they'd run a credit check, too. This kept getting better and better. He opened his mouth to say, *Screw you*, but glanced at Logan and thought better of it. They had the drop on him, and he hated how it felt.

About as crappy as saying "no" felt good just moments ago.

Well, there would damn well be a negotiation, whether she wanted one or not. "Six hundred thousand," he said.

Her eyes widened just a little. Maybe she thought he'd be too impressed by the number to try and negotiate. "No."

"Fine," Quinn said. "Five hundred, but I keep the metal case."

"What metal case?"

"The one in Rudy's top drawer."

Kiara reached for it, but Logan cleared his throat. "Let me, Lieutenant." A military title. That explained the good posture.

Logan gave him a hard stare. Then he reached over and edged the drawer out, enough that he could look inside. "What the—" He slid the drawer open, picked up the case he'd had in his jacket. "My glasses."

He wrinkled his brow. Finally, a crack in the stony facade. "How did you do that?"

Quinn shrugged. "Do we have a deal?"

"Fine," Kiara said. "Six hundred thousand."

Logan tucked the case back inside his jacket and buttoned it, watching Quinn all the while.

"That case felt like titanium." He smirked. "What kind of specs do you have in there?"

"None of your damn business."

"Guess I'll have to take them again."

Logan smiled. "Try it."

Kiara looked at Quinn. "So, Mr. Bradley?"

Quinn turned back to her. "Let me get this straight: you won't tell me who I'm working for."

"No."

"And you won't tell me *where* I'll be working."

"No."

"And you can't tell me what kind of performance you're looking for."

"Before you sign the NDA? No."

"But you'll pay me six hundred thousand dollars."

"Yes." She gave no indication there was any more coming.

He had two choices, because he wasn't going back to Rudy.

It was this or the foreign guy, who'd been even less forthcoming. But a jack of spades wasn't a paycheck.

"Then I guess we're agreed on terms. When do I start?"

"You already have," she said.

They left by the theater's back door before Quinn had a chance to tell Rudy anything. It let out into the narrow alley between the theater and a strip mall. An SUV with tinted windows waited there, the engine already running. Kiara went around to the passenger's side. Logan opened the back door for Quinn, closed it behind him, and got behind the wheel.

"Seat belts," he said.

Quinn buckled his and checked his watch. Almost midnight. "I need to pack a few bags."

"What do you need?" Kiara asked. She had her comm device out again. It looked like a next-gen smartphone, one of the autoencryption models. They weren't supposed to hit the market for another year.

"I don't know. Clothes, toiletries."

"Anything special?"

Six months was a long time to be gone, but he didn't have much in the way of personal possessions. Every dime he'd had went into the illusions. The materials didn't come cheap.

"I guess that's all," he said.

"We'll take care of it."

"Do you need my address, or . . ."

Logan snickered.

"No," Kiara said.

Logan turned onto the 592, headed west. They passed Caesar's Palace, then The Palms. Away from McCarran Airport. *I guess we're not flying*, Quinn thought. He turned to watch their lights fade. Couldn't help it, any more than he could ignore the heartbreak of getting so close, only to have Kiara get in the way.

"We've got a friend, Lieutenant," Logan said. "Black sedan, three cars back."

Quinn looked over his shoulder.

"Damn it, Bradley, don't look!" Logan said.

"You have tinted glass, and it's dark out," Quinn said. No way anyone could have seen him turn.

Logan shook his head and muttered something about "amateurs."

"How long have they been on us?" Kiara asked.

"Almost from the start."

"Lose them."

Logan hit the gas, and the SUV leaped forward. They went from forty to eighty in about two seconds. Had to be a V-8 under the hood.

"Did you contact anyone since we met?" Kiara demanded.

"No," Quinn said.

"No phone calls or texts to anyone?"

"Nothing. Here," he said. He took out his phone and offered it to her.

She took it, glanced at the screen, lowered her window, and threw it out.

"Hey!" Quinn said. "Aw, hell. I just got that!"

"We'll get you a new one."

"I want a better one." He couldn't help sounding petulant about it.

"Fine," she said, and he was pretty sure she rolled her eyes. "Now, keep quiet."

"Hang on," Logan said. He braked hard and swerved onto a side street.

The momentum threw Quinn against his door and window. "Jesus!"

Kiara's comm unit beeped. She checked it. "Thirty seconds."

"Thirty seconds to what?" Quinn asked.

She ignored him. They shot past a couple of car dealerships. Orange pylons started flashing past. Quinn looked out the front, saw a construction crew and a cement truck working in the other lane ahead. One of the workers held up a stop sign. The truck rolled across, toward their lane.

"Shit, watch the truck!" Quinn shouted.

Logan gunned it through the gap. God, it was close. Quinn caught a glimpse of the guy with the stop sign as they passed. He didn't look angry, or even surprised. It was like he didn't even see their SUV at all. Quinn looked back, saw the crew drag a wooden barricade across. The sedan screeched to a halt, horn blaring.

"Relax, Mr. Bradley," Kiara said. "They're with us."

Not for the last time, Quinn wondered who the hell "us" was. Logan eased off the gas. A chain-link fence rose up on the right side. They turned into an entryway and paused at a guard booth. Kiara flipped open an ID case and held it where the guard could see. He waved them past without a word, into the small airfield beyond.

Maybe we are flying.

A private jet was on the runway, getting ready to take off. Logan drove right up to it. Right out on the tarmac. Quinn was shocked they were allowed out here, but he kept his mouth shut. After the construction site, he figured he shouldn't be surprised by anything. Logan put it in park, but left the engine running. He and Kiara got out. Quinn would have followed, but his door was locked. He knocked on the window.

"Whoops," Logan said. He opened the door from the outside.

Quinn climbed out and gave him a dirty look. He doubted they'd locked him back there on accident. Another SUV pulled up beside theirs. A young guy in a suit got out and jogged around to the trunk. He lifted out a black suitcase and handed it to Logan without a word. A woman got out of the passenger seat and got behind the wheel of Logan's SUV. They drove off, one right after the other.

Kiara was already boarding the jet.

"Shake a leg, Bradley," Logan said. He shoved the suitcase at him. "Don't forget your suitcase."

Quinn grabbed it by instinct. He saw the American flag label, and the neon-green shoelace he'd tied on the handle last year. It was full, too. Probably with his own stuff.

"Son of a bitch," he said. So they *hadn't* needed his address. They hadn't even needed his keys. He walked up to the jet, and noticed the company name on the side. "CASE Global Enterprises?"

"Your new employer," Logan said.

CASE Global was a billion-dollar corporation. Quinn couldn't guess what they wanted him for, but one thing was certain.

I should have asked for more money.

> "Nothing spreads across a continent
> like disruptive technology."
>
> —R. HOLT, "RECOMMENDATIONS
> FOR GATEWAY PROTOCOLS"

CHAPTER 2

FLIGHT

Fourteen hours later, they rode in an unmarked helicopter over some island in the South Pacific. Quinn sat on a bench in the cargo bay, trying to keep his lunch down. Already regretting that he'd said yes. Kiara and Logan sat across from him, stoic as ever. They might as well have been out for a pleasure cruise.

Kiara pressed her headset to her ear, listening to something the pilot was saying. She signaled to him and Logan: *we're landing.*

Thank God for that.

A gust of wind buffeted the chopper as they descended. Quinn fought another wave of nausea. Jet travel he knew. Helicopters were another beast entirely. The whole thing seemed so . . . *fragile*. He was glad when they touched down.

A security team awaited them on the helipad, four men cut from the same cloth. Big shoulders, short hair, dark suits, and excellent posture. Quinn caught the glint of brushed aluminum under their jackets.

Machine guns. Sweet Jesus.

Kiara and Logan held up badges that got a careful look, but then they were waved past. Two of the security men came forward and took Quinn aside. He started feeling nervous. These guys were *huge*. Probably bigger than Logan, and that was saying something.

"Quinn Bradley?" one of them asked, with just a faint accent. German, maybe. He was even bigger up close.

"That's me," Quinn said.

The man consulted a small notepad. No, a legal pad. His hands only made it seem small. "Who was your favorite high school teacher?"

Quinn was surprised by the question, though he found himself answering without hesitation. "Mr. Ribbing." His high school physics teacher, the one who'd first gotten him interested in engineering.

"Where was your mother born?"

"Lebanon," Quinn said.

The man just stared at him, unblinking.

"Uh, Beirut," Quinn added. He doubted the question was an accident. When were they going to get over the fact that his mom was born in the Middle

East? It ticked him off a little, but not enough to talk back to these guys.

The man lifted a hand to speak into his wrist. "Clear Bradley." He waved Quinn past to where Kiara and Logan waited.

"Good security you have here," he said to Logan.

"You'll be hard-pressed to find any better."

"How do they know that stuff about me?"

"We told you: we ran a background check." Logan shrugged. "Besides, they know everything about everyone. Oh, almost forgot. Here's your ID." He handed Quinn a security badge. It had his driver's license photo and the words "CLEARANCE LEVEL: 0" stamped in red on the front.

"Level zero? Seriously?" Quinn asked.

"Won't get you in anywhere except the cafeteria."

"What's your level?"

"A lot higher."

A dark-haired woman in a white lab coat had hurried out from a nearby building. She got to the helipad and started sneezing. Kiara gestured at her. "Quinn Bradley, meet Dr. Veena Chaudri."

"Welcome," Chaudri said.

Quinn shook her hand, impressed by the strong grip. She was almost as tall as him, too. "Nice to meet you."

"Likewise." Chaudri turned abruptly to sneeze again. "Oh! Sorry. It's my allergies."

Kiara and Logan started toward the building, which was long and low like an army barracks. Quinn fell into step beside the newcomer. She looked to be in her mid-thirties. Had to be from India with a name like that, but the accent was puzzling. Not Indian, but not British colonial, either. "Are you a medical doctor?" he asked.

"Not quite. I'm an anthropologist. What about you?"

"I'm an entertainer," Quinn said. "A stage magician."

"Really?" She didn't seem terribly surprised. "They certainly have thought of everything."

Whatever the hell that means. . .

The interior of the building belied its outward drab appearance. The corridors were brightly lit, the floors polished. Everything was spotless. It looked more like a research laboratory than anything else . . . if research laboratories had state-of-the-art security.

Quinn had trained himself to look for cameras, microphones, and other forms of surveillance—the secrets behind his stage tricks were too valuable to put at risk—and right away, he knew they were being covered from multiple angles. Most of the cameras were stationary, but at least one or two pivoted to follow their progress as Kiara took them in.

The company was watching.

They stuck the magician in a secure conference room while Kiara briefed the executives. Logan waited for her outside the briefing room, looking over the file on Bradley's father. Both the parents were dead, but the father had worked for the State Department. Sometimes that meant CIA. Kiara had told him to pull the file, to make sure it wasn't a cover.

Her briefing took longer than it should have. Logan knew how it had gone the second she marched out the door. He saw the tightness in her jaw, the too-stiff posture soldiers adopted after a good chewing out.

"That bad?" he asked.

"They're not happy with how it went in Vegas."

"Why not? We got the magician they wanted," Logan said.

"We were exposed. Someone knew we wanted to recruit him," Kiara said.

"Any word from the cleanup team on who they were?" Logan asked.

"No, but I have my suspicions."

"Raptor Tech," Logan said. CASE Global's largest competitor. They had a huge presence in the defense industry, and were doing their best to infringe on every market CASE Global dominated. Mostly by black hat stuff, and this fit the bill.

"The sooner we're mission-ready, the better," Kiara said. She saw what Logan had been reading. "Is that the file on Bradley's father?"

"It looks legit," Logan said. "He worked as a cultural attaché in Beirut when Hezbollah bombed the embassy in '83. Spent twelve hours under the rubble, and then a month in the hospital. I saw the records."

"Hard to believe he stayed after that," she said.

"I think he'd met the mother by then," he said.

"She'd applied for asylum a couple of times, but couldn't get it. He smuggled her out in '86. Got a write-up for it."

"Her family filed a complaint, too," Kiara said. "Our sources over there say they disowned her after that."

"For joining the infidels?" Logan asked.

"That, and the fact that she'd been promised to someone else."

Logan grunted. "No wonder he got the write-up. State benched him after that. Put him behind a desk in Nevada."

"Reassignment to somewhere boring," Kiara said.

"The government's favorite kind of punishment."

"Any red flags on the mother's family?" she asked.

"No ties to any radical groups. She came over alone. Wasn't on any watch lists."

That was the main concern. Not that she was a terrorist—the company couldn't care less about that— but the possibility that feds could be keeping tabs on Bradley. Tapping his phone, monitoring his travel. Just because of where his mother had been born. The fewer satellites keyholed to the island compound, the better.

"All good news," she said. "So why do I feel like you still have a problem with him?"

He kept his face still. She'd had a tough briefing and he didn't want to do this now. "You know where I come in on this, Lieutenant."

"Pretend I don't."

"I never liked the idea of bringing in a civilian,

much less one without any training. I'd rather bring a couple of my guys."

"We need someone Holt doesn't know already. Someone he won't expect. An ace in the hole."

Logan doubted that was a play on words. He was pretty sure Kiara had never uttered a joke in her life. "Oh, I'm sure he won't expect us to bring a Vegas performer along. Mission accomplished."

"If you have a more creative idea, say the word."

Logan said nothing.

"Good. One last thing: the executives want us to make sure he's not in touch with any of his father's old contacts from the State Department. If not, we can read him in."

Quinn faced Kiara and Logan across a small conference table. It hurt to keep his eyes open, but they'd insisted on the briefing right away. The conference room was modern and functional, the table a single sheet of glass on metal legs. The walls were bare except for a security camera with a steady red light. How many did that make? Quinn had lost count. The level of surveillance had him on edge.

"First things first," Kiara said. She slid over a thick document in a manila folder. "The nondisclosure agreement."

Quinn scanned through the pages, wishing he'd thought to consult a lawyer. Too late for that now.

"This agreement went into effect the moment we met, and never expires," Kiara said.

"What if I don't sign it?"

"They'll never find your body," Logan said.

Quinn wasn't sure he was kidding. "Not taking any chances, are you?"

"Everyone signs one of these. It's standard protocol."

"Right."

"To be fair, your background has some of the executives nervous."

Oh, delightful. The Lebanese question again. "Look, I never met anyone from my mother's side of the family," he said. After she'd married his father, none of her relatives would even talk to her. She'd almost never spoken about them, either.

"So it would seem. Telecom records only had the occasional call from her sister."

"Really? I—I didn't know." Once, while still in high school, he'd come home early and caught her in the kitchen, whispering into the phone. She'd hung up right away, wiped her eyes, and never said a word about it.

"Yes. But it's not your mother I was talking about," Kiara said.

"What?"

"It's your father."

Now *that* one Quinn hadn't seen coming. He was behind the curve again, and he hated that. "Why would he make them nervous?"

"He worked at the State Department."

"Yeah, that's how they met," Quinn said. "But he was

an office worker. Boring stuff. He said so all the time."

"Do you know what he was doing in Beirut?" Kiara asked.

Quinn shook his head. "He never talked about it." His father hadn't been a big talker. Hell, the company probably knew more about his past than Quinn did. Knowing that added fuel to the smoldering anger against CASE Global. They'd sabotaged his career, dug into his past. God, it was almost like they were *trying* to piss him off.

"You're not in touch with any of your father's old coworkers, then?"

"Why does it matter?"

"Answer the question," Kiara said.

"Like I said, he wasn't a big talker. And we don't get a lot of federal government types out in Nevada—not a lot of foreign dignitaries in the desert. So, no."

Kiara pressed two fingers to her ear, as if receiving instructions. Which he realized was probably exactly what she was doing. Her eyes flickered to a large mirror on the wall. The surface wasn't as reflective as it should be. Had to be a one-way. No one knew mirrors better than magicians.

She stood. "All right, Bradley. It's time you saw where you'll be working."

I guess I passed.

Quinn followed Kiara and Logan down a stark corridor. A group of soldiers strode past, headed the other way. At least, they looked like soldiers, from the bearing and confidence. And from the way they saluted Kiara as they approached. Two men and two women. Dressed in black. With swords at their belts . . .

Quinn did a double take.

Yep, swords. He was about to bring it up when they hit the security checkpoint.

There was a heavy steel door, flanked by two security guards who cradled automatic weapons. They stiffened when Kiara approached, but made no salute. She slid back a panel in the wall. She put her palm on a gray panel. It lit up blue at her touch. "Lynn Kiara," she said.

Biometric scanners and voice recognition. So, she did have a first name. *And it was Lynn.* Quinn smiled. He'd never have guessed that in a million years.

The panel flickered green, and then the guards broke composure to salute her. The steel door hissed open.

Quinn stepped close to Kiara, so that the guards knew he was with her. The chamber beyond surprised him. It was cavernous, easily the biggest room he'd seen in the complex so far. The air was heavy and smelled of . . . *wet stone?* The reason became apparent when he saw that the back half of the chamber was raw bedrock, carved out around a steel-and-Plexiglas door.

"What you're about to see was discovered fifteen years ago by a local shepherd," Kiara said. "He'd been missing for days. Limped home to his family raving about it. He was dead within a few hours."

"Of what?" Quinn asked. He started holding his breath, just in case it was some kind of disease.

"Frostbite," Kiara said.

Logan appeared beside him. He wore a heavy coat in brown wool, and held out another for Quinn. "Put this on."

Quinn took the coat and tugged it on. It wasn't really wool, but some kind of synthetic fiber. The coat itself was actually plain and shapeless. Like the world's warmest poncho. He'd been in caves before, and they were cold, but this seemed a bit excessive.

Kiara had bundled up as well. She entered a command at the computer terminal on one side of the cavern, and strode over to join him. "This is CASE Global's single most important asset."

The Plexiglas door slid open. Behind it, the wall of the cavern was translucent and gray. It shimmered as he watched. The air in the chamber had an energy to it, like the buildup of static electricity. It made the hair on Quinn's arms rise.

Kiara walked into it. The grayness swallowed her, like she'd slipped through a waterfall. Quinn gasped.

"Your turn," Logan said. And he shoved Quinn right after her.

Cold. That was the first thing he felt. He stumbled on a hard stone floor and caught himself against the wall. The rock was rough under his hands, and it drained the heat from them. He jerked them back and put them in his pockets. Logan appeared behind him. Quinn had an urge to shove the man right back, and would have done it if he thought it would have moved the man an inch.

And if he thought Logan would let him that close to begin with.

"This way, Mr. Bradley," Kiara said. She stood at the mouth of a tunnel, and from the brightness behind her, it must lead outside.

Quinn followed her down a short passage. The stone walls were marked with odd symbols. Hieroglyphics, maybe. The paint looked ancient, but had a sheen to it. Like it might glow even in total darkness. They turned a corner and were greeted by the near-blinding whiteness of outdoors.

"Sweet Jesus," Quinn whispered.

A snow-covered landscape fell away from the mouth of the cave. It was like looking down the side of a mountain. On the horizon, other peaks loomed out of an iron-gray sky.

"What is this place?" he asked.

"This is where you'll be working," Kiara said. "The inhabitants call it Alissia."

Quinn felt vaguely aware that he hadn't spoken for a long time. Logan had guided him back through the odd portal to the company facility. Took his coat off, and walked him to the conference room again. He stepped out and closed the door, leaving Quinn alone with the mirror and whoever was behind it.

The door banged open again, startling him.

Chaudri backed in, her arms occupied with a tray of refreshments. She heaved it onto the table and sat down. Quinn's stomach rumbled at the smell of food.

"I know that look," Chaudri said. She set out a pair of ceramic mugs and started pouring coffee. She slid one over. "You're going to need this."

He accepted a mug and leaned back, inhaling the steam. He ventured a sip and sighed. Some kind of tropical roast, strong but faintly sweet. Something normal, for once, and it helped. "God, that's good."

"So, I take it you've been read in," Chaudri said.

"Kiara and Logan took me through this . . . thing."

"The gateway."

Quinn spread his arms out. "I don't even know what it is."

"We're not certain ourselves, if that makes you feel any better. Some of the consulting physicists think it's a wormhole, between our world and theirs."

"Their world . . ." he said, bemused. "Kiara said it's inhabited." The coffee was starting to kick in, because he made the leap. "And you're an anthropologist."

"Yes. I've been studying Alissia for ten years."

"Wow. And it's been kept secret all this time?"

"Have you *seen* the NDA?" she joked.

"It was pretty serious." He sipped more coffee. "So, how many people live there?"

"We have a good idea, but I'm not allowed to tell you," Chaudri said.

"How come?" Quinn asked.

"You don't have your clearance yet."

But the woman knew; Quinn could see that. And anyone with a number fixed in her mind was malleable. "I didn't see anyone while I was there. So I'd say less than ten thousand."

Chaudri exhaled faintly. A scoff. *Far too low.* "As I said, I can't—"

"A hundred million."

"Ah, I'm not permitted to divulge exact numbers." The jaw tightened, but the eyes widened just a little. Quinn knew he was too high, but in the ballpark. Two or three questions more and he'd have it narrowed down.

He'd done more than enough readings as a "medium" to infer a number. Chaudri was the perfect mark.

Logan and Kiara barged in before he could press Chaudri any further.

Just when I was getting started, too.

"I see you've recovered your spirits, Mr. Bradley," she said.

"Somewhat," Quinn said. He settled back in his chair, watching her. Something about her manner always made him feel like he should find a place to hide. Or toss a smoke bomb and disappear. "I have a lot of questions."

"Undoubtedly," she said. "But you should know that much of the information on Alissia is given out on a need-to-know basis."

She was stonewalling him. "But you haven't told me

anything!" Quinn said. He pointed in the direction of the chamber. "For example: What the hell was that?"

Kiara touched the corner of the table. Light bloomed under her fingertip. A high-def projector flicked on, casting a sharp image of the snow-blanketed mountains he'd seen from the mouth of the cave.

"What you saw is barely a glimpse of what lies through the gateway," Kiara said.

More images flickered past on the wall, aerial footage of windswept prairies, rolling hills, pristine shorelines. It was beautiful, once you got past the snow. Pure.

Massive.

"How big is it?" Quinn asked.

"Based on our curvature measurements, nearly as large as Earth," Chaudri said.

Quinn couldn't look away; he was riveted. There were settlements, thatch-roof cottages for the most part. Three men leaning against a stone wall, their armor polished like chrome. A crowded bazaar packed with people and animals. Everything looked so real.

But how could it be? It made no sense. One thing in particular seemed off.

"OK, let's back up," Quinn said. "You said a shepherd found this fifteen years ago. So how do I not know about this already? Shouldn't it be on CNN?"

"CASE Global owns this entire island," Kiara said. "We've managed to keep the gateway's existence a secret."

Quinn was incredulous. This was getting harder and harder to believe . . . except that he'd seen the proof. Then again, he had just shown people he could turn out Las Vegas by snuffing some candles, so incredulity was an integral part of his makeup. "OK, then let me get this straight. You found a portal to a whole other world. With *people* in it. And you've just been, what, sitting on it?"

"We've been studying it from every possible angle," Chaudri said.

There had to be an endgame here. Billion-dollar companies didn't study things. They profited from them.

More importantly, he needed to know where he fit in.

As if anticipating that question, Kiara tapped her control panel. The image changed again, to a photo of a man in a white lab coat. He was middle-aged, maybe a little older, with wire-frame glasses and a pronounced nose. Looked like a cardsharp, the kind of guy who's always thinking two moves ahead.

"This is Richard Holt," Kiara said. "The head of our research team since this project started."

"He's a nice-looking man, I suppose."

Kiara scowled.

"Six days ago, he went rogue, and disappeared through the gateway," Logan said.

Quinn stole a glance at their faces. Kiara's was cold calculation, almost hidden animosity. On Chaudri's, sadness warred with admiration. Interesting. "Maybe he just needed a vacation," he said.

Chaudri barked a laugh. It came out nervous. "Dr. Holt didn't believe in vacations."

"He also took a backpack full of technology that's not allowed on the other side of the gateway."

"What technology are we talking about?"

"That's above your clearance level."

That excuse is starting to get real old.

"Whatever his reasons, the executives want him retrieved," Kiara said. "Quickly and quietly."

Quinn made a face, to show that he wasn't happy about the clearance thing. "That sounds like Logan's department."

"It is," he said.

"And we have Chaudri, for the cultural angle," Kiara said.

"I guess you're all set, then," Quinn said. He still didn't know why they'd brought him here, why they'd shown him something that was clearly a tightly held secret. They wanted something—something worth more than a half million dollars.

Kiara sighed. She almost seemed to agree. "Some of our superiors are concerned because we've all been working with Holt for a long time. He knows our tactics. Our tendencies."

Ah—the reveal at last. "But he doesn't know me," Quinn said.

"Exactly," she said. "And given their preindustrial technology level, your talents for illusion might be useful in a tough spot."

"It certainly is an interesting way to go," Logan said.

Kiara frowned at him.

So they did want a performance out of him. "The logistics would be tough," Quinn said. "I'm used to working on a stage."

"You'll have substantial company resources at your disposal," Kiara said. "Materials, schematics, a fully trained engineering team. Pretty much whatever you need."

"I guess I can draw up some ideas," he said.

"They don't even have to be your own. If any of your competitors have something that would be useful, we can have the details for you in twenty-four hours."

"Good luck with that," Quinn said. "Magicians are a secretive lot, from what I hear."

"You're one of the most secretive, and we got you here in, what, fourteen hours?"

"Touché," he said.

"We'll provide you with virtually anything you need to create the best magic that you can muster. And trust me, it'll have to be convincing."

Something about her seriousness raised his hackles. "Why is that?"

"Because Alissians have the real thing."

> "I never went for craps or
> blackjack or poker. If I want to
> take a gamble, I do it onstage."
>
> —ART OF ILLUSION, OCTOBER 6

CHAPTER 3

HAZARDS

Two weeks later, Quinn clung to the pommel while his mare plunged through the snow after Kiara's. Chaudri rode behind him, followed by the packhorses. Logan brought up the rear.

God, it's cold here. He tried to pull his fur-lined riding cloak tighter around him. The snow blanketed everything perfectly, like a Thomas Kincaid painting. And the air was completely still. There was only the sound of their horses' hooves as they crunched into the snow.

Kiara reined in suddenly. "Something's wrong," she said.

Besides the fact we just walked through some kind of dimensional portal?

But Quinn knew what she meant. He pushed down his hood for a better look around. They were on the top of a small rise, with tall, leafless trees towering above them. Wintry landscape fell away in every direction, into an endless sea of semi-open forest. Not a trace of movement anywhere. Not a sound.

"There's no wind," he said. "Is that unusual?"

"Very," Logan said. He made some kind of hand signal to Kiara.

"Earbuds," she said softly, and pressed a finger to her ear to activate hers. Quinn fumbled off one of his gloves and activated his own. The tiny speaker crackled as it came to life. These little gems had come out of the company's prototyping lab. Rechargeable, encrypted frequency, and a range of about two miles. You could even mutter into it and be heard clear as day.

Kiara's voice seemed to whisper right in Quinn's ear. "We're going to ride down into the trees for some cover. Keep your eyes open."

They set a good pace down the slope, but slowed as the trees thickened around them. Kiara took them along what appeared to be a game trail among the trees. When the cave had fallen from view, she halted. "Logan, check our backtrail."

He wheeled his horse and broke away from the track they'd been following, moving northwest to come at the cave from another angle.

"Approaching the clearing," came his voice, a baritone that buzzed in Quinn's ear. "No sign of pursuit. No hiding our tracks, though. Should I lay some false trails?"

"Not there. I don't want you out in the open," Kiara said. "It would be obvious that we're headed south in any case."

"Who do you think might be after us?" Quinn asked.

"Hard to say. Could be a competitor, or the government. Or any number of protest groups that are constantly railing against the company and its practices." She frowned, as if weighing a decision. "Logan, check the gate."

"Yes, Lieutenant," Logan said. A moment later he checked in again. "I'm in the cave. Looks clear."

"Set a couple of proxies," Kiara told him.

"Already on it, Lieutenant," Logan replied.

Quinn looked at Chaudri and mouthed, "Proxies?"

"Proximity sensors, I think," Chaudri said. "Infrared motion and heat detectors. They'll go off if anyone comes after us."

Logan's voice came again. "The gate is blocked."

"Say again?" Kiara said.

"The gateway is nonfunctional."

Quinn felt a stab of terror. He looked at Chaudri, who was wide-eyed and probably thinking the same thing. No way back.

Kiara pursed her lips. "Get back here right away," she ordered.

They waited in uncomfortable silence for half an

hour, while the horses snorted white puffs of air. At last, Logan's horse trotted into view.

"So?" Kiara asked.

Logan shrugged. "I went to stick my head through the gate. Couldn't cross the threshold. It was like trying to walk through Plexiglas."

"Foxtrot protocol?" she asked.

"Must be."

"Wait, I'm sorry," Quinn said. "What is Foxtrot protocol?"

"A security lockdown procedure," Kiara said. "We have means to physically seal the gateway from the other side."

"For how long?" Quinn asked.

"Until the threat has been addressed," she said.

"What if we drag Holt all the way back here and it's still locked?" he demanded.

"It won't be," Kiara said. She sounded confident, but how could she know?

"I hope you're right," Quinn said. He damn well didn't want to spend the rest of his life in this place. It might be pristine, but he doubted they had a strip like Vegas.

It wasn't long before they encountered the first of Holt's little surprises. Twilight was already approaching; according to Chaudri, the days and nights between here and Earth were never quite in sync. Logan gave no indication that they'd stop even in darkness. They

THE ROGUE RETRIEVAL 45

had LED globes disguised as torches, for when it came to that.

They were riding single file in dense woods when Logan collided with an invisible barrier.

"Oof!" The impact of it nearly tossed Logan out of the saddle. Kiara sawed her gelding's reins to keep from plowing right into him. Quinn jerked back on his, as did Chaudri. It was like a medieval six-horse pileup in slow motion.

"What?" Kiara demanded.

"What the hell—" Logan nudged the horse sideways and kicked out with a leather boot, getting a dull thud for his effort. Then he had his sword out and probed at it. "There's some kind of a barrier here."

Quinn saw it now, a slight distortion of the forest ahead of him, as if looking through an old leaden window. It appeared to extend left and right as far as he could make out. Logan dismounted, stepped close to give it a look. "Not sure what I'm looking at."

Kiara's face was a mask of concern. "Let's backtrack and try another way."

Logan jumped back on and spurred his horse past them. They all wheeled and followed. A quarter mile away, some distance to the southwest, they hit the barrier again. Same thing to the southeast.

"It wasn't here two months ago," Logan said. "Our scouting party came right along this trail."

He made a dedicated effort with his sword, and then a crossbow. Nothing could penetrate the barrier.

Kiara dismounted. She found a branch and threw

it at the barrier; it bounced off harmlessly. She stepped close to inspect it. "Alissians don't even have lead-free glass yet. Must be some kind of magic."

Finally, Quinn thought. A problem that Logan and Kiara couldn't solve right away. Time to show that he could be a team player. He'd been waiting for a chance to try out some of the equipment anyway.

He wound up his right arm like a pitcher and made a throwing motion. A melon-sized ball of fire flew from it, roared through the air, and slammed into the barrier. It made for an impressive show, even if it had little effect on the barrier itself. And caught part of his sleeve on fire, which he quickly patted out.

"Wow!" Chaudri said.

"Impressive, Bradley," Kiara said. "Unfortunately, I don't think it helped us."

"It was worth a shot," Quinn said. He wound up and threw another fireball, this one at the leaf-strewn ground beneath a tall conifer near the barrier. The needles and dried twigs flared up immediately.

"Your aim needs a little work," Logan said. He moved over to stomp out the flames.

"Leave it," Quinn said. He slid out of the saddle. "I want the smoke."

Logan grunted and stood back. The fire grew. When enough of the brush had caught, Quinn snuffed it out with handfuls of snow. Steam rose with a hiss, hugging the inside of the barrier. It rose straight up but then began to curl over their heads, back in the direction from which they'd come.

"See that? It's concave," Quinn said. "Like a bubble. Whatever made this thing is probably right in the center of it."

"Good thinking, Bradley," Kiara said.

Logan was already mounted again. "Based on the curvature, the central point should be this way."

It was near dark by then. A pale yellow moon shone between the trees. Quinn heard the yipping of some animal; it sounded almost like a hyena. Another one yipped back at it. "What is that?" he asked.

Logan and Kiara exchanged an ominous look. "Alissian wild dogs," Logan said.

"Should I be worried? They're just dogs, right?"

"The Alissian version is bigger than a wolf. Pack hunters, too. Sounds like they're inside the barrier. I'm guessing that's no accident."

Oh. Perfect.

"We need to get that barrier down," Kiara said.

Ah, yes, ordering the obvious. She was ex-military for certain.

Logan spurred his mare to a gallop, and the others followed.

They rode in open woods near the cave clearing; the epicenter of the barrier seemed to be just north of it. More yipping rose to the left, and then to the right. The pitch was higher now, almost excited.

"They have our scent," Chaudri said. "They're hunting us."

Quinn thought about making a break for it then. He could probably find his way back to the cave, if the dogs didn't catch him. This whole mission was a mistake. Logan was right. He wasn't safe here, not by a long shot. And yet even with the danger, his curiosity overcame his survival instinct.

Ahead was a small clearing, awash in yellow moonlight.

"This should be it," Logan said. He approached the edge, slowing his horse to a canter and loosening his sword in its scabbard. "Whoa!" He yanked his horse around at the tree line. "Fall back!" he whispered fiercely.

A moment of confusion followed as they got the horses turned around and backed up. Logan signaled that they should dismount. Then he put a finger to his lips and led them up to the edge of the trees.

Logan pushed aside a branch so they could see into the clearing, which held a massive nest the size of a dump truck. Perched above it was a green serpentine creature whose body shone like metal in the moonlight.

"What the hell is that?" Quinn whispered.

Even coiled up, it was the biggest reptile he'd ever seen. By a factor of ten. The body was muscular, the neck thick. It had to be, to support that big triangular head. A thick line of spikes ran down the spine to the tail, which whipped back and forth like a snake's.

"Wait . . . is that a goddamn *dragon*?" he asked.

"Looks like a northern wyvern," Chaudri said. "Strange to find one with a brood here. Usually they nest in colonies up in the mountains."

Logan had out his night-vision binoculars. "How much do you want to bet that whatever made the barrier is in that nest?"

Behind them in the shadowed woods, more of the wild dogs were yipping. They were *close*.

"We need a look at it," Kiara said.

"I think the dragon's going to have something to say about that," Quinn said.

"*Wyverns,*" Chaudri corrected, "are territorial. Probably just moving into view in that clearing will be enough to bring her over."

"Good idea," Kiara said. "You and Bradley try to draw it off. Logan and I will go for the nest."

"Wait, why do *I* have to act as bait?" Quinn demanded. He felt his survival instincts kicking in. They were screaming at him to stay as far away from the dragon, or wyvern, as he possibly could.

I've had my fill of curiosity.

"If you have better ideas, I'm ready to hear them," Kiara said.

He racked his brain, but couldn't think of anything on the spot. There was just no preparing for this sort of thing.

"Give us three minutes to get into position," Kiara said. She and Logan mounted and started off.

"Wait, wait!" Quinn said. "What do we do once we have the wyvern after us?"

"Make it disappear," Logan called. "That's your specialty, isn't it?"

Chaudri cleared her throat. "The wyvern will—"

"Will you stop calling it that?" Quinn asked.

"I'm sorry?"

"I know I'm not the world expert," Quinn said. He pointed his finger out into the clearing. "But that thing out there is a dragon."

"If Dr. Holt were here, he'd ask you to defend your position," Chaudri said. She spoke as if making a wish.

"But he's not here. Hell, for all we know, *he's* the reason that *dragon* is here. I'll play your game, though. For starters, it looks like a big reptile. It's sitting on a nest. It has scales and claws. All we're missing is a pile of gold."

"And fire-breathing capability, which these do not have. Hence: wyvern." Chaudri checked the wooden bracelet on her wrist. These were company issue, and concealed both a watch and a wrist-camera. "Almost time."

Quinn shook his head, still in disbelief that things had gone this far. But he wasn't about to let his first job become a failure. *No matter how ridiculous it might be.* "Let's get this over with."

They rode out from the trees; almost instantly, the wyvern was in a crouch, its massive head turning to track their movement. Two hundred yards of open clearing separated them from the nest.

"She's not moving," Quinn said.

"We need to get her attention," Chaudri said. She put her hands to her mouth. "Hello there!"

"Hey!" Quinn shouted. He waved his hands like he was trying to land a jumbo jet.

Nothing from the wyvern. She just watched them with unblinking eyes. There was intelligence there, and curiosity.

"You said they're territorial, right?" Quinn asked.

"Quite. It's strange that she's not moving yet."

"Maybe she doesn't consider us a threat. Draw your sword."

Chaudri's blade rasped as she pulled it from the scabbard. The swords they carried were actually hollow, with a titanium endoskeleton that made them strong but incredibly light. The blades were cast from a proprietary alloy right out of the company's R & D lab, so sharp you could shave with them. Quinn had one, too, though Logan had made it clear that he should avoid a swordfight at any cost. More accurately, he'd said that even a twelve-year-old from Alissia would "carve you like a turkey."

But if I see any eleven-year-olds, watch out.

Quinn had something better anyway. He rummaged around in his saddlebags, until he found what he wanted: a metal cylinder about the size of a cigar. "I knew I'd have an excuse to use this."

He held it up, found the switch, and flicked it on. A narrow beam of green light hummed into being, about a yard long and two inches wide. He slashed the air in a figure eight, wishing they'd had time to add the sound effects.

"I'm sorry, is that a *lightsaber*?" Chaudri asked.

"Like it?"

"I wouldn't mind one of those."

"They're only for Jedi," Quinn said. He couldn't keep a straight face. The lightsaber had no substance to it; it wouldn't even melt butter. It got the wyvern's attention, though. Her catlike eyes had narrowed.

They urged their now-terrified mounts a couple of paces forward, and that was enough. The reptile crouched low and then leaped into the air. Wide, leathery wings unfolded from her back.

"It can *fly*?" Quinn asked.

"I guess I should have mentioned that."

"Oh, shit!"

They turned their horses and fled back to the tree line. Quinn wasn't sure they were going to make it. He could already feel the wind from her wings.

"Stay with me!" Chaudri shouted. She plunged down the trail they'd followed up here. The wyvern was still right over them, her claws just above the tree-tops. They lost the trail and got into denser woods. Branches started whipping Quinn in the face and body. One nearly slapped him right out of the saddle. He crouched low and just let his horse run.

Part of the last two weeks had been intensive horse training. At this pace, they risked breaking a horse's ankle, but there was nothing to do about it. Any slower and the wyvern would drop down through the trees like a bird of prey. If he fell or the horse went down, that would probably happen anyway.

God, it was better not to think about it.

"Knew I should have asked for more money," Quinn

shouted to himself. He ground his teeth together and spurred the horse onward.

He couldn't say how long it was before the wyvern finally broke off and flew back toward her nest. Evidently she'd put enough of a scare into the interlopers to satisfy any territorial ambiguity. Quinn and Chaudri reined in, panting for breath. Their mounts licked at the snow, their flanks lathered and heaving.

"Think we gave them enough time?" Chaudri asked.

"I hope so. I'm not doing that again," Quinn said.

They picked their way back to the rendezvous point. Quinn was drenched in sweat, but the cold quickly seeped in to chill him. And it still hurt to breathe.

A few hours in, and I definitely hate this place.

On the bright side, Logan and Kiara rode up a moment later. Logan had something in his arm, a white sphere about the size of a watermelon. "Look what we found."

That had to be it. Quinn didn't know a thing about Alissian magic, but the sphere was too symmetrical, and gave off a slight hum. "Thank God," he said.

"Wasn't easy to get, either," Logan said. "Hatchling in the nest tried to bite my arm off." He chuckled and shook his head. "Tough little fella."

"Please," Quinn said. "You should meet his mother."

> **"The den was about four hundred
> square feet and littered with bones.
> Some of them were fresh, and a
> few looked to have been horses."**

—R. HOLT, "SURVEY OF THE
ALISSIAN HIGHLANDS"

CHAPTER 4

EGGBREAKING

The wild dogs had fallen quiet during the wyvern's
show of force, but something told Quinn they were
still nearby.

Logan held up the egg so they all could see it. "Feels
almost like glass," he said.

"Maybe it's a miniature version of the barrier,"
Quinn offered. "Like a voodoo egg."

"In voodoo, you break a curse by burning or de-
stroying the effigy," Chaudri said. "Will it burn?"

"No, but it might break," Logan said. "I'll have to do it on the ground."

He dismounted, found a bare patch in the snow for the egg, and drew his sword. Then the yipping of the wild dogs rose up again. All around them—and they sounded hungry.

"Make it fast," Kiara said. "Bradley, covering fire!"

Quinn took up the bow lashed to his saddle. It was a modern compound disguised as an Alissian longbow. A high-tensile resin gave it a seventy pound draw, with a concealed cam to provide the let-off at full draw. He'd learned to bow-hunt with his grandfather, back in Nevada. Made the mistake of mentioning that to Logan, and now look where it got him.

He fumbled an arrow out of the quiver and nocked it. The familiar grip of the bow was comforting, and the glow of the fiber-optic pins was just enough to aim by.

He drew to his cheek, just as the first wild dog lumbered into view. It had a shaggy coat of gray-brown fur, bared teeth, and moved with the easy gait of a predator. It halted for just a moment, sniffing the air. Quinn checked the range and loosed. The bow thrummed, but the wild dog hunched low at the sound. His arrow struck high shoulder. Probably not fatal, but enough to send it whining into the night. Kiara fired a crossbow, cutting down a second member of the pack.

Logan raised his sword with both hands and brought it down like a hammer. The glass sphere shattered. Blue lightning crackled up the length of Logan's blade. He shouted and dropped it before it reached his hands.

Quinn couldn't stop to help; he was trying to find a target for his next shot. The dogs were wary now, slinking among the shadows where it was harder to see them. There were at least four or five still hunting. Quinn picked one at random, aimed, let the arrow fly, but missed.

"Damn!" he muttered. *Got to aim lower.* He'd spent about half of his first quiver, and he only had two. No time to regret that now. He bit his lip and drew again.

Then the rest of the pack rushed right at them, growling and snapping at the legs of their mounts.

"Protect the horses!" Logan shouted. He had his sword back and was trying to scramble into the saddle.

The mountain pony whinnied in fright as a dog circled it. Quinn drew again, aiming low, and fired. His arrow hit center mass and pinned the dog to the ground.

The dog yelped and whined. The rest of the pack fell on it in a frenzy.

"That's our cue!" Kiara shouted. "With me!" She turned her horse and took off. Chaudri was right after her.

Quinn jerked the mare around and Logan was with him, the pack animals in tow. They galloped to catch up. One or two of the wild dogs started to follow, but most of the pack was with the frenzy. They stopped and loped back.

After half a mile or so, Kiara slowed them to a trot.

The horses were tired, but still jumpy. Quinn couldn't blame them.

"I *hate* dogs," Logan said. "There's no way my daughters are getting a puppy. I don't care how bad they want one."

"Never seen a dog attack a horse before," Quinn said. "That was unreal."

"That's probably what they were after, more than us," Logan said. "One would feed their pack for a week, and who knows how long they'd been trapped within the dome." He rode forward to confer with Kiara.

Chaudri dropped back. "So, what do you think of Alissian wildlife so far?"

"Everything I've seen has tried to eat me. So, not really a fan."

"You should see some of the data our biological surveys have returned. Alissia seems to have undergone fewer of the mass extinction and evolution events than Earth did. There's an incredible diversity of wildlife here. A lot of it we can't even classify."

"Have they done any DNA testing?" Quinn asked. "Does that even work on Alissian creatures?"

"It works on anything with DNA, and most species here seem to have it. But the company's been very cautious about that kind of thing."

"For safety reasons?" Quinn asked.

"I think more for secrecy. Someone gets ahold of it, and even a grad student could tell you that we have access to a new ecosystem."

They halted at the spot where the barrier had

stopped them before. Logan moved forward tentatively, his eyes on the ground.

"Think it worked," he said. He pointed down at a clean line in the snow that crossed the trail. "Here's where the barrier was."

Quinn felt coolness on his left cheek; a sound whispered through the treetops. "Wind," he said. "The wind is blowing."

Logan threw a stick through where the barrier had been, and nothing happened. That was enough to convince Kiara.

"Let's get going. We're way behind schedule," she said.

They crossed the line where the barrier had been without incident. The only thing Quinn noticed was a faint smell of ozone.

"This barrier, the wyvern, the dogs," Logan said. His voice came in across the comm link, clear as day. "It's too cute to be circumstantial."

"I agree," Kiara said. "And I sense Holt's hand in this."

"I can't picture him wrangling a wyvern into position by himself."

"Not to mention the casting of the barrier," she said.

"I'm guessing he had help."

"I don't know much about the magic or the mythical creatures," Quinn interjected. "But it looks like Holt's been planning this for some time."

"That was his way," Chaudri said.

"If you're not sure why he left, can you at least

tell me why the company wants him back so badly?" Quinn asked.

"You don't have the security clearance," Kiara said.

"Screw the clearance. I'm in here now, same as you."

"This is still the company's domain," she said.

"Really?" Quinn asked. "In that case I want to file a complaint about unsafe work conditions. I almost got eaten by a dragon back there."

"A wyvern," Chaudri said.

"Call it whatever you want," Quinn said. "But you guys brought me here, so I'd like to have some idea of what we're up against."

Kiara sighed. "All right, Bradley. When Holt left, he took a backpack with him."

"What's in it?"

She had her console out and must have pulled up a list. "Genetically modified corn, soybean, and wheat seeds. A butane lighter. Waterproof binoculars, ten times magnification. A compact portable generator. Military frequency scanner, infrared goggles. A solar-chargeable laptop."

"And a Beretta .45 caliber handgun," Logan added.

"Jesus, is that all?" Quinn asked.

"It's enough," Kiara said.

They made camp at around two in the morning, by Quinn's best guess. He'd have checked the watch but he almost didn't want to know.

Logan unpacked four shoebox-sized bundles that

proved to be self-assembled, insulated pup tents. Each one came with a tiny portable heating unit about the shape and size of a grapefruit.

"Know what powers these?" Logan asked.

"I'm guessing a battery that will be in my cell phone in two years," Quinn said.

"Nope, but close. Hydrogen fuel cells."

"Are they safe?"

"Nope, but close," Logan said.

"Don't listen to him," Chaudri interjected. "I've been assured that they are."

"Even so," the big man said, "I'm sleeping on the far side of the tent from it."

Far side of a pup tent. That was all of two feet.

Quinn hoped it was enough.

Kiara had a wood-framed device about the size of a King James Bible in her hand. It had to be digital, from the sound of the soft, persistent beeping. Logan wandered over to check on her. Quinn followed.

"Any signal on Holt?" Logan asked.

"Nothing yet," she said.

"Wait," Quinn said. "You can track him?"

"We can track anyone who spent time at the island facility," Kiara said.

"How?"

Kiara ignored him. Logan said, "It's an isotope with a long half-life. They put it in the food on the island."

"I've been eating that food!" Quinn said.

Kiara glanced at her console. "I can see that."

"Aw, hell." Yet another little surprise the company hadn't bothered to read him in on.

"It's perfectly harmless, Mr. Bradley," Kiara said.

"Big corporations say that all the time."

"Relax, Bradley," Logan said. "Been eating it for years, and look how healthy I am."

"You're also twice the size of a normal person." He turned to Kiara as Logan chuckled. "Next time you put radioactive stuff in the food, I'd like to know in advance."

Once the tents were set and warming up, Logan established a perimeter around their little camp. For this he had six identical metal stakes that he drove into the ground with a rubber mallet. Each housed an infrared heat/sensor grid and short-range transmission chip. Facing outward, the stakes provided a hexagon-shaped field of surveillance about fifty yards in each direction.

Anything giving off heat and movement triggered an alert to consoles carried by Logan and Kiara. Pinhole zoom cameras from the company's covert surveillance division would feed videos to the consoles Logan and Kiara kept at hand.

"Get some rest, everyone," Kiara ordered. "Daybreak is in about six hours; we'll get moving then."

"Should we set a watch, Lieutenant?" Logan asked.

"Let's rely on the sensors. I want everyone fresh tomorrow."

No such luck.

An hour after they turned in, something set off the

infrared sensors. Quinn woke reluctantly to a persistent beeping noise in his communicator, followed by Logan's voice.

"Sensors picked up something. Stand by."

Quinn heard something crunching heavily through the snow.

"Looks like a bear," Kiara said. "Logan, hit the pulse."

The infrared sensor posts also had an ultrasonic emitter, something Logan called a "pest deterrent." In truth, it was about a hundred times more powerful than similar devices sold for home use. The frequencies were just beyond the range of human hearing.

"Seems to be working," Logan said. "He's moving off. Wait, I was wrong. Who left their food out?"

"Hit it again," Kiara said.

The ultrasonic emitter kept the bear away from the tents, but only just. Try as he might, Quinn couldn't go back to sleep with a golf-cart-sized carnivore just outside and a persistent beeping in his communicator. Logan gave him a little update each time.

Beep. "Just the bear again."

Beep. "Just the bear."

Beep-beep. "Oh, now we have two bears."

The bears didn't bother them, or the horses, but they kept Quinn up most of the night. He thought Kiara might push back their timetable, since no one had gotten a good night's sleep. But no, wrong again. She had them up and moving just after daybreak.

Quinn crawled out of his tent, already missing his bunk on the island complex. The Alissian sun was almost white; it cast the open woods around them in grayscale.

"Morning all," Chaudri said. She stood and drew a deep breath. "I love the sunrise here."

"You're chipper this morning," Quinn grumbled.

"Why not? With that portable heater I slept like a baby."

"What about the bears, and the constant alarm beeps?"

"There were bears? Oh. Sorry." She winked at Quinn. "Must have switched off my comm unit."

"I believe I asked you to keep it turned on," Logan said.

"Of course, of course. Won't happen again."

Wink.

Kiara, already dressed and armored, had engrossed herself in her digital console and the map of Alissia. The material was woven cotton, just like U.S. currency. It proved lightweight, waterproof, durable, but felt remarkably similar to good quality Alissian parchment. Graphite ink added to the illusion that it was drawn by hand.

"Still nothing on Holt," she announced. "We're going to need intel if we want to track him down anytime this year. We'll make for the nearest village. It's called Wenthrop."

Quinn couldn't wait to meet some Alissians. He hadn't decided whether or not they counted as aliens. Maybe on this side of the gateway, *he* was the alien. One thing was certain: they'd not yet met a Vegas illusionist, which meant he had a completely naive audience.

Also known as a magician's favorite thing.

"Here's the deal," Kiara said. She'd called a halt in the slushy mess that counted for a road in Alissia's rural areas. Two hundred yards downhill, a village crouched beneath a haze of smoke. "We like the Wayfarer because it caters to travelers. It's the only place in this area that we can resupply. But it does attract a rough crowd."

"Define 'rough,'" Quinn said.

"Mercenaries, cutpurses, bounty hunters, and smugglers," Logan said. "Any of 'em would gut you like a pig if he thought he might find a few coins in your pockets."

"Sounds delightful. I think I'll wait here," Quinn said. Logan had showed him some video footage of street fights and muggings he'd recorded while on scouting expeditions here. The idea of entering a building crowded with violent criminals was terrifying.

"We're all going," Kiara said. Her tone said there would be no argument.

"How do I keep from getting gutted like a pig, as you so delightfully put it?" Quinn asked.

"Stay right by me, and don't stare at anyone," Logan said. "Make yourself invisible. You're supposed to be good at that."

"Great," Quinn said. Helpful as ever.

The village was nothing more than a dozen ramshackle buildings that squatted on either side of the slushy road. All of them were wood, but no two looked alike. They were practically on top of one another in hodgepodge fashion, like a city inspector's nightmare. The thatch roofs were at least a foot thick, maybe more, and sagging under the weight of the snow.

The whole village looked like it could collapse any minute.

The area outside the Wayfarer boasted a variety of animals lashed to wooden posts. Most were mules and half-starved packhorses, but a few stood out. They were armored in some kind of animal hide, and bristled with swords, spears, even longbows.

"Merc horses," Logan said.

"That's a lot of weapons," Quinn said.

"They'll have even more inside. Good weapons are sort of like a mercenary résumé."

"Why do you think they're here?" Quinn asked. Armed men weren't exactly his first choice, if he had to meet the natives. Just seeing their horses made him nervous.

"Hard to say. Anyone with a level head is probably looking for work farther south where it's harder to freeze to death."

Which, sad to say, sounded perfectly reasonable.

They secured the horses to a set of hitching posts, as far away from the other animals as possible. Kiara pulled open the inn's stout wooden door. The inside was poorly lit. The warm air reeked of soot, sweat, and ale.

"Make sure your weapons are visible," Logan muttered across the comm link.

Quinn loosened his cloak enough that the hilt of his short sword poked through. Chaudri and Kiara did similar with their blades. It was a casual but concerted gesture; more than a few of those in the common room took notice that the newcomers were well-armed. Not to be trifled with.

One such cognizant fellow was the proprietor, a slender, middle-aged man wearing a white apron. He greeted them with the nervous smile of a guy who doesn't want any trouble.

Logan held up four fingers, and then led them into the smoky back half of the common room.

Quinn did his best to keep his eyes to himself, but he couldn't help but glance around. *Alissians.* They looked human, albeit grubbier and with a good bit of facial hair to go around. The men had untrimmed beards and long hair that blended together into shaggy dark manes about their faces. The women had their hair pinned up, which explained why Kiara and Chaudri had done the same to theirs before coming through. Now Quinn understood why they hadn't let him shave since he'd come to the island. A man with a clean-shaven face would stand out here.

All of the tables were full, so they stood up against the bar. Quinn did his best to appear casual. The innkeeper came over and plunked down four heavy mugs. Logan paid him with odd-shaped metallic coins from a leather purse at his belt. Then he took another fistful of coins and casually dumped them into the innkeeper's apron pocket. The man moved away without seeming to notice.

"What's that about?" Quinn whispered.

"Don't let his manner fool you," Logan said. "Old Sy keeps a squad of bruisers with steel-wrapped cudgels on the other side of that door. If there's trouble, we just bought their allegiance."

"For how long?"

"Daybreak . . . or as long as no one outbids us."

God, hired thugs with clubs waiting in a back room. They weren't kidding about this being a rough place. Quinn couldn't get out of here fast enough.

Kiara left her ale on the bar untouched. "Logan and I will make the rounds. You two stay out of trouble."

Quinn picked up his mug and hefted it. The ale was honey-colored and frothy, the glass cold to his touch. "Is it safe to drink?"

"One way to find out," Chaudri said. She leaned back and took a sip.

"You look like you're on vacation," Quinn said.

"I am, in a way. It's one thing to study the data. Quite another to be over here collecting it firsthand." She frowned, her eyes distant. "Dr. Holt did most of the fieldwork."

Quinn looked around the smoky common room, taking care not to stare at anyone for too long. The smoke helped with that—the air was thick with it. Men and women crowded the tables, drinking and laughing and shouting at one another. Like a scene from King

Arthur's court. *Guess that makes me Merlin.* He could see the appeal of a little fieldwork.

He thought more about what Chaudri had just said, about Holt doing most of it. "Did you work closely with him?"

"For most of my career," Chaudri said. "He recruited me, trained me. Took me here for the first time." She smiled in a kind of shy way.

Not for the first time since he met her, Quinn thought, *Maybe there's a little more to this relationship than she's letting on.*

"Does he have a family?"

"I don't think so. His work was his top priority."

"His name was on most of the briefing documents," Quinn said. "Must be a pretty sharp guy."

"Probably one of the smartest men I know," Chaudri said. She took a long pull of the ale. "He lived and breathed this place. Spent weeks here at a time. Not to discount the efforts of the whole research team," she added quickly. "But Holt was sort of our visionary."

"You know, through all of the briefings and strategy meetings, no one's ever mentioned to me *why* he left."

Chaudri raised a hand purposefully and leaned her head on it, tapping off her communicator. Quinn did likewise.

"Just between you and me, I think he got wind of something that the company was planning, and he didn't like it."

"What are they planning?" Quinn asked.

Chaudri paused. "You saw the armory, didn't you?"

"Of course. I spent two weeks there proving my martial incompetence to Logan. You must have every medieval weapon ever used in there."

"We have even more in storage, and hundreds of mercenaries who know how to fight with them. Not to mention the siege engines on the roof of the armory."

"Like catapults?"

"Catapults, mangonels, siege towers. Even a pair of trebuchets. All built by your friends in the prototyping lab to be lightweight and portable."

"Does that make you nervous, at all?"

She offered a dismissive wave. "I think they're just being careful."

"Maybe it's more than that."

"Like what?"

"I don't know, an invasion?"

"That would be a fascinating thing to see."

"Fascinating?" Quinn was aghast. "How do you figure?"

Chaudri shrugged. "A small but technologically superior force against a larger native population. It's not like it hasn't happened before, in our world."

Quinn shook his head. "Wow."

"That's the difference between Dr. Holt and myself. He always got too close," she said. "To the work, I mean."

Oh my God, I think she's blushing.

Then Logan leaned into view from halfway across the common room, caught Quinn's eye, and tapped his ear.

"I think Logan wants us linked back in," Quinn said.

They both leaned against their hands and turned their communicators back on.

"So, Bradley," Chaudri said, with a forced cheerfulness. "How did the company ever get you to go along with this?"

Quinn smiled and shook his head. "A check and a threat."

"Were you in Atlantic City?"

"Vegas. Have you ever been?"

"Oh, heavens no. What sort of tricks were you doing?"

"You name it. Disappearing acts, sleight of hand, optical illusions. A lot of flash and razzle-dazzle. That's what they want in Vegas."

"You don't sound as high on yourself as you did when you came here."

Quinn sighed. "I have to admit I'm a little nervous. I mean, you guys have me posing as this magician and we know so little about them. How am I supposed to act? What things do they usually do?"

"We're not sure, to be honest. All we've been able to dig up is that they seem to take a lot of naps."

"I'll be sure to run that one by Kiara."

They sat in silence for a minute, and Quinn let the hum of conversation wash over him. Two heavyset men at the next table were arguing over whose turn it was to pay the bill.

"Son of a bitch," Quinn said. He leaned toward Chaudri. "They speak English!"

"No, they don't," Chaudri said.

"I'm talking about these two," Quinn said. He tilted his head slightly in the direction of the fat guys. "I can understand them."

"I expect so. That's the effect of the polyglossia."

"The poly-what?"

"Polyglossia. Universal comprehension of spoken language," Chaudri said. "It's one of the phenomena here that we don't understand. And it works in both directions, too. They can understand us just as easily."

"How is that even possible?"

Chaudri shrugged. "Like I said: we don't entirely understand."

Quinn frowned. The list of things they didn't entirely understand just kept on growing. But he felt a wave of exhilaration just the same. He could *talk* to these people. "What about writing?"

"Well, there's the rub. The polyglossia is limited to spoken language. We've had to learn Alissian writing the hard way. Took our best linguists more than a year."

"Ooh." Quinn made a face. "You know, I'm not sure I can spend that much time here."

She took him too seriously. "No need to worry. The prototyping lab set us up." Chaudri took out a metal case that looked a lot like the one Logan had had in Vegas. She flipped it open to reveal a pair of thick-framed reading glasses.

"The nosepiece has a tiny optical scanner. Whatever you're looking at, it captures the text and runs it through our translation programs in real time. The top halves of the lenses display it in English."

"Get out," Quinn said.

"Here, take them. I have another pair."

Quinn did, and chuckled. Looks like he'd snagged what was in Logan's case after all.

Just then the big man reappeared, with Kiara right behind him. Their faces looked grim.

"We're leaving," Kiara said.

"What's wrong?" Quinn asked.

"Someone outbid us with Sy's bruisers."

"Already?" *That doesn't seem like a good sign.*

"Yes. Quickly now."

They started for the door. Quinn set his mug down and started to follow. Of course, that's when the men stood up, and the steel came out. Four of them. Four mercenaries, each holding a long dagger. Logan and Kiara retreated, moving back toward the bar. Two mercs pressed them. A third was on Chaudri. The fourth came for Quinn.

He thought about the sword, but knew he'd be less than useless in a fight. Especially at close quarters. Better to get out in front of this.

"I'm not with them," he said.

The man had a narrow face and close-cropped beard. A pale white scar ran from one cheekbone nearly to his chin. "You came in with them."

"We entered at the same time. That's all." Quinn

leaned toward the man and lowered his voice. "I'm actually working right now."

The man took a step forward. He held his knife low enough that it wasn't in plain sight, though Quinn could see it. "Doing what?"

Quinn took half a step back. He felt the wood of the bar against his back. No way around it. This was going to end just like one of Logan's cautionary tales.

"I'm the entertainment." He threw his legs over and climbed up on the bar. Every eye in the room turned to look at him.

Quinn gave his best walk-on smile. "Who wants to see a magic trick?" he said.

> "The best illusions aren't a matter of
> technology, but of performance. First,
> you open the minds of the audience.
> Then you fill them with exactly
> what you want them to know."

—Art of Illusion, March 5

CHAPTER 5

THE POWER TO SAVE THE WORLD

From his vantage point atop the bar in the Wayfarer common room, Quinn got his first good look at the crowd. Most of them hadn't noticed that three of the mercenaries had Kiara, Logan, and Chaudri pinned against the bar. That, or they chose not to care.

He tried to forget everything about his current situation—the mission, the danger, the Alissian world—and pretend it was just another stage.

"I have in one of my hands the power to destroy the world," he proclaimed. That turned some heads. "And in the other, the power to save it. Who among you is brave enough to guess which is which?"

No one stirred among the crowd.

"You, sir!" Quinn called. He pointed to the white-aproned innkeeper, who'd appeared behind the bar, looking nervous. He knew.

"Choose a hand to save the world," Quinn said. He held both hands out, fists clenched, palms down, right in front of the man.

Old Sy looked dubious, but at last he pointed at Quinn's left hand. Quinn turned and held both fists up to the crowd. "He says left. What do you say?"

Mutters in the crowd. Some were nodding, others were shaking their heads. That was part of why this trick worked so well. Everyone favored a hand.

"I say right!" someone called from the back of the room.

"Right!" another man echoed.

"Two say right," Quinn said. He raised the right fist slightly higher.

"No, left!"

"Right!"

The crowd was getting into it, shouting out their preference. A scuffle broke out on one side of the room where two groups of bearded men seemed to disagree.

"It sounds about even," Quinn said. He lowered both fists down, right to the face of the man who was waiting for him. "I'll let you decide, my good man. Choose a hand to save the world."

The mercenary's lips curled into a sour expression,

but the crowd was hollering at him, everyone trying to shout down his neighbor. He raised a mail-gloved hand, started to choose Quinn's left fist, but changed his mind and tapped the right.

"He chooses right," Quinn said. He dropped his left fist by his side, raised the right one up to his face.

"Shut your eyes," he whispered over the comm link. He rotated his hand, and made as if to peer in between his clenched fingers. The room fell silent now. He laughed out loud, held the fist up to face outward. "He chose wrong!"

He opened his hand and squeezed his eyes shut. A dazzling white light poured from his palm. Ten thousand candlepower. Everyone in the room was blinded, stumbling backward away from him. Men were shouting, falling on top of each other. Logan, Kiara, and Chaudri rushed past the mercenaries. Quinn ran along the top of the bar, jumped for it, and landed hard behind them. They ran out.

They slammed the door closed behind them. Logan dragged over a heavy crate and shoved it beneath the handle.

Quinn saw the door shaking as he scrambled into the saddle and followed Logan down the road out of the village. They fled at a full gallop for about half a mile.

At last Kiara called for a halt. She gave Logan a signal, and he rode back to scout behind them.

"What the hell was that, Bradley?" Kiara demanded.

"A simple trick. What we in the trade would call

a looky-loo." Quinn showed her the small glass-and-metal contraption. It was one of the company's super-LEDs, the kind used on emergency vehicles and radio towers. About the size of a matchbox car. Only worked if someone was looking right at it, so he'd had to make sure they were. Usually, the "Power to Save the World" was just a coin that he'd work for a few minutes with sleight-of-hand. More entertaining, but far less distracting.

"You shouldn't have drawn attention to yourself," Kiara said.

"Hey," Quinn said. He wasn't about to take flak for this. "I'm pretty sure I saved your asses in there. Those guys weren't screwing around."

Logan reappeared. "No one following us. Looks like there's a full-on brawl happening at the Wayfarer, though."

"Wonderful," Kiara said. "Bradley's already causing riots."

"You hired me to play magician," Quinn said. "That's what we do. We improvise."

"In any case, I want a warning the next time you plan to go off script."

I didn't know we had one. "Know what, Lieutenant? You take the fun out of everything."

The one redeeming point about the Wayfarer debacle is that it yielded the first intel on their quarry.

"Old Sy said Holt stopped in about a day after he

went through the gateway," Logan said. "Bought a horse and asked about the situation on the Kestani border."

"Crossing the mountains is tricky this time of year," Chaudri said.

"Think he'll head for one of the bigger passes?" Logan asked.

"I would. Probably Nevil's Gap."

Kiara consulted her map and made a quick measurement with a stainless-steel ruler. "Should be about a week's ride. That's long enough to know for certain which way he's headed."

"Guess we'd better get moving, then," Logan said. He tossed Quinn the reins of the mountain pony and took point. Kiara was after him, then Quinn, then Chaudri and the other packhorse.

They rode for five or six hours at a stretch, dismounting occasionally to walk the horses. Otherwise, they stopped only at midday for a brief rest and then to make camp at night. This wasn't R & R time, of course. Once the pup tents were up and a perimeter set, it was training time for Quinn.

Usually that meant Logan drilling him in the finer points of swordplay or knife-fighting—often literally. Sometimes Chaudri would take a break from her reading to join in. For a self-proclaimed academic, the woman certainly knew how to swing a broadsword. She and Logan would spar with Quinn in a three-sided melee, an exercise that usually meant welts and bruises on two sides instead of one.

"You're getting a little better," Logan told him, after their fourth night of sword practice. "Might take an Alissian teenager to skewer you now."

"As a general rule, I try to avoid teenagers."

"It's the girls you've got to watch out for."

Quinn chuckled. "You say that like you know. You have daughters?"

Logan sighed. "Four of them. No boys."

"Wow."

"Yeah, wow. The oldest just turned fourteen."

"Ooh." Quinn made a pained expression. "How do you survive?"

"Mostly by staying in the basement. And invading other worlds."

The thought of this battle-hardened soldier hiding out in the basement from his wife and daughters made Quinn smile. "I didn't realize you were such a family man."

"That's the first thing they teach you in basic. If you have a girlfriend, marry her. If you have a wife, start a family."

So he is *ex-military.* "How'd you end up doing this?"

"That's classified."

Of course it was.

Kiara kept trying to raise someone on her long-range transponder. It might reach the gateway cave, if the lockdown protocol was lifted and a receiver unit came through. None of her transmissions brought a reply, though. No one talked about it, but Quinn could tell that the lack of communication had her concerned. As did the clouds in the distance.

The storm hit about four days later. The barometric pressure—updated hourly on the communicator Kiara had strapped to her wrist—had been falling for almost a day. It was early afternoon when the first storm clouds began to gather. Logan began making little forays ahead of the group to search for shelter.

"Got a clump of evergreens close to the road, about a half mile ahead," he said.

Kiara glanced at the wall of dark sky that loomed toward them out of the west. "Can we make it before the storm hits?"

"If we ride hard."

The horses were tired, but Quinn had no trouble spurring his mare to a gallop. She seemed to sense the urgency of the situation. The mountain pony tossed his head a couple of times but eventually followed suit. They plunged along the hard-packed dirt road behind Logan and Kiara in a growing shroud of twilight.

Logan raised an arm to signal and they broke east toward a dark patch of forest. Then the hardwoods gave way to blue and green conifers. Their branches were already draped in snow. The ground was clear except for a thick layer of fallen needles.

Quinn tried to ask where they planned to put up the tents but took a branch to the face instead. Shaking his head, he opened his eyes to find them reining in at a small natural clearing. By then the wind had become a steady roar.

"Secure the horses!" Logan shouted.

Quinn half fell to the ground, but he managed to keep hold of all the reins. He looked around for a good trunk or branch to tie off to, but the snow-covered conifers had nothing to offer. Chaudri rummaged in one of the saddlebags, came up with a handful of metal spikes and a claw hammer. She drove enough spikes into the ground to get the reins secured. The mounts were snorting, showing the whites in their eyes. A primal fear of what was coming had them in its grip. Quinn and Chaudri struggled with hobbles for the horses' feet so they wouldn't bolt in the storm.

Meanwhile, Logan and Kiara had assembled a series of telescoping metallic rods about seven feet long. They drove these into the earth at regular intervals around the small clearing. Out came a long roll of ultrafine wire mesh from one of the saddlebags. They wrapped it around the perimeter of their clearing, then draped more of it overhead, supporting the mesh with more telescoping rods like the poles of a circus tent. Logan unwrapped a plastic-covered bundle about the size of a small shoebox, revealing an electric console disguised as a jewelry box. He and Kiara fitted wires from this to the fine-mesh layer.

"Everyone stand clear!" Logan shouted.

Kiara flipped a series of switches on the console, and the fine mesh began to hum. Quinn was half-blind from the blowing snow, but he could have sworn a faint blue glow emanated from the mesh. And within their little clearing, the wind died.

"Don't touch the mesh," Kiara said.

"Wasn't planning on it," he said. *I'm not a moron.*

The sounds of the storm had grown muted, as if shutting an open window on a downpour. Only this was a tempest unlike any Quinn had ever seen. He'd grown up in the desert; he'd seen summer squalls and even a sandstorm, but nothing with the raw fury of this storm. It was like a living thing that clawed at the very ground and shook it furiously.

"Is this a typical storm?" Quinn asked. His voice sounded strange in the clearing's numb silence.

"For northern Felara, yes," Chaudri said. "The straight winds aren't so much a danger as the electrostatic charges. Incredibly disruptive to just about every electronic device that we carry. Not to mention the interference with neural function."

"Neural as in neuron? As in my *brain*?"

"Yes—for what it's worth." She smiled, but Quinn was feeling his head, as if he might feel the storm attacking his mind. She took a wrist and gently pulled his arm down. "It's perfectly all right, Quinn. Alissians seem to have a natural resistance to the interference, but we don't. So we have this," she said, gesturing at the wire mesh all around them.

"It looks . . . expensive."

"CASE Global made it a priority investment. The charged plasma keeps debris off of us, too."

Like a deflector shield, straight out of *Star Wars*. As if sensing his doubt, a wrist-thick branch from a nearby tree was ripped loose by the wind. It skittered once across the top of the protective barrier, only to tumble away.

"Case in point," Chaudri said.

"So nothing can get to us?"

"Oh, I doubt it would withstand a crossbow bolt. But it's good for just about anything else."

"Hopefully the storm won't start shooting at us."

"I'd say we're reasonably safe."

Quinn leaned back and stretched. It felt like the first time in ages he didn't have that tension in his shoulders. "Why aren't we using this all the time?" He might even get a decent night's sleep for once.

"It's an energy hog. Emergency-use only, that's right in the protocol. The solar chargers will need a few days to replenish the power we're burning right now."

"Too bad."

She leaned close to Quinn and lowered her voice. "There are security reasons, too. The plasma generates an electromagnetic field. Building a sensor to detect it would not be difficult . . . for someone who knew what he was doing."

"Like Richard Holt," Quinn said.

"Exactly."

A jagged line of steep, snowcapped mountains separated Felara from New Kestani to the south. The research team had been unable to determine what happened to *old* Kestani, or if it had even existed. The fact that mountains formed a physical barrier between Felarans and Kestani seemed a good thing, as the two city-states had remained in a state of open conflict since well before the gateway was first discovered.

The main strategy for both sides was to control the mountain passes, of which there were about a dozen. Possession of these changed hands every few months by military action or treachery; sometimes even by strategic intent. According to Logan, Kestani currently controlled the largest pass, called Nevil's Gap.

"Border crossings are touch and go," he said. "The key to getting across without too much trouble is to minimize your threat and have a good story."

He dug into one of his saddlebags and came up with two hooded robes of plain brown with white stars embroidered over the heart. "So here's part one. You two are going to pose as Friars of the Star."

"Who are they?" Quinn asked.

"Sworn pacifists," Chaudri said. "They take a series of oaths not to use weapons except in the defense of their own lives."

"It makes us look less like a small military squad," Logan said.

Quinn took the cloak and paused. "Won't it seem a bit odd, since we're . . ."

"What?" Chaudri asked. All innocent, too.

Please don't make me say it out loud. "You know."

"A woman and a man?"

"Well, yeah," Quinn said.

"The friarhood is open to both."

I'll be damned. "Very forward-thinking of them."

"Alissia scores better than Earth in some areas. Gender equality is one of them."

Quinn tugged on the robe over his cloak. He was all about blending in, and not seeming a threat. "How should I play it?" he asked.

"Just let Chaudri do the talking," Kiara said.

Great, she wanted him to take a vow of silence. "Sounds like fun," Quinn said. "You know, I *do* act for a living."

"Then act like Chaudri is doing all the talking."

The somewhat regular vista of mature forest gave way to rocky terrain as they headed south. One morning, after the fog had cleared, Quinn saw the distant peaks of the mountains that marked the border between Felara and New Kestani. Another day and night of riding put them well into the foothills. Despite Kiara's sense of urgency, they had to slow down here; the hard-packed dirt road had become gravel, and Logan disliked the reduced visibility of the road ahead. More than once he called a halt while he rode around blind turns or scouted ahead over the next ridge.

But this was Alissia, so of course it didn't matter how prepared they were.

The attack came at the worst time and place possible. The road had narrowed to little more than a goat trail sandwiched between a steep ridge on their left and a precipitous drop-off to the right. Logan had the lead, Chaudri the rear, with Kiara and Quinn between them. Their only warning was the soft rattle of some gravel tumbling down the ridge just ahead of them. Out of nowhere, two gray-clad men hidden among the rocks jumped out in front of Logan's horse. One of them swung a sword at Logan; the other went for his horse's reins.

"Ambush!" Logan shouted.

No shit. Quinn wondered if he should draw his sword or keep up the pretense.

Logan leaned back and away from the blow, sawing at the reins to turn his horse around. The animal snorted and kicked one of the attackers; he tumbled over the edge and out of view. Then Logan had his sword out.

Quinn turned, saw two more figures in gray running up to box them in. "Behind us!" he shouted. Chaudri turned to engage the attackers. A small avalanche warned of more men coming down the rocky slope. Two of them. Kiara cut the first one down with her crossbow. The second charged right for Quinn.

"Shit!" Quinn said. *Survival trumps pretense.*

He fought to get his sword handle free of the robe disguise. He drew the blade just as the man was on him. Quinn made a weak attempt at a thrust. The man knocked it aside—this was definitely not a twelve-year-old boy. The returning slash should have taken off Quinn's arm at the shoulder, but instead glanced off the hidden armor. It hurt like hell. It also put the man off balance. He fell down in front of the mare. Instinctively Quinn spurred her, hard. She rode him down.

Quinn lashed the sword to his saddle and took up his bow. Logan had killed two more attackers; his sword was spattered red. Kiara turned aside a sword blow and ran a man through with her saber. Chaudri was locked in contest with another attacker. Quinn drew an arrow, put the sight pin on the man's back, and just loosed. Didn't even think about it. At ten yards, he couldn't miss. The shaft struck center mass. The man collapsed. Chaudri sagged in relief, and nodded her thanks.

Then all was still, but for the stomps of the horses and the panting riders atop them.

"Everyone all right?" Kiara asked. Two ragged forms lay motionless below her.

Chaudri had a nasty gash on one arm, and her hands were shaking. Quinn couldn't stop himself from looking back at the trampled mess of the man he'd ridden down. It had all happened so fast, and he was just trying to stay alive. But he had always been a creator. He made things: his tricks, his magic, the excitement of an audience. On the ground was something he'd *destroyed*. He felt his stomach roiling. He half fell out of his horse and threw up in the weeds.

Logan dismounted and checked one of the bodies. "Looks like an old Felaran uniform. Must be deserters from the battle for the gap," he said. "They couldn't have picked a better place for an ambush. We were lucky."

"Lucky?" Quinn said. He wiped his face with a sleeve and fought another wave of nausea. "How do you figure?"

"If they'd had bows, we'd be dead right now."

Quinn's stomach lurched on him again. He dry-heaved for a few minutes. Nothing came out; he was completely drained.

"Pull yourself together, Bradley," Kiara said.

I'm trying.

She and Logan helped Chaudri climb out of the saddle. The gash on her arm wasn't as bad as it looked. Logan broke out the med kit. They shook hemostatic powder onto the wound to stop the bleeding, and wrapped it up tight with bandages. Logan wanted a look at Quinn's shoulder next. The skin was already black and blue where the sword had hit him.

"Not much I can do about this," Logan said. "It's going to hurt like hell tomorrow."

"Great. That gives me something to look forward to," Quinn said.

"Look at the bright side," Logan said. "It'll remind you to keep your guard up next time."

> **"Felarans and New Kestani are Alissia's answer to the Hatfields and McCoys."**
>
> —R. HOLT, "ALISSIA: POLITICAL OVERVIEW"

CHAPTER 6

BORDER CROSSING

Two days after the ambush, the mountains pressed in all around them.

"We've been spotted," Logan said quietly. "No, don't look around. Ridge to the northwest. They're good, whoever they are."

"The Kestani at last," Kiara said. "Remember the story, people. We need to sell this just right."

Within ten minutes, there were watchers on both sides. According to Logan, at least. Quinn didn't see anything, but he was under orders not to "look around like an idiot."

At Kiara's signal, they slowed the horses to a walk. It

wasn't long until a squad of pikemen in maroon-slashed uniforms materialized on the trail to bar their way.

"Can I help you?" Kiara asked. Her voice had a sudden inflection to it, almost a hint of British royalty.

"Name and purpose," one of the soldiers said.

She turned up her chin. "I'll give you my name, soldier, when you give me yours."

Quinn tried to hide his rising panic. What the hell was she doing? These soldiers were going to butcher them like cattle.

But something about her retort had changed things with the soldiers. "Apologies, my lady," the one said. He straightened. "Captain Darenko, Kestani advance guard."

"And I am Kiara. Now, move your oafs aside so we can be on our way. We have a schedule to keep."

"Sorry. No one from Felara is permitted through."

"Are you deaf as well as blind? We're from Valteron!"

"I meant no off—"

"You may slap yourself later for the offense, intended or not. Now, out of our way."

"You'll have to speak to the commander before going through."

Kiara scoffed in perfectly feigned disgust. "I don't have time to speak to unwashed soldiers all day. We'd like to clear the pass before nightfall."

"Everyone speaks to the commander. No exceptions."

Kiara waited a moment as if considering this proposal, then sighed. "Very well. Lead on."

The man who'd spoken and another soldier beckoned them forward, deeper into the pass. The other two fell in behind Chaudri once they'd passed. They seemed peaceful enough, and theoretically Quinn had the protection of his assumed brotherhood, but the thought of the spears behind him made his back itch. Ahead, the pass widened into a small canyon into which the Kestani—or possibly the Felarans, before being routed—had built a considerable fortress. They rode past lines of sharpened stakes buried in the ground, pointing outward at an angle like spines on a porcupine. Logan muttered something about "horse killers."

Beyond these was a stockade wall, peppered with slits manned by archers and crossbowmen. Above and behind them were wooden platforms with machinery that Quinn recognized as catapults. These were loaded and ready to fire, pointed toward the north end of the pass. He sucked in a sharp breath, wowed by the display.

A low, square building squatted beside the catapult platform. The soldier who'd led their escort excused himself and ducked inside to retrieve the commander. He returned with a thin, energetic man with dark hair and a goatee speckled with gray.

"Are you in command here?" Kiara demanded.

Her imperious tone washed over this man like a wave crashing on shore. He spent a long moment taking them in, frowning as he looked at the weapons strapped to their horses. "I am."

"Commands and those who give them are a thing of war," Chaudri said. "Peace has no need of either."

Quinn had to bite his lip. Chaudri knew what she was doing, all right. Came out of nowhere and just *sold* it. No one even blinked. She'd really missed her calling on the stage.

The commander cleared his throat. "Well said, sister. But peace is a long way off for us."

"Peace is right in front of everyone, if they could look for it," Chaudri said.

Kiara coughed into her hand, and the message was pretty clear: *Dial it back, Chaudri.*

"Your man says that we have to see you before going through the pass," she said. "So here we are. Have we wasted enough of each other's time yet?"

"Where are you from?"

"Valteron, of course," she said.

"Why were you in Felara?"

"The same reason I go anywhere. To buy and sell and make a profit."

"I see," said the commander. He walked past her and along the horses, looking it all over with a sort of casual air.

"Do you?" Kiara asked. "Because every moment I waste here costs me money."

The commander seemed to notice Chaudri's bandaged arm for the first time. "Looks like you had some trouble on the road."

Kiara flicked a hand at Logan, as if the discussion of such things was beneath her.

Logan cleared his throat. "If I may, Commander?" he asked. Polite, deferential. That was good. Play to his ego, since Kiara had trodden all over it.

The commander perked up a bit, and gave Logan a curt nod.

"We were attacked by bandits about a half day's ride from here," Logan said. "Six men in old Felaran uniforms."

The man grunted. "Deserters. I'm not surprised, given the routing we gave them. Did you lose any men? Or cargo?"

"We fought them off, thanks to the good brothers here," Logan said. He nodded at Quinn and Chaudri.

"Our arms can swing a sword," Chaudri said. "But only with sadness."

"Great sadness," Quinn echoed, in a low tone. He just couldn't help himself.

Logan coughed, covering his mouth with his hand.

"How fortunate," the commander said. "In any case, we'll send a patrol down to ensure that there were no survivors."

"Good," Kiara said. "We'll be on our way, then."

The man strolled back toward her, rubbing his chin. "See, the thing is, we're looking for three Felaran spies."

"Good for you," Kiara said.

"A large man with dark skin. A studious, quiet one. And a woman in charge."

Uh-oh. This was starting to feel like another one of Holt's little surprises. Quinn slid a hand into his sleeve and brushed his fingertips against the mechanism there. If push came to shove, he could surprise these soldiers. Maybe buy them a little bit of time to flee back down the mountain . . . no, not with the defenses they'd seen. These soldiers weren't screwing around.

Damn.

"I'm not sure I like what you're implying, Commander," Kiara said.

He shrugged. "We get a warning like that, we pay attention."

A few more soldiers had materialized around them, all of them holding hooked spears. Quinn recognized them, too, from his training. They were for pulling riders out of the saddle. Kiara had told him in no uncertain terms to stay quiet, but he didn't have much of a choice.

"I killed a man today," he said.

His words caught the commander by surprise. Kiara threw him a sharp look.

"It was my own failing," Quinn said. He made his face a mask of pained regret. "Just as letting those Felarans escape was yours."

"We're not the ones who attacked you. Blame Felara," the commander said. But the corner of his eye trembled, almost like a nervous tic.

Quinn pounced on him. "You drove them upon us!" He was using his stage voice now, and the words carried. Other men in the encampment turned toward them. Then the lyric just popped into his head. "So now we've come to you, with open arms. Nothing to hide." He held out his arms, palms open, imploring him. "Believe what I say."

The soldiers around them hunched a little at his words. Lowered their weapons just a fraction, too.

"Yes, well . . . I suppose that's true," the commander said. "But we still got the warning."

Kiara had stopped glaring at Quinn, and now pursed her lips. There was blood in the water, and she was circling.

Yes, Quinn thought, trying to will her to action. *Go for it.*

"Let me guess," Kiara said. "A graying fellow, traveling alone, with a backpack and a borrowed horse."

The commander's eye trembled again. Oh, what a delightful tell that was.

"I knew it," said Kiara. "His name is Richard and he's my biggest rival in Valteron."

"He warned us that—" the commander began.

"Of course he warned you. The bastard would say anything to slow me down by a day, with the kind of cargo I'm carrying."

"And what is that?" the commander asked. Still suspicious, but more circumspect about it.

"Mostly gems," Kiara said. She nodded at Logan.

He reached into a bag—slowly, as a few of the guards tensed—and produced a leather satchel filled with polished stones. Rubies, emeralds, amethysts. From what Quinn had been told, they were worth a fortune in this world, even if they'd been synthetically created back in the company laboratory. Kiara beckoned Logan over, selected a ruby about the size of a robin's egg. "Perhaps a contribution to your war effort would speed this along?"

The commander wavered a moment, but the way he stared at the gem said plenty. A mark was a mark. Quinn's tense shoulders started to loosen.

"Your support is appreciated," he said at last. He took the gem, held it up to the sunlight for a look. Then he tossed it to a soldier. "Strongbox."

"With your permission, Commander," Kiara said. She picked up her reins. "The sooner I'm off Felaran soil, the better."

The perfect thing to say. If he could have, Quinn would have applauded her.

The commander allowed a tight smile. "Now there's a sentiment I can agree with. Speak of what you've seen to no one, even in New Kestani. Felarans have spies everywhere."

"You have my word, Commander. Not a whisper to anyone." She tapped a finger on her chin. "My competitor. Did he happen to say where he was headed?"

"Can't say I recall."

Kiara flipped him another gem, this time an emerald. "How's your memory now?"

"Getting better." The commander scratched his head. "Still foggy, though."

Quinn fought the grin that wanted to take over his face. This guy had some balls.

Or jewels, as it were.

She tossed him a sapphire about the size of Quinn's thumb. Now there was a substantial bribe; that gem could probably fund the entire garrison for a month.

"South, I believe it was," the commander said. He looked to one of his soldiers, who nodded in agreement. "Back to Valteron, just like you."

"Thank you, Commander," Kiara said. She made a sour face. "I do hope your memory clears up faster the next time."

"I'm sure it will, my lady," he said. He handed her a small square of parchment with a maroon wax seal at the bottom. "This will get you through to New Kestani." He put two fingers to his forehead and gestured to Chaudri, then to Quinn. "Brother. Sister."

Quinn gave him a solemn nod. It was all he could trust himself to do.

They rode slowly out of the battlements and began winding their way out of the canyon to the Kestani side of the pass.

"Really went on a limb out there, Bradley," Logan said quietly.

"I had to say something. They were about to string us up."

"Maybe avoid the Journey lyrics, next time."

"I hope there isn't a next time," Quinn said.

Logan chuckled. "Don't stop believing."

At two narrow funnel points in the road they encountered squads of soldiers, but their wax-sealed parchment got them through without delay, and a thought occurred to Quinn: they might even be gaining on Holt. He felt a thrill, thinking about it.

I can't wait to meet this guy.

Logan had to admit that they were making good time. Nevil's Gap put them at the narrowest point of New Kestani, squeezed between the border mountains and an inlet bay shared with the city-state of Tion to the south. That was if Kiara's maps were accurate. Holt might have tampered with the Alissian geographical data. Logan didn't trust the maps, didn't trust anything the man had touched before he left, and had voiced that numerous times.

The lieutenant was unfazed. "The survey teams went over them twice with their notes. They couldn't find any significant changes."

Logan shrugged. "Holt's too smart to leave a trail." *And we usually don't catch on to his little surprises until it's too late.*

They rode on.

The trail widened enough that he could drop back to ride beside the magician. "How are you holding up?" he asked.

Bradley shrugged. Didn't say anything, where normally he'd have a joke or a smart-ass reply.

"You did well in the ambush," Logan said. "Only forgot about half of what I taught you."

"I'm glad I didn't drop my sword," Bradley said. "They just came out of nowhere and were on us."

"Hate to tell you, but that's usually how it goes," Logan said. "Even back home. Middle Eastern fighters are all about guerilla warfare. Roadside bombs, sneak attacks, assassinations. You don't get prep time or warnings. That's why we train the way we do."

Bradley looked down and away from him. "When I shot him, I—I didn't even think about it."

"That's good," Logan said.

"How is that *good*?"

"You relied on instinct, and you stayed alive. That's all that matters."

"I guess," Bradley said.

Logan would have told him that it got easier, that he'd get over it. But that would be a lie, so he left Bradley to his haunting thoughts and rode up to check on Kiara's progress with the radioisotope scanner. "Anything yet?"

"Nothing," she said.

"He must have some way to circumvent the isotope." Logan wouldn't put it past him. Holt had been two or three moves ahead since the day he'd left. Probably before that.

"At least we know where he's headed."

"I'm worried about that, though," Logan said. "He's too smart to let something slip by accident."

"We catch up to him before he crosses the border, and it doesn't really matter what he's planned," Kiara said.

Logan didn't think it was that simple. Holt had never done anything half-ass. "Hope you're right. I'm tired of dancing for him." *Just as I'm tired of this horse, of this world, and of being away from my girls.*

"Then we should try to get ahead of him. What's the fastest way south?"

"Probably by sea, this time of year. We might even beat him to Valteron." If that's where he was truly headed.

"For all we know, he's done the same," Kiara said.

"Might as well check the closest port city, then," Logan said.

"Very well," Kiara said. "You know the one I want, Logan. Take the lead."

"Roger." He nudged his mount into the lead and began whistling a sea chantey. Bradley rode up to take his place.

"What's got him so excited?" he could hear Bradley ask.

"The thing that enlisted men live for, and every officer dreads most," Kiara said. "Shore leave."

He couldn't help but grin.

> **"If we spent half as much on cultural research as we did security, we'd know the Alissian world as well as we do our own."**
>
> —R. HOLT, "INVESTMENT IN ALISSIA"

CHAPTER 7

CAPTAINS

Seven days of hard riding put them in smelling distance of the ocean. The mountain peaks had steadily dropped behind them, fading at last into the indistinct clouds of a bruised-gray sky. According to Chaudri, ninety percent of Kestani lived within ten or twenty leagues of one of the borders, be it the mountains, the seacoast, or the capital city near the borders with Tion and Caralis.

Now they rode into a steady southern breeze that carried the hint of brine, and laid eyes on the largest Alissian settlement Quinn had seen yet.

"Bayport," Chaudri said. "Population of about ten thousand, give or take a few depending on the trading fleet and naval presence."

The port city and the bay beyond looked like an old painting of Hong Kong. Wooden buildings piled on one another amid a sea of thatch-roof houses, more than Quinn could count. Beyond them was an even more crowded harbor, first with rowboats and single-masted sailcraft, then larger junks and eventually the traders: deep-hulled ships with two or three masts.

Chaudri used a pair of compact binoculars to inspect the flags and sigils at their masts. "Kestani and Valteroni craft for the most part," she said. "I see a few Caralissian traders, too. There's a Pirean ship—they're a long way from home. If Holt came here, he could catch a ride anywhere."

"He could still be down there, waiting to catch a ride," Logan said.

Kiara checked the radioisotope scanner. The look on her face was frustration, as best Quinn could gauge. He was still trying to work out her tells.

"I don't like going into a crowded city, but it's probably worth a look," she said.

"I know a stable where we can stash the horses," Logan said.

"Good," she said. "We'll need to find the port master, and then we make a round of the captain's taverns along the waterfront. If Holt passed through, someone might remember him."

They reached the city limits in late afternoon, when

the setting sun made black skeletons of the masts in the harbor.

"Watch your purses and saddlebags," Logan said. "It tends to get a bit crowded in here."

The city had no wall, which meant no gate—apparently the Kestani felt comfortable with few land defenses here because of the ships. A steady flow of travelers entered the city from several directions at once, most of them on foot. The occasional wagon or horse cart rumbled past, loaded with tubers or livestock or materials Quinn didn't even recognize.

Most of the people were Kestani; he could tell by a quick glance because of the colorful garb. There was no wrong answer when it came to colors or styles for Kestani dress. Neon green and bright orange? No problem. Bright blue and rich purple? Go ahead. Somehow the Kestani made it all work. He felt drably attired by comparison, a plain raven in a flock of tropical birds.

Eventually they were forced to walk the horses, as Alissians pressed around them in the narrow streets of the port city. Quinn looked out across the people and the cottages and marveled at how *many* of them there were. He had been in big cities—hell, Vegas could have ten times this number on the Strip alone—but it wasn't the same. Bayport was a city bursting at the seams. The layout of the city, the garb, the chatter of those passing by, emphasized how much this world differed from his own. They passed the open door of a squat stone building where a wave of heat washed out, along with the steady ring of hammer on metal. A blacksmith. Quinn shook his head. Unbelievable.

Chaudri was getting into her element. She strolled casually along, chatting with Alissians as they passed, asking questions, even bargaining with a street vendor for some mystery-meat concoction served hot off a heated iron brazier. Were she not following Quinn's horse, the woman would probably have lost herself in the crowd and not even cared.

Logan finally turned them away from one of the main avenues and down a side street to a high stockade fence. He banged on it with an armored fist until a boy unlatched the door to let them in. The fence encircled what seemed to be a sort of horse parking lot. It had a couple of guards, several hitching posts, and a smell that Quinn could only describe as authentic. Bits of hay and manure were scattered about the entrance to a small stable crowded with pack animals, cart horses, and a few riding mounts.

"Nice little parking lot," Quinn said.

"You're looking at one of the most profitable businesses in port cities," Chaudri said.

"Horse and buggy storage," Quinn said. He was dubious.

"They charge to store the horses, and then they rent them out during the day," Chaudri said. "Not ours, of course."

"We pay extra, I'm guessing," Quinn said.

"They sell the manure, too. Makes for decent fertilizer."

Quinn tried to keep his breathing shallow. "I'd hate to live downwind."

Chaudri gave a shrug. "Smells like money to me." Logan had finished hobbling the horses, then lashing the swords and bows up in canvas. *Probably a good idea to keep those away from prying eyes.* He came over to Quinn and Chaudri, and tucked a carbon dagger into each of their boots. "This is a port city. Keep your wits about you," he said.

Quinn feigned surprise. "So Bayport's a port city? Get outta here."

Logan glared as Quinn hurried past.

On the way out, Kiara pressed a couple of coins into the boy's hand for an extra careful watch over their mounts and saddlebags. They regrouped outside the gate, which the boy closed and barred behind them.

Kiara pulled up a rough map of the city. "The port master's office is on the north end of the harbor. Most of the captain's bars will be on the south."

"Have to split up to cover them all," Logan said.

"Chaudri and I will try the port master," Kiara said.

Quinn rubbed his hands together. "I guess Logan and I are hitting the bars, then."

"For information *only*," Kiara said.

Quinn didn't try to hide the disappointment from his face. He realized he could really use a drink.

"Ah, perhaps they could be permitted a bit of indulgence, Lieutenant," Chaudri said. "In the name of field research."

She sighed. "Very well. But keep it in moderation."

They arranged to meet that evening at an inn called the Lost Lady. Comm units were checked, but Kiara wanted radio silence unless there was an emergency. She and Chaudri set out to track down the port master, whose offices were at the south end of the city. Logan and Quinn made right for the waterfront.

"Captains love to talk, but they'll want something in return," Logan said.

"I could give a little performance," Quinn said.

Logan shook his head. "That will draw attention. We'll just spread some coin around, buy a few drinks."

"So once again I'm absolutely useless here."

"That's what I've been trying to say all along."

"As long as we're on the same page."

Logan almost smiled at that as he dug out a brown leather purse and handed it over. Quinn shook out a handful of heavy round coins into his hand. Some gold, some silver. They had the heft of value to them, like premium poker chips. "Good. I could use a drink."

"You're buying, not drinking."

"Trust me, I know how to work a crowd."

"This isn't Vegas."

Quinn stepped right into a fresh pile of horse manure. He grimaced. "I'm well aware of that."

The streets grew crowded as they neared the waterfront, and carried the potent smells of brine and urine. The people, too, were more downtrodden and ramshackle. Funny that he'd started thinking of them that way. They looked *human*. Even the outfits didn't seem odd any longer. Fewer of the Kestani bright colors were visible here; loose shirts of what appeared to be sail canvas were far more common. Nearly everyone walked with the rolling swagger of lifetime sailors.

"Most of them are on shore leave," Logan said, as if hearing his thoughts. "A day or two of drinking, gambling, and other vices until their pay is gone. The captains will be holed up in one of these drinking parlors."

"How will I know what a ship captain looks like?" Quinn asked.

"Oh, you'll know."

The first drinking parlor was a dive for certain. It was a squarish room, poorly lit by round lamps that flickered and gave off oily smoke. A haze hung over the bar, a wooden monstrosity carved to resemble the hull of a ship. A handful of men lounged in high-backed chairs beside it. They were cleaner and more expensively attired than anyone Quinn had seen so far. There were other patrons in the room, some drinking at low tables, others playing cards, but these men were the centerpiece.

Mostly because of the hats they wore. These were made of crushed velvet or a similar material, broad-rimmed, and studded with tropical feathers.

"Oh my God, it's the cast of *Don Quixote*," Quinn whispered.

Logan laughed. "Told you," he said. "Now, put your people skills to work and find out if anyone's seen Holt."

Quinn strolled up to the end of the bar, digging a few silver coins from his purse as he did. The man on the end had a dark mustache and goatee; his red cap had a shockingly bright purple feather. Like the other captains, he appeared to have been drinking and smoking for most of the day. Quinn held out a silver coin in the palm of his hand.

"Buy you a drink, Captain?"

The captain looked Quinn up and down, hardly glancing at the coin. "That won't buy what I'm drinking."

Quinn had figured as much. "Ah, sorry. Of course." He snapped his fingers, then spread them wide; now there were two coins in the hand. "Perhaps this is better. No, on second thought—" Another snap, another coin appeared. He could do this all day.

"Now you have my attention," the captain said. "Landorian ale." He gestured at a small, ornate cask on a shelf behind the bar. "Probably cheaper to melt silver down and drink it, but I just can't help myself."

"Let's make it two, then," Quinn said. He got the barkeeper's attention and ordered two of the ales.

"You're not a seaman, I can see that," the captain said. "Not Kestani, either. I'd wager my beard on it."

The barkeeper set two ales in front of them in heavy, cloudy glass mugs. Then he made Quinn's coins vanish as quickly as any magician could.

"I'm a traveling performer," Quinn said, which was essentially true. He dipped a finger in the foam of his glass and traced it around the rim. "A trick here." He tilted the glass to a precarious angle so that the ale threatened to spill over the rim. Then he pulled his hands away, and the glass held fast. "A trick there."

The captain raised an eyebrow over his ale. "Not bad. Then again, I've seen the real thing."

He had to stop himself from a sharp intake of breath. "You've met a magician."

"A couple of them, as it were."

At last, a hint of the real reason he'd come. The true promise of Alissia. "Maybe I know them."

"Nah, this was years ago."

Damn. Quinn took his glass and had a sip. Carefully. He sniffed appreciatively and raised his glass. "You've good taste, Captain."

"I've made it my business to try every ale the city-states have to offer. The farther away they're from, the better they taste. Without exception."

"Not a bad way to get along," Quinn said. "Is yours a trading vessel, then?"

"Aye. Three-masted Kestani sloop."

"Mmm," Quinn said, stroking his chin appreciatively, though he had no idea what the man was talking about. "Sounds like a fine rig. You ever take passengers?"

"On occasion, if the price is right. They take up room I'd otherwise use for cargo. Doesn't come cheap."

"A friend of mine was looking for a ride down to Valteron. I wondered if he'd found a berth. Older fellow, goes by Richard?"

"Not with me, though I can't speak for the other captains. Did you say Valteron?"

"Yes."

"I'm not sure your friend wants to go there right now."

"Why not?"

The captain drained his ale with a flourish. "That was a fine drink."

"Have another. This time, you're buying," Quinn said. He reached into the captain's hat and found three more silver coins somewhere in the vicinity of the outrageous purple feather.

"You're a sly one," said the captain. "Very well. Another ale."

The barkeep was already pouring it from the cask on the shelf. He slid it over, took the coins, and was gone again. A perfect performance, as far as Quinn was concerned. Everything about the captain's bar was that way. He really should look into the whole captaining thing.

The captain took a sip of his new ale, licked his lips. He leaned close. "Truth be told, I was supposed to head to Valteron with this cargo. Now I'm looking for a different port to take it to instead. At a loss."

"Are things that bad?" Quinn asked. He took another sip of the ale, and had to remind himself to slow down.

"Hard to know what's going, now that the Prime is dead."

Quinn nearly choked on his ale. *That sure as hell wasn't covered in my mission briefings.* "I'm sorry, did you say—"

"Dead."

"I hadn't heard," Quinn said. He wished Chaudri were here, to weigh in on the implications. "I didn't think he was terribly old." In fairness, he didn't know a thing about the Prime, except that he ruled Valteron.

"It was unexpected, that's for damn sure. I'm told things are dicey down there."

"I'll bet, with the Prime dead," Quinn said. He had to tell the others as soon as possible. "I should find my friend, I suppose. Good luck to you, Captain."

The man lifted his glass in salute. "Thanks for the drink."

Quinn turned, saw that Logan was waiting for him by the door. He gave him a nod, like *Let's go outside*.

They stepped out of the captain's room. Quinn briefed him on what he'd heard.

"Damn," Logan said. "That explains why none of the captains I spoke to were heading south. None of them said why, though." He gave Quinn a hard look. "How did you get that out of him?"

"Just my natural charms."

"Right."

"I'm a people person."

"You're something, all right," Logan said.

"Do you think Holt changed his plans?"

"Hard to say," Logan said. "A city-state without a leader isn't the safest of places to hide out."

"The chaos might help him, though," Quinn said.

"So he'll either have made a different plan, or be harder to find."

The sun had dipped below the horizon; twilight cast a pall gray on the buildings along the bay. It was dim enough that Quinn didn't initially recognize the men loitering in the alley beside the captain's room. Then he saw the nearest man's face.

It had the same sour expression as when he'd chosen the hand to destroy the world, back in that common room in Felara.

> **"There will always be detractors.
> If you don't have them, you
> don't matter enough."**
>
> —ART OF ILLUSION, APRIL 1

CHAPTER 8

STREET MAGIC

"**S**hit, it's them!" Quinn hissed . . . but too late.

Two of the men jumped Logan. Or tried to. The nearest got a slash on his forearm for his trouble— Logan's knife seemed to come out of nowhere. They backed off a moment and moved to attack from two sides. Meanwhile Sour Face drew a dagger and came at Quinn. He held it in a fist, blade-down. That was bad news.

If Logan had taught him one thing and hammered it home, it was that Quinn was a dead man in a fair fight. *So let's forget "fair."*

Bravado seemed a better option here.

"Didn't you learn your lesson?" Quinn sneered. "Magicians are not to be trifled with."

"No tricks this time, boy!" he hissed.

Quinn circled him, keeping out of reach. Maintaining eye contact and a mask of contempt. "You obviously don't know me. Because anyone who does wouldn't question it."

The man hesitated. "You're no magician." He came again.

Quinn backed away, trying to keep the panic from his voice. All of his great magic trinkets, and none where he could get to them! This fellow was going to take convincing, so he pushed the act even farther.

"Do not presume to know the ways of magicians!" he spat. "I don't want to hurt you, but I will." He raised his free hand and waggled his fingers together in intricate motions and started mumbling utter nonsense under his breath. Just total bullshit. But if the man thought he was working a spell, it might keep him cautious.

Meanwhile Logan threw one of his attackers into the wall. But the other one pounced at him. *No help from him, then*—in the dim light and close quarters, they were keeping him at bay.

All Quinn had was his stage presence. Maybe he could back that with the elemental projector strapped to his wrist. It had slipped up too far, though, and he couldn't get a grip on it. The edge was slick metal and the nylon band tight against his arm. And time was definitely a factor. The man pressed his attack—Quinn backed up until his back hit the rough stone of the building. *Sour Face is clearly not a believer.* He slapped his arm against the wall enough that the control button slid into his searching fingers. Finally.

Let's give him a reason to believe.

He sighed, and stood up straight. "You leave me no choice."

He held out his hand, palm-up. A ball of white-orange flame appeared above it. The heat from it was uncomfortable, but he kept his face still. Just a reluctant magician forced to reveal his craft.

The mercenary had been about to lunge. Now he backpedaled, his eyes wide. The two others attacking Logan were suddenly aware of the grapefruit-sized ball of fire in the palm of Quinn's hand. They hesitated, too. Logan took that opportunity to slash at the other fellow, the one who wasn't yet bleeding. He cursed; they backed up to where they could keep an eye on both Quinn and Logan.

"I'll give you to the count of five," Quinn said, using his stage voice and a confidence he didn't feel. If they attacked, the fireball wasn't going to help much. He had to sell it. "This is no ordinary fire. It burns a man from the inside out. Starting with the crotch." He lowered the hand with the fireball, praying that the projector's charge didn't run out.

The men looked at one another as if indecisive.

"One!" Quinn said. He moved his arm back in a slow, windup. The fire hissed through the air, crackling. "Two!"

The men broke off and fled down the alley, with Sour Face giving Logan a wide berth. Once they rounded the corner, Quinn let the flame dissipate. He'd probably drained half of the juice in the elemental projector, so he needed to save what he could. The engineers had been working on a refill pack, but when the mission got moved up, they couldn't finish in time.

"Nicely done," Logan said. He moved catlike to the corner of the building and glanced around it. "Looks all clear."

"Those were the same mercenaries as before," Quinn said. "God, I'm glad that worked."

"Yeah, you're getting a little bit smarter. Remembering some of the stuff I taught you."

"Not like I had a choice. You're not much of a bodyguard."

"I had my hands full, and you managed to be clever. Take the win." Logan unmuted his comm unit to report to Kiara what had happened. She and Chaudri had just found the port master but the conversation was a bust. He either knew nothing of Holt or had been too well paid to say otherwise.

"Everyone stays in crowded areas until further notice," she said. "Keep working the captains' bars. Follow up on the Valteron rumors; if it's true about the Prime, we'll have to reconsider the plan. And find me someone who's talked to Holt." Logan agreed and shut the comm unit off before they joined the crowd on the avenue that ran along the shoreline.

"Great to hear her concern at our almost-demise," Quinn said as they walked.

"That *was* her being concerned," Logan said.

Between the raucousness, the stink, and the general press of people, it reminded Quinn of Bourbon Street. At Logan's suggestion they stuck together in each captain's room now, throwing around silver, buying drinks whenever they could. Word had gotten around about the troubles in Valteron, and it turned out few of the captains were planning to head south. Surely one of them was willing to gamble for profit despite the risk. But so far, Logan and Quinn had been coming up empty.

The last drinking room stood a bit off to the others; the architecture and red-and-white stone made it even more unique. And whereas the doors of the other places were open and inviting, this building had a door of steel-belted hardwood, and it was closed.

"Are you sure this is a captain's bar?" Quinn asked.

"Not just any. The Valteroni one," Logan said.

"Wow. Fancy."

"Valteron builds one in every port their ships serve, for use by ships' captains and naval officers. We'll be lucky to get in. Noncitizens are up to the doorman."

Logan took off his glove and knocked five times. It was the most polite thing Quinn had ever seen him do—almost dainty. The man looked *nervous*. Now that was frightening.

The door opened about a foot, wide enough for a

distinguished man with graying hair, dressed entirely in black, to look upon them with a disdainful expression.

"Evening," Logan said cheerfully. "I thought we'd come in and buy the good captains a drink or two."

The doorman seemed unconvinced. "This is a Valteroni bar."

"Where else to find the finest captains in Bayport?"

The doorman raised an eyebrow. "Do you have the coins? We only serve Valteroni liquor. Four silvers a glass."

"We have the coins," Logan assured him.

"You don't look like it."

This bar was their last shot for getting a line on Holt. Quinn could just picture the frown Kiara would give them if they failed to get in. He'd spent plenty of time around doormen and bouncers. It wasn't enough to have money here. They had to be interesting. He just hoped the coins had enough iron in them.

"Looks can be deceiving," he said. He brought his hands together, pulled them apart, and a silver coin appeared in his palm. He turned his hand over, and the coin danced across his fingers. Another joined it, then another. He made a fist. Here came the moment of truth, when he'd either seal the deal or fumble everything.

"Money has a way of . . . growing, when we're around." He let the coins fall from it one at a time. Each one held fast to the coin above it, till they dangled edge-to-edge from his fingertips. *Oh, yes.*

With his other hand he flicked the bottom-most

coin so that it spun around and around. He smiled. Logan matched it. They looked up at the doorman. The spinning coin fell off then, but hopefully the effect was enough.

The man's face never changed. Damn. Maybe he should have gone for a flashier trick. He kept forgetting that a magic trick that charmed in Vegas might not make anyone blink here. They had the real thing.

Finally, though, the doorman said, "Welcome to the House of Valteron." He unlatched a hidden chain that had secured the door. Warm air and the potent smell of alcohol washed over them.

Oh, yeah. Still got it.

Where the other captains' bars were nicer than Quinn might have expected, the House of Valteron took opulence to a whole new level. Oil lamps in reflective sconces lined every wall, but most of the light was cast by an impressive chandelier that hung from the ceiling of the chamber. Sumptuous furnishings were scattered tastefully throughout the room. To Quinn, it resembled the lobby of a Victorian-style hotel.

"Your weapons, please," the doorman said.

"I'm sorry?" Logan said.

"You have a knife on your belt and another one in your boot. They stay with me, or you go right back out." He stood with his hand in an alcove beside the door. Probably had a loaded crossbow back there, or something worse. For all his dapper appearance, the doorman seemed oddly capable of violence. Perhaps only to preserve the sanctity of House of Valteron, but that was what they were threatening, so he was threatening back.

Quinn unsheathed both of his knives and handed them over; they were more dangerous to him than to anyone else. Logan grumbled but did the same. The doorman disappeared into a small room. He returned and handed each of them a carved wooden marker.

"Don't lose it," he said. Then he went back to take his position by the door.

Three women in exquisite gowns lounged on two of the couches, speaking quietly among themselves and giggling occasionally. No matter the world, no matter the technology level, Quinn knew a professional when he saw one.

"How much is our budget for tonight?" he asked.

"Not nearly enough for that," Logan said.

All of the men were at the bar, a massive slab of black marble atop a dark wood base. The marble was a foot thick and looked to be a single piece. Probably as heavy as it was expensive. Three shelves lined the wall behind the bar. Each held about a dozen silver chalices, in which rested round, corked glass bottles of Valteroni liquor.

"We'll blend in here if we're drinking," Quinn said.

"All right, but I'm not carrying you out of here," Logan said.

"Such a gentleman," Quinn said.

Chaudri was going to be green with envy. She'd

spent a long time lecturing Quinn on the protocols for storing and transporting Valteroni liquor. Like, a *really* long time. The rules made French vintners look easygoing. Apparently the research team had taken numerous samples over the years, subjecting them to chemical and mass spectrometry assays to determine the origin of these expensive distillations. As yet, they were unable to unravel the complex structure of the liquids, or even determine the source. What they did find out, though, was that Valteroni liquors were prized for individuality—no two kinds had the same viscosity and taste. There were even subtle differences from one bottle to the next.

The wooden stools along the bar were about two-thirds full, so they claimed a pair and sat down. The marble was cold to the touch, almost like ice.

Like the captains he'd seen in other drinking rooms, the men and women at the bar wore hats with overlarge feathers on them; it seemed to be a mark of captainship in this part of Alissia. The only difference was that where the others' feathers were simply dyed to their obnoxious hues, those worn in the House of Valteron were naturally beautiful. Some resembled the peacock feathers from Earth, others surely came from birds unlike Quinn had ever seen. Regardless, they all spoke to a certain exotic origin.

A good illusionist could read faces and body language as most people can read billboards. Those skills seemed to translate fairly well to Alissians, though as a general rule they seemed more guarded with their emotions. Even so, Quinn picked up a universal vibe among the Valteroni captains drinking at the bar. No matter how well they tried to hide it.

"They're nervous," Quinn said quietly.

"How do you know?" Logan asked.

"I can just tell."

"Was it here before, or did they become that way when we entered?"

"Not sure. I was too busy being frisked by the doorman."

"And ogling the ladies."

"I was trying to get a read on them, too."

"I bet."

Quinn shrugged, and made another surreptitious look about the bar. The man on Quinn's right had the look of a ship captain.

Time to drum up a little information.

"Evening, Captain," Quinn said.

The man gave him a slight nod. His silk-and-leather jacket was studded with silver thread and decorative jewels; the feather in his soft gray hat looked like that of a pheasant: brown with black stripes and red near the tip. Quinn resisted a sudden, likely suicidal urge to reach out and touch it.

The bartender, an attractive brunette in a spotless white apron, came over to take their order. Quinn tried valiantly to remember what he could about the liquor from Chaudri's briefings. Now was not the moment to come off as a hayseed.

"What can I get for you, gentlemen?" she asked.

"Something off the dark end," Logan said.

"How about you, handsome?" she asked Quinn.

Quinn felt his cheeks heating, but a moment of inspiration came. "Gold and cold," he said casually, as if he'd ordered it a hundred times before.

She smiled; he knew he'd won a point or two with that one. From beneath the bar she produced a delicate glass tumbler for Logan, identical to the others being sipped at along the bar. She poured three fingers of dark liquor the color of motor oil into it. That would be Logan's drink, and it suited him.

For Quinn, she opened a wooden cabinet nestled among the shelves that lined the back wall. The bottom half of the cabinet was a solid block of ice. Above it rested a wire shelf with frosted, gold-rimmed tumblers. She used a pair of wooden tongs to pluck one of these from the rack and set it on the bar in front of Quinn. His drink cost about twice as much as Logan's, if he wasn't mistaken, but the result would be worth it.

The bartender retrieved a round glass bottle from the top shelf and uncorked it. She poured it into the frosted tumbler from beneath the bar. The liquor was clear when it came out of the bottle, but turned a honey-gold color when it hit the glass.

"Beautiful," Quinn said.

The captain beside him took notice, and gave a nod of approval.

"Perhaps one for the good captain?" Quinn asked the bartender, daring to flash her a wink as well.

"Mmm, handsome *and* generous," she said. "Not bad for a northerner."

She poured another frozen glass of the "gold and cold" for the captain and slid it in front of him. Quinn took his glass at the same time as the other man. They clinked glasses and drank.

The foremost Alissian experts, Richard Holt included, had attempted to describe exactly what Valteroni gold liquor tastes like. Half of them could not put it into words. The other half couldn't agree on them.

Quinn expected it to feel cold at first, given the frosted glass and everything, but there was no real sensation of temperature, hot or cold. The liquor simply flowed across his tongue, stimulating taste buds he didn't even know were there. He understood right away why the research team had struggled so much. This one, as far as Quinn could best describe it, tasted like sunshine.

The ship captain's drink might have been similar, because it made him smile. "Thank you for that," he said. "I love the golden stuff, but if I let myself drink it without occasion, I'd be bankrupt."

"I don't drink any other kind," Quinn said. Technically, it was true since this was his first glass.

"That, my friend, is an opulent lifestyle," the captain said.

Quinn shrugged. "Fortune has smiled upon me, and life is short. Why have anything but the best?"

"I'll drink to that," the man said. He took another sip, savoring it. Meanwhile, Logan's drink seemed to make him angry. It was either bad luck with the dark liquor, or else he got what he paid for.

It occurred to Quinn that they hadn't paid for anything yet, despite being about twenty pieces of silver in to the bartender. He had some vague recollection of how one was supposed to pay for drinks in Valteron, but couldn't dredge it up. Hopefully Logan would remember.

The captain chuckled to himself. "Strange coincidences."

"What's that?" Quinn asked.

"I'm just lucky, that's all. Two strangers have bought me drinks inside of a week. Not even Valteroni, either."

"Someone else was in here buying drinks?" Logan asked.

"Sure was. Serious fellow, and he was throwing some silver around buying drinks for all of the captains. Wanted to get to Valteron right away." His face clouded.

"His name wasn't Richard, was it?" Logan asked. "Balding fellow, middle-aged, talks like a poet?"

"Ah, you know him."

"He's an old friend," Logan said.

"Nice fellow. We talked for a couple of hours. Knew even more about Valteroni liquor than I do."

"I'm not surprised," Logan said. "He always could talk my ear off. You know, I'd like to catch up with him, actually. Is he still around?"

"Don't think so. He eventually persuaded old Jock to sell him passage south, back to Valteron."

"What kind of ship?"

"Coast-cutter."

Logan smiled, though it was visibly forced. "He's a persuasive guy, isn't he?" He rested a fist on the bar, with the thumb between two of his fingers. One of the basic hand signals he'd taught Quinn; this one meant, *Time to go.*

Quinn pretended not to see it. "Did he seem nervous at all?" he asked.

"Distracted, more like. And eager to get to Valteron."

That had to mean something. Quinn just couldn't figure out what it was. Surely Holt had heard the news by then. "A shame about the Prime," he said.

"Heard about that, did you? Bad news travels fast." The captain made an odd gesture, pouring just a drop of his liquor onto the counter, dipping a finger, touching it to his forehead. "Gods look after the Prime. He was a good man."

The barmaid came back. "See anything else you like?" she asked. She met his eyes when she said it, and Quinn liked that. He liked her smile, too, and the way she sort of leaned over the bar a little bit toward him. He'd be happy to buy another round, or ten rounds, but Logan cleared his throat a little too loudly.

Quinn sighed. "I suppose I should settle up."

Her smile faded just a little, but he tipped enough to bring it back in spades. Maybe on the way back, Kiara would grant them some shore leave. He wouldn't mind spending a little extra time here.

He put his hand on the captain's shoulder. "I'll pray for Valteron, Captain."

The man gave him an odd look. "You sound like a brother of the Star."

"I used to be one," Quinn said.

They took their wooden markers back to the doorman and reclaimed their weapons. Logan made a big show of unsheathing and inspecting his knives, while the doorman pretended not to notice.

But Logan found nothing to complain about, so the doorman ushered them out into the cool night air. The door closed firmly behind them. Logan made sure that no one was around, and then activated his comm link to raise Kiara.

"We've got something," he told her.

"Better be good," Kiara said. "I just spent two hours buying drinks for naval officers who didn't know anything."

"Holt was in the House of Valteron buying drinks a few days ago. Seems like he caught a ride south."

"How good is the intel?"

"Bradley can offer his own opinion, but I think it's legit."

"I'm with Logan on this," Quinn said.

"What sort of craft is he on?"

"A coast-cutter."

"Damn."

"My thoughts exactly."

"Well, that settles it. If he goes by sea, so do we. Go get us passage on the fastest Valteroni ship you can find."

"Will do," Logan said. He tilted his head back toward the House of Valteron's door. They knocked again. The same doorman answered. He looked at them with that same appraising, disdainful stare. "This is a Valteroni bar," he said.

"You've got to be kidding me," Quinn said.

> "Valteron is the most powerful of
> Alissian nations, owing to their
> trading fleet and navy. Perhaps also
> contributory is the omnipotent role of
> a single ruler: the Valteroni Prime."
>
> —R. HOLT, "SUMMARY OF
> ALISSIAN CITY-STATES"

CHAPTER 9

SEA LEGS

Of course it had to be their drinking buddy from
the House of Valteron who had the next ship headed
south. Something about his conversation with Quinn
and Logan had made the man homesick. That didn't
stop him from accepting two more rounds of Valteroni
liquor before he agreed to take them on.

Quinn and Logan reunited with Chaudri and
Kiara back at the Lost Lady, a two-story inn located
uphill, and more importantly upwind, of the crowded

waterfront. The liquor had Quinn's head swimming by then.

The building featured a small common room, stout wooden doors, and a communications relay hidden on the roof. The lieutenant wanted a good signal—they'd probably be out of range while at sea. The inn's proprietor was a slight fellow of fair complexion; he couldn't be more than twenty-five. He arranged for a late-night meal while his brother, a much stouter version of the same stock, cleared the drunken sailors from the common room.

The food was good. Quinn remembered that much. The thick white soup reminded him of clam chowder from back home, savory and piping hot. There were loaves of bread, the heavy brown kind. He ate as much as he could, hoping to soak up some of the alcohol. He finished his bowl and another one after that. Chaudri had two bowls; Logan put away three without breaking a sweat. Kiara promised to rouse everyone by sunrise, so Quinn didn't waste any time after that. He found his tiny room near the attic, feeling dizzy but sated. The Valteroni gold gave him strange dreams filled with sunshine and pretty barmaids.

As usual, it was Logan's fist on the door that woke him.

"Up and at 'em, ladies' man," he said.

Quinn groaned. His head was pounding, and the rest of him felt like he'd been hit by a truck. "Ow."

"Told you to go easy," Logan said.

"Can I have another hour?"

"Sorry, we got a boat to catch."

He dressed slowly and followed Logan out, wishing for sunglasses. The sunlight made his headache even worse.

They met their captain at the end of one of the docks, where two husky dockworkers were loading a wooden crate. The ship was a two-master with plenty of sail, deep-hulled but in good shape. Logan and Chaudri had given it a thorough inspection. The horses were already on board; Kiara had arranged for them to be brought right to the dock. All but the mountain pony, because there simply wasn't enough room in the hold. The captain wasn't happy about having any of the "crap producers" on his ship at all until his purse was heavy with lab-created emeralds.

His name was Legato and he'd been running the trade routes between Valteron and the northern city-states for fifteen years. Apparently Valteroni liquor had absolutely no effect on him. Quinn hadn't even finished his second one, and he was already feeling the start of a brutal headache. Weak as the late-year sun was, it seemed much brighter on the water. He stepped on the deck of Legato's craft and groaned.

Logan clapped him on the shoulder. "Ever been on a sea voyage?"

"A couple of sunset cruises on yachts. How similar will that be?"

Logan laughed and followed the lieutenant below. Quinn couldn't make himself follow just yet.

Chaudri put a hand on his shoulder. "Rough morning?"

"My head's killing me."

"You got us a ride, though. We're lucky to have one."

"You'd think the company would have built us a ship."

She glanced around and lowered her voice. "We tried that once. It didn't go well."

He was curious enough to nearly forget the pain. "Really?"

She pulled a notebook from her satchel and flipped through to a page with a sketch of an old clipper ship. "Here it is. The *Victoria*."

"Looks like a whaling ship."

"Only on the outside. The inside was state of the art. Kiara's predecessor, Captain Relling, had it built in-world with native timber."

"So where is it now?" He'd have killed for a modern bed in a dark, dark room.

"Relling and her crew disappeared on their maiden voyage, along with the ship."

"No wreckage or anything?" Quinn asked.

"Nothing. We searched for months and never found a trace of them."

"Oh," Quinn said. "Sorry to hear that."

"We took it hard. Kiara especially."

"I can imagine," he said. The lieutenant didn't seem one to take failure very well.

Chaudri was about to say more when the captain marched up the gangplank. He spotted them and bellowed a laugh.

"How are you this morning, my friend?" He shook

Quinn's hand vigorously, causing little spikes of pain to begin jabbing at his temples. "What a night we had last night, eh? Look at what I brought to keep us entertained, thanks to your prompt and generous payment."

He lifted the lid of a small wooden crate nestled inside the ship's rail. In it, carefully packed with straw, were four bottles that looked all too familiar.

Oh, no, Quinn thought. He shivered involuntarily. "I hope that's not—"

"Valteroni gold!" Legato said. He saw Quinn's mouth hanging open and laughed. "I knew you'd be excited. Gods, it feels good to be heading home."

Within the hour, Legato's men had raised sail and tossed off the dock lines. Steady wind filled the sails; the ship shuddered into motion. Quinn disliked the sensation of the deck moving slowly, ponderously, beneath him. He found it far more comfortable in the generous quarters Legato had set aside. Apparently the man had decided that Quinn's taste in liquors meant he could only get by with the finer things. He, Logan, Kiara, and Chaudri had four small cabins at the rear of the craft.

Quinn found his bunk to lie down, which quickly proved a mistake. Once out of the bay's protected waters, the ship began rolling and falling with the seas, which were just high enough to give Quinn a sense of vertigo every ten seconds or so.

Not exactly the rest he had been looking for.

He came up on deck after they'd been under way a couple of hours. Kiara was on the deck talking to

Legato. Logan stood near the mast, watching the crew while pretending not to. Quinn ambled over to him, close enough for a quiet conversation.

"What's going on?" he asked.

"The captain just told the crew that we're headed to Valteron," Logan said. "They were . . . surprised."

"I'd think they would be glad to head home. Legato certainly is."

"It's risky making port in a city that just lost its leader. Every other ship is headed the other way, and the crew knows it."

That explained the stiff actions of the sailors, the way they shared dark looks with one another as they worked.

"Should I be worried?" Quinn asked.

"Don't know yet."

Quinn stretched and looked around, trying to count how many sailors it took to work the sails and the rigging. At least four or five per mast, and the ship had two. They knew their business, though. The sails bulged with wind, and prow of the ship sliced through the sea with the sound of rushing water.

"What's the worst-case scenario?" Quinn asked.

"You don't want to know."

"Try me."

"They kill Legato, cut our throats, and feed us to the sharks."

"Can't we hole up in our cabins, if it gets bad?"

"Sure," Logan said. "But then we have no control over where they go."

They needed the crew on their side; that was certain. If there were a mutiny, the passengers would be the first to die.

"Let me perform for them," Quinn said.

"Why?" Logan asked.

"Entertainment. Keep their minds off the destination," Quinn said. And maybe make them wary of him, which could be useful.

Kiara turned away from Legato long enough to weigh in. "I don't like this idea. The more attention we draw, the more they'll remember us later."

Quinn was disappointed, but not really surprised. Kiara liked to keep him under a tight yoke.

"I think it might be worth a shot, Lieutenant," Logan said. Surprising him. "Their mood's getting darker by the hour. They could use the distraction."

Kiara seemed to weigh her options for a while. "Fine. But I want him to bring it up. The captain seems to think they're best friends now."

Quinn knew how the man would have to be convinced, and his stomach churned at the thought. But Legato was far more pliable with drink in him.

"Captain!" Quinn called, over the rail. "How about a drink tonight?"

Legato grinned. "I knew you'd get your thirst back."

Half a night and three rounds of golden liquor later, Quinn had gotten Legato to sign off. That night was shot, of course, as was the morning. Meanwhile the crew's grumblings increased in frequency and volume. If he was going to change the tone of the conversation, he'd have to do it soon.

He needed a stage, of course, and so Legato tasked a couple of sailors to help him build one near the bow of the ship—more grumbling. But it was necessary if his act was going to work. Nothing special here; Quinn just had to quietly install some screw-in wire loops, magnets, a stepping platform colored to blend in with the deck, that sort of thing. Just the basic props of a street magician, nothing more. Kiara insisted on low-tech since he'd be under close scrutiny.

Meanwhile, Legato's ship was under full sail heading due south, driven by a cold wind out of the north. They stayed in view of land for much of the journey, but never too close. Keeping to the deep channels had them tacking out and back again, balancing between keeping land in sight while not running aground.

The wind was good but time was against them. The coast-cutter that Holt was on, according to Logan, was a shallow-draft, single-mast craft with a keel that could be raised or lowered at will, allowing it to glide across the shallow flats in a straight line toward the southern ports. They'd already gotten a head start and would gain another day on speed alone, a day and a half if her captain was good. And Quinn guessed that her captain was one of the best. Holt would probably have a nose for such things.

Even so, Quinn tried not to dwell on the mission and instead focused on the magic. Everything he'd done in Alissia was impromptu, either to distract or impress or save his own skin. Now, with a bit of planning, he could bring out some of the better illusions he and the engineers had cooked up back on Earth.

For a moment his thoughts flickered to the engineers. He'd spent weeks getting to know them, and building the equipment to bring along. The head of the prototyping lab was a guy named Julian Miller. Turned out he was a bow hunter, too. Big game up in Manitoba. He'd been the one to put a laser rangefinder on Quinn's bow.

That was weeks ago now, and Kiara had still received no signal from the company since coming through. Quinn hoped to God that Julian and his crew were all right.

And that it wasn't my fault. . .

He shook that thought from his head. All that mattered now was making sure the sailors didn't cut their throats and feed them to the sharks.

He was ready near sunset, just after the evening meal. Legato's crew normally underwent a shift change then, but the captain allowed all but a skeleton crew to assemble in the front of the ship to watch. The sky was a backdrop of blaze orange and pink; the seas for once were blessedly calm. Quinn took the stage and turned to assess his crowd.

The body language told the story, and the muttering about whether or not this would be a waste of their time.

"Perhaps the captain has told you already," Quinn

pronounced, his voice raised to carry to the crewmen at the back of the mainmast. "I'm not from Valteron, though I love your fine city-state." He won a couple of nods from that. "I've been beyond the shores of Alissia. I've seen things no Alissians have seen."

While he was talking he put on the gloves, one white and one black. This audience wouldn't know from experience to watch the white-gloved hand or the other, but the instinct would come naturally. That was one thing Quinn loved about magic. Done well, it captivated the naive and the jaded with equal wonder.

"The captain's a decent fellow," Quinn said. "And he loves his liquor, doesn't he?"

A few soft laughs from the audience; they knew well enough.

"But he was kind enough to lend me a bottle for this performance. Thank you, Captain." Quinn raised a round, corked bottle in salute. Legato nodded, the very picture of genteel grace. Pandering to the venue owner always, *always* paid off. Even if this one was oblivious to the mood of his crew.

Quinn took out a metal cup with a handle, the kind most of the crew used for their water rations. "A plain cup," he said. He brought it to the nearest crewmen and let them inspect it. "Here, have a look." They turned it over in their hands, tapped on it, nodded and gave it back.

He uncorked the bottle. "When we first met, I bought your captain a drink. Well, several drinks, if I'm being honest."

Amusement rippled through the sailors; he was warming them up.

He began pouring the liquor into the cup. He kept pouring, kept pouring. After a moment it was clear even to the dullest mind on deck that he'd poured far more than the cup should be able to hold. The bottle was half-empty, two-thirds empty. He upended it over the cup, letting the last drops fall.

"You know what I learned? When the captain's around, liquor has a funny habit of . . . disappearing."

He turned the cup over and nothing came out; it was empty. The crew hooted with laughter and clapped appreciatively. Even Logan raised an eyebrow.

Kiara had come on deck; when Quinn saw her, he nearly dropped the cup entirely. She'd changed from her riding clothes into a long skirt and tunic. She had her hair down, too. It was longer than he'd guessed, and fell freely past her shoulders. She stood next to Logan, seemingly at ease and enjoying the show. Quinn had to look away to clear his head.

"So where did it go?" he asked the crowd. "Any guesses?"

"The captain's belly!" someone shouted.

"That was just my guess," Quinn said. He stepped down from the stage and walked over to the captain. The crowd parted to let him pass.

"What do you say, Captain?" Quinn asked. It would have been far easier if Legato were in on it, but then he wouldn't be nearly as impressed. The captain had no idea what was coming, and it showed on his face.

"I've known a cup of liquor or two," Legato said. "But it wasn't me. This time, at least."

"I'm not sure I believe him," Quinn said. "If you're innocent, Captain, could I have a look at your hat?"

"I suppose," Legato said. He took it off with just a touch of reverence and handed it to Quinn.

"What's this?" Quinn asked. He turned the cap over, and a stream of clear liquid poured out, right into the mouth of the empty bottle. And the proof was evident, for when it touched the glass, the clear liquid turned to gold.

He had to inspect the captain's boots next, and found even more liquor in each of them. Another bit in one of his sleeves. The crew loved it, and the captain himself got quite into it, bellowing louder each time.

He's probably just relieved to be getting his precious liquor back.

Quinn figured he might as well test out some of the equipment, as long as the crowd was hot, so he made a full show of it. He made things around the ship appear and disappear. He put a dagger through a flask of brandy without leaving a mark or spilling any of it. All of the equipment that he and the engineers scrupulously designed performed without a hitch.

He wanted something impressive for the finale, not a sleight of hand trick but a true illusion. This had been the most delicate bit of business, because he'd had to make surreptitious preparations on the ship. Now he faced the crowd, and felt their rapt attention on him.

"So now we've come to the end of the show, and

I have one last trick for you," he said. He lowered his voice a little, made it serious. "I want to thank you all for your help on this voyage, and more importantly, for your *discretion*. The less you wag your tongues about us when we come into port, the more likely we'll have success. So thank you, in advance."

You could have heard a pin drop, while the crew pondered this. Quinn took his position near the back of the stage, against the mast. Dusk had fallen, and at his request they'd not lit any of the whale-oil lanterns in the middle of the ship. A bit of fuzzy vision was required.

"It's said that a man at sea lives his life for a few little moments. A special sunrise, a quiet breeze, maybe even a liquor-induced hallucination."

He nodded vaguely in Legato's direction to the general amusement of the crowd. "For my last illusion, I'd like to give one of those moments. To each of you. In honor of the Valteroni Prime."

He slid the elemental projector into the palm of a hidden hand, found the button he needed. He leaned back, spread his arms out.

The jet of liquid was soundless, and invisible to those on the deck below. So was the tiny apparatus he'd hidden on the mast overhead, a funnel with amplifying microfluidics. Into the funnel it went, through a tube, and then out hundreds of specially drilled holes. Tiny droplets of it spilled down to patter on the ship's deck. Everyone looked at the sky, eyes wide and mouths open in wonder. This was the moment Quinn savored most, when a performance really took the crowd by surprise.

He held out the metal cup, catching enough of the droplets to make a sip. "Cheers, Captain!" he called, and he drank. Then everyone realized the real twist of the performance, something that made it clear this was no well-timed natural phenomenon. It wasn't water that fell.

It was Valteroni gold.

The applause was lively but short. Every sailor on deck scrambled for a drinking cup. Quinn remained on his little stage, enjoying the wonder and chaos. Maybe it wouldn't be so bad to be stuck here in this world. He could probably make a killing.

As long as someone doesn't kill me first.

The performance had cost him about a quarter of the elemental projector, and wasted a small fortune of Valteroni liquor, but it did two things. First, it drained most of the tension from the crew, gave them something else to talk about other than the gamble they took by sailing to Valteron. Second, it won him points with the rest of the team. Not quite as important as surviving the voyage, but nearly so.

Logan found him the next morning, while Quinn stood at the rail and watched the shape of the distant coastline roll by.

"Look at you, awake and sober," he said.

"Well, I managed to get rid of most of Legato's stash

in the performance," Quinn said. "I'm a little worried he expects me to recover it at some point."

"Just tell him it's the price of doing business."

Quinn turned and made a survey of the deck. Legato was at the wheel himself. Kiara was there, too, chatting him up again. "I think the lieutenant might have a man-crush," he said.

Logan chuckled. "Don't count on it. She grills every ship captain she comes across. Hoping to hear some hint about the *Victoria*."

"Oh, right," Quinn said. "I'm surprised she hasn't written it off already. It's probably at the bottom of the ocean."

"I wouldn't suggest that to her, if I were you," Logan said.

"It's not like it didn't work out for Kiara. She got Relling's job, didn't she?"

Logan gave him a quizzical look. "You don't know, do you?"

"What?"

Logan muttered a curse. "Relling wasn't just her predecessor. She was Kiara's older sister."

A week of fair winds brought them south and east to the shores of Valteron. Nearly every ship they'd seen had been heading the other direction. Legato tried more than once to communicate with other captains using signal flags, but most of them were unresponsive. What little information he did get made him nervous: unrest in Valteron city, a blockade of the harbor, maybe even some armed conflicts.

Logan had made certain arrangements with Legato before their voyage began, ensuring that no passengers would be entered into the manifest. This was a cargo-only ship, as far as the documents were concerned. It helped minimize the risk of Holt learning of their arrival. Chaudri was sure the man knew how to get the records from Valteroni port masters.

"I don't enjoy working with smugglers," Legato had told Logan. "But it's part of the business. Not every shipment can be profitable once Valteroni taxes are involved."

"Part of the business," Logan agreed. "I'm sure you pay nearly all of the duties for your cargo. You're a good citizen of Valteron."

Quinn was pretty sure he said it with a straight face.

A day's sail from Valteron city, Legato steered closer to land. The shoreline was pocked with coves and inlets, their backwaters hidden by the dense stands of mangrove-like trees along the water. Legato ran up a certain set of flags, reefed the sails, and waited.

An hour later, a small ship slid out of some hidden cove. It was single-masted, maybe half the length of Legato's vessel, but a good bit rougher around the edges. Trading that polished appearance, Quinn guessed, for quick sails and hidden compartments.

When the craft arrived, Legato invited its captain aboard for a drink and a hefty purse, while members of the smuggler crew helped Quinn, Bradley, Kiara,

THE ROGUE RETRIEVAL 145

and Logan aboard. Legato's crewmen used the crane to move their horses into the other ship's hold.

The smuggler captain, who'd never offered a name, disguised his ship as a fishing vessel. Quinn wasn't sure how he did it, but the smell was certainly convincing. It threatened to gag him in the tiny closet where they'd stashed him, hoping that the trust and exchange of silver between the captains was enough to guarantee their safety. At least he was better off than Logan, who'd drawn the privilege of hiding in the bilge and didn't sound very happy about it over the comm link. Quinn thought he was somewhere off the hold, while Kiara was behind a false door in the captain's closet, and Chaudri in a sort of oubliette beneath a pile of grimy sail canvas.

He didn't even want to ask where the horses were.

In this fashion they made the two-hour journey to Valteroni shores, a time Quinn intended to forget. Something told him the fishy smell might linger in the clothes and belongings for days, if not longer.

The smuggler captain offloaded his "catch" with their equipment and horses at a disused fishing dock on the southern coast. The structure was dilapidated but sound enough that when the smuggler's vessels bumped against it, there was only the faintest of shudders. Once ashore, Logan checked to be sure all of their equipment had made it, while Kiara thanked the captain for his silence with a heavy purse and quiet warning that made the man's face lose a bit of color.

Since it was near the planet's equator and bordered

on three sides by the sea, most of Valteron knew no true winter. With mild weather came a clear sky. So while they'd come ashore under cover of darkness, Chaudri was able to take their rough position with a sextant.

Kiara consulted her map. "About a day's ride to Valteron City," she said.

That proved an optimistic estimate. For while the evening was moderate, the weather was uncomfortably warm when the sun was out, especially as they got farther away from the coast. The horses tired more easily, and they had to constantly ride around putrid-smelling marshes and water pits.

It beat the seasickness, though, and Quinn actually found he was glad to be back in the saddle atop his mare. He'd visited her in Legato's hold a few times with bits of fruit or grain, and tried to build up a little camaraderie. Between that and the steady practice, she actually started responding to some of his commands. Maybe one in three. He took what he could get.

At last they trudged out of the marsh to more solid ground in the fertile valley where Valteron City lay. They crested a ridge, and the land spilled out before them. They'd emerged on a sort of peninsula at the mouth of a massive bay. Across the water was a huge settlement, easily five times the size of Bayport. It hung beneath the specter of a charcoal-dark cloud that stretched out over land and sea. A line of ships fanned out in a wide arc to enclose the bay. They were stouter and deeper-hulled than Legato's, and had the look of warships. Between that line and the city wharves, burning or charred hulks littered the water. The wind changed then, coming toward them, carrying the heavy odor of acrid smoke.

"I'm no expert," Quinn said. "But I think that's a bad sign."

> "Disappearance comes far
> easier than conjuration."
>
> —ART OF ILLUSION, JULY 22

CHAPTER 10

CIVIL UNREST

The news out of Valteron City backed Quinn's hunch.

Logan and Kiara spent two hours talking to refugees that were streaming out of the city. Most of them told the same story. The Prime of Valteron had died unexpectedly more than a month ago. Within hours of his death, there were at least six candidates vying for the office. Each of them backed by a faction of supporters.

Cue the riots and looting. Two of the candidates died in the fighting. Another was poisoned. Two days passed before enough of the Valteroni fleet arrived to establish some semblance of order. A flotilla of merchant ships had even attempted to blockade the harbor, hoping to secure the office of the Prime for their candidate. Most were fired or sunk, for daring to impede navy vessels. Troops and officers came ashore to establish martial law until the new Prime was chosen.

"Hard to know if Holt made it in or not," Logan said. "For all we know, he could be dead."

"We'll make camp outside of the city," Kiara said. "I don't want to be inside in case there's more violence, and they're not likely to welcome four non-Valteroni strangers in any case."

Logan found them an abandoned farmstead within walking distance of the city. What had happened to the family that lived there, no one could say. It looked as if they'd left in a hurry, and someone had tried in vain to fire the place. Kiara spent an hour giving out orders to make it defensible. They reinforced the front door, took out a wall, established a few escape routes. Then Logan set his infrared perimeter sensors with a control pad in the main room of the farmhouse.

He left at midday to trek into the city and see what he could find out. They saw the occasional refugee while he was gone. All of them kept their distance. The poor souls only now trudging out of Valteron City had lost too much already, and wanted no trouble.

Logan returned right at sunset. "There's good news and bad news," he said. "Bad news is the military's got the city on lockdown. I had a bit of trouble talking my way in, especially without Mr. Magic Fingers to provide some razzle-dazzle."

"I offered to come along," Quinn said. He fanned

out the cards he'd been shuffling in one hand. "Hey, Logan, pick a card."

"I'll pass," Logan said.

"You said there was good news," Kiara said.

"They picked a new Prime," Logan said.

"Who was it?" Chaudri asked. "The merchant?"

"No idea. They're announcing tomorrow."

"Any leads on our target?" Kiara asked.

"Not a whisper. I made a quick survey of the ships in the bay. There wasn't a coast-cutter among them."

"That city is massive," Quinn said. "I don't know how easily we're going to find him."

"If Dr. Holt is anywhere near Valteron City, he'll come for the announcement," Chaudri said.

"Think so?" Logan asked.

"So many Alissians in one place, with the fate of a city-state in the balance." Chaudri's smile was faint, her eyes distant. "He wouldn't miss it for the world."

Quinn was starting to wonder if there was more to the Chaudri-Holt thing than there appeared.

The rough outline of a plan came together that night over dinner. Logan unrolled a black nylon satchel that Quinn hadn't seen before; that probably meant it had been stored in the small armory that he kept in his saddlebags. Inside were four glass-and-steel devices, each tipped with a narrow metal cylinder.

He took out one and folded down a lightweight aluminum handle. "These are pneumatic tranquilizer handguns," he said. "CO_2 powered, effective range of about ten yards." He opened a smaller metal case to reveal several glass darts tipped with hypodermic needles.

"What's in there?" Quinn asked.

"Genetically modified botulinum toxin," Logan said. "Near-complete paralysis for about two hours."

"Botox?" Quinn asked.

"Not as long-lasting, so don't get any ideas, baby face," Logan said. "So much as scratch your finger with one of these and you're a rag doll. City like this, you'll end up naked in the gutter. If you're lucky."

"You always paint a delightful picture," Quinn said.

Kiara ignored their banter. "We'll sedate Holt and get him back to the farmhouse. Then Logan can arrange for transport on the quickest boat we can catch north."

"We'll have no trouble finding one of those," Chaudri said.

It occurred to Quinn that his time in Alissia was about half-over. Once they grabbed Holt, Kiara would want to make a beeline for the gateway. The realization made him a little bit sad. More than he'd expected. And anxious, too. He was no closer to finding a bit of magic to bring home.

Then again, if anyone knew where to find magic here, it was Richard Holt.

The haze of smoke still hung over Valteron City, trapped by an overcast sky that never seemed to break. On foot, dressed in garb that showed no hint of wealth, they joined a steady throng of people headed toward the bay. Word had gotten around about the day's announcement, and suddenly the flow of humanity was reversed. More refugees than Quinn thought possible were trudging back home to hear their fate decided.

Logan made quiet inquiries of the other travelers while they rode. No one had heard much of the new Prime, but there was a hint of optimism on their faces, their mannerisms. A new person in charge—whoever it was—would be a return to normalcy.

"Keep alert, people," Kiara said. "Holt could be anywhere. He recognizes Logan or Chaudri, and we're in trouble."

"Do you think he knows we're after him still?" Quinn asked Chaudri.

"Dr. Holt never deals in certainties. He'll find it improbable because of all the chaos, but he'll have a plan ready just in case."

Sounds like this guy would make a great magician.

The great influx of returning citizens allowed them to get into Valteron City without attracting too much attention. The gates were thrown wide open, and guards had long given up doing anything about the crowd other than move them along. Logan led them down a narrow avenue to the stable yard behind a small inn. The owner was a stout woman with her hair in a tight bun and two small children clinging to her woolen skirts. She saw Logan's face and smiled, almost in a motherly way.

"Lem, fetch some oats and water for the horses. And get your brother out of the hayloft to help you."

Soon the boy and his near-identical brother were running about, dodging the horses and filling feed troughs with hay and oats. A few more children made the mistake of revealing themselves in the hayloft and were quickly barked down by the inn's mistress to help out.

"Is Richard with you?" she asked. "I know he's got a taste for Caralissian ale, and we've a fresh keg."

"Ah, no, sorry," Logan said. "We're traveling separately. In fact, you haven't heard from him, have you?"

"Not for a couple of months. Who are your friends?"

Logan introduced them by first names only. "Everyone, meet Briannah. She's the mother I never had."

"Don't go pouring honey on your words for me, Logan," she said. It was an act, though. Her eyes were smiling. "At least you brought a tame animal this time, the gods be praised."

She took the reins of Logan's horse and wrangled it back toward the stable. This was the animal that had been trying to bite Quinn the whole trip. A goddamn warhorse, and mean as hell—*How the hell is it tame for her?* But it lacked either the time or the spirit to resist Briannah as she tucked it away back into a stall.

"You going to hear the announcement?" she asked.

"We think so, yes."

"Best to get moving, then. The boys told me the plaza's getting crowded."

They left the inn and joined the crowd filing toward the square, which was already packed. More people were steadily coming in. Quinn had been assigned the easternmost entrance, which was the least busy. He tried not to take offense at this; the others had known Holt personally. Logan pointed him in the right direction with a last warning to stay out of trouble.

Back in Vegas, the crowd was always changing. People came, gambled, usually lost, and went home. It was never the same faces in the theater, except for a few regulars. So Quinn never spent much time memorizing faces. He focused on the emotions and reactions of the crowd. That's what mattered most.

Even now, though he'd stared at a picture of Holt all night, he felt the details of the man's appearance slipping away, like water through cupped hands. If the man had any kind of disguise, Quinn would be less than useless at spotting him.

Probably should have mentioned that earlier. . .

The others checked in by comm link as soon as they were in position.

"I'm here," Logan said. "God, it's crowded."

"*Gods,*" Chaudri corrected. "And I'm in position as well."

Quinn scanned people's faces as they came in. There were almost too many to keep track of, but he did his best. The buzz of the crowd already in the square was distracting. There was a definite feel of energy to the place.

"Plenty of newcomers on the west gate. None of them look like Holt," Kiara said. "There might be too many. I'm starting to second-guess our plan."

Quinn couldn't argue with her. Holt could be anywhere in Alissia. His file had said that he was a chess player. No wonder he'd been a move or two ahead of them at every turn.

The pitch of excitement in the crowd rose. Something was happening toward the front of the square, on the steps of the white marble amphitheater reserved for the use of the new Prime to address the public. Chaudri said the position came without pay, not that it mattered. The Prime of Valteron ruled supreme over the most powerful city-state on the continent. No amount of wealth could buy that.

On the balcony of the impressive manse was a huge speaking-cone of some kind. A small figure stepped to this and yelled, "Welcome!"

His voice boomed over the square; the crowd fell silent. Quinn glanced around and recognized the subtle designs of an architect who knew his acoustics. By shouting through the cone, the speaker on the balcony—usually the Prime, in all likelihood—could be heard by anyone in the square.

People not already in the square started to hurry. It was a near-stampede to be in place for the announcement.

"What a mess," Logan muttered over the comm link.

"We're running out of time here," Kiara said. "If we don't have eyes on Holt by the time they make the announcement, plan to meet back at the inn to regroup."

Quinn took a moment to get his bearings so he could find the way back. He looked out into crowd of people . . . and there he was. Tall, bald, just past middle age, and striding purposefully into the crowd. His hood was up, and a brown cloak streamed out behind him. He carried himself with such purpose, such confidence. It could only be Richard Holt.

"Son of a bitch," he said. "I think I see him. Stand by."

He hurried down from his vantage point, keeping an eye on the hooded man as best he could. The man's long strides weren't easy to catch up with, especially given the haste of the crowd. Quinn's palms were sweating; he wiped them on his pants and checked the hilt of the pneumatic pistol tucked inside his jacket. His finger brushed the trigger and he jerked the hand away quickly. If he accidentally shot himself with that thing, he'd blow the mission. And worse, Logan would never let him live it down.

The tall figure had come up against the press of people and fallen still. Quinn had a moment to catch up. He grabbed a shoulder, his hand ready to draw the pistol and fire. This was the moment.

He tapped him on the shoulder. "Richard?"

The man turned around, surprised, and his face was that of a stranger.

"Oh. S-sorry," Quinn stammered. "I thought you were someone else."

"Who did you think I was?" the man asked. His eyes nearly made Quinn take a step back they were so intense. Blue-green, like the color of the ocean.

"No one. Just a friend I was looking for."

"Richard Holt?" the man asked.

Quinn felt a surge of excitement. "You know him?"

"Rather well," the man said. He gave Quinn a considering look. "You seem familiar."

"No, I'm sure we never . . ." Quinn began. But the man had turned toward him, and his cloak fell open enough to reveal the bright blue sash beneath. "Uh, met," he finished. He glanced from it to the near-identical sash of his own costume. The thing Chaudri had insisted would help mark Alissian magic users. Could it be?

"Now I remember," the man said, though his tone said he'd never quite forgotten. "You look like someone I've been sent to find. A man who claimed to be a magician."

Uh-oh. "No, that wasn't me," Quinn said.

"You were never in Bayport."

He hesitated a second too long. Missed that split-second chance to lie. Where was his goddamn poker face when he needed it? He'd been away from Vegas too long. "No, I was . . . I just—"

"Gods be good, you *are* him." The man laughed. "Oh, this is too rich."

"I think there's been a mistake," Quinn said. "I'll be on my way now."

The man whispered a word. And Quinn's boots stuck to the ground as if glued there. And the crowd parted naturally around both of them, never looking, as if they didn't see them at all.

"Mayday," Quinn said. "Mayday, mayday."

The comm link was quiet. He couldn't even hear the static.

"Let me go. Help!" Quinn shouted. But no one in the crowd around seemed to hear him. He didn't dare draw his sword, or try the elemental projector. He could reach the pack of cards in his sleeve. That was about it.

"Impersonating a magician is a serious crime, as I'm sure you know."

Maybe he could talk his way out of this. "Who says I'm not one?" Quinn asked.

"A fair point." The bald magician pressed a finger to Quinn's temples and held him fast. His touch was like ice. A chill flowed down from his hands. It felt like he was slowly freezing Quinn to death from the outside in. His face went still, his ears numb, his shoulders quivered.

Some part of him fought this. Deep in his gut he clung to the only warmth he had. Almost like a hot meal in the stomach, but deeper. The cold from the magician's fingers pressed against it. Did it recoil, even? Yes. Quinn found the source of it and *pushed*. Then the heat was emanating outward, shoving back against the cold. Surging into his shoulders, his face. The balding man's eyes widened. His arms were flung away. He stumbled a step backward and stared.

"Gods," he whispered. "How?"

Quinn wasn't sure himself, but he had this guy on the ropes and intended to take advantage. "Release me, and I'll tell you."

But the man only moved closer to him, and threw a cloaked arm over his shoulders.

"Wait," Quinn said. "What are you doing?"

The magician ignored him. He looked down, muttered a command. Quinn felt a surge of panic—or rather, *another* surge of panic—and started to struggle, but the magician's arm was like stone. He couldn't break his grip. He worked a few cards out of the pack and let them fall. Then he tugged the jack of spades out enough that he could press his thumb down on the switch. Not that he thought Thorisson could help, but he was desperate.

The plaza flickered around him. The magician's arm held him like it was made of steel. A light flashed, blinding him.

He fell into darkness.

"Bradley, report," Logan said. He stood on the balls of his feet, ready to start moving the second he got confirmation. But Bradley hadn't said a word after "Stand by."

On the marble steps, a man's voice boomed through the speaker. "Our troubles are over!"

"That's Admiral Blackwell," Kiara said. She sounded surprised. "Top commander of the Valteroni fleet. They're certainly bringing out the big guns for this one."

"Maybe he's taking over," Logan said. It wouldn't be the worst thing. This dump of a city could use a leader with some discipline.

"The Prime must be a civilian," Chaudri said. "It's one of the few restrictions."

Still no word from Bradley, but he'd probably

forgotten to unmute his comm link. In the background, Blackwell was speaking ponderously about all that Valteron had lost in the days of unrest, the dead, the damages.

"All of that is behind us, my fellow citizens," the admiral said. "Leading us into the future is a man that many of you know. Someone who was born here. Who understands what Valteron needs. A man who will ensure that we remain the greatest power in Alissia for another century!"

"This is quite an introduction," Chaudri said.

"Let me delay no more. We have suffered long enough." Blackwell paused for effect here.

He's already contradicting himself.

Chaudri must have had a flicker of insight; her voice came over the comm link. "Oh my *God!*" She'd even forgotten to make it plural.

Something in her tone gave Logan a feeling of dread. He connected the dots then. A day late, as usual.

"The new Prime of Valteron," the admiral boomed. "Richard Holt!"

For the first time since Logan had known her, the lieutenant had no words. Either that or she'd fainted, but he didn't consider that very likely.

"All right, everyone," Logan said. "Let's regroup at the inn. Get there as quick as you can."

Holt's voice came over the amplifier and it fixed him to where he stood.

"People of Valteron," Holt said.

Chaudri gave a soft gasp.

"Jesus," Logan whispered. It was him, all right. He'd know that voice anywhere.

"All of us are orphans," Holt said. "My predecessor, the former Prime, was like a father to us. Without him we've been like a ship without anchor."

Not a bad metaphor for these people, Logan had to admit.

"Consider the course righted. There are days of change ahead. Days of growth and prosperity like none that Valteron has ever known. I have seen things in our future. Ships that move without sails. New sources of heat. Advanced weapons for the admiral and his fine navy."

Logan sighed. He hoped that didn't mean what he thought it did.

"Go back to your homes, your shops," Holt was saying. "The admiral has been kind enough to reopen the harbor, starting tomorrow."

Men in feather caps cheered. The more shabbily dressed seamen muttered curses.

Logan didn't wait to hear the rest. He began shouldering his way toward the exit. Kiara and Chaudri were silent across the comm link. He let the flow of Alissians carry him out of the square. They were jubilant, most of them. Excited about a new future, and talking about Holt as if they knew him well. Funny how just yesterday no one had ever heard of him.

Valteron City still had a charred smell to it, but at least the sky had opened. The fog was lifting, and the city was vibrant.

> **"Magic is like a religion to Alissians. The practitioners are revered and secretive. Either that, or they're avoiding us."**
>
> —R. HOLT, "QUESTIONS ON
> ALISSIAN MAGIC"

CHAPTER 11

TAKEN

When Quinn could see again, he was somewhere else. A clearing surrounded by forest, and the trees were the largest he'd ever seen. They towered like California redwoods, the tops of them lost in low-hanging clouds. Some time seemed to have passed; it was near evening here. A footpath lined with round stones led away from the clearing, deeper into the forest. He thought he heard the distant sound of ocean surf.

He whirled on the magician. "Where are we?"

"We are no longer in Valteron, I will tell you that. This is a place not found on any maps."

"What kind of place?" Quinn said.

"Call it a home, call it a school, call it whatever you will. This is where we come to be with our own. With magicians."

Oh my God, oh my God, oh my God. . .

"Let's take a walk, shall we?" The man started down a path lined with round stones. Not looking back to see if Quinn followed.

He was unrestrained; he might have tried to run away. But he had no idea where he was. And he was as curious as he was frightened. So he followed.

"Tell me your name, son," the magician said.

"Quinn." He said it automatically, not thinking to use the cover identity that Chaudri and her team had assigned to him. *Damn.* "Well, I was born Thomas More. But I go by Quinn."

"You have a strange way of speaking, Quinn," the magician said. "You're not from Valteron, are you?"

"You didn't tell me *your* name," Quinn groused.

"You may call me Moric."

"I have a few other things I'd rather call you."

The magician didn't seem to move, but a burning sensation lashed across Quinn's wrists. He cried out, rubbing them against his chest.

"That's for your impertinence," Moric said. "You shouldn't speak that way to magicians. Particularly after masquerading as one."

He went cold when he heard that. The man's tone was light, but the accusation was there. "Maybe I did indicate that I had certain abilities. It was only to save my own skin. There were these mercenaries—"

"It's still a crime. One that true magicians take rather seriously," Moric said.

Quinn sighed. He should have known that posing as a magician in a world where real ones existed was going to get him into trouble. "I didn't hurt anyone."

"I'm aware of that. If you had, this would be a far less friendly conversation."

The man kept looking at him sideways while they walked, as if Quinn were a strange animal or something.

They turned a bend in the path and climbed a hill. Quinn hadn't been imagining the sound of surf; aquamarine water glinted at him through the woods to their left. He tried another angle.

"Where I come from, you're innocent until proven guilty."

"You come from a soft place, my friend."

Quinn considered making a run for it again—this time he was sure he didn't *want* to find out what was going on. And maybe Moric was tired from his recent exertions. He'd climbed the hill with no difficulty, though, and seemed perfectly hale to the appearance. Looking closely at him, Quinn realized the man wasn't as old as he'd thought. He was middle-aged, probably in his late forties. The shaved head added years.

"This is just too weird," Quinn said at last. He didn't know how else to put it.

Things rapidly got stranger. A flock of massive birds flew overhead. They were the size of small airplanes, and wheeled and dove with one another with a strange sort of intelligence. Quinn studied them for a second, shook his head, kept walking.

"How did you make the fireball?"

"What fireball?" Quinn asked. He had to be careful here.

"A witness claimed that you conjured a globe of fire. Like this." He raised a hand, shook the sleeve of his robe clear, and curled his fingers together. A ball of blue flame appeared at their tips, hissing and curling. Quinn could feel the heat from it on his face. Then Moric let his fingers fall apart, and the ball dissipated.

"I definitely never did anything like that," Quinn said. Blue flame. He wished he'd thought of that one. There was just something intimidating about fire in such an unnatural color.

"Fire is destruction personified," Moric said. "Wielded only with the greatest care. It builds nothing, it only consumes."

"It cooks things," Quinn said. "That's a kind of producing, if you ask me. And you can use it to reshape metal."

Moric pursed his lips thoughtfully. "You're not quite as foolish as you've been acting. And you've managed not to try and run away, though I could see you were thinking about it. That's good. It prevents an awkward situation in which I must drag you back by your ears. Or strip you bare and let you float along beside me."

"What can I say? I'm a fast learner."

Moric smiled, though there was no humor in it. "You'd better be. If I'm right about you, you're as dangerous as anyone who's ever come to this island."

So it was an island. That was something useful, if disappointing. It meant that Quinn wouldn't have any luck escaping on foot unless he got hold of a boat. A big boat. The research team's reports on predators in the Alissian seas had been simply haunting.

"What makes you think I'm dangerous?" he asked.

"Because you've either been masquerading as a magician, or you have a talent that we don't understand."

Quinn shook his head. "I'm not threatening anyone. All I wanted was to stay alive."

"So you say," Moric said.

The stone-lined path led out into a large clearing. A group of children sat together on the grass some distance away, listening to a shaggy-haired old fellow who was showing them something in tree bark. Moric and Quinn walked about a quarter mile, passing low stone buildings and huts, a small section of farm plots, and an outdoor farrier's yard. It was like a tiny little community here. They had a bit of everything.

"Is everyone here a magician?" Quinn asked.

"For the most part, yes."

Quinn made a quick mental tally, like a blackjacker counting cards in the casino. About forty people were in view, including the children. At the estimated rate of magic capabilities in the population, this was beginning to explain why magic users had been so difficult to find.

"I didn't realize how many of you there were," he said.

"Few do. We prefer it that way," Moric said.

"Which hut is yours?"

Moric chuckled. "Oh, I don't live here. This is one of our farms. A place of peace and contemplation."

One of their farms? Quinn shook his head in wonder. The company researchers weren't a little bit off about the numbers of magicians here. They were off by an order of magnitude. Finally, he knew something that they didn't. And he liked how it felt.

Moric steered him along the road, where some of the other islanders—that was how Quinn thought of them now—called out a greeting to him. They eyed Quinn strangely, but said nothing.

This was the highest point on the island. The ground stretched downhill before them for a quarter mile and then dipped out of view, perhaps into a steep vale. Quinn could see water on either side. To their left was an inlet bay, dominated by several docks to which ships were unloading boxes of cargo. Strangely, there were no dockworkers carrying the boxes out on their shoulders. Instead, two gray-robed men stood waving their hands, moving the boxes around in midair with complex gestures. The crates sailed out of the holds of squat cargo ships and stacked neatly on the docks.

Beyond them, in the deeper part of the inlet bay, was a tall sailing ship with a deep hull and three masts. Like something out of a storybook. Only this craft looked out of place compared to Legato's trading vessel and the other ships Quinn had seen. There was a sleekness and style about her that didn't fit in to this place.

And it looked familiar . . .

Recognition clicked. It had to be the *Victoria*, the company's lost ship. His mouth fell open; he almost said it out loud. But he didn't know what Moric had in store for him, whether he was a friend or an enemy.

All Quinn could think about was Kiara. Was her sister here, and alive?

"Do you know what happened, when I touched your temples back in the plaza?" Moric asked suddenly.

"I know it was cold," Quinn said.

"Yes, that's how it feels for some. What else?"

"I pushed it away. The cold. It felt like you were turning me into a block of ice."

Moric grunted. "That test should have gone differently. It should have numbed you completely to my touch. Instead, I felt a resistance in you. A resonance. When I tried to cast a delving, you pushed back." He chuckled. "I admit that surprised me a little."

"What does it mean?" Quinn asked.

"What it usually means is that you have the magic in you. The gift, the birthright. It means you've come to this island to be trained as a magician. Or else I'm wrong, and you were simply pretending to be a magician without cause. In which case you'll most likely face death. Either way, I'd say we have some exciting times ahead."

"Oh," Quinn said. *How is that even possible?* "Crap."

"Yes, there will be some of that. It usually isn't pretty when we get someone as old as you. Too spirited, too stubborn. Much harder to set straight and put on the guild path."

"What guild?" Quinn asked. He'd not heard of anything like that in his briefings. And it worried him that there seemed to be no kind of timetable in Moric's words.

Most of all, he was still reeling from the idea that he might have magic in him. *Alissian* magic.

Moric had been talking while his thoughts scrambled to find purchase. " . . . collection of all magicians in Alissia. At some point, most of them come here to be evaluated and taught. We seek them out as children, they come here to train, they leave as guild magicians. Some stay to help with the business of the guild. Like myself."

"Right, you're the magic muscle."

Moric turned to look at him. "That's a peculiar expression. I prefer to think of myself as a creative problem solver."

"You've got the creative part right, at least."

Mission *failed.* That was all Logan could think about as he joined the crowd streaming out of the plaza. Holt was now the most powerful—and untouchable—man in Alissia. How he'd managed to get himself down here and elected on the brink of a civil war, Logan couldn't begin to understand. Nor could he figure out why the admiral had called him a native Valteroni. None of it made sense, and he felt the beginning of a headache creeping up.

He usually left these political complexities to the eggheads in the research department.

There was a distinctive, upbeat hum to the people here. Most were Valteroni, which wasn't surprising, but Logan picked out a few foreigners as well. Kiara hailed him over the comm link.

"Yes, Lieutenant?"

"I can't raise Bradley. Have you heard from him?"

"No. Maybe he took out his comm link," Logan said, but a cold feeling began to form in his gut. Something was wrong. "I'll start heading over to his spot."

"Chaudri just joined me. We'll meet you there," Kiara said.

Logan turned and fought his way against the flow of humanity until he was back in the plaza. Many would-be revelers had lingered there, and members of the city watch were outnumbered far too heavily to do anything about it. Well, Holt would have his first test of leadership soon.

He tried the comm link one more time. "Bradley, can you hear me?" Only static answered him.

By the time he'd reached Bradley's post, most of the crowd had thinned out. That's how he noticed the men following him. Three of them. They stuck out because they were armored and well-fed, whereas most of the people in the square were neither.

"I've got some trailers," he said softly.

"City watch?" Kiara asked.

"No," Logan said. Watchmen usually carried clubs or steel-wrapped cudgels, the kind of weapons you'd use for crowd control. These men had swords, and looked like they knew how to use them.

"See if you can lose them," Kiara said.

Already way ahead of you, Lieutenant.

Logan waved at a random person ahead in the crowd, and hurried forward as if to greet him. He skirted around a group of Kestani merchants sharing a bottle of wine, chanced a look back. The men had sped up to follow. Now there were four of them, and they'd given up any pretense otherwise.

He reached the mouth of a narrow avenue exiting the plaza—what had been Bradley's post. There was no sign of him. No blood on the ground, though. At least that was something. The swordsmen were twenty paces out.

"Heading up the street. Don't think I can lose them," he said. "Permission to engage?"

"Try not to hurt anyone. We're almost there."

No promises.

He ducked into the first alley and drew his sword, putting his back to the wall. The alley was narrow enough that he might avoid being surrounded. Boots pounded toward the corner. Logan counted to himself. Three. Two. One. He swung low, catching the first one across the shins. Down he went, even as Logan engaged the second pursuer. The man parried his first slash. They locked blades, hilt to hilt. Logan threw a shoulder into him. He stumbled back out of the alley into the arms of his companions. The first attacker was trying to stand. Logan kicked him in the side of the head. He went down like a sack of bricks.

The three others kept their distance. They were looking behind him. Logan spun, already slashing, but it was only a woman. She wasn't armed, or armored. A trick. He started to look away, but she raised her hands in a complex gesture. It *was* a trick, and a very dangerous one. She spoke some words he couldn't understand. An invisible weight pressed all around him. *Son of a bitch!* He tried to warn the others, but he couldn't move, couldn't even speak.

Chaudri appeared out of nowhere and bowled into two of the swordsmen, taking them down in a tangle. Kiara approached the third; to Logan it seemed she was holding her sword awkwardly. As if she could barely hold the weight, and fear was written on her face.

The third swordsman smirked. "Just you, little lady?"

This should be entertaining.

He sauntered toward her, holding his own sword almost casually. Thinking her an easy mark.

One more step, Logan thought. The man complied.

Kiara's blade whirled in her hands, even as she spun and slashed him across the shoulder. He cursed and stumbled back. She was on him instantly, her sword flashing. He recovered enough to parry the worst of her cuts. She wasn't trying to kill the man, or he'd be dead already.

Logan felt the cold tip of a dagger against his throat.

"Stop!" the woman called. "Or your man dies."

Kiara glanced over, saw them both, and backed off. The man she'd been attacking leaned against the wall, panting. Chaudri scrabbled away from the other two as they regained their feet. Logan tried to shake his head. *Go*, he wanted to tell them. Better that two get back to the gateway than all of them be captured. His head wouldn't move, though, so he rolled his eyes. Kiara saw it, but she shook her head. He would have cursed if he could.

"That's better," the woman said. "We're not supposed to harm you."

"If that's true, then release him," Kiara said. She kept her blade up.

"Put your steel away."

Kiara paused, not giving in straightaway. That was good. Show some backbone. After a long moment, she slid her blade back into the sheath on her belt. Even as she did, the invisible bonds around Logan lifted . . . for the most part. He could move, though every motion felt sluggish, as if he were moving through water. Kiara gave him the hand signal. *Stand down*. His knuckles were white around his sword, but he obeyed and put it away.

"What now?" Kiara asked.

"The big man wants a word."

"And which big man would that be?" Kiara demanded.

"The Valteroni Prime."

> "The gateway is a secret we cannot
> hope to keep forever. Sooner or
> later, someone is going to talk."
>
> —R. HOLT, "WHAT IS OUR ENDGAME?"

CHAPTER 12

THE VALTERONI PRIME

Richard Holt's new residence, the palace of the Valteroni Prime, dominated the great plaza in Valteron's capital city. Everything about the structure seemed to defy physics and architecture. The alabaster roof curved like a sail over the main structure, supported by great stone chains stretching from a seemingly too-thin marble pillar hundreds of feet tall. The building was shaped like a half moon, both sides curving up from the ground. From a distance it looked like a fat cargo ship balanced precariously on the plaza, its bow pointed to the ocean.

This structure had astounded the CASE Global's

consulting architects, as it was unlike anything they'd seen in Alissia. They were all but certain that a stiff breeze should knock it over, but the structure had stood firm for decades. And the cost of the materials to make it, the labor required, spoke to the kind of wealth Valteron had amassed by dominating the Alissian seas. The Valteroni Prime was one of the most powerful leaders in Alissia. The fact that the former Prime had died shortly before Richard Holt got here was a little suspicious, but Logan still couldn't picture the studious, scholarly man planning an assassination. *Not really his style.*

Granted, Logan's own recon teams might have helped. They had infiltrated the libraries and archives throughout Alissia, creating the fictitious backstory for Holt and other researchers. This allowed them to assume the roles of scholars, priests, and teachers—all backed by planted documents and altered records.

Barely an hour had passed since the announcement was made, but already the city watchmen had cleared would-be revelers from the plaza. Wagons and horse carts were trundling in to sell produce and livestock. Maybe the city wouldn't starve after all.

They ascended an exquisite marble stair from the plaza to the front of the palace. Logan noticed archer slits cleverly concealed in the ochre walls; a dozen uniformed soldiers guarded the main entrance beneath an iron portcullis. He knew, too, from assets inside the palace, that the roof of the structure was studded with catapults and mangonels. A standing army of at least two hundred soldiers manned the ramparts and entrances and murder holes at all times. It might look like a cargo vessel, but the palace was a warship through and through. There would be no getting Holt out of here by force.

For a hopeful moment, it looked like the guards would challenge their mismatched party. With just the right amount of discord, Logan might be able to slip away. Only he couldn't see Kiara's face, and they dared not risk the comm units while being so closely watched. Besides, there would be no getting Chaudri away quietly. Not until she saw Holt.

The woman magician barely slowed down, though. She showed some kind of parchment with a wax seal. "The Prime is expecting us."

Soldiers parted ranks so that they could pass. They marched up a narrow hallway—more arrow slits here, and a few murder holes—to an immense receiving hall. It had to be three stories tall, with great bay windows overlooking a courtyard that lay beyond. Everything here spoke of incredible wealth, at least on Alissian terms. Lamps burned in dozens of alcoves around the room, casting a warm glow on oil paintings and rich tapestries. Logan had eyes for none of it, though. He was too focused on the man who stood gazing out one of the windows, apparently lost in thought.

"Hello, Richard," Kiara said.

He turned at the sound of her voice, but wasn't startled. That little bit had been rehearsed, then. He wanted them to know he felt secure. "I hoped it would be you, Kiara. I trust my associates were not unkind?"

"No more than we had to be, your eminence," the magician said. Her tone was softer now, deferential for the first time. "They didn't come easily."

"I warned you about that," Holt said. "Any injuries?"

"One of your men got hurt. The big one surprised him."

Holt smiled at that. "I think she's talking about you, Logan. That's as close as you'll get to a compliment, from one of the guild." He moved away from the window and came over to look Logan in the eye. He still kept a healthy distance between them. "You look well."

Anger simmered in Logan. "Not as well as you."

Holt smiled in his infuriating way. His gaze flickered over to Chaudri, who was still muddy and a little dazed from her tumble with the swordsmen. She pushed an errant strand of dark hair aside and met his gaze.

"Dr. Chaudri," said Holt.

"Dr. Holt."

"You managed to get your hands dirty."

Chaudri wore a hint of a smile. "Just following your advice."

"I can see that. And I'll bet you're enjoying it, too." Holt looked at Kiara. "But where is the fourth member of your party? This *magician* I've been hearing about."

He put an emphasis on the word, like he guessed at Bradley's game. Kiara said nothing.

Holt looked at the woman magician, who seemed uncomfortable with the attention. Strange to think someone with her abilities would be nervous around him. "Well?" he asked.

"We only saw three of them," she said.

"There's a fourth. Find him," Holt said.

She took her men and left down a narrow hallway.

Kiara waited until the door closed, then she turned on him. "Richard, you must know why we're here."

"I hope it's not for the seafood. Most of the fishermen fled when the navy arrived."

"You've broken nearly every gateway protocol."

"I know that quite well, having written most of them."

"Enough games, Richard!" she snapped. "What the hell are you doing here?"

"Running the most powerful nation on the Alissian continent," he said.

"So it would seem. I look forward to learning how you pulled that off when we get home."

"Home?" He shook his head. "This is my home, Kiara."

He gestured out the window toward the bay, where a pair of ships with colorful sails were gliding into harbor on a steady breeze. "Look at this place! A world without pollution. Without landfills or nuclear weapons. Alissia has given me the greatest joys of my life. It seems only right that I should do something in return."

"We have orders," Logan said.

"Orders from a faceless company," Holt said. "Don't get me wrong. I'm grateful for what they've done. But I fear that the executives don't have the interest of *Alissians* in mind. Do you have any idea what they're planning?"

"That's not our concern," Kiara said. Too quick, maybe. As if she were worried that he might go on. Which made Logan wonder: *What does Holt know?*

"It's not *your* concern. It certainly is mine. They have shareholders to think about. Millions—probably billions—of dollars invested. Eventually, they're going to exploit this place, the way Earth has been exploited."

"You have no reason to believe that," Kiara said.

"Haven't I? What about the core samples from all over the continent? They're predicting crop yields, from those soil analyses. And what about the terrain surveys, the ultrasonic scans? Tell me why they're all tuned for precious metals."

"We've been doing those surveys for years," Kiara countered.

"It's not the surveys that changed," Holt said. "It's CASE Global's Earth-side acquisitions. Two timber companies in Brazil. A Texas refinery. The top metallurgy firm in Germany. They've also doubled the number of mercenaries in the past six months. That's when I knew I had to act."

"You're reading too much into those things," Kiara said.

"No. They're gearing up for an invasion. And the people here are defenseless to it. That's why they need me."

"You can't stay here. No matter what you believe."

Holt said nothing. Instead, he strolled back to the window, looking almost distracted.

Logan ran a quick scenario. If they grabbed him here, they'd have to get back down that narrow hallway, past the guards. There was probably a magician somewhere around here, too. But that might be manageable. Especially with the element of surprise. He eased a hand beneath his cloak to the handle of the short-range dart gun. How much did Holt weigh? About one-eighty back home, but he looked like he'd lost a few pounds. All they had to do was get him out of the palace. And they might not have another chance.

Kiara caught Logan's eye; she was thinking the same thing. She gave a curt nod. He drew the pistol quietly, aimed at the center of Holt's back, and pulled the trigger. The dart flew wide, missing Holt by just an inch. He'd missed. Damn! He fired again. Another miss.

Kiara, alarmed, drew her own pistol and fired. This time the dart hit the window frame and stuck there, quivering.

Holt barely spared it a glance. "You needn't bother. Do you know how many times the Valteroni Prime has been assassinated in the past century?"

What the hell is going on? They all looked at Chaudri.

"Not once," Chaudri said. "They all died of natural causes. There were numerous attempts, of course. None succeeded."

Holt turned to face them. "Seems peculiar, doesn't

it? In medieval Europe, most monarchs lasted less than two decades."

"Some less than a year," Chaudri said.

"I'd long suspected that the Valteroni Prime had certain protections. Now I have the proof," Holt said.

Wonderful. The man had some kind of magical shield. Logan considered just grabbing him, but the failure of the dart gun made him wary. Where was Bradley when they needed him?

He almost shuddered at that last thought.

Kiara took a different approach. "It will go far easier on everyone if you come willingly," she said.

"Easier for you, certainly," Holt replied.

"I've been authorized to offer you immunity. Complete access to your research files for the rest of your life."

Holt looked back out the window.

"A financial settlement as well," Kiara said. "Ten million, transferred to your account the moment you set foot back through the gateway."

"Free to return here whenever I want?" Holt said.

Kiara's expression grew pained. That was the weak point of the offer, and she knew it. "I can't promise that."

"What would happen to Valteron, if I agreed?" Holt asked. "Here's something I can promise *you.* There'd be another civil war. Thousands would die, both of violence and hunger. The populace is already on the brink of starvation."

"Richard—" she began.

"No," he said. "You've made your offer, which I decline, but let me give you a counterproposal. Admiral Blackwell has been so kind as to hold a package for me, to be opened in the event of my death or disappearance."

"What kind of package?" Kiara asked.

"The most damaging kind. Information. Everything the Alissians need to know to disable the gateway, and sufficient motivation to ensure that they do."

Kiara's face was neutral, but Logan knew that look. Cold fury.

"How about giving us the contraband back?" Logan asked. "The weapons and the disruptive technology make everyone back home pretty nervous."

"They were meant to," Holt said. "Imagine if I put them into the right hands. The craftsmen, or the guild of magicians."

"You wouldn't dare!" Kiara said.

"I have no desire to interfere with the course of Alissian civilization," Holt said. "But I'll do whatever I must to protect Alissia's future."

"Yes—you're so altruistic, Richard."

"I'm not claiming I'm a saint. But 'benevolent supreme ruler' is far better than what these people had before." He shook his head. "I don't expect you to understand . . . and honestly, I don't care if you approve or not." He clapped his hands twice. A contingent of uniformed guardsmen appeared from the hallway and took up position around Logan, Kiara, and Chaudri.

"And here's your escort," Holt said. "They'll see you back to the plaza. Please send word before you enter my city again. I won't ask my people to be so gentle, next time."

"This isn't over, Richard," Kiara said.

"It is for today, I'm afraid." Holt turned back to the window. "Valteron has need of me."

Logan half expected the soldiers to escort them to a prison cell. That's what he'd have done in Holt's shoes, to eliminate and contain the threat. That is, if he didn't want to simply eliminate the threat once and for all. True to the man's word, however, his troops showed them back to the plaza. The squad's commander, a solemn man of middle years sporting an oiled mustache, touched Kiara's shoulder as she passed.

"One officer to another," he said quietly. "Make yourselves scarce. The Prime's given clear orders for if we see you again."

"Understood, Commander," Kiara said.

She beckoned the others and set out quickly across the plaza, eager to put some distance between them and Richard Holt's new seat of power. None of the soldiers followed, but Logan marked a few shadows moving parallel to them. Whether these were Holt's men or someone else's, he couldn't say, but he wouldn't be surprised if they were a little of both—people who get an audience with the new Prime so soon after his ascension would be of interest to any number of people.

Either way, they were keeping their distance.

"Where the hell is Bradley?" Kiara whispered over the comm link.

"I was hoping that Holt's people nabbed him, and we'd find him in the palace," Logan said. He doubted Bradley would have fought his way free. *He's more dangerous to himself than anyone else, when it comes to fighting.* And yet Holt was still looking for him, which meant Quinn Bradley was on his own in Alissia.

God help us.

Chaudri had been quiet since they saw Holt; now she spoke for the first time. "It occurs to me that if there's one magician in Valteron City, there might well be others."

Logan drew in a sharp breath. "If he tries some of that sleight of hand stuff on a real magician . . ."

"Let's hope he didn't," Kiara said.

"We can hope that, but I'm telling you. It's his go-to move," Logan said. "To be fair, that's why you brought him in the first place."

"I brought him to help avoid altercations with people *other* than real magicians. I can't imagine how an encounter *with* one would go down."

Logan glanced at Chaudri. "What would happen if he did?"

"You know the law as well as I do."

Logan shook his head. "It was a mistake to bring him."

"What's done is done," Kiara said. "The only thing we know for certain is that Holt doesn't have him."

"Let's go back to the east gate," Logan said. "I think I saw something."

They returned to the east entrance to the plaza, where Bradley had been posted. Right out in the middle of the plaza, Logan found what he'd glanced before: a red-backed playing card stuck in the mud. "Got something," he said. He picked it up. "Ace of spades."

"Here's another one," Kiara said. She plucked it from the mud. "Ace of clubs."

"Got one, no, make that two," Chaudri said. She plucked them from the wheel ruts that crisscrossed the plaza. "Both eights. Clubs and spades."

They searched for a few minutes, but found no more cards.

"Not much of a trail," Kiara said.

"I think it's a message," Logan said. "Aces and eights."

Chaudri looked at him, her eyes questioning.

"Dead man's hand," he said.

Kiara found a lonely section of the plaza to talk strategy. Their watchers hovered nearby, visible but out of earshot.

"We need to regroup," Kiara said. "Let's get back to the inn, and figure out a different way to grab Holt."

"A different way?" Logan asked. He jerked a thumb toward the palace. "Last I heard, we were told to get out of town."

"Of course he wants us gone. He considers us a threat."

"What about the part where he jumps Alissian

technology ahead by about five hundred years?" Logan asked. "Or tells them about the gateway?"

"He was bluffing."

"I don't know," Chaudri said. "Something's different about him. I'm not sure what he might be willing to do."

"If we get him out clean, he won't have a chance," Kiara said.

"Don't see how we're going to do that, Lieutenant," Logan said. "The palace is a fortress, and he's got people shadowing us. If there's a magician with them, all bets are off. Holt has every advantage here."

She paused. "Maybe we should think about removing him from the equation."

"How?" Logan asked. "We can't get anywhere near him."

"We might be able to intercept some of the supplies going to the palace," Kiara said. "Food, in particular."

Son of a bitch. "You brought R-117, didn't you?" Logan asked.

Kiara didn't deny it.

"What's R-117?" Chaudri asked.

"A bioweapon," Logan said. "Tuned to one person's DNA."

Chaudri was aghast.

"Damn it, Logan, she's not cleared for this," Kiara said.

"She'd have to know, if you were serious. Which I hope you're not." Surely even she wouldn't be that coldhearted.

"I want no part in this," Chaudri said.

"Neither do I. It's cowardly."

"It's efficient," Kiara said.

"We can find another way, Lieutenant."

Kiara clenched her jaw. Logan knew how she felt; he hated a failed mission. But sometimes you had to cut your losses, and move on to the next one. He'd carry her out of the square bodily if it came to that.

A soft, persistent beeping noise saved Logan from looming insubordination charges. It came from the comm unit strapped to Kiara's wrist, the one disguised as a wide metal bracer.

"Thank God. Command is up," she said. Relief flooded her face. But it was short-lived. The stiffness came back.

"What's wrong?" Logan asked.

"There's been another breach at the facility. A team of gunmen has infiltrated the gateway."

"Into Alissia?" Chaudri asked.

"Yes."

"How many combatants?" Logan asked.

"Several. Bravo Team came in after them."

"Should be over quickly, then." He'd trained every man on Bravo himself. They were good.

"Maybe not. They've been in pursuit for two days."

"Where are they headed?"

Kiara's brow furrowed, and she checked her map again. Twice. "Right toward us."

"How is that possible?"

"I don't know. But they want us to make for Felara to help intercept," Kiara said.

Before they figure out how big this place is.

"What about Bradley?" Logan asked.

"He'll have to hold out on his own for a while."

"I don't like leaving him. He's still new to this place."

"Holt let us go unharmed. That's a good sign," she said.

"Would be, except that Holt doesn't have him," Logan said.

"We can monitor the isotope scanner while we head north. That's all we can do."

Logan frowned, but orders were orders. Bradley had proven himself resourceful so far. A bit of time on his own might be good for the greenhorn. "Covering that distance is going to take some time. And our rations are about spent."

"Chaudri and I will restock while you get the horses. We'll rendezvous at the base camp in two hours."

"Will do."

Kiara and Chaudri headed back toward the plaza, where the first tents from farmers and vendors had already gone up. Valteroni were already mobbing those tents; the cost of food would undoubtedly be enormous were it not for severe laws against price gouging. Logan wondered if Holt would keep those in place; he'd always been fascinated and a bit puzzled by Valteron's peculiar brand of economics.

He worked his way through the city, moving considerably slower since most Valteroni were out in the streets. They seemed to be celebrating their new Prime in a city-wide revel. Ironically, in this crowd it was easier to pick out the tail, a dark-haired man in a drab cloak who'd been following him since the square. More than one drunken citizen shouldered Logan hard as he passed, no doubt hoping to pick a fight. He might have indulged a couple, if he could have spared the time. He'd barely had a chance to warm up against Holt's men before the magician sewed him up like a stocking. None of the recon teams had ever engaged with a magic user before, and now it seemed that such avoidance had been a good idea. But it had got him riled up—just as missing Holt with the dart gun had— and he was definitely itching for some action. It took all of his training not to thrash the next drunk who bumped into him.

An open alleyway was just ahead. Logan knew he could cut over a few hundred yards to a smaller street running north-south. The next push from a swaggering Valteroni couldn't have come at a better time. He looked like a brawler: heavyset, with a beard and mustache that couldn't quite hide the ugliest nose Logan had ever seen. The thing must have been broken four or five times, and here came this fellow asking for another.

He lurched into Logan in a manner that wasn't quite clumsy enough to be accidental. "What?" he demanded, when Logan looked at him. His breath reeked of *jennah*, the rougher form of hard liquor that sponsored many a poor decision in southern Alissia.

"Do you know that fellow over there, in the gray?" Logan asked.

The bruiser peered in the direction of Logan's tail, who had paused to haggle with a street vendor while waiting for Logan to continue on. "Don't think so. What's it to you?"

"Nothing. He said he knew you."

"Never seen him in my life."

Logan shrugged. "He said something about you owing him money."

"That a fact?"

"You didn't hear it from me," Logan said. He slipped back into the crowd.

Moments later he heard a scuffle behind him. "You in the gray! Heard you been talking about me!"

Logan sighed contentedly. "Ah, Valteron." That should be about it for the tail. They were a touchy lot when it came to money. Owing anything to anyone else was a source of shame here.

Briannah's inn was one of the more defensible establishments in the city—with a high stockade and its own stable—but that wasn't why Logan had chosen it. He'd been wounded on a raid some years back. Barely made it away from the docks alive. Briannah had found him in the alley behind her stable yard. He was a complete stranger then, bleeding and half-unconscious, but she had her stable hands carry him inside.

For two weeks she looked after him, until he was

well enough to catch a trading vessel bound for New Kestani. Since then he'd visited her whenever he could, paying handsomely for a room he hardly used. Briannah liked to boss him around, but God, she could *cook*. He'd never eaten so well anywhere else in Alissia. More importantly, she knew how to keep her mouth shut. To others, at least. That was a rare thing among innkeepers.

Lem, one of the stable boys, answered almost immediately when he banged on the gate. "Hi, Logan!"

"Hi, Lem." Logan made sure no one in the alleys or street was watching him, and then entered the tiny stable yard. "Keeping out of trouble?"

"Mostly."

"Mostly, eh?" Logan went to ruffle his hair; the boy ducked nimbly out of the way. Most of those Briannah took in were orphans. She fed them, kept them reasonably clean, and gave them a safe place to sleep in this rough port city. Lem had come a long way under her care. For the first couple of years that Logan had known him, the boy hadn't spoken. Gods knew what kind of horrors he'd seen.

"Briannah told us to keep a lookout for you. She wants a word."

"Just one?"

The boy giggled. Logan wanted to check the horses, but thought it better to see Briannah first. He found her in the kitchen making a kettle of fish stew. The spicy kind, his favorite.

"It's about time you got back," she said. "Here I was thinking you were in the bay with your throat cut."

He couldn't help smiling. "Aw, you were worried about me."

She glanced away from her cooking long enough to note his disheveled condition. "What happened to you?" she demanded. "Picking fights with the locals again?"

"Wasn't my fault, I promise," Logan said. He kissed her once on the cheek and took a whiff of the stew. "Smells good." He reached for the spoon and got a hand smacked for his trouble.

"It's not ready yet, and your hands are filthy."

Logan went to the sink and washed up; there was no point in arguing with her. She added something else to the kettle that looked suspiciously like a lump of butter.

A serving girl came in and began slicing bread. She was young, perhaps twelve, nearly as old as Logan's eldest daughter. Seeing her made him think of home.

"Lessa, put another log on the hearth in the common room."

"I just added one," she protested.

"Lessa!"

The girl left, but not without rolling her eyes in the most condescending way possible. *Where do teenage girls learn that one?*

"Someone tried to steal your horses this afternoon," Briannah said.

"Again?"

"I warned you about bringing animals that fine to these stables. You're not the only one with eyes for them. And people talk around here."

"Do I need to go out to the stable and count them?"

She *tsked* at him. "Of course not. We're even more careful when you're here."

"And the saddlebags?"

"I had the boys lock them in your room. I know how particular you are about those," she said.

That was a relief. Logan wouldn't have wanted to write that particular report on lost equipment. With everything they'd brought for the retrieval mission, the executives would have had a fit.

"Thank you," he said.

"Don't thank me, thank the boys. They've been keeping watches, whenever you're around."

"I didn't ask them to."

"They did it on their own. They look up to you, though I can't say why."

"Maybe because you treat *me* like a stable boy."

"Ha! Well, you owe them this time. They ran off the thieves before I could even get out there with a wooden spoon."

"Good lads." All of the company mounts were thoroughbreds, all descended from championship horses. They were incredibly useful to take in the field, but there simply was no hiding their quality.

"Where's that handsome friend of yours?" she asked.

"Huh?"

"The new fellow? About half your size but a much nicer smile."

"Oh," Logan said. Bradley's charm apparently knew no bounds. "We got separated, after the announcement."

"You should bring him to the common room for a spell. Might be nice looking at a face other than yours. Just keep him away from my serving girls!"

"What makes you think he's single?" Logan asked.

"I can always tell. Just like I pegged you as a man raising daughters."

He still hadn't figured out how she guessed that one. "Well, you don't have to worry about him. If you see him, though, tell him I've headed back north, will you? I'll bring his horse, just in case."

She looked up from the kettle, frowned. "You're leaving already?"

"Wish I could stay longer. There's an urgent situation."

She ladled a healthy portion of the stew into a wooden bowl. "I won't have you leaving on an empty stomach."

It did smell good . . .

"I could eat," he said.

"When in doubt, bluff."

—ART OF ILLUSION, FEBRUARY 27

CHAPTER 13

THE ENCLAVE

Quinn knew he was in over his head.

Moric had escorted him for almost an hour on foot while they made their way to the center of the island. The stone-lined path led over a grassy hillock, beyond which the land fell away into a wide valley. A blue ribbon of water wound through it, glinting in the sun. Nestled in the middle of that was an island within an island, a settlement unlike any Quinn had seen in Alissia—or anywhere, for that matter. The buildings were cut from a pale gray stone. Seven crenellated towers encircled the town. Bright, colorful banners—one for each of Alissia's nations, apparently—flew at their peaks. Above them towered a single, elegant spire topped with a flag Quinn had never seen before in any of the research materials or briefings: a white hand clutching a golden star, on a field of royal blue.

"This is the Enclave," Moric said. "The heart of Alissian magic beats here."

"Unreal," Quinn said. The number of people that must live there. Hundreds upon hundreds of magicians, and the company knew nothing about them. Did Richard Holt? He couldn't help but wonder. The rogue researcher turned Valteroni Prime certainly had been able to contract their services, something the company briefings on Alissian magic hadn't covered.

"I had the same reaction when I first came here," Moric said. "That was a long time ago, but I remember it like it was yesterday."

He led Quinn to a pile of flat stones the size of coffee tables. One of them slid from the top of the pile with a grating noise as they approached and settled softly to the ground. Moric stepped onto it and gestured that Quinn should do the same.

Quinn hesitated. "What's this?"

"Fastest way down into the valley. Come, come, we're wasting time!"

Quinn stepped on reluctantly. "Is this even *safe*?"

"On my word, no one has ever been injured on these in recent memory," Moric said. He muttered a command; the stone lifted and began to skim down the slope into the vale.

"In recent memory" had the kind of ominous tone that worried Quinn. He was certain he'd fall off, but the stone was as solid as he could have wanted. The effect was still unsettling. They coasted down the slope, gaining speed. The Enclave's towers had seemed impressive from a distance. Now they towered overhead, impossibly tall. The air had a warm stillness to it.

The effort it took to guide their stone down the slope seemed little distraction to Moric. They leveled off and shot across the valley floor. They passed another person heading the other direction, an intense young man in crimson robes. He waved to Moric as they shot past one another.

They neared the river and glided along it toward the city proper. Moric set it down at the base of the nearest of the seven towers. It was a massive thing of stone and mortar, and like most castles, seeing it up close revealed its age. There was ivy growing along the base.

"This way." Moric stepped unceremoniously from the stone and marched up to a round wooden door at the tower's base.

Quinn followed on his heels. The door opened silently on well-oiled hinges to receive them, though Quinn saw no one on the other side. Their boots clicked on tile floors. The walls were some kind of polished glass; they glowed with a soft light, like underpowered neon signs. A spiral staircase led up to higher levels within, but Moric bypassed this and took him down a narrow hallway instead. There were doors on either side, and when he came to the fourth of these, Moric pushed it open.

The room was simple. Sleeping cot, mismatched

table and chair, a pitcher of water, and a wooden desk. But there were *books* on the desk—thick volumes bound in leather or pigskin. Quinn's fingers twitched, but he resisted the urge to pick one up and try his glasses.

Moric snapped his fingers, and a fire bloomed in the hearth on the far side of the room. Light poured in from a round window, though the glass was opaque.

"I need to sleep," Moric said. "Stay in this room until I come for you."

Quinn frowned. "So I'm, what, a prisoner?"

"Think of it as a cherished visitor."

"You can't keep me here," Quinn said.

Moric turned to look at him. "Oh? You don't look like much of a swimmer."

He stewed there in the tiny room for hours. He'd have tried the door, but Moric might have done something to it. He'd have read the books, but that would require the glasses. And Moric might have someone watching him, in any case.

To pass the time, he took out his deck of cards and practiced shuffling. He was five cards short, now that he'd left that message for the others to find. Even if they did, they had no idea where he'd been taken, or why. Riffle, cut, riffle, cut. The routine was familiar enough he could almost forget where he was. Or how much trouble he was in.

They had no proof that he'd claimed to be a magician, other than the ridiculous blue sash that he'd worn. He could deny it. But Moric had recognized him, which meant they had a witness. Even if they hadn't, this wasn't the kind of place that had developed a modern justice system.

He could claim it was true. Maybe that was the better way to play this. The magicians were more likely to trust him, more likely to let him snoop around. Less likely to execute him, too, let's not forget that.

He just had no idea how to prove it.

Moric returned a couple of hours later. "Good, you stayed," he said.

"You told me I had to," Quinn said. He didn't look up from his shuffling. Riffle, bridge, stack.

"I wasn't sure you would."

"What if I had tried to leave?" Quinn asked.

Moric chuckled. "It would have been unpleasant."

Quinn looked up and was taken aback by the change in Moric. The man was more than refreshed; he looked about two years younger.

"Wow. That was some nap you took!" Quinn said.

"I admit I was feeling haggard. Too much magic, not enough sleep."

He made the two sound connected somehow. Quinn filed that away for later. He tucked the deck of cards back into their box. He held it up so that Moric could see it, scissored his hands, and made it disappear into one sleeve.

"Oh, I think you're ready," Moric said.

"For what?" Quinn asked.

"To learn if you're one of us."

Quinn and Moric sat across from one another in a grove of broad, scraggly trees that overlooked the valley. The trees were in full flower and the perfume nearly overpowering. Quinn kept sneezing, which seemed to ruffle Moric's concentration.

"Hold still, will you?" he groused.

The magician had poked and prodded him with numerous small enchantments. He couldn't get any response like the first time. It didn't disappoint the man; it intrigued him. He was full of ideas.

"A hot and cold treatment might shock some magic out of you," he said.

"What's that involve?"

"Oh, it's quite simple," Moric said. "First I set you on fire, then dunk you in a tub of frigid water."

"I'd really prefer not to be set on fire. Even if you had water to put me out with. Which you don't. I'll pass on the dunking, too, for the same reason."

Moric put the tip of his finger on the ground, tracing a circle. "Water can be had." Where his finger touched, a puddle formed in the dirt. It welled up like a small geyser, soaking both of them.

"I *do* find it a bit hard to control," he admitted. "There are others more talented."

"How many people are on this island?" Quinn asked.

"Oh, about—" Moric caught himself; he seemed to sense Quinn's eagerness. "Well, let's just say that there are many. More than you'd guess."

"I knew that much already," Quinn said.

"Where are you from, if I may ask?"

Quinn had expected this; he'd been silently rehearsing his cover story since the moment they'd arrived. "Wyndham Bridge," he answered. "North Landor." The company had placed scrolls in the tiny hamlet's library that would vouch for him.

"I've never heard of it."

"It's near the coast. Boring place. That's why I left."

"What do you do for a living? Other than pretend at magic, of course."

Quinn bit back the excuse; it was time to start playing into this. "I was going to apprentice with my father. Carpentry."

"What happened?"

"He died. I left," Quinn said. He put a pained expression on his face. "If it's all right with you, I'd rather not talk about it."

"Magicians rarely have easy childhoods. Many of us here are content to leave the past in the past."

"What about you? Where are you from?" Quinn asked.

"I was born in Farbor, in the Pirean tip. My parents worked the nets, like everyone else there." He held up his hands; the palms were laced with old scars.

Pirea. Northeastern part of the continent, sparsely populated. Very little arable land, but the cold, deep coastal waters held some of the best fisheries in the world. The information just popped into Quinn's head out of nowhere. "Son of a bitch," he said. They'd had these headphones in his room, back at the island facility. He'd had to put them on at night. Kiara called it a memory consolidation program, but it was clearly more than that. What the hell else had they stuck in his head?

Moric was frowning at him. "I'm sorry?"

"Nothing. Sorry," Quinn said. "So, how did you end up here?"

"I was twelve, working the boats with my family. A storm caught us too far from the harbor. I knew about my abilities by then, but I'd kept them hidden. Didn't practice. I couldn't save anyone else."

"I'm sorry," Quinn said. He was surprised at how much he'd meant it. He knew what it was like to lose both parents at once. He knew the darkness it brought.

"It was a long time ago," Moric said.

A chime sounded then, almost like a doorbell, though Quinn couldn't pinpoint the source. The sound seemed to be coming from everywhere at once.

"What was that?" Quinn asked.

"A summons," Moric said. He stood. "The council meets today. No doubt they want a report on you."

"Do you know what you're going to tell them?"

"I haven't decided yet."

"I'd like to speak on my own behalf," Quinn said.

"The council is closed to outsiders, I'm afraid."

"You're not going to make me sit here all day, are you?" Quinn asked.

"I expect you to make your way back to your room. Can I trust you in that?"

"Fine," Quinn said.

"I'll find you when the meeting ends," Moric said. He strode out from the copse of trees. Once clear, he jumped and glided down the slope of the vale like a snowboarder. He didn't even bother with a stone this time. Robes flying, shaven head glinting in the sun. He was an odd bird for certain.

Quinn had said he'd go to his room.

I just didn't say I'd go there right away.

He really wanted to go to the docks for a closer look at that sailing ship, but that might look like he was trying to get off the island. So instead he found his way back to the stone-lined path that led around the vale. The climate was absolutely perfect. About seventy degrees, slight breeze, sunny. It was like southern California.

No wonder the magicians like to keep this island private.

He climbed to the highest point of the slope he was on to get a better vantage point and try to see the full island. A jumble of rocks and boulders littered the high point of the land, so he started free climbing them. Not being careless, but glad to have the chance to do something on his own. He gained the top of the pile, exhilarated . . .

Only to find that the highest rock was already occupied.

A fair-haired girl sat there, with her back to the vale, looking out across the water.

"Oh. Hello," Quinn said. He looked past her for a moment and fought a wave of vertigo. Beyond the boulder's edge was empty space; the ground dropped away a few hundred feet to where waves crashed on rocks below.

She turned slowly as if coming out of a trance. Not startled at all, which said she'd heard him climbing. Not a girl, either, but a young woman. Probably not as old as him, but it was harder to tell with Alissians. She had a freckled, youthful look and she was, hands down, the prettiest Alissian he'd seen so far. "Who are you?" she asked.

"My name's Quinn," he said. "I'm new here."

She went back to looking out over the water. He waited a minute. "And you are . . ."

"Jillaine." She brushed a strand of golden hair from her face. Her eyes were violet; Quinn had never seen anything like them.

"Are you a magician?" Quinn asked.

"I'm a chandler."

A candle-maker. Often kept bees as well. He hated that he knew that. "So, you make candles?"

"And soap, among other things," she said.

Quinn locked eyes with her and smiled. "You never answered my question."

She ignored him and looked back over the water. Her fingers fluttered slightly; Quinn saw the movement and waited. A light, floral aroma wafted to him on the breeze; it smelled faintly of roses. It grew powerful, nearly enough to make him dizzy, then it changed to the smell of warm bread. More scents assaulted his nose: cinnamon, lavender, hemp, vanilla.

There was something he could only describe as new rain on stone. Then a strong scent of pollen. It caught him off guard, and he sneezed.

She smiled faintly, but never so much as looked at him. Apparently "Bless you" wasn't a custom here.

"That was *incredible*," Quinn said, and he meant it. Not just because she was pretty.

"I find it useful sometimes." She turned back to him. "What can you do?" she asked.

"Nothing so grand as that, I'm afraid," Quinn said. He gestured to the stone beside her, and raised his eyebrows in question.

She nodded; he sat down. Not too close, but not far away, either. He produced his deck of cards and began shuffling one-handed. She watched the cards move as well as any mark back in Vegas.

He held the deck out to her. "Pick a card, any card."

She touched a card in the middle, thought better of it, and took one from the very edge. A choice that hinted at suspicion, though her face was hard to read.

"Memorize it, and then put it back in my hand," Quinn said. He held out the fan of cards toward her, and looked the other way. He felt her slide the card back in. Right away he began shuffling, with both hands this time, riffling and churning the cards for show. Dealers in Vegas learned this on their first day; shuffling cards the way most people did it would have them worn out in half an hour in a real casino.

The wind picked up suddenly and nearly blew them out of his hands. Jillaine had her little smile again, and he couldn't help but think she might have had something to do with it. He spread the cards in a line on the stone between them, just enough that the symbols showed.

"Do you see your card?" he asked.

She scanned the deck carefully, giving away nothing. She looked back at him before answering. Smart. "Yes."

"Good." He swept up the cards again, shuffling efficiently this time. Riffle, cut, riffle. Then he made another spread. "How about now?"

She looked again. It took longer this time, because her card wasn't there. "No. It's gone," she said.

"Are you sure?"

Her mouth opened a little. She was surprised he'd questioned her. "I'm sure."

"Maybe the wind took it," Quinn said. He began searching the area where they were sitting. Jillaine hadn't moved; she was watching him.

He came up empty, of course. "What about under your boot?" he asked.

Her boots were ankle-high, cut in some kind of soft leather. Maybe suede. She lifted the one closest to him, and there it was. A single red-backed card, facedown on the ground beneath her. She gasped in a soft, girlie way. Adorable. She snatched it up.

"Is that your card?" Quinn asked. It would be, of course. She'd picked the queen of hearts.

"No," she said.

"It's *not*?"

She handed it over. It was a queen, all right, but green instead of red, and the hearts had been changed to something else. It took him a second to recognize them. Candles. Oh, she thought she was so clever. But it wasn't the first time a mark had tried switching a card on him. He had another queen of hearts at the ready. He made the switch and held it up for her to see.

"I think this *is* your card," he said.

She smiled and rolled her eyes. "Still wrong."

He flipped it over; now *this* card had candles on it. "Hey!"

She laughed then, a soft and delicate laugh. He laughed, too.

"How long have you been on the island?" he asked.

She groaned. "Too long. My father rarely lets me leave."

Ah, yes, a father. She'd have one around, and he'd probably keep a tight watch on her. "He's a magician, too, I take it," Quinn said.

"Of the most boring kind. He's been here, like, forever."

"What does he do?"

She shrugged and looked back out across the water. "Something or other for the council."

Oh, no. Please, no. "What's his name?" Quinn asked. Hoping desperately he didn't already know the answer.

"Moric."

Of course it was.

> **"Alissians might not recognize a thoroughbred, but they know a good horse when they see one."**
>
> —R. HOLT, "OVERVIEW OF
> ALISSIAN HUSBANDRY"

CHAPTER 14

PESTS

Logan made the rendezvous just in time. Kiara and Chaudri had arrived earlier and erased all signs of their presence from the abandoned farmstead. They'd bought about a week's worth of provisions, mostly in the form of local nuts, figs, and cured meat.

"We had to wait in line to get it, no matter the price," Kiara said.

"Too many people, not enough food," Chaudri said. "Even with Dr. Holt's intervention, things will be difficult here for some time."

"That reminds me," Logan said. "Briannah said someone tried to steal the horses."

"Did they get anything?"

"Don't think so. Lem and the boys were all over them."

"When this is over, we should have another look at the security at Briannah's inn."

"It's not as bad as it sounds. And we can trust them."

"I suppose the food is decent," Kiara said.

"*Decent?*"

Chaudri leaned over. "You smell just like her kitchen. She was cooking, wasn't she?"

Logan shrugged. "I have great timing."

"Did you bring me some?"

"Ooh, sorry," Logan said. "Not like I had any Tupperware." Yet another item on the company's doesn't-go-through list.

Chaudri's face fell.

Logan handed her a bundle wrapped in wax paper. "Brought you some of her honey rolls, though."

"Oh, Logan! You're a knight of honor," Chaudri said. She was all grins, which was fitting. Briannah's baking was the only thing equal to her cooking.

Kiara and Logan wandered over to where the horses were hobbled. "I assume that's to keep her busy while we drug the animals?" she asked quietly.

"Not sure she'd be thrilled about it. You know how she is with the horses."

Logan dug into his saddlebags and came up with

a sealed leather pouch. The tech team had crafted it to look like the kit of an Alissian surgeon. The vials inside held a proprietary solution derived from South American tree frogs. The natural substance was called dermorphin, and often used to dope racehorses. The company's synthetic isoform was more potent, though, and longer-lasting. They'd even gone so far as to match doses to each animal based on gender, weight, and genetics.

Logan read the reminder label inside the kit. " 'Emergency Use Only.' "

"This qualifies," Kiara said.

The horses didn't protest the needle prick like Logan feared. He supposed that as company investments, they saw regular blood draws, antibiotics, and supplements to keep them in pristine health. And they came from good stock, too, which couldn't hurt.

They mounted. Chaudri took the reins of the packhorse, and Logan handled Bradley's mare. He gave the isotope scanner a quick glance. Nothing was on the scope but the three of them. Holt had defeated the system somehow—Logan forgot to ask him about that—and Bradley was still MIA.

Great: all this tech, and it's useless when we need it.

It's one of the reasons they'd brought Bradley in the first place, and now he was lost. Logan had left instructions with Briannah in case the magician wandered back that way. He hoped to hell that he would.

But he wasn't holding his breath.

Drugged-up horses made incredible time.

A week of hard riding put them in north Valteron, approaching the border. Kiara set an aggressive pace; they stopped only to feed and water their mounts. The animals didn't seem to tire, thanks to the frog juice, but they still had to refuel. Logan, as the heaviest member of the party by half, had alternated riding his own mount and Bradley's mare to spare the animals.

The fact was, though, that the ride was harder on Logan, Kiara, and Chaudri than it was on the horses. Too bad CASE Global didn't have a serum for its soldiers as well. The company had one in the works, of course, but it wasn't yet ready for prime time. Which was a shame, because they could have used it. He was exhausted, and even the lieutenant looked a little worn.

Not that she'd ever admit it.

What surprised him was that even though Chaudri was dragging, she voiced no complaint, either. She'd been uncharacteristically quiet since encountering her former mentor. She'd been more awed than indignant during their encounter, which was intriguing. Logan would have thought she'd be the angriest of all of them.

Word of Holt's ascendancy must have spread quickly, because most of the people on the road were heading south. The majority of them were walking and not riding, though they passed the rare wooden cart with two wheels and a mule.

Hard to tell what nationality they were, but they were refugees for certain. It showed in the possessions strapped on their backs, the dirt and road grime that coated all of them. A lot of groups of women and children. Must have left their men behind, when the fighting started. Now they were headed back to reunite. Or to bury them.

They came to a shallow creek that crossed the road, and stopped to water the horses.

"What's the status of Bravo Team?" Logan asked. It was easier to talk when they weren't riding; the timbered north of Valteron often had them riding single file. He knew she'd been in touch with Command, but nothing had merited an update so far.

"They're making slow progress. Felara just had a snowstorm, one of the worst we've ever seen. The snowdrifts are chest-deep in some places."

Logan had out his lightweight parchmap of Alissia. A hell of a lot of work had gone into these. There was no satellite coverage here, no long-range aircraft. Once upon a time, charting the main Alissian continent ranked among the most dangerous jobs in Project Gateway. He didn't miss it. Sudden winter storms in the north, when the temperature dropped forty degrees and the sky dropped four feet of snow. Caralissian sinkholes. Packs of wild dogs that would kill your horse right under you.

Bravo Team had played a part in that. Logan had trained every single one of them. They were solid guys. Tough. Whether or not the company had decided to send another Vegas magician to accompany them wasn't clear, but he doubted it. A hostile party slipping through the gate merited only one kind of response.

"Any word on the infiltrators? Who they are, what they're doing?" Logan asked.

"Two to seven individuals, based on the tracks. As for who they are, I have my suspicions."

Logan chewed his lip. A few organizations had the resources to raid the island compound and breach the security protocols CASE Global had in place. Most were governments, and that made them more likely to try a soft approach first. Legal actions, casual blockades, inquiries from state departments. A raid was far more direct, but riskier, too. It had to be someone with a lot to gain from CASE Global, and that meant only one thing.

"Raptor Tech," Logan said.

Sabotage, espionage, stock manipulation . . . nothing was out of bounds for them. If anything, he wished CASE Global would hit back harder sometimes.

"I had the same thought," Kiara said.

"Did they do a head count at the company?"

"Right away," Kiara said. "Everyone's accounted for, except for a janitor with limited access."

"I don't think a janitor managed to evade Bravo Team for this long," Logan said.

"He might have been taken, or bought off," Kiara said.

Logan guessed they'd find him stuffed in a closet. Or several closets.

"I'll keep an eye out for anyone in blue coveralls," Chaudri offered.

Over the next week, they continued to push the horses hard. They crossed into the city-state of Tion, a marshy and sparsely populated kingdom between Valteron and New Kestani. They'd avoided this trek by catching a ship from Bayport while heading south, and with good reason. In every bit of Tion that he'd scouted, the ground was a constant form of muck and the air smelled like stagnant water. You wouldn't want to mention that to the Tioni, though. They didn't seem to notice the smell, and took offense if an outsider brought it up. Bugs were bad here, too; biting flies of the dime-sized variety swarmed their horses whenever they slowed.

Kiara's communicator-bracelet made a coughing noise. Urgent message. She looked at it, and her brow furrowed. "Video coming in from Command," she said.

Logan fell back beside her. The video was footage from external security cameras at the island facility. A shadow swept across the frame. Airborne, triangular, and moving incredibly fast. Then it stopped in midair and just hovered there.

"It's jamming the island radar systems," Kiara said. "Broadcasting a high-band signal at the facility, too."

"You were right about Raptor Tech," Logan said. "But that's a bird I've never seen before." Not a surveillance-only model, either. It had the bulky shape of a weaponized aircraft. Just looking at it had him reaching for his holster.

"Recommendation?" Kiara asked.

They must want her to give an order. Logan might be in charge of mission security, but Kiara was the top dog for the gateway island. The tough calls always came to her, no matter where she was.

Logan weighed the options. They could ignore the drone, or track it without opening any gun ports. With a bird like that, though, it was better to hit first, and hit hard. "Show them our teeth," he said.

Kiara tapped in a brief message. Logan recognized the code. *Weapons free.*

The island was equipped with a new generation of antiaircraft weaponry in the form of the Russian-made S-400 Triumf system. The launcher held thirty-two long-range surface-to-air missiles controlled by a mobile command center. The panoramic radar system was almost impossible to jam. Even by a next-gen military drone. The missiles were accurate enough to take out ICBMs, according to the Russians. Entire battalions of these systems ringed Moscow, so they had to put some stock into it. It helped that the crewmen who ran the S-400 had actually trained there.

"They're locked on. Fifteen seconds," Kiara said. Two contrails appeared, streaking toward the drone. The first closed within a hundred yards. Couldn't miss . . .

Then the drone flipped over and dropped, like a swooping bird of prey.

"Son of a bitch!" Logan said. He'd never seen a drone move like that.

The missile shot past it and crashed into the cliffs behind. The second one, three seconds behind it, missed the cliffs and circled around. Good. It was hard to see what happened as it came back, but it ignored the drone entirely. Came right at the camera. Logan sucked in a breath. Then a flash and the video feed became a snowstorm.

They stared in silence for a long, uncomfortable minute.

"I'll be damned," Logan said. "Rerouted the damn missile."

The communicator beeped, and Kiara exhaled. "They're all right. Asking for suggestions."

"They might try something low-tech. Anyone there have a deer rifle?"

"I'm sure they can drum that up."

"It'd help if we had the specs on that bird."

Kiara frowned. "We can reach out to our contacts on the Senate Arms Committee, but that'll take time."

"There are less official ways to try to get them," Logan said.

"I wish we had you there."

"Then we'd better get going."

They pressed the horses farther; they were holding up well. Bravo Team sent an update. The infiltrators, whoever they were, had acquired horses. Certainly not the stock that Bravo Team had—more thorough-breds from the island stables—but enough to make it a chase. They'd changed directions, too, and turned east toward Landor.

"It's odd that they'd set a new heading," Logan said. "How are they even getting their bearings here?"

"You can ask that when we intercept them."

"We'll need a new route to head them off," he said.

"What do you think about cutting back over to New Kestani?" Kiara asked.

"The border could slow us down. Especially with Holt's little warnings."

Chaudri cleared her throat. "What about going through Caralis?"

Logan mulled it over, trying to ignore the darkness he felt when he heard that name. "Longer ride that way."

"But the terrain is virtually flat. We'd make good time."

"They have a local militia," Kiara said. "We've had a few run-ins with them." Which was putting it lightly.

Chaudri waved it off. She didn't know about Logan's failed mission there. "They're in harvest season. They'll be busy. If you want to get north fast, that's the way to go."

Kiara looked at Logan expectantly.

I swore I'd never go back there. But duty called. He took a breath and gave her the nod.

"Caralis it is," Kiara said.

> **"Quick fingers get you only so far."**
>
> —Art of Illusion, December 30

CHAPTER 15

THE PROVE

Moric woke Quinn up with bad news.

"You've been summoned to appear before the council."

Quinn sat up and rubbed bleary eyes. He'd been here a week, and still not gotten the knack of sleeping in the Enclave. It was too dark at night, too quiet. All those late nights in Vegas had him trained to sleep in daytime, lulled by the sound of jumbo jets and the occasional sirens. "When?"

"Today."

Shit. "Should I be worried about this?"

"Absolutely," Moric said. "I'd hoped to buy some time, to keep working on you. But I caused some consternation by bringing you here in the first place."

"I thought you were on the council."

"They prefer to do things a certain way. My influence goes only so far." Moric's eyes narrowed just so. "I don't remember telling you that I was a member."

"Word gets around."

"You've been checking up on me, eh? I suppose that's only fair. We sent word to Wyndham Downs about Thomas More."

His cover village. God, he hoped the company's false identity would hold up. "I thought you said magicians left the past in the past."

"Your case is different. You've been accused of a crime."

The impersonation thing again. Damn it, he should have listened when Logan warned him. "I look forward to seeing the proof of that."

"The council is not obligated to prove anything. We'll base our decision primarily on our assessment of you."

"Have they been wrong before?" Quinn asked.

"Not often."

"Have *you* been wrong?"

Moric hesitated. "I personally have not. There were others who made mistakes. Most often, a parent with the gift can't accept the idea that his or her child doesn't have it. We humor them with a testing, and break the news as gently as possible."

"Does the ability tend to run in families?" Quinn asked.

"Not as often as most of us would like. Perhaps one in six children of a magic user will have it."

"I guess Jillaine beat the odds, then."

That caught him off guard, because Moric missed a step. "How do you know about my daughter?"

Quinn smiled. "Like I said. Word gets around."

"So it does. Yes, Jillaine is an exception." He smiled. "In many respects."

"I met her, actually. She's nice."

Moric put an arm around him and squeezed his neck—not hard, but enough. "You're a grown man, and you've seen some of the world. I trust I don't even have to voice what I'm thinking right now."

Quinn didn't want to press his luck. He needed Moric on his side. "You don't have to say a thing," he said with rapidly diminishing air.

"Good," Moric said, letting go. "Now, there are some things about this testing that you should know. It's an open meeting, so anyone on the island can come. But it's the council you'll need to worry about."

"How do I know which ones they are?"

"It should be obvious. We'll be the ones examining you, asking you questions. The first half of the hour is for us. The second half is yours."

"To do what, exactly?" Quinn asked.

"Prove yourself." He shrugged. "Or beg for mercy."

Moric came to get him just before midday. His room was in the base of the tower flying Landorian colors. He couldn't think that was an accident. A worn staircase led to the levels above, but he hadn't been permitted upstairs. A few of the tower's other residents had passed him; they were friendly enough, but they never lingered. In his days here, the longest conversation he'd had with someone other than Moric had been with Jillaine.

And he hadn't seen her since.

He followed Moric outside. They set out on foot toward the center of the city. Quinn still couldn't get over the architecture. The structures hadn't been built; they were carved from what must have been a huge block of the dark gray stone. The material seemed to shimmer when viewed from afar, as if some echoed image was hidden beneath. It had the effect of a hologram that never came into view. Not quite the show of wealth he'd seen in Valteron City, but still impressive. It made him think of Kiara, Logan, and Chaudri.

"I never heard who they picked for Valteroni Prime," he said. "Was it the admiral?"

Moric looked at him, as if in disbelief. "You don't know?"

Quinn glared at him. "You took me before they announced it."

"Yes, but you said you were his friend."

"Whose friend?"

"The new Prime."

"I'm confused," Quinn said. It was like Moric was talking in circles.

"When we met, you said you were looking for

Richard Holt," Moric said. He shrugged. "I assumed you'd know of his ascension."

Quinn shook his head. "Wait a minute. *Holt* is the new Prime of Valteron?"

"Yes."

God, Kiara must have had a fit.

"I take it you don't know Richard well," Moric said.

"He's a friend of a friend," Quinn said. He still couldn't believe it.

"Ah," Moric said. He looked disappointed.

"What does the Enclave think of all this?"

"The council has no official stance on Valteron's choice of leadership."

Quinn knew a deflection when he heard one. "Fine. What do *you* think of him?"

Moric seemed to mull this over. "I think he will be good for Valteron. Certainly better than some of his predecessors. Not everyone on the council agrees with me. Some believe that he poses a serious threat. That perhaps we should distance ourselves, rather than offering an olive branch."

A worrisome thought came. "Has he been here?" Quinn asked.

"Gods, no. We've always met on neutral ground."

They've always *met.* It took every fiber of Quinn's will not to ask about that. He'd read every one of Richard Holt's reports concerning magic, and the man had never mentioned Moric. Or the Enclave.

How much else had he hidden from CASE Global?

They joined the foot traffic on a rather crowded thoroughfare. People were out and about, visiting shops, sharing mugs of hot cider on the steps of their houses. The dress was a hodgepodge of styles from all over Alissia. It seemed as if everyone brought a piece of home with them, to live in apparent harmony among the unnatural buildings. Unified by their rare and wonderful talents for magic.

He saw little signs of it everywhere. A long train of baskets floating behind a baker making deliveries. An alley where children lobbed different-colored sparks through an iron hoop.

"Have you decided what to tell the council about me?" Quinn asked.

"I'll tell them the truth. That I felt the resonance in you, and think you have a latent ability."

Latent may not begin to describe it.

"Maybe that will be enough."

"It may be for my friends on the council, but not all members fall into that category."

Quinn didn't like the sound of that. "You have enemies."

"That's too strong a word for it. I prefer to think of them as friendly rivals. They'll be the hardest to convince, in any case. Sella is the one who matters most. If you win her over, you'll be just fine."

"What if I can't prove myself?" Quinn asked.

Moric hesitated. "It would not go well for you. The Enclave must enforce its laws."

There was a finality to his words that made Quinn feel cold inside. "I see." So much for mercy.

"This trial is about character as much as it is ability," Moric said. "You seem like a decent man who was in a tough spot. Convince the council as much, and you might win your life."

"So generous of you," Quinn said.

Moric gave him a sharp look. "We must protect ourselves first, and outsiders second. Not everyone in Alissia admires what we can do. Some consider magic abilities a curse."

"You don't say," Quinn said.

"Magicians have been attacked, even killed."

"I'm sorry to hear that," Quinn said. Alissia's own version of the Salem witch trials, apparently. But hard to feel bad for people who were basically planning his execution.

"That was before we formed the guild. If anyone harms a magician, or even threatens one, the guild knows. Their response is swift and direct. Believe me, no one makes the mistake twice."

"Good to know," Quinn said. He wouldn't mind having that kind of protection. But he doubted he could pull it off, even if he wanted to.

"We're giving you a fair chance here," Moric said. "The latter half of the hour is yours. During that time, no one else can use magic."

"Why?"

"So there's no question of interference."

"Does this apply to the council, too?" Quinn asked. Not daring to hope.

"Of course."

Now *that* was something he could work with.

Quinn's trial had his biggest audience ever, and undoubtedly his most important one.

The council of Alissian magic met in a small amphitheater at the base of the central spire. This, too, was cut into the same gray stone as everything else in the city. Quinn had guessed there might be a few dozen interested citizens with nothing else to do. He couldn't have been more wrong. There were hundreds of people filling the seats. Men, women, and children all were present. There seemed to be no age limit.

"Good crowd," Quinn said, almost by instinct.

"They're intrigued," Moric said. "You're older than the typical candidate."

"Which one is Sella?"

"She'll be the last to arrive."

Right on cue, an old woman strode into the amphitheater. Her white hair floated in gentle orbit around her head, as if she was under water. She was dressed head to toe in purple, a color made even brighter by the cluster of dark-robed magicians following in her wake.

"She knows how to make an entrance, doesn't she?" Quinn asked.

"She knows a great deal more than that."

The delicate scent of roses touched his nose, and then the heady smell of the ocean. It was Jillaine's way of saying hello; she smiled at him from the third row. Quinn waved at her.

Moric frowned at him.

"What? You said I was intriguing," Quinn said.

"That wasn't what I meant. Wait here." Moric strode over to join a cluster of serious-looking magicians in the front row. A different set than the ones that came in with Sella. They all wore ankle-length robes in mundane colors. They conferred quietly, with Moric doing most of the talking. There seemed to be some argument going on there.

I hope those aren't his friends.

Moric returned and stood facing the crowd; silence fell among them. Quinn felt the weight of their eyes on him. He heard the sound of an infant crying momentarily from somewhere up in the stands. The breeze, which had come steady out of the west, died. *Oh no*, he thought. He needed that breeze.

Moric muttered something and drew a small circle in the air; it solidified into an opaque disc. "Welcome," he said. His voice boomed around the amphitheater; a number of people covered their ears. He grunted. "Too much."

He waved a hand through the opaque image and repeated the spell; this time, he drew the circle a bit smaller. "Welcome," he said again.

Still loud, but there weren't any complaints this time.

"We're here to evaluate Quinn, who comes to us from north Landor." He put a hand on Quinn's shoulder; it was surprisingly warm. The heat from it spread across Quinn's torso. What was he up to?

He recounted the story of their meeting in the square for the announcement of the Valteroni Prime. How he'd recognized Quinn, tested him, and felt the resonance.

One of the council members stood. He was old but not elderly. Gaunt, with a queue of gray hair down his back. "He's too old. The ability should have manifested by now."

"Unless it's a latent ability," Moric said. "Friends, if I'm right about Quinn, it means that some of our assumptions about the manifestation are incorrect. There may be others like him, who appear far too old to be tested."

A few of those in the front row shifted in their seats, muttering to one another. Obviously the council was not unanimous on this point.

"Others may disagree," Moric said. "If I'm wrong, it must be said that he was pretending at it. He's admitted as much."

Quinn nodded. No point in denying it.

"But I'm confident that he belongs here," Moric said. He gestured with both hands to the Enclave magicians. "I leave it to the council to decide."

The robed magicians in the front rose and drew their hoods. Moric did the same. It was a rather ominous gesture, like that of a phalanx of headsmen. They glided forward to encircle him. They began chanting softly, rhythmically. He didn't feel anything at first. Then the air grew heavy. It was hard to breathe. He tried to move and found that he couldn't. They had him trussed up like a calf. The warm feeling in his chest dissipated, replaced with cold fear.

The pressure changed somehow. He still couldn't move, but he could feel them poking around. Prodding at his head, trying to find out what was in it. He tried to clear his thoughts. He didn't want to make his secrets any easier to find. It felt like trying to hold a box closed, with someone else trying to force it open. And they were strong. He fought them.

Then came the searing heat, all over his body. Freezing cold followed right on its heels. He went from sweating to shivering. Beneath it all was that pressure, the relentless push to open his mind. He tried to keep them out, but it was like fighting the wind. Their search went around him, through him. Pried at his thoughts. The sheer invasiveness of it started to piss him off. Anger turned to that familiar warmth, deep in his gut. He tried to snatch it and push at them, but they were too strong together. His warm resistance stayed deep in him. He found the edge of it. He brought it up slowly this time. Got a good grip, and heaved it at all of them.

The chant fell apart as two of the robed magicians stumbled. The spell broke. All of the pressure abated. God, what a relief. He couldn't see most of faces under the hoods, but the frowns were easy enough to discern.

"I suspect that will be enough for now," Moric said.

The council members returned to their seats. Some of them glanced back to look at him. Moric lingered long enough to share a private smile. "You've sparked some interest, I'll wager," he said. "Don't squander it."

Quinn tried to ignore the crowd and the sheer strangeness of the entire situation. They were marks, nothing more, an audience to be dazzled and entertained. So far they hadn't searched him; thank God for that. If they did, they'd find about half a million dollars of advanced equipment hidden about his body.

He couldn't quite duplicate what Moric had done with the circle speakerphone, but the comm units had a portable amplifier disguised as a metal amulet. What looked like flecks of obsidian were actually tiny solar cells. He'd kept it on his windowsill since arriving, and prayed that doing so had given it a full enough charge.

"Magicians of the Enclave," he said, and his voice thrummed out of the speaker, startling those in the first few rows.

He took two breaths to steady himself. He had to do this perfectly. Otherwise, he'd never have a chance to learn the truth behind Alissian magic. When this job was over, that might be his key to success. The things he'd seen Moric do, and Jillaine, they were beyond any of the best illusions on Earth. He could write his own ticket back home, and make a fortune.

And it would also mean he was still alive. *Yet another bonus.*

"I will need a volunteer," Quinn said. He looked up

at the stands. None of the council magicians stood, but others in attendance seemed to understand his request. A few raised their hands. Jillaine was one of those.

He knew better than to choose her. Moric was his only ally in the Enclave, and he was obviously protective of her. She was smart, too, and just as likely to sabotage his illusion as help it along. She was pretty and alluring, but he definitely shouldn't choose her.

He did anyway.

"How about this young lady right here?" he called.

Moric said something to her as she passed by him, on her way to where Quinn stood.

He'd been practicing a little monologue, but he watched the way she walked toward him—taking little steps on her toes, like a dancer—and the words nearly left him. Damn, she looked incredible. How had he wanted to start it? He had a moment of panic, and then it came. Landor.

"As Moric said, I came from the north of Landor," he said. "A cold place. A hard place, as anyone from there can tell you." There was truth to that. The people in Quinn's supposed home village worked the iron mines in the foothills of the nearby mountains. That was a dangerous career in modern times, let alone a world without electricity. He even saw a few nod, and wondered for a moment if there were others from that region here now.

If so, then they'll love this next bit. . . .

"There's a saying about the mountains, back home," Quinn said. The last word had a sort of echo to it. *Home, home.* "They take life and youth, but give two things in return."

Jillaine reached him. He made a fist and wrapped her hands around it. She smiled faintly. He turned her so that everyone could see them both. She *did* smell like roses. And that couldn't be magic, either, because it was forbidden here.

Stop thinking about how good she smells.

"Ready?" he asked her softly.

She nodded.

He looked back to the crowd, raised his voice. "Iron. And snow."

With that, he triggered the microfan at his wrist. A narrow stream of white stuff fountained from his hands where Jillaine held them.

"Come on," Quinn muttered. Where was the breeze? The damn thing had died again. He needed it desperately. Just the tiniest stirring of air. That's all he asked for. Just a gentle little breeze—yes! There it was. And the cool on the back of his neck told him the direction would be perfect.

He'd never done this trick outside before, and the compressed foam—a proprietary company material used by ski resorts—handled well in the humid air. The particles expanded to nearly a hundred times their compressed volume, almost weightless as they fluttered in the humid air. And with the breeze, thank God for that, the opaque cloud spread far and wide over the stands. A blizzard for an island that—unless

Quinn missed his guess—had never seen snow before. The crowd uttered a collective gasp.

The entire island was filled with magicians; that worked to his advantage. They saw what they wanted to see.

Only Jillaine seemed underwhelmed. She let her hands fall, stared at him for a long minute, and walked away. Not back to her seat, but out of the amphitheater. He had the weirdest flashback then, to the moment those talent scouts had walked out of the casino the night he'd met Kiara and Logan. Not much he could do about it now, though.

A thrilled audience had a certain sound to it, a certain *feel* of palpable energy. This crowd had it. Some whistled in appreciation; others cheered. The stands hummed with excitement.

Quinn stood watching them, keeping his face neutral. He had to admit, the effect was incredibly realistic. A few of the robed council magicians held out their hands to catch the delicate flakes. Even before Moric caught his eye and gave him the slightest of nods, Quinn knew he had them.

He was in.

Then the magician in purple, the one called Sella, appeared in front of him. Her eyes were dark as obsidian, and it was all he could do not to take a step back.

"Interesting performance," she said.

He tried his best grin on her. "Did you like it?"

"Not particularly."

"Oh."

"Perhaps you could do another. Right here, right now."

He had a deck of cards in one pocket, and a couple of coins that might serve. But something told him sleight of hand wasn't the right way to play this. He shook his head.

"I didn't think so."

"It's not that I don't want to," Quinn said. "It just doesn't come easy."

She looked at him a long while, her face as unreadable as a stone. The orbit of white hair around her head was distracting. He tried not to stare at it.

"I teach a class for students who have difficulty accessing their magic. An hour after midday. Starting tomorrow, you will be there."

"I will be there?" Quinn asked.

"You will be there," Sella said.

"I look forward to it."

> "We've found few veins of precious
> metals. Iron is plentiful, as is copper.
> The mines for such metals are
> carefully watched and protected."
>
> —R. HOLT, "BRIEF SUMMARY OF
> ALISSIAN NATURAL RESOURCES"

CHAPTER 16

AMBUSH

Caralis represented a unique political structure in Alissia, a feudal monarchy centered around agriculture. The hilly country was well-suited to their orchards and vineyards. Apples, berries, grapes, and other sweet fruits were the principal crops produced. Not that the people of Caralis subsisted on these. Virtually all fruits were funneled to the central province, where they were fermented to make the monarchy's single export.

Caralissian wine.

The vintners of Caralis had a method for fermentation that impressed even modern winemaking experts. The company had sent samples to a number of these—through third-party intermediaries—for evaluation. The cover story had been one of a guy brewing wine in his garage, who wanted to know if it was any good.

Half of the winemakers came back with a job offer.

Good wine meant good trade, which in turn meant some of the best roads in Alissia. Finally, Logan had a chance to see what the horses could really do. They were four days out of Valteron when the drug's effects began to wear off. The veterinary team had warned about this—the animals were developing a tolerance. Logan gave the next dose two hours earlier than expected, just before crossing into Caralis.

As Chaudri had said, the country was well into harvest season, so the Caralissian workers hardly noticed as they thundered past down the hard-packed dirt roads. The horses found a groove on the smooth, flat surface. It was like they'd been waiting for it. Logan grew up around horses and he'd been riding as long as he could remember. It was part of why he'd made the team for the early Alissian missions. Horsemanship was a dying art in the modern world. Here, it was thriving.

It was still hard to believe that he'd landed this gig. That he'd gotten a glimpse of this world that CASE Global seemed determined to hide from the rest of humanity. If the company got serious about establishing a military presence here, it would require a real paradigm shift in their recruitment program.

Maybe they knew that. Maybe that's why the lieutenant recruited me in the first place.

He tried not to dwell on that, though. His job in the here and now was to keep everyone safe. The only time they got any notice from the locals was when they encountered a wine caravan. Ten wagons, each pulled by a pair of draft horses. These were hardly visible behind the mounted riders that escorted them, who happened to be some of the hardest mercenaries that Caralissian gold could buy. They looked up at the sound of the approaching horses. Hands went to sword hilts. Two of the men reached down into the nearest wagons, probably for spears or loaded crossbows.

"Caravan coming at us," Logan warned over the comm link. He slowed his mount and moved to the side. "Keep your hands visible, no sudden moves."

The mercenaries knew their business—they only got paid if the shipment arrived safely. Their casual positions only *looked* haphazard. If Logan were to attack, three or four would engage him from multiple angles. An equal number would stay with the wagons. And a few would ride for the nearest Caralissian outpost for reinforcements. Bandits tried raiding wine caravans from time to time. Some even got hold of a cask or two, but they rarely made it far enough to enjoy a taste.

The caravan moved on, the rear riders keeping their eyes on Logan and the other two the entire time.

They were half a day's ride from the Landorian border when they lost contact with Bravo Team. It couldn't have come at a worse time. Bravo had tracked the infiltrators halfway across the Alissian continent, and were only just closing in enough to learn about them. It was a small group, four or five men at the most. They were on their third set of stolen Alissian horses. Judging by the tracks, these were starting to falter as the others had. South Landor was rugged, sparsely populated country. There weren't any horses to steal.

Where they were headed, and why they'd changed direction a couple of weeks ago, remained a mystery.

They almost certainly knew they were being followed. The first time Bravo Team had made visual contact, the raiders were topping a distant ridge just after sunrise. It was a tactical blunder; now Bravo Team knew their bearing and location. A quick look at the parchmap for this region said that they could be intercepted by following a ravine northeast. They tried it, leading the horses and moving double time. Got to the far end, though, and found no infiltrators.

It had been a ruse, and put them half a day farther behind.

Bravo was quiet for a while after that. They were riding hard, trying to make up ground. Then communication broke off entirely. Kiara tried to raise them, but got no reply.

"Any luck?" Logan asked, after she'd tried a third time.

"No," she said.

"When were they due to check in?"

"Two hours ago."

"Maybe they went radio quiet."

"Do you think that's what happened?"

He had been on too many missions to be that naive. "Not really."

They rode for another hour. The terrain flattened here in the extreme north of Caralis, and rose steadily toward the Landorian plateau. Kiara still couldn't raise Bravo Team. "Something's wrong," she said.

Logan couldn't argue with her.

Her communicator beeped with an incoming. "Command hasn't heard from them, either. They're sending the communications log."

Just ahead, the hard-packed dirt road running north into Landor widened. They reined in here so that they wouldn't block the way; another wine caravan might suspect an ambush. On the east and west were the last of the Caralissian orchards. The trees were mostly bare, as the plums and apples that once decorated them were likely already undergoing the fermentation process.

Chaudri held the reins of the horses while Logan and Kiara spread out their scale map of Alissia. They plotted the bearing and distance of Bravo Team's transmissions, both from Command and their own communicators. The intersection of these vectors marked Bravo's actual route as they pursued the infiltrators southeast from the gateway. It was more or less a straight line of travel—this made Logan frown.

"I know that frown," Kiara said. "What's wrong?"

"It's just not what I'd do, if I were the raiding party. A straight line of flight is too easy to follow."

"They've doubled back a few times. Laid some false trails," Kiara said. "Even pulled that head-fake and gained half a day on Bravo."

"Yeah. They're good. That's why their route now bothers me. It's like they're trying to seem predictable. If it were me, I'd be worried about the exact vise we're trying to put them in."

"If you'd done as they had, breached a portal into a completely new area, what would you do?"

"Evade, survive, evaluate. The mission's not about sabotage, or they'd have just destroyed the gateway. They had to have some idea of what the gateway did. They're here for the intel."

"Doesn't do them much good, unless they can report back. The company's reasonably certain the signal isn't coming through, but we don't want them back near the gate."

Logan cursed. *Why didn't I see this before?* "It's the perfect time to double back. Maybe that's why we haven't heard."

Kiara took a measurement and pointed at a spot in southern Landor. "They should be somewhere in this region."

"That's about six days from here, if we push it."

"We're going to push it. And I hope you're wrong."
She rolled up the map and took her reins back from
Chaudri. They mounted.

"Me, too," Logan said. But he doubted that he was.

This time they had to drug the horses four hours ahead
of schedule. Logan began to see the toll that this ride
was taking on them. Their legs shook with muscle fa-
tigue, and their coats were matted down with sweat.
They walked with the nervous excitement of racehorses after a derby.

"We're killing the horses," he told Kiara when
they'd stopped to water the panting animals. "They
won't hold up much longer."

She nodded slightly, but didn't tell him to lessen the
pace. There was still no word from Bravo Team.

Chaudri hadn't complained; she knew the urgency
of the situation. Even so, worry lined her face as she examined her mare. She spoke quietly to the animal, and
slipped her an apple when she thought Logan wasn't
looking. The animals weren't supposed to eat native
flora, but there was no point in reminding her of that.
Might as well try telling the horses when and where
to crap.

"One more push should have us on Bravo's last
known location," Kiara said. "Mount up."

They complied wearily. Landor's roads weren't
quite as nice as the Caralissian ones, but at least the

terrain was relatively steady. Soon the ground began to rise more sharply, though, as they approached the southern edge of the Landorian plateau. Two hours later, Kiara picked up a signal on the isotope scanner.

"One of ours on the scope," she said.

"How far?" Logan asked.

"Two kilometers, give or take."

Logan loosened his sword in its scabbard. He was more worried than he was willing to admit. Bravo Team was good. They'd trained hard, and they knew the terrain well. But they'd also pursued four or five men the company knew nothing about, except that they didn't belong in Alissia. He had the lead, with Chaudri bringing up the rear. Kiara rode in the middle, mostly focused on the isotope scanner.

It dawned on him that it was odd that they only had one signal; Bravo Team should have stayed together. *I'm liking this less and less.*

"Logan," Kiara called suddenly. The terrain had just leveled off; they'd gained the edge of the Landorian plateau. She lifted the isotope scanner to swing it back and forth. She pointed left off of the road. "There."

Rocky terrain dotted with scrub brush didn't seem ideal for his horse. Drug-induced euphoria or not, the mare looked like she might collapse where she stood. Logan dismounted, unlacing his crossbow. He'd gotten to bring this murder-piece only after Bradley proved a surprising competence with the bow. That weapon had a range of sixty, eighty yards. This one could flat-shoot a hundred yards with precise accuracy. It might as well have been a gun.

The tech team hadn't skimped on craftsmanship, either. Alissians seemed to prefer the simple longbow. The crossbows here were masterpieces of wood and metal; most were owned by wealthy nobles and used for sport. Logan liked the feel of the wooden stock. He could hide it under a table or carry it beneath a long cloak. It was powerful, deadly, and he could crank it back in twelve seconds.

He worked slowly through the brush, placing each foot carefully. Kiara and Chaudri were back-to-back, watching the road, with the extra horses between them. She tracked his progress on the scope. "Another ten meters."

Logan saw him then, a crumpled form at the base of a large boulder.

"Man down," he whispered. "Stand by while I sweep the area."

He raised the crossbow and sidestepped, working around the boulder. This was a perfect situation for a trap, and one he'd seen before in jungle countries, Earth-side: position an enemy soldier—wounded or dead—in plain view, and pick off his comrades when they came for him.

That didn't seem to be the case today.

"All clear," he said. He approached the fallen man, trying to ignore the cold tightness in his gut. "Ah, O'Toole. Damn it."

Charles O'Toole was the youngest member of Bravo Team. Twenty-six, with two tours in the Middle East under his belt when he came to work for the company. He loved fishing; the facility's location in the South Pacific had been what sealed the deal.

Bravo's tech specialist still clutched the portable comm unit in one hand. The thing was in pieces, and with a small screwdriver on the ground nearby, it looked like he'd been trying to make some repairs. That began to explain why Bravo had been out of touch. Logan didn't need to check the man's pulse. At least it had been quick. He knelt close to him and got a look at the wound. "Lieutenant, you'll want to see this."

"Already behind you, Logan," she said. She had her crossbow out and was covering his six. He hadn't heard her approach at all.

She knelt beside him. "Christ, that's a gunshot wound." He saw Chaudri come into the clearing behind her, leading the horses.

O'Toole used to tinker with ham radios, back on the island. Gods, the kid could get any scrap of electronics to work. No. He couldn't think about that now. Logan crouched beside Kiara. "Double tap, small caliber," he said. "Might be an MP5."

"How would that have gotten past the gate security?"

"Don't know. How did they even know about it in the first place? None of this makes sense."

"Maybe it's been a little bit off since Holt disabled it," Chaudri suggested.

She shook her head, either in disagreement or because she didn't like what it implied. "Fully automatic weapons on this side of the gateway. God help us."

"His mount's gone, too," Logan said.

"Maybe the rest of the team took it."

"Let's hope so." But it was clear from her tone—and the lack of signals on the isotope reader—that she didn't really believe it.

"Think I might be able to pick up their trail, at least," Logan said.

Business first, though.

He went to a packhorse for the shovels, and then he and Chaudri dug a shallow grave. They laid O'Toole into it. Logan said a quiet prayer. They buried him and piled rocks over the grave. An hour lost, but none of them suggested leaving him.

There was a certain understanding among the people who braved this side of the gateway. Everyone got to return home, one way or another.

Kiara set a pulse-transponder on top of the pile. The company would send a retrieval team here, disguised as priests who cared for the dead.

They picked up the trail and followed it northwest. An hour later, Kiara tried her isotope scanner out again. "We're getting a couple of signals. I think they're together, and moving."

Jackpot.

"Bravo Team," Logan said. "We find them, and we'll find the infiltrators."

"Let's finish this."

They remounted and rode north, not pushing the horses any more than they had to. The isotope scanner gave a decent signal, but they were in unfamiliar terrain, with possible hostiles waiting in ambush. Logan made a number of forays to scout ahead, and to check their backtrail. When they made camp at night, they did so under a full security protocol. Decoy tents, proximity sensors, hobbles on the horses, everything. Logan wasn't taking any chances.

The isotope signals for Bravo Team grew stronger. Two days later, they found two more of its members. Their position hadn't changed at all, based on the isotope scanner's readout. The signal led them away from the road to the lip of a narrow defile. Kiara and Chaudri held a covering position between it and the road, along with Logan's mount, while he crept forward to investigate. There was some risk of an ambush here, so he kept his eyes up.

The sky was overcast; dark clouds and lightning threatened on the western horizon. Between that and the late-afternoon hour, twilight shrouded the bottom of the defile. Logan crawled up to the edge to hazard a glance down. Once his eyes adjusted, he could make out the bodies. Four of them, and not a one moving. One was on a shelf perhaps twenty feet below; the rest were at the bottom.

"I've got four bodies," he said over the comm unit.

"Only two on the scanner," Kiara replied. "Any sign of the raiders?"

"It looks clear. I'm going to climb down."

"I want your safety harness on," Kiara said.

He made a face but complied; the last thing he needed was a broken bone. He wished he'd thought to test the new paracord the tech team had put together under happier circumstances.

He secured one end to a large tree trunk and clipped the carabiner to an alusteel ring at the waist of his custom armor. The sides of the defile were some kind of porous rock, possibly volcanic. It allowed a good grip, so he reached the shelf without incident.

"Status, Logan," Kiara said. There was tension in her voice.

"I'm at the first body," Logan replied. "It's Keene." The man's tar-black hair and thick beard were unmistakable. Kiara made a noise over the comm unit; it sounded like a muffled curse. Keene was the Bravo leader. He and Logan had served together on a couple of tours. Logan had recruited him once he got out. He'd have been with the first retrieval team, if the executives hadn't sent Bradley. Keene's crossbow lay in two pieces on the rocky shelf; his quiver was empty. His body was riddled with bullets.

"More gunshot wounds," Logan said. "I'll check the others."

He left the man to belay to the floor of the defile. He reached the nearest body, facedown in a puddle of blood. He rolled it over and recognized another Bravo Team member, Hank Magrini. He was the weapons specialist, an ex-tank-gunner. "It's Hank the Tank."

Hank's body had numerous wounds. His combat knife was nearby. It was bloody.

Logan stepped over him to the others. These appeared different from the others; they didn't have Alissian clothing. They wore black tactical vests over dark fatigues, and both were strapped with MP5 machine guns.

"You're not Bravo," he said, and that explained the lack of an isotope signal. They *were* dead, though. Each man had a company-issue crossbow bolt in his chest.

"Who are they?" Kiara demanded over the comm unit.

"Two of the hostiles," he said.

"Good," Kiara said.

He searched them, but found no identification. Just ammunition and tactical gear. He hadn't really expected to find anything, but he was trying to be thorough. The men had the short hair favored by ex-military, but he didn't recognize them. He cut the straps of the MP5s and tied them to his pack. He took the clips as well. The rest of it might seem strange to an Alissian, but didn't represent an advance in technology. He snapped their photos and scanned fingerprints.

He climbed out to give Kiara the good news. Two of the MP5s were in hand.

More importantly, the last member of Bravo Team might still be alive.

They buried Keene and Magrini as the sun set on the Landorian plateau. Logan tried to say a few words about the fallen men, but his tongue felt numb. He took only a little bit of solace in the fact that they'd managed to surprise the raiders, and kill two of their number, with the very weapons he'd trained them to use.

He made them a silent promise that he'd finish the job.

It was a better prayer than anything he could have said aloud anyway.

They walked the horses for a bit, until the rim of the defile was out of view. No one had the energy to press on in full darkness. They made a quiet camp without a fire and slept ten hours.

Logan woke just after sunrise, feeling strangely rested. These past few days had been draining on all of them, but they seemed to have bounced back. The horses, too—and now they snorted, their breaths making frost in the chill air. Logan strapped on their feed bags of grain while they stamped impatiently. They were eager to get moving. Kiara was awake already, fiddling with the isotope scanner. Even Chaudri was stirring, and before the coffee was made.

I bet Bradley would still be asleep.

"I've got the signal," Kiara said. She frowned. "It's strong. Almost looks like two signals."

Logan hurried over for a look. The fourth member of Bravo Team was Julio Mendez, their scout. He was a young kid, twenty-seven, but tough as alligator skin. He'd come over from Cuba at age five, on a raft his family made out of inner tubes and plywood. They had to *swim* the last half mile . . . something little Julio had had to figure out in the moment. He was a survivor.

Mendez had gone into the foster care system, a childhood only marginally better than what he'd have had in Cuba. At eighteen he signed up for the Marines. Company recruiters had lured him away only after promising to help get the rest of his family out. Apparently they thought it might be a handful of aunts and uncles. The last Logan heard, it was forty-one Mendezes and counting. There were jokes that CASE was one of the biggest lobbyers in getting the US to normalize relations with the island country—it would be cheaper than bringing over more of Julio's family.

The signal from the isotope was unmistakable: north across the plateau. And close. Chaudri had made coffee—she might have woken up before it was made, but she wasn't going to function without it. She brought Logan and Kiara each a cup.

"I feel like I slept for two days," she said.

"For once, that's not true," Logan said. "I do feel strangely rested, though."

She pursed her lips. "Dr. Holt used to talk about stumbling upon anomalies like this. Where wounds heal faster, and sleep counts more. He called them 'rejuvenation zones.'"

"That's exactly how I feel. Rejuvenated."

"Let's hope we were the only ones to get this advantage," Kiara said.

There was a natural spring nearby; the water looked clear. Logan took a sample and ran it through their chemical/microbe test kit. The readouts were almost too good to be true; the water was incredibly pure. He refilled their canteens, and then let Chaudri bring the horses down. They drank heavily. Saddles were tightened; weapons were checked.

"Ready, Lieutenant," Logan said.

Kiara hadn't moved her eyes from the isotope scanner. "Mount up," she said.

> "I want the same thing anyone else in entertainment does. I want access."

—ART OF ILLUSION, JUNE 8

CHAPTER 17

OLD MAGS

Quinn hadn't been executed yet, which he took for a good sign. The council meeting that had featured his trial had dissolved into an impromptu social gathering. Magicians lounged in their seats, mingled with one another. He took that time to work the crowd, a part of the business that Vegas magicians had to learn early. Something felt different about the way the islanders spoke to him now. They shared a common bond, accepted him as one of their own.

He had the distinct feeling that life here would be a lot more tolerable.

Moric had conferred quietly with the magicians, tolerated Quinn's schmoozing with the islanders, but was plainly waiting for him. Once the crowd thinned out, he ambled over.

"Well done, Quinn," he said. "I'll walk you back to your quarters, if you don't mind."

"Wow. You make it sound as if I have a choice in the matter."

Moric smiled. "You've always had a choice. You could tell me to go jump in the ocean."

Quinn looked at him sidelong. "Something tells me I shouldn't do that."

"Well, I would advise caution when it comes to council members. I'm told we can be a bit on the grouchy side."

"Duly noted."

"Besides, you're likely to need rest. Magic takes a toll on the body."

"I am rather tired," he said, remembering Moric's nap when they first arrived. It wasn't exactly true—he was tired, but it was more the exhaustion of coming down from the high of a show, and not because he used up some sort of internal reserve of power. Knowing he'd need to keep up the charade, though, he asked, "How much sleep are we talking about?"

"An hour or two, for most enchantments. You'll need to pace yourself, though. The more powerful the spell, the more rest you'll require."

Quinn noticed a pack of giggling children had swept much of his foam-snow into a large pile. Moric looked upon them fondly, smiled with a sort of indulgent pride. They built it up to about waist-high, and then took turns running and jumping in the stuff. The best part about this foam was that it was biodegradable. The next significant rainstorm would wash it all away.

"I grew up with a lot of snow, in Pirea," Moric said. "I remember it being heavier. And colder, too."

"I did the best I could," Quinn said.

"It wasn't bad, for a novice. Our art is much harder than it looks."

You have no idea.

They strolled away from the amphitheater and the tower that loomed above it, back in the general direction of Quinn's guest quarters—which was starting to feel a bit less like going back to prison. The breeze had picked up into a steady wind; it looked as though they might have a storm. Idly he wondered how well the islanders could withstand a typhoon, if it happened to come to that. Hadn't Moric said something about a threshold? Perhaps that shielded the island from the worst of it.

"Strange that you were so adamant about not having the gift, only to use it so compellingly, when pressed," Moric said.

"I suppose I just got lucky." He felt a little guilty for pulling one over on this crowd. Magic was clearly a precious thing to them.

Moric pursed his lips. "Perhaps. But I believe I may understand what's going on here."

That worried him. "Oh, yeah?"

"Some magicians who are just learning their art

aren't able to call upon it easily. Often it requires a desperate situation."

"I tend to do well under pressure. That much is true."

"You're an unusual man, Quinn. And I certainly hope that won't change, now that you're a member of our society."

"It's official, then?"

Moric nodded. "You'll no longer be locked in your guest quarters, and we won't have someone shadowing you at all times."

"I didn't think there was. I spent a lot of time alone, if memory serves."

Moric shrugged. "You were never truly alone. In any case, you may go where you wish on the island."

"Can I leave the island if I want?" Quinn asked.

Moric's lips curled, as if made unhappy by the question. "Yes," he said. "We have means of getting back to the continent. Nothing so disorienting as the way you were brought here, either. You need only say the word, and we'll get you on a ship to the mainland."

Back to Valteron. He wondered what the others would be doing now. Surely the mission had continued, even after he was taken. He seriously doubted they'd drop everything to track down their missing entertainer. Then again, the fact that he wasn't able to use his comm unit had probably made them fear the worst. They might even have left, and headed back north without him. If he got back on the main continent, he'd *probably* be able to make contact. There was no way to know for certain—and he definitely couldn't ask Moric about it.

It occurred to Quinn that he had little to contribute to the primary mission, now that Richard Holt was the Valteroni Prime. No doubt Logan and Kiara would still try to haul him back to the gateway, but they didn't need a magician for that.

They needed a miracle.

Besides, wasn't the company's principal goal to learn as much about Alissia as possible? Chaudri had admitted that they knew very little about the magic here. None of his briefings had mentioned the guild or the island or anything.

Here he was, right in the thick of it. Surrounded by people who were capable of *real* magic, and accepted as one of their own. Free rein of the island might even let him get down to the shipyard for a better look at that ship.

"I'd like to remain in the Landorian tower, if possible," Quinn said.

Moric smiled; he seemed genuinely pleased. "Excellent. I'm sure you'll enjoy staying here a while longer."

"I want to learn everything that I can," Quinn said.

"I know just the place to start," Moric said.

The guild of magicians kept its library in the central spire. More accurately, its library *was* the central spire. It contained, if Moric was to be believed, the most extensive collection of scrolls, books, and written documents in Alissia. The magician had offered to accompany Quinn for his first visit; he seemed unusually excited about it.

"How long has it been here?" Quinn asked. Maybe that would give him some idea of how long the island community had been around.

"Two hundred years, give or take," Moric said. "It's grown considerably since my time here."

"I'm surprised it all isn't crumbling into dust," Quinn said. Alissian paper was rather primitive, made from the fiber of a cotton-like plant grown mostly in Valteron.

"Ordinarily they would be, were it not for our arts. Old Mags has a particular knack for the preservation spells."

"What's Old Mags?" Quinn asked. It sounded like the name of a tavern, which he really hoped it was.

"She's the head librarian, and a fellow council member."

"How old did she have to be to get that nickname?"

"You should ask her," Moric said. His face was carefully neutral.

"Maybe I will," Quinn said. Granted, asking any woman about her age seemed unwise in Earth or Alissia. "If I do, I'll be sure to tell her it was your idea."

Moric folded like a card table. "Don't do that! I'm in enough trouble with her as it is."

"Romantic trouble?"

"Ha! Don't be foolish." Moric looked around, as if he feared Old Mags might be lurking somewhere nearby. "I may have borrowed a few parchments. Old treatises on a topic dear to my heart: the art of forced disappearance."

"That sounds a lot like what you did to me in Valteron."

"What? Oh, not exactly. I'm talking about causing things to disappear. To cease their existence entirely."

"I've done that, actually. Made things disappear," Quinn said.

Moric's eyebrows went up. "Permanently?"

"Not quite." Just long enough to be convincing.

"That's the tricky part. I had made some progress on it, though I'm sorry to say that it came at the tangible expense of the scrolls themselves."

"Is there any way to get them back?" Quinn asked.

"Yes. Unfortunately, the instructions for that particular bit of magic were, well . . ."

"On the scrolls, too?"

"Exactly."

They skirted around the amphitheater, where remnants of Quinn's performance danced and whirled in the gusting wind. The base of the central tower was massive, probably fifty or sixty yards in diameter. Despite its size, there was only a single entryway not much wider than a man. The iron-banded wooden door was shut firmly from the inside, too. The tower itself was supposedly stuffed with papers and other flammable items.

These people clearly didn't understand much about fire codes.

Moric didn't try the door. Instead, he pulled on a rope cord dangling beside it. There came a faint sound of bells ringing from somewhere inside, muffled by the thick wood of the door. Quinn stole a glance at the tower wall; it seemed to be of brick-and-mortar construction, but polished nearly as smooth as glass. He brushed his fingers along it and could barely feel the edges of the bricks. The building itself felt cold, almost icy.

"Feels cold, doesn't it?" Moric asked as if reading his mind. His voice sounded an octave higher than usual. "It's a side effect of the preservation spells." He was fidgeting while they waited.

He's nervous . . . and he can fly.

Quinn couldn't *wait* to meet this librarian.

A grating noise came from the far side of the door. Someone was unbarring it. The door opened wide enough to reveal an ancient woman with a graying bun. Her eyes were bloodshot.

"Hello, Mags," Moric said.

She grunted at him.

"This is Quinn, the newest member of the Enclave."

"I know who he is." She looked Quinn up and down. "I'm still picking your snow out of my hair."

"Now, Mags," Moric said.

"Don't you even start," said Mags. "I'm missing three parchments. Some of the same ones you were asking after, just last week."

"I'm sure they'll turn up," Moric said. A bit too quickly.

She stared at him, unblinking. Almost like a fish.

Moric cleared his throat. "In the meantime, I was hoping to show young Quinn here what it looks like."

Quinn jumped in to help. "I'm told you've done wonders with the place." He flourished with both arms and produced a white-and-yellow flower out of nowhere. This he offered to her with a bow. "For you."

She looked at it like it was a dead animal. "I've got a lot of work to do. No time for foolishness."

He let the flower tumble from his fingers. It disappeared in a puff of smoke, just before hitting the ground. No reaction.

Tough crowd.

"Moric, I'll be needing to search you on your way out, so keep that in mind."

"I'm sure we'll both enjoy that."

She turned to shuffle with agonizing slowness down a narrow hallway just as wide as the door.

"I think she likes you," Moric whispered.

"I think she likes you, too."

Moric smiled ruefully. He gestured, so Quinn followed.

The hall led to an open chamber several stories tall. Lamplight shone on a great spiraling staircase that wound up the core of the tower. The walls around it were lined with shelves, and every shelf crammed with books or papers. There were thousands in view, and likely even more in the floors above. A dusty but faintly sweet smell permeated the air. The smell of old books. Here was a wealth of knowledge about Alissia and its history. Chaudri would have been salivating over it.

"I don't suppose there are any maps?" Quinn ventured.

"Fourth floor," Moric said. He gestured at the staircase in a mock imitation of Quinn's bow. "After you."

Quinn ascended without hurry, still marveling at how much the library contained. He'd always had the impression that there simply wasn't a lot written down in this world. Yet the first three floors alone contained more parchments, more stacks of papers, and even more leather-bound books than he imagined could exist in Alissia.

The fourth floor, the map room, was even more impressive. The map of Alissia was a hand-painted mural that dominated the entire fourth-floor wall. The mountains and forests and coastlines were sketched in painstaking detail. The company's map of Alissia had ports and capital cities, as well as a few dozen other settlements.

This mural had *hundreds*.

And the details! Even down to simple hamlets represented by a cluster of tiny cottages. Without thinking about it, Quinn's eyes flew to the area in north Felara where the gateway was located. This, to his great relief, was one thing the map was missing.

There was something else, too, that the map might have contained. He searched the waters and the coasts for it, but came up empty. His disappointment must have been obvious.

"You were hoping to see something here," Moric said. "Perhaps the very island on which we stand?"

Quinn shrugged. "I know you said I could leave, but I'd still like to have some idea of where we are."

"You won't find the Enclave marked on any maps, I'm afraid," Moric said. "Revealing its location might bring unwelcome visitors, of the sort who would try to exploit our arts for personal gain. Or worse."

"I can't imagine that you'd let anyone catch you by surprise here," Quinn said.

"Oh, we wouldn't make it easy. But should one of Alissia's more powerful nations take an interest, we could be in trouble."

"Like Valteron?"

Moric smiled. "We don't need to worry about Valteron, as long as I'm on the council."

"Because you're friends with Richard Holt."

"Something like that," Moric said.

Quinn laughed, suddenly nervous. "You didn't, ah, have anything to do with his rise to power, did you?"

Moric did not answer.

> **"Alissians have much to
> teach us about loyalty."**
>
> —R. HOLT, "UNDERSTANDING
> ALISSIAN ETHICS"

CHAPTER 18

CONFRONTATIONS

Logan was in a dark place. The faces of the dead Bravo Team members played over and over in his head. He'd been a soldier for all his adult life. He'd lost brothers before. But when you recruited and trained them yourself, you felt more than just a loss. You felt the guilt. It was just as bad as that shit-storm in Caralis years ago.

No—worse.

Kiara motioned for him to scout ahead. The isotope signal had remained strong. They were in Landor still, though closer to the Felaran border. That made everyone nervous; it seemed their quarry had given up all pretense and were making a straight shot back toward the gateway.

Now, suddenly, the source of the isotope had gone still. If Bravo's last surviving member was tracking the infiltrators, it meant they'd stopped somewhere. Maybe to set an ambush. Kiara had ordered silence on the comm units; the raiders might be listening in. One of the fallen men had been missing his earbud.

Logan dismounted and slipped forward for a look over the ridge ahead. He rested a hand on the stock of the MP5. Bravo Team had managed to put them on close-to-equal terms with the raiders, though at great cost. She and Logan had the guns; Chaudri now carried Logan's crossbow.

Kiara estimated the signal was about a quarter mile ahead. As he looked now, he could make out a dense cluster of evergreens on a rocky outcropping. *Distance looks about right, too.* It was slightly uphill from his position, and his field glasses couldn't penetrate much into the dense wall of trees. Anyone hidden there, however, had a view for miles around. He scooted down the ridge and jogged back to confer with the others.

"Are they up there?" Kiara asked.

"That's where I'd be," he said. "You could hide a small army in those trees, and they have good visibility. There's no way we'll approach without being seen. In daylight, at least."

"What if they have night-vision equipment?" Chaudri asked.

"Then we're at a major disadvantage," Logan admitted. He hoped they wouldn't have it, though. That kind of gear was heavy, and they'd had no reason to suspect they'd need it when they raided the island facility.

"We'd better proceed as if they do," Kiara said. "It's about four hours until nightfall. As long as they stay here, we'll hit them tonight."

They gave the horses their feed bags to keep them quiet, and began to draw up a plan.

Logan hid behind a boulder twenty yards south of the tree line. It was almost midnight. They'd seen no movement in the evergreens before darkness fell, other than a thin curl of smoke. Someone had built a campfire. He doubted it was Mendez; the scout wouldn't risk revealing his position. Either the remaining raiders had grown lax, or they meant to lure someone in.

Kiara was working in from the east, to try for a better fix on the isotope scanner. Chaudri had taken a position to the west, fifty yards from the trees. She wouldn't move in unless called; her job was to make sure that no one slipped away north or west. Logan had found a suppressor on one of the bodies in the defile; he screwed it into the muzzle of his MP5 now. It would hide a muzzle flash and muffle the sound, but cut the effective range of the weapon considerably. If he used it, he'd better be close.

Which he damn well intended to be.

A tiny signal flashed to his right. Their beacons

were small LEDs, matched to the fluorescent green of the Alissian firefly. From a distance, it was hard to tell the difference, except that these flashes happened to be Morse code. She had a fix just inside the wood line. Thirty yards. He sent back three dashes, then dash-dot-dash. *OK.* A cloud drifted in front of the Alissian moon; the wind provided some cover noise. He rose and sprinted for the trees.

Fifteen yards, ten yards, five. He rolled in under the foliage of the evergreens. The mat of fallen needles made no sound. He came up into a crouch, MP5 at the ready. No movement. Mendez shouldn't be far in. He might be asleep, or unconscious. Kiara flashed an update. Ten yards. He crept forward, closing the distance. Something clicked ahead. Logan tensed. It was a cigarette lighter; the man was lighting up.

"Hey!" Logan whispered. "Mendez!"

The man paused. He looked over, clicked the lighter again. Then Logan realized something.

Mendez didn't smoke.

The cigarette had been a distraction. With his other hand, he'd raised the dark shadow of a handgun.

Shit!

Logan dove over and down as the suppressed muzzle spat bullets at him. He rolled prone behind a fallen tree. The man was up and walking toward him. He was wearing a powder-blue jumpsuit. He fired again, splintering the wood in front of Logan's face. And he kept coming.

Logan lifted the muzzle of the MP5 just over the

wood. The man reared back in surprise, trying to scramble away. *I guess he didn't expect to face a gun.* Logan didn't take any chances. He aimed for center mass and put four in the man's chest. He was dead before he hit the ground. Logan stood and hurried forward, still covering him with the MP5. The fallen cigarette smoldered in the leaves. He stamped it out, then rolled the man over.

"This is interesting," he whispered.

"What?" Kiara's voice asked.

"It *is* the goddamn janitor."

A hundred yards to the east, Kiara watched Logan sneak into the woods. She had the isotope scanner trained on a source just inside the wood line. Presumably that was Mendez, hiding in the deep cover. Hopefully he hadn't come this far just to bleed out. It was critical that Logan reach the last member of Bravo Team alive. Not only would he have priceless intel on the infiltrators and their movements, but his survival would offer some consolation, some payoff, for the lives taken from the other three.

Logan had been trying his best not to show it, but their deaths had hit him hard. Yes, he was a professional soldier; he'd seen killing before. But it didn't stop these things from hurting. It just meant he covered his emotions. He focused on the task at hand.

And the moment he got close to those responsible, he'd be like a tiger off the leash.

She'd specifically ordered him to try to take one of them alive, but that was unlikely to happen. Not that Logan wasn't capable. He was a brawler and always had been, from the day she'd recruited him out of the service. But losing soldiers under your command was the most devastating thing that could happen to an officer. These were men and women you trained, gave orders to, felt *responsible* for.

On a mission, no one obsessed more about security than Logan did. Half of the equipment that the prototyping lab designed for Alissian use—such as the perimeter stakes—were things that he had dreamed up. None of it had saved Bravo from the raiders. Logan would kill them to a man if she let him.

And he might even if she *didn't* let him.

They'd cross that bridge if and when they came to it, though. For now, Kiara scanned the tree line for any hint of movement. As she did, she reconsidered their tactical options. Judging by the curl of smoke they'd seen earlier, the raiders had made their camp another few hundred yards north. They were surrounded by dense forest on three sides, and a rocky drop-off to the north. It was a fairly defensible position, with the advantage of elevation and visibility. Two or three raiders remained, and they'd proven themselves dangerous.

She looked back to Logan just in time to see the gunfire. *Christ! What's going on?* She heard a faint sound, like the *pfft-pfft* of a silenced handgun. The suppressor covered most of the flash, but not all of it. A moment later came the soft putts of Logan's MP5. She cursed and ran for the woods, praying that Logan wouldn't accidentally shoot her.

Chaudri crouched in the long grass to the west of the wooded outcrop. The stock of Logan's crossbow felt clumsy and uncomfortable in her hands. She tried her best to concentrate on the mission and her orders, but there were so many distractions. She'd spent the better part of her career studying Alissia. Poring over manuscripts, reading reports, studying maps and histories. The prospect of an entire new world, one for which new data were constantly pouring in, thrilled her as nothing in archaeology had. And Richard Holt had inspired her as no one else could. He didn't just read about something to study it. He inserted himself into the experiment. Studied it inside and out. Almost got married, just to understand what it was like.

Meeting him in the palace of the Valteroni Prime . . . that had been something. Holt had been as confident and calm as ever. He showed no remorse for what he'd done; if anything, he was even more self-assured. Chaudri was beginning to understand why. There was an *enchantment* to this place. Even now, when she placed her palm against the hard, rocky earth, she imagined she could feel its pulse.

Movement from the trees broke her out of her reverie. A man hurried through the woods, south toward Logan's position. No, two men. It looked like they were carrying machine guns, and moonlight glinted off of some gear on their heads.

Are those night-vision goggles?

Chaudri reached for her comm unit, but remembered that Kiara had confiscated it. Knew she'd be tempted. If she could get close enough, she might be able to warn them with the flash signal. Her Morse code was a bit rusty, though; she began running through it, just in case.

Kiara hadn't really told her what to do in this situation. Her job was to watch and report if men fled. *How I'm supposed to do that without a comm is still beyond me.* At this range, she wouldn't be able to hit either man with the crossbow, so she was useless. She started working her way south, keeping behind the grass or bushes whenever she could. Shadowing the men in black clothing. Her boot snapped a dry twig; the noise seemed to echo in the night air. She froze. The men in the woods paused. They'd heard it, of course.

Will they come this way? That was the real question.

If they did, she gave herself very little chance of killing them both. The crossbow would give her a good chance at one, but the second man probably wouldn't come within sword range.

Then again, it had slowed them, which gave her an idea. She shadowed their movements for another few minutes, then found a stone and hurled it into the woods behind them. They certainly heard that. Both of them crouched low, half turned to look for a threat behind them. Chaudri remained completely still. In low visibility, movement gave away more than anything else. She was a stump, or a stone. Nothing more.

At last they moved on, and faster than before. Some urgency drove whatever they planned. Chaudri nearly had to run to keep up with them. She came to a ditch running east-west. It would give her enough cover to get near the tree line, and the raiders were already past it. She'd have to be closer to be useful to Logan and Kiara anyway.

She cut left, trying to keep low. Gods, but she hoped they wouldn't turn around. The crossbow was getting heavy.

Logan crawled on his belly under the branches of evergreens, working his way toward the enemy camp. He hadn't lingered near the dead janitor. If the other raiders had heard the gunfire, they'd be coming fast. The blue jumpsuit was another piece in the puzzle; it explained the isotope signal here and how the infiltrators had gotten past security and through the gateway. Security on the Earth-side wasn't Logan's responsibility, but he saw how it could happen. Big company, lots of layers of security codes and scanners and such, but you need someone to clean up after closing time. Those trash cans didn't empty themselves. Janitors had access to almost everything. A well-placed agent posing as a janitor could help himself to the files and reports undoubtedly left lying around.

Some of the smartest scientists in the world, and they don't know anything about information security.

The worst part was that it *hadn't* been Mendez. Bravo's scout would have really turned the tables on this mission. Logan and Kiara had been counting on the *intel* and the extra manpower. The idea that he might still be alive had kept Logan better in line. Who had he been kidding? The kid was probably dead, just like the rest of his team. Another awkward letter to send about an "unfortunate training accident."

He probably should have retreated and regrouped with the others. More planning, more chasing. More bodies probably left behind as the raiders burned their path back toward the gateway. That's what Kiara would have wanted him to do. But now his blood was up, and there was no Mendez to save.

That only leaves one thing to do.

He paused for a moment to put on the infrared-sensing lenses. They didn't help with seeing in the near-darkness, but they'd give him a warning if the enemy had night-vision equipment. The moon was enough for him. He edged toward the center of the woods as he went. Sixteen rounds in the clip, three of them spent on the janitor. That left thirteen. Would it be enough? He paused long enough to pull the clip and add three more rounds. No sense going into a fight without a full mag.

The clip slid back into place. He tried to muffle the sound when it seated, the soft metallic *click*. The wind died at the exact wrong moment. The click sounded too loud in the silent woods. He held completely still, listening, waiting. Good. He took a step forward.

Gunfire erupted from the left, from the shadowed woods. He dropped flat, but not in time to avoid a graze across the shoulder. *That was close.* He couldn't see the muzzle flashes—the trees were too thick here. He scrabbled away on a diagonal. Bullets flew again. He was forced to take cover behind a tree. They had him pinned. More gunfire, now coming from the two positions. One to the left, one almost north of him. They were flanking him. He resisted the urge to shoot back; that would only give away his position and they had the drop on him already. He slouched low to the ground, putting the tree between him and the shooter on the north. He brought the stock of the MP5 to his shoulder and quieted his breathing.

Footsteps. To the left, approaching with deliberate slowness. Logan still couldn't make him out; there was too much foliage. But he was close. Maybe thirty yards. Red beams flared on his IR lenses. Shit! Night vision—Chaudri had guessed it after all. Logan was already sweating; he'd be lit up like a Christmas tree. Farther west came a deep *clack-thrum*. Something about the sound was familiar to him, but he couldn't quite place. But he recognized the grunt that followed, especially when the raider fell to his knees. The man saw Logan then, under the foliage. Started to bring his gun up. Logan shot him four times in the chest. He tumbled over backward.

The tree behind his head exploded into splinters. Logan rolled and returned fire, shooting blindly. More shots caused him to bury his head in the pine needles to protect his face from the flying wood. He shot again.

Empty.

Worse, the impotent *click* gave it away. The man heard it and, like a seasoned vet, charged while Logan fumbled for another one. The damn thing caught on the edge of his pocket. He fought with it, couldn't get it free. His arm was half-numb. The graze must have been worse than he thought. The last raider came into view, crouched low, scanning left and right with night-vision goggles. He saw Logan struggling. He took a knee, brought a weapon up to his shoulder. Logan wouldn't make it in time. He closed his eyes, thinking of his girls.

Thump. The raider crumpled forward. Kiara stood behind him, her MP5 held like a club. Logan exhaled.

God, that had almost been it.

"Cutting it a bit close, Lieutenant," he said.

She hardly spared him a glance as she knelt by the fallen man to check his pulse. "You're still alive, aren't you?"

"I suppose."

"Good."

Logan stood slowly and reloaded the MP5. His hands were shaking.

The trees behind him shook suddenly, as if mimicking his hands. A figure burst from between them, crossbow pointing around wildly.

Chaudri.

Logan held up his hands. "Easy, easy!"

"Oh. Logan." She sagged with visible relief.

"Jesus, Chaudri, you scared the hell out of me."

"Sorry. I didn't think I'd make it in time. Thank God."

"Gods, you mean," Logan said.

"Right. Gods." She leaned against a tree, shaken. "That was unpleasant."

> **"Most illusions are a matter of timing and misdirection. The best part is that the audience knows it."**
>
> —ART OF ILLUSION, AUGUST 1

CHAPTER 19

THE HARBORMASTER

Quinn woke before sunrise to find the island wrapped in fog. He dressed quietly, threw on a heavy cloak, and slipped out of the tower into gray anonymity. Visibility was no more than twenty feet. The Enclave had a few early risers, shadows that moved almost imperceptibly in the semidarkness. He drew his hood and became one of them, walking with purpose down toward the island's docks.

He wanted a closer look at that sailing ship he'd seen in the harbor.

It hadn't left, or even moved, while he'd been on the island. The docks were often a busy place, though, and it was hard to tell from a distance whether or not they were guarded. There was no better time than now, when most of the Enclave slept and fog hid him from the rest.

Especially the ones who'd been shadowing him. They were careful about it; they never did it openly. But he kept seeing the same faces. They never returned his wave, never smiled. Never did anything but stare at him. Moric had said they weren't his people—that he no longer required an escort—and that worried Quinn even more.

A single road led down to the docks through a natural cleft in the rocks. The click of his boots echoed off of the cleft's sides, but the wet heavy air muted the sound. There were luminescent globes strung along the tops of the wooden dock posts, almost like Christmas lights. Fog enshrouded them; their fey light didn't quite reach the surface of the water. No one seemed to be about.

He walked casually along the dock, as if out for a morning stroll. The wooden planks creaked beneath his boots. The air smelled fresh here. Almost pure. And strangely absent of the odors of dried seaweed and rotting fish that pervaded every body of water he'd seen Earth-side. Up close, the docks were the cleanest he'd ever seen. There was no hiding the sturdiness of the docks, the clean anchor lines, and the harbor waters that were completely free of debris.

He reached the end of the docks, and there she was. It had to be the *Victoria*. They'd moored her in the deepest part of the bay; a small white rowboat currently tied up at the docks must serve as a tender. He bent close to look at it; the boat wasn't locked. A simple rope secured it to the rock post, and it bobbed alluringly. He could probably be on board in five minutes, well before anyone noticed. But what then? He knew even less about sailing than he did about swimming.

Instead, he took out a pair of compact binoculars. These were about the size of opera glasses, and disguised as an ornate snuffbox with a lacquered lid. Snuffboxes were private possessions in this world, almost like handkerchiefs. No one would open it without being invited to.

At ten-times magnification, the sleek lines of the *Victoria* leaped into view. Captain Relling's shipbuilding team had done their job well. Maybe too well. All the angles were perfect, the finish was spotless, and not a single bit of metal had begun to rust. He couldn't think that it was some kind of magical protection offered by the Enclave magicians, because other than parking the vessel here, they didn't seem to have touched it.

If this was the company ship, then where was the crew? He'd been hesitant to ask Moric about it. Expressing any interest might clue him in that Quinn recognized it. That was a risk he wasn't willing to take.

Timbers creaked behind him. Someone was coming. He tucked the snuffbox away in his cloak and began whistling to himself.

A woman in a heavy woolen coat strode down the

docks toward him. She spotted Quinn, and seemed just as surprised as he was.

"Oh. Hello," she said.

"Hello," Quinn answered.

"Who are you?"

"Quinn. I'm—" he began, and then he got a good look at her face. He knew that face. The stern countenance, the eyes. It was Kiara's sister, Captain Relling. He wanted to say who he was right away, but some instinct screamed at him for caution. "I'm new here."

"You're a little old for a student."

He grinned at her. "So Moric tells me."

"One of his, eh?" She gave him a sidelong look, as if reappraising him. "Well, students aren't permitted down by the docks."

"Sorry." Quinn shrugged. "He said I could go wherever I want."

"Well, you tell Moric that everyone checks in with the harbormaster before entering the docks." She stalked past him and climbed into the tender. "He has a problem, he can take it up with the council."

"I didn't even know we had a harbormaster," Quinn said.

She took up the oars and started rowing out toward the ship. "You just met her."

Jillaine was avoiding him. Quinn had seen her once or twice since his testing, always from a distance. He'd waved at her but she never slowed. She never seemed to run, either—that was the crazy part. She'd turn a corner or something and just be gone.

So he climbed up to the highest part of the vale, the pile of rocks where he'd first met her. And he waited.

He never heard her climbing. Never saw her approach. He'd been distracted by the view, and wondering about how his team was doing on the mainland. Then he heard her little huff of surprise when she saw him.

"You've been avoiding me," he said.

She brushed an errant strand of hair from in front of her face. "I have not."

So that's how she was going to play it. "Did I do something wrong?"

"How should I know?" she asked.

She was impossible to read, and he wasn't sure if that vexed him more as a man or as a magician. "Well, I wanted to say thanks," Quinn said. "The council agreed to let me join."

She didn't answer him, and he didn't want to seem needy.

"That's all," he said. He stood and brushed past her to climb down. Trying to ignore the faint rose scent of hers as he did.

"I didn't feel anything," she said, without warning.

He paused in his descent. That could mean a lot of different things. "What?"

"During your trial," she said.

"Did you expect to?"

"I was touching your hands. I should have."

"Well, you felt the wind, didn't you?" he asked.

She paused, as if reluctant. "Yes."

He shrugged. "How else do you explain it?"

Trickery. He could sense the word on the tip of her tongue. Damn it, she *knew.* He should have been more cautious. All that bragging and celebrating, and he'd never realized that the one closest to him onstage would end up suspicious.

"Could you do it again?" she asked. "Here, and now?"

"I don't think so." Repeating a trick was dangerous, especially at the request of someone who wasn't convinced. She'd only look for the flaws in it. Besides, even if he wanted to, he'd used most of the foam, and the microfan wasn't charged.

"Hmm," she said.

"I'm not like you. I can't just summon magic whenever I want," Quinn said.

"I see."

"So we're OK, then?" he asked.

"Yes," she said. "As soon as I talk to my father about it."

Quinn hurried across the Enclave grounds. He was barely going to make class on time. He wasn't certain what Jillaine had told Moric, but the man had been asking him a lot of questions. Told Quinn he was the oldest newcomer in more than a century, and that he'd like to find others like him.

Quinn hoped to hell that would never happen.

He still hadn't figured out what to do about Captain Relling. There was no easy way for him to bring it up with Moric without showing his interest. All he knew was that she was here, alive, and working for the Enclave. What about her crew? The questions were piling up, and he had fewer and fewer answers.

And now he was going to try to learn actual magic.

Today his seven classmates perched precariously on rocks in the middle of a narrow, fast-running stream that fed the river. They were all about twelve or thirteen, and new to the Enclave. Just beyond them, the water tumbled over a twelve-foot waterfall. Sella seemed to enjoy putting her class in harm's way, in hopes of "lighting the spark of magic."

The stream was fed by an underground spring, and was ice cold. The thought of taking a dunk in it wasn't very appealing. He hesitated. Maybe skipping today's class was a good idea.

"Quinn is here!" one of the students called. *Judas*.

"Quinn, you're the last to arrive," said Sella. She was in purple, as always, with the white hair floating about her head. Since the first class, she'd made it clear that she saw no difference between Quinn and his classmates. They were all untrained magicians trying to "cross the threshold," to call upon magic whenever they wanted. The ability supposedly improved with age and practice; he certainly had the former, but was in desperate need of the latter.

"That last rock is yours," she said. She pointed with the long bamboo-like stick that she always carried; it served a variety of purposes . . . including disciplinary ones. Any time she started tapping it against the palm of her hand, someone was about to get the switch.

Quinn didn't think he was late enough to merit a lash, but stepped lively just in case. The last rock was one of the smallest, and it perched a scant two yards from the edge of the fall. He found the wooden plank that students used to reach their assigned stones and laid it across the water, resting the far edge on his rock. He scurried across it to the rock and nearly overshot his destination; the stone wobbled and grated beneath his boots. A few of the other students giggled at this. Most, though, were preoccupied with keeping their own balance above the frigid water.

Sella waited until he was settled before making a small flicking gesture with her stick that sent the wooden plank back to shore.

"Water magic is one of the most fickle arts you'll ever study," she said.

Quinn had to strain to hear her voice over the roar of the waterfall. There might be a test after this.

"You'll spend years mastering even the most basic enchantments and manipulations. Unless you happen to be one of a gifted few with a talent for it," she said, and seemed to smirk just a little bit.

He missed what she said next, because the comm unit made a burst of static in his ear. Startled the hell out of him. The thing had been absolutely silent since Moric had brought him here. He'd thought it broken, but he wore it all the time, on the off chance that he might pick up a signal from the others.

He pressed a finger to his ear. "Logan?" he nearly shouted. "Kiara?"

Silence answered him.

Sella had heard him, though. "Something to add, Quinn?" she asked.

"Uh, no," he called. "Sorry."

She spared a moment to frown at him, and went on. "Many of the guild's contracts require a water specialist. Deciding where to dig a well, or how best to dam a stream, can affect an entire village."

Guild contracts. So they did more than just kidnap people. They must have kept it quiet, though, because the reports he'd read had said nothing of it. Unless CASE Global knew, and had kept it from him. God, if he ever got back he was going to demand more access. There was just too much they might have decided he didn't have clearance for.

"Of course," Sella said, "water magic can be destructive as well."

She began tracing little swirls on the surface of the water with her whipping-stick. A circle, then a figure eight. Her lips moved faintly, but he heard no sound. The water around his stone seemed to increase in speed. It rushed and gurgled beneath his stone. The noise from the falls behind him seemed to increase.

One of the other students, a girl, squeaked and stumbled back. She went down with a splash. She flailed for the rock's edge, but the current had her. She

shot past Quinn and over the edge of the falls. Screaming all the way. The other students watched it happen
with wide-eyed looks of terror. Sella seemed not to
notice; she never broke from her enchantment.

The water began to rise. There was a sound to it, a
quickening that set his heart to pounding, his thoughts
racing. *Even if I can figure out how to swim enough to survive, and even if there are water magicians at the base of the
falls, what if they aren't prepared for a grown man? What if
they're too busy catching the other students?*

That's when the perfume hit. A heady rose scent
that overwhelmed him without warning or explanation. Oh, perfect. Jillaine must have come to watch today's lesson. The scent changed; now it was oranges
and cinnamon. He chanced a quick look around and
nearly tumbled into the drink because of it. She wasn't
on the shore, at least not within plain view. It had to be
her, though; only Moric's daughter sent smells by way
of greeting.

Sella continued her enchantment. She drew wider
circles now, sweeping her stick around and around as if
stirring a pot of stew. The water churned past Quinn,
sloshing across the tops of his boots. The sheer force of
it made his rock even more unstable. Another student
went down, one of the towheaded identical twins; the
water swept him away so fast he didn't even have time
to cry out. Now all he could smell was black licorice,
and it was strong.

Jillaine really wanted his attention.

The youngest student in the class was a tiny brown-haired girl named Meera. She looked like she'd be next. She teetered on her stone back and forth. Then she fell forward. He knew the water would take her; the girl couldn't weigh more than seventy-five pounds. But the water shrank away from her. Like an amoeba reacting to fire. She tumbled on the mud bottom of the stream-bed, as stunned as those around her.

Sella still didn't look up, but the hint of a proud smile played on her lips. Meanwhile Quinn pivoted as best he could on his stone, trying to spot Jillaine's hiding place while she assaulted him with a barrage of fragrances, and not all of them pleasant ones. She wouldn't stop until he found her; this was one of her little games. He heard a faint giggle. It sounded like it came from *behind* him. That simply wasn't possible, unless . . .

There she was, floating just over the edge of the wa-terfall and off to one side. How? She blew him a kiss. He lost his balance then. The stone gave. The water didn't magically part for him, either, no matter how much he wanted it to. The cold hit him everywhere at once. It knocked the wind out of him. He went over the edge and had a gut-wrenching moment of weight-lessness. He tried to take a breath and got a mouthful of cold water.

He felt a massive, invisible hand wrap around him. It slowed him as he fell. He was barely moving when he hit the pool at the bottom. Not that the magicians kept him completely dry, of course. They let him flail around for a bit while the falling water pummeled him before dragging him to the shore. He got no further attention, as two more of the students came over the falls.

Quinn looked up to find Moric standing there. "No breakthrough, I take it?"

"Not the one I was looking for, at least."

The two magicians behind Moric lifted the most recent victims to the shore of the waterfall pool.

"Where's Meera?" Moric asked.

"She did something with the water. It parted like the Red Sea for her," Quinn said.

"What's the Red Sea?"

"Right, sorry." Quinn held up his hands and split them into a V-shape. "It went like this, with her in the middle."

"I'll be damned. Little Meera a water magician. That's fantastic!"

"Yeah," Quinn said. He took off his boots to empty out the water. Damn these tests. He'd officially been burned, chased by a wild animal, and nearly drowned in a class that was designed for twelve-year-olds.

"I'm sure Sella's quite pleased about it. She's a water magician herself, you know," Moric said.

"Yeah, I picked up on that," Quinn said.

He was starting to dry out by the time he found Jillaine, perched on her usual rock at the island's high point. She was faced out to sea, but had her eyes closed. He paused to just look at her a moment, without the distraction of her staring back. She was more than pretty; she was serene. Not a worry line on her. Not an ounce of tension in the set of her shoulders. She was as careless and free as the strands of red hair that drifted back and forth in the sea breeze.

"You made me fall," Quinn said.

She kept her eyes closed, but smiled. "I never touched you."

"You know what I mean."

"I was only trying to help you find your break-through."

"Why would you do that?" he asked. The last time they'd spoken, she didn't seem ready to help him do anything.

"It's why you've come here, isn't it? To find your magic?"

"Technically, I came here because your father kidnapped me."

"But you could leave, if you wanted."

"Yes."

She opened her eyes and held him in place with them. "I want to come with you."

It was the last thing he expected her to say. He struggled for a minute, working his mouth and trying to find a word to reply. He was pretty proud when he came up with "Why?"

"I want a change of scenery. And my father won't let me go to the mainland on my own. Even though I can take care of myself, and have for years."

She said it with a bit of a petulant tone. He couldn't

blame her, any more than he could blame Moric for wanting to keep her close. Alissia was a rough place, even for magic users.

"What makes you think he'd let you come with me?" he asked.

"He likes you."

Quinn didn't think that mattered much, when it came to Jillaine, but he didn't want to argue. "It doesn't really matter right now. I don't plan to leave until I can win Sella over." He had to do that before he set foot off the island. If he didn't he was sure she'd make it impossible for him to come back.

And he wouldn't leave until he was sure he could return.

"So win her over," Jillaine said.

"I'm trying to!"

"You're doing it wrong."

"What's the right way, then?" He couldn't keep the irritation from his tone.

She tried to read his face, as if she thought he was kidding. "You really don't know, do you?"

"If I knew, I wouldn't be soaking wet right now."

She shook her head. "She's trying to help you reach your breakthrough. And all you do is complain."

"Because it's not *working*," Quinn said. "I'm afraid it never will. That I don't really belong here."

"That's not her fault. She's doing her job."

"So what am I supposed to do? Thank her for throwing me off a waterfall?"

"That would be a start."

"I don't know why I should do that."

"You both want the same thing, don't you?"

He bit back a snarky reply, because she was right. Even if he didn't agree with the approach, he had to admit that everything Sella did was aimed at helping the students call on their magic. "I suppose so."

"If you really want to impress Sella, show her that you want it as much as she does."

Moric found him that afternoon and dropped a bombshell.

"We've just had a message from the new Prime of Valteron."

Quinn sat up straight and put down the book he'd been secretly photographing. "From Richard Holt?"

"Yes."

"What did he want?"

"A protection detail."

He was careful to keep his face neutral, because he was thinking about Kiara and her mission. And what she'd probably be willing to do to complete it. "Has something happened? An assassination attempt?"

"No." Moric looked at him in a searching way. "You needn't worry about that, you know."

"Why not? He's a powerful man. I'm guessing he has enemies."

"That may be, but the Prime is under certain protections."

From the Enclave, no doubt. This quiet alliance

ran deeper than he'd thought. But he had to tread cautiously here. "I hope Richard appreciates all that you've done for him."

"We do this much for every Prime."

"That's generous of you," Quinn said.

"It's a small price to pay for stability."

Ah, there it was. The first hints that the Enclave wasn't playing an isolation game here on their island. As much as he wanted to ask how many other political leaders got this deal, he knew that might be pushing it—and he was pretty sure he already knew the answer. *You back the man with the power.* And in Alissia, there was no greater power than the wealth of Valteron. "Why does he need protection, then?" he asked.

"It's for some friends of his who are journeying north, by way of Landor."

It took all he had to keep his poker face then. To play it cool, because he knew Moric was watching. "Anyone I know?" he asked.

"He didn't offer their names," Moric said. "But the Prime believes them to be in some kind of danger. He's asked us to ensure that they make it to Felara."

And back out of the gateway, no doubt. How thoughtful of him. Quinn couldn't imagine Kiara just deciding to cut and run. Or Logan, for that matter. Something must have happened. God, they might just ride through the gateway and seal it permanently.

"Sounds kind of boring," Quinn lied. "If you wanted my opinion."

"I've already agreed to the contract," Moric said.

"Then why are you telling me this?" Quinn demanded. Here he'd thought Moric actually wanted his opinion.

"I was only being polite."

"Thanks a lot."

"The council had a similar reaction when I told them, if it makes you feel any better."

"Not really, no," Quinn said. If Moric got the boot, he'd probably be next.

"Sella only agreed on the condition that she be part of the team. So I suppose I'll have some face time with her."

Quinn chuckled. "Well, that should be fun."

Moric wandered over to Quinn's hearth, as if distracted. "Sometimes the guild brings students out on contract jobs. It's an educational experience."

"It's free labor," Quinn said.

"That, too."

"I think they'd be a liability, though," Quinn said. From what he'd seen in his classmates, twelve-year-old magicians were a mess.

Moric waved this off. "What better way to teach our students what the world is really like?" He shook his head. "Regardless, I'll be undertaking the mission, and I've decided to bring along a student observer."

"Who's it going to be?"

"I haven't decided yet," Moric said.

He had to know how badly Quinn would want it. A chance to get off the island, collect some intel on Holt, and maybe find a way to impress Sella. If such a thing was even possible.

So Quinn yawned. "Well, good luck with that." He stretched out on his bunk, picked up a book, and flipped it open.

Moric's eyes widened. "Sweet gods, is that a library book?"

"Oh, this old thing?" Quinn asked. Old was the word for it, too. The cover was animal skin, and the pages near-transparent vellum. By his guess, the book was at least a hundred years old.

"I know that book. It's *Fundamentals of Magic*. One of only three copies in the world," Moric said. He sounded like he was going to be sick.

"Yeah, it's all right," Quinn said. "Mags let me borrow it." At first he'd done so just to try out the reading glasses. The translation program was pretty good, though it couldn't always decipher the handwriting. Once he'd gotten the hang of using them, though, the book had gotten interesting.

"*Borrow* it?" Moric spluttered. "She hasn't even let me *look* at it in ten years!"

"I've got it for the rest of the week," Quinn said. He'd photographed nearly every page as well. If he ever managed to get back to the gateway, Chaudri was going to have a field day.

Moric's incredulity was gone; he was all curious now. "May I ask how you managed that?"

Quinn shrugged. "I'm good with people."

"You're a mysterious man, all right," Moric said. He lowered his voice. "Say, could I have a look?" He leaned over Quinn's shoulder.

Quinn put the book to his chest. "Sorry, can't help you."

"What?"

"Library policy. Mags insisted." Quinn didn't fight the smile. This was just too fun.

Moric stood up straight and rubbed a hand over his bald head. One of his tells. He had so many it was getting hard to keep track. "Perhaps we could reach some kind of arrangement."

Quinn began reading again. Best to keep it casual, and not seem too interested. "What do you have in mind?"

"An hour with that book might be a good start."

Quinn couldn't begin to guess why Moric wanted this particular book. He seemed to have his fundamentals covered rather well. An hour was nothing, since he had it for the week. But in Vegas, you never took an opening offer.

"Five minutes," Quinn said.

"You're not the only student on this island," Moric said. "Many would be interested in witnessing some guild work."

"Ten minutes," Quinn said.

"Fifteen," Moric said.

"Done," Quinn said. He set the book on his table and started pulling on his boots. "See you in a bit."

"Where are you going?"

"Out for a walk. I'll leave my book here. Due to library policy, I must request that you don't read it while I'm away."

"Oh, come, Quinn. Mags will never know."

"She'll know. Trust me," Quinn said. *She can read faces as well as any cardsharp.*

Moric looked uncertain. "Better safe than sorry, I suppose. Off with you, then."

Quinn stepped out. A thought occurred to him just then, so he poked his head back in. "You'd already picked me for the job, hadn't you?"

Moric smiled. "Of course. The rest of your classmates are children." He settled down into Quinn's chair.

"You played me," Quinn said.

"Well, I have been around a while."

"So it's you, me, and Sella?" That was going to be interesting.

"We'll bring a fourth to handle the workload. Someone young, most likely."

Quinn hesitated, but figured he might as well throw the dice. "You know, I could make a recommendation."

"Oh?"

"I know a talented young woman who'd probably be useful." *Not to mention good company.*

Moric gave him a stern look. "Did my daughter put you up to this?"

"Not at all. I just think she might like a change of scenery."

"I'll find it easier to concentrate if I don't have to

keep an eye on both of you. Are you willing to give her your spot?"

And miss out on seeing Logan, Kiara, and Chaudri again? "Not really."

Moric smiled. "I didn't think so."

"Well, it was worth a shot." *Sorry, Jillaine.* Quinn turned to leave again.

Moric touched the book's cover gently, almost with reverence. When he opened it, though, the first page was blank. So was the second. He flipped through more of them, finding only empty pages.

"Quinn, get back here!"

> **"We cannot hope to equal the fighting
> prowess of those born here."**
>
> —R. HOLT, "ASSESSMENT OF
> ALISSIAN MILITARIES"

CHAPTER 20

PRISONERS

They had tied Mendez to a tree in the middle of camp. Dried blood crusted the side of his face. His arms and legs were mottled with bruises. He was conscious, though. He'd managed to get a piece of rope between his teeth and was gnawing it steadily, like a rat trying to chew itself free of a trap. Maybe a rabid dog was more accurate. He shook his head, growling. No other part of him moved, just his head.

Logan clasped both hands over his mouth and gave the soft hoot of a white-winged owl. Mendez cocked his head, listening. Logan hooted again.

Mendez spat out the rope, licked his lips, and gave

a long, warbling call. *All clear.* No one from the other side of the gateway would recognize these calls; they were from Alissian birds.

Logan moved forward, sweeping left and right with the muzzle of the MP5. The fire pit near him had burned down to coals. Bits of charred leaves littered the periphery.

"You look like hell," Mendez said.

Logan felt himself grinning. "So do you. Were you going to chew through twenty loops of paracord?"

"Hey, fiber's good for you. You should try it sometime."

Logan took out his combat knife and began sawing through the cord. "I'll get right on that."

"Did you take care of the mercs?"

"Of course. No problem."

"I guess that's why you're the Alpha Team."

"Yeah." Logan finished cutting him free. "Janitor almost got the drop on me, though."

"He's not a janitor."

"I figured that out when I saw his submachine gun. Can you walk?"

"I've been slung over a horse for almost a week. I could run a marathon," Mendez said.

He was still in his armor, a lighter version of the alusteel suit that Logan himself wore. They'd beaten him pretty soundly; the bruises that weren't fresh were yellow around the edges, probably days old. Logan knew he wouldn't complain. When you've been to hell and back on a raft from Cuba, you go through life with a different perspective.

Logan handed him a canteen and a sidearm they'd taken from one of the men. Mendez took the gun first. He dropped out the clip, checked the ammo, slammed it home, and chambered a round. All of that in about four seconds. Then he tucked the weapon into a concealed carry holster strapped to his ankle.

"That company issue?" Logan asked.

"Not exactly. I know guns aren't allowed across, but I can't even sleep without the feel of the holster on my leg."

"I know what you mean."

Mendez nodded at Logan's MP5. "I know *that's* not company issue."

"Borrowed it from someone."

They didn't talk about the other members of Bravo, but one look at Mendez's eyes told Logan that he already knew. It was too soon, too fresh, to bring it up now. They still had work to do. When the mission was over, and the men's remains were brought back Earthside, then they could remember. And grieve.

"Don't get attached to the gun," Logan said. "The lieutenant wants to be rid of them as quickly as possible. You been practicing with the sword?"

"Every day. I'm probably as good as you now. Maybe better."

"Christ, we'd better get you some food," Logan said. "I think you're delirious."

Logan poured a stream of frigid water on the prisoner's face. "Wake up!"

The man spluttered awake, tried to move, and found that he could not. His wrists and ankles were bound with flexsteel ties. They were like zip ties, but made of a company-developed polymer that was virtually unbreakable. He struggled only for a moment, and then grew still. He looked around, assessing his captors, the environment, everything. Most normal people would have panicked.

Training always tells.

They were in the enemy camp, or what was left of it. Two of the raiders' horses were exhausted beyond recovery; Logan had had to put them down. He added their deaths to the mental tally he was keeping; this man had a lot to answer for.

He crouched in front of the prisoner. "Who are you?"

The man met his gaze and held it.

Logan stood and delivered a hard kick under the rib cage. The manual on field interrogation called this part "Establishing physical dominance."

He tried asking again, once the man had recovered. "What's your name, soldier?" Logan asked.

"Thorisson. Lars Thorisson." He had a slight accent, probably Nordic of one kind or another. Raptor Tech loved to hire these Andal types; they were good for show on the private security details. Some of them really knew how to handle themselves, too. "How many men were on your team?"

Thorisson didn't answer.

"Five?" Logan asked. "That's counting the janitor."

The man's face gave something away at the mention of the janitor. How had they gotten someone in, so close? To say CASE Global did intense background checks was a hell of an understatement—they made colonoscopies seem noninvasive by comparison.

Yet another mystery to unravel once they returned.

"What are your mission objectives?" Logan asked.

"Untie me first."

"No." He'd done enough damage here already.

"Am I under arrest?"

"Let's call it detained," Logan said. He smiled without humor. "Suspicion of trespassing."

The way the company saw it, they owned the island, so they owned the gateway, so they owned everything through the gateway. Of course, there was no legal precedent for such a situation, and a fair number of Alissians would take issue with being owned by anyone. Yet another fine line they walked that required absolute secrecy. As far as the gateway went, at least, the company's lawyers had offered the adage that possession was nine-tenths of the law.

"I want a lawyer," said Thorisson.

"Got one in your pocket?"

Thorisson scowled.

"Listen, man," Logan said. He tried to make his voice reasonable, when all he really wanted to do was beat this man to a bloody pulp. Kiara and her damn orders. "We're taking you back with us, back to the company facility."

"Where's that?"

"None of your business."

"And where are we now, exactly?"

"Also none of your business. Listen, I don't think you're quite getting it. You're our prisoner," Logan said. "We've got a long way to go and I'm not going to play babysitter the whole time. You do what I say, you answer our questions, but otherwise you keep your mouth shut."

"What's in it for me?" Thorisson asked.

"I won't cut your throat right now and leave you here to rot. Like you did to three of my men."

"So you're with them, eh? The bearded one and the bruiser?"

"That's right. You son of a bitch. And we're not the only ones, so give me your answer." He put a hand on the hilt of his combat knife. If the man didn't agree, he'd use it no matter what Kiara said. This was a security matter. They couldn't afford to risk a captive constantly trying to escape or undermine the mission.

"I agree to your terms," Thorisson said.

He wanted to kill the man anyway. The guy deserved it; all of them did. But Logan's comm unit was back in, and Kiara had probably been listening. He put his knife away and hauled the man to his feet. Maybe a touch rougher than necessary. "Let's see if there's a horse you didn't manage to kill."

There was a contentious debate about where to head next.

"I think we should go after Bradley now," Logan said, out of earshot of Thorisson—he had Mendez watching the prisoner. "It's been almost a month since he pulled a Houdini on us. He's not prepared to last that long on his own."

"I want him back, too," Kiara said. "But we don't even know where to start looking. He could be anywhere between here and Valteron."

"The trail's only going to get colder," Logan said.

"There *is* no trail. We're talking a grid search at best, and that won't be easy while we have to keep an eye on Thorisson."

"I've got a solution for that."

"And as I told you, I want him alive. Too many questions have gone unanswered," Kiara said.

"Good luck getting any answers out of him," Logan said. "I know what it would take, and I doubt the company is willing to go that far. That's all besides the fact, though. If we're right about who took Bradley, his information will be far more valuable."

"As long as we get him back. If magicians do have him, then we're facing an even more difficult problem," Kiara said. "The one we encountered in Valteron had our number pretty quickly."

Logan frowned, remembering his mistake in not taking the slight woman seriously. A moment's hesitation, and she'd sewn him up like a throw pillow. "We'll be ready for that, if we encounter another magician. Their magic can't protect them all the time, from every angle."

"Tell that to Holt."

Ultimately the company executives ended the argument. The moment they learned that Kiara and Logan had captured one of the raiders alive, they sent a new set of orders. Bradley was officially placed on the back burner. Getting Thorisson back to the gateway was priority one.

They put Mendez on Bradley's horse, and Thorisson on the packhorse. That way Logan could keep the reins; the packhorse had followed his mount for most of the journey anyway. Logan bound the prisoner's boots to the stirrups. They'd had to bind his hands in front of him—which Logan wasn't happy about—so that he could hold the high Alissian pommel enough to keep from falling.

Letting Thorisson ride was the backup plan—they'd tried sedating him, but the drug hadn't worked. Either it was a bad batch, or Raptor Tech's team had taken countermeasures before the mission.

My money's on the second explanation.

He'd searched the man for weapons twice, first while he was unconscious and later while the man was hog-tied. He'd confiscated the handgun—now in Mendez's possession—and a SOG tactical folding knife, the kind favored by Special Forces. The second search turned up a small Leatherman tool, another military favorite.

But he still wouldn't put it past the man to have something hidden somewhere. That's why the best policy with any prisoner is diligence.

Kiara took the lead. They'd stashed the MP5s in her and Logan's packs. She wanted swords and crossbows from here all the way back to the gateway. They tied Bradley's bow to the saddle of the packhorse. Logan moved the quiver of arrows to his own horse, but hoped the sight of another ranged weapon might discourage any bandits or militias they'd meet along the way.

Logan and the prisoner were in the middle. Chaudri rode just behind them, with a bolt loaded on the crossbow and express orders to shoot Thorisson if he tried anything. Mendez insisted to Kiara that he was fine, and played the role of the scout. He took quick control of Bradley's mare; they worked well together. He ranged ahead. He checked their backtrail. Somehow he even found time to catch a pair of Alissian rabbits and skin them to roast for dinner.

He did everything but look in Thorisson's direction.

Thorisson clammed up for the next two days. He refused to answer any questions about his mission, or who had sent him. Logan would have applied more persuasive techniques, but there wasn't time.

The updates from Command weren't encouraging. Raptor Tech's drone continued to harass the island facility, disrupting communications and thwarting every attempt to shoot it down.

Mendez appeared over the rise ahead and reined in to wait for them.

"Barometric pressure has been dropping all day between here and Felara," Kiara said. "Eighty percent chance of a storm."

"We should stop soon anyway, to rest the horses," Logan said.

"Agreed," Kiara said. She got another beep on the comm unit, skimmed it, and didn't look happy.

Logan gave Mendez a hand signal. *Shelter.*

Mendez flashed an answer.

"There might be a spot about half a klick ahead," Logan said. "I'd like to scout it first." Landor's capital was on the far side of the country; bandits and highwaymen were the rule in this area.

Kiara glanced up. "Do it," she said.

Logan untied the packhorse's reins from his mount and lashed them to Kiara's instead. Chaudri moved up to cover Thorisson with the crossbow.

"If he gives you any trouble, shoot him," Logan told her. The reminder was more for Thorisson than Chaudri, and he kept his eyes locked on the prisoner's just to make sure he heard him loud and clear.

He joined Mendez and they rode ahead. The wooded hollow wasn't far from the road. They split the perimeter and met on the far side.

"Looks all right," Logan said. The hollow was bowl-shaped, with a rather steep side of hard earth on the western side that might provide some cover from the approaching storm.

"There's a lot of angles to cover, but I figure you still have your dog fence," Mendez said.

"That's a roger."

Logan tapped off his comm unit and signaled for Mendez to do the same. They were both alone for a minute. "How are you holding up, soldier?" he asked.

"Just fine."

He was tough as nails, always had been. But Logan had still been there. "When the mission's over, it'll be rough for a while."

"Trying not to think about it," Mendez said.

"You'll get past it," Logan assured him. "Haven't seen your skills dip at all, which is good. Stay focused for now, and tell me if you have any problems. Understood?"

"Understood, sir."

Logan tapped his comm unit back on. "Don't call me 'sir.' I work for a living!"

Mendez laughed. "Roger that."

"It's all clear, Lieutenant," Logan said over the comm unit. Treetops leaned and sighed in a strong gust of wind. "You'd better make it double-time."

> "We came here thinking the people might dream of the things we take for granted. Peace, democracy, freedom of speech. Instead, most Alissians simply pray for rain."
>
> —R. Holt, "Reevaluating Alissian Assumptions"

CHAPTER 21

PRISON BREAK

Logan and Mendez established a base camp and got to work on the plasma field. The wind picked up; they were having trouble even stretching the netting by the time Kiara and the others arrived. The horses were exhausted and panicky. Kiara and Chaudri fought to secure them with hobbles while Logan and Mendez tied the prisoner to a sapling in the middle of camp.

They barely got the plasma field up before the storm

hit. The wooded hollow offered some protection, but the tempest thrashed against it like a wild animal in a cage. Kiara allowed a small fire; they all more or less collapsed around it. Even Mendez seemed to have run out of steam; he offered to take watch but started nodding off almost right away.

Two hours later, Thorisson made his move.

His hands were bound behind him, but he arched his back enough to reach his boot. The heel twisted off. Hidden inside was a thumb-sized cylinder. The laser torch cut through his flexsteel bindings like they weren't even there. He rose silently. The fire had burned down to embers; the chests of everyone in camp rose and fell slowly. Logan had been snoring for half an hour; he snorted. Thorisson froze in a half crouch. The big man rolled over, and resumed snoring in a steady rattle.

Thorisson began to move again. He paused over the sleeping form of Mendez, as if considering finishing the job his team had started. He moved on, though, stepping noiselessly away from the fire. He didn't go near the horses; there would be no getting one of those loose and away without waking the others. He slipped away toward the trees that were still whipping back and forth in the grip of the wind.

He was two paces from the edge of the plasma field when something tapped him twice on the shoulder. The stock of a loaded crossbow.

"You going somewhere?" Logan asked. He lowered

the crossbow so that the tip of the quarrel pressed into Thorisson's back, right at the kidney.

Thorisson's shoulders drooped. He emitted a string of violet curses, most of them in a language Logan didn't understand.

"Sorry, I don't speak German," he said.

"It's Swedish, you bastard!"

"Ah. Thanks for telling me."

The man's face was a mix of frustration and disbelief. "You were *asleep!*" he hissed.

"Just because I was snoring?" Logan laughed softly. "My sergeant taught us that one, back in basic."

Logan confiscated the laser cutter and searched the prisoner's other boot heel, turning up a small pocketknife. He'd put a static burst out on the comm unit, once Thorisson was in hand. It woke the others. Well, except for Chaudri, whose comm unit had *accidentally* fallen out again. No matter, Logan had given her a gentle nudge with the toe of his boot. They'd bound his wrists and ankles with new flexsteel ties, and set a real watch at night. Mendez or Logan kept a loaded crossbow pointed at him at all times.

"A word, Logan?" Kiara asked. They stepped away from the others while Mendez took prison guard duty.

"How did you know he'd try to get away?"

He shrugged. "Just played a hunch. It's what I'd do."

"You could have told me about it," she said.

"If I had, you wouldn't have slept."

"That's not your call." She'd never admit it, but she was upset at herself for letting the prisoner nearly escape under her command.

"You're right, Lieutenant. Won't happen again."

She gave him a nod; that was that. They returned to the fire. Chaudri, irritable as she was at being roused, had another suggestion. "What about a bell or something?" she asked. "They did that with medieval prisoners sometimes. Tied them up in ribbons and hung bells on them, like they did the fools of royal courts."

"I think we're a little short on ribbons and bells," Logan said.

"I've got an IR beacon," Mendez said. "Seems to me it would serve the same purpose." Every team sent to Alissia carried these, to help locate one another in a crowd, or rendezvous at night in the rough country. It stood to reason that Alissians wouldn't have the technology to see infrared, but Logan wasn't so sure about some of the nocturnal predators. That was part of why they hadn't used theirs yet.

If a wild dog or something got ahold of Thorisson, hey, that was just bad karma.

Of course, the prisoner would damage or toss the IR beacon the first chance he got. If he knew about it. Logan sauntered over to where Thorisson lay hog-tied. "Got anything else you're holding?"

Thorisson didn't answer. Logan searched him anyway, half to check for weapons or tools, and half to attach the IR beacon—a small disc, about the size of a quarter—on his back. He'd be easier to find now, if he slipped away. They couldn't obsess too much more over security. They had bigger problems in front of them.

The Landorian plateau ended not far to the west, with a mountain range that marked the Felaran border.

> "Most stage magicians work
> alone. We have trust issues."
>
> —ART OF ILLUSION, DECEMBER 12

CHAPTER 22

HIDDEN THINGS

Quinn didn't have much to pack. He'd returned his book to the library, and assured Mags that it never left his possession. She glared at him all the while. It was like she could *smell* Moric's fingerprints on the pages. Beyond that, his possessions were meager. He almost wished he had a saddlebag or a suitcase, just to have something to do other than pacing in his chambers.

Then the rose perfume hit him. *Uh-oh.*

Jillaine stood in his doorway, with her hands on her hips. She wore a light, diaphanous dress that was the color of moonlight.

"Hi there," Quinn said. He smiled to cover the nerves. An old stage trick.

"You're leaving."

"Yes. Moric agreed to let me come on the mission."

"To where?"

"No idea. They're not exactly consulting me on this stuff."

"At least you get to go."

"I tried to get him to bring you."

"Did you?"

"Of course." He spread his hands out. "I talked you up as much as I dared to."

"I can guess how that went."

"Yeah." He elected not to tell her about the choice Moric had given him. *I'm in deep enough as it is.*

"How long will you be away?" she asked.

"I don't know, a week?"

She glided into his room and made a survey of it. "So why does it look like you're not coming back?"

He'd packed everything and even tidied up. *I guess it does seem that way. Damn.* He looked at her and just couldn't lie outright. "I'm not sure when I will." *Or if I will.*

He was fairly sure he wanted to, despite the lack of progress, but it really wasn't up to him.

"Don't take too long, or I might not be here," she said.

Two things happened at once: she stood right in front of him, and he discovered he couldn't move. Not even a little finger. "What—"

She stood on her toes and kissed him. A soft, warm, lingering kind of kiss. Her perfume filled his nose.

It was like time stopped. He wanted to put his arms around her more than anything in the world. But he might as well have been made of marble. She pulled away.

No, no, no, no. . .

But he couldn't even speak. She gave him a little smile, turned, and left. It was a good five minutes before he could move again.

He doubted that was by accident.

Moric's security team assembled on a grassy ridge overlooking the Enclave settlement. Quinn hadn't been up here since his involuntary arrival nearly a month ago. So much had happened; it felt like months.

And Jillaine . . . wow. She knew how to tell a man goodbye.

He hadn't made much progress on the magic yet, but he still had one hell of a briefing for the lieutenant. Of course, that assumed she and the others were still alive. And that they'd be able to catch up to her.

Two other magicians rounded out the team. There was Sella, of course. She had her hair wrapped into a tight bun and wore a plain gray cloak; it took a moment for him to recognize her. The other was a young man, slender and pale-haired, who went by the name Leward. Quinn had heard of him; he had a reputation for fire magic. He looked young for a full-fledged magician, a fact he'd tried and failed to address by growing a goatee. A water witch and a fire wizard. Moric sure liked to cover his bases.

Guess that makes me the token impostor.

The bald magician himself appeared a few minutes later, leading four stocky animals that looked suspiciously like mules. "Our clients are mounted, it seems, so we'll need these to keep a close eye on them."

And here Quinn thought he'd gotten away from the horseback riding. But he was the student-trainee, so he bit his tongue and kept quiet. Moric took them higher up the ridge to a wide, round stone. A perfect circle was etched into the stone's surface, as well as other runes in some strange language. The symbols and markers looked unlike anything he'd yet seen in the library. He wondered if the reading glasses would work on them.

"We're headed to a place on the northern edge of the Landorian plateau," Moric said. At his gesture, they all stepped on the stone. In the shuffle, Quinn snuck a photo of some of the symbols with his wrist-camera.

They managed to fit the animals on the stone as well, though doing so involved putting one of their rear ends right up next to Quinn's face. He couldn't think that was by accident, but had no chance to call Moric out. The magician had already started an incantation.

The light was just as blinding as he remembered, and after-images played across Quinn's vision. He felt the cold first; they'd traveled from the island's persistent summer to late autumn in northern Alissia. The air was dry here, and thin. A bleak gray sky stretched overhead. He shook himself and rubbed his arms;

Moric's arcane teleportation disconcerted him. The mules were unaffected by it, though, as were Leward and Sella.

Other than Quinn, then, only Moric was slightly worse for wear; the effort of bringing them all here had exacted its price from him. Quinn guessed he'd need sleep before long.

"Lew, a concealment spell, if you'd be so kind," he said. He must have seen the interest on Quinn's face. "It's a minor enchantment that helps keep us hidden from prying eyes."

"So we'll be invisible?" Quinn asked.

"Not entirely," Sella said. "We'll blend in better to our surroundings, and be harder to pick out from afar. Someone might still spot us, though."

"True invisibility requires a far more powerful bit of magic," Moric said. "I'm sure Leward could do it, but he wouldn't be much use to us afterward."

The young magician had begun an incantation while he walked in a slow circle around the rest of the group.

"It will help him if you remain still," Moric added.

Quinn held his breath. His skin tingled, as if building up static electricity. Lew completed the circle, made a gesture with one arm, and ended his spell. There was a *settling* to it, like a light but unseen cloak wrapping around his shoulders.

"It's done," Leward said. "I, uh, hope it's all right."

"A bit abrupt for my taste, but it will do," Sella said.

His face fell, until Moric said, "Relax, lad. We're a big group."

Quinn couldn't help but feel relief that Sella was as hard on others as she was on him. He held out his arm in front of him. The gray of the cloak darkened to the rich brown of the mud beneath his feet. He lifted the same arm up high, and now it became a lighter gray, almost matching the heavy clouds. "That's spectacular!" he said.

Leward blushed. "Thanks."

"You'll have to teach me that one."

"It's not so difficult, really. Just a matter of—"

Sella cleared her throat. "I'm sure you'd prefer to leave instruction to the Enclave instructors, wouldn't you, Leward? We wouldn't want Quinn losing a foot out of carelessness."

Leward bowed his head. "By all means."

"We need to get moving, in any case," Moric said. "Into your saddles, please." He leaped onto the nearest mule in a manner that almost certainly defied physics. Sella floated up and into her saddle with precise elegance; Leward had scrambled into his own saddle and then looked embarrassed to have not done so with the use of magic. Quinn found the stirrup with one foot and mounted in a single movement, careful not to catch himself on the unusually high pommel. All of that practice with Logan was paying off.

Sella noticed it, too. "You've ridden before, I take it," she said.

"Some," Quinn admitted. He looked around, momentarily puzzled. "Where are the reins?"

"Reins?" Moric laughed. "These are Tioni mules," he said, as if that were enough explanation.

"Well, how do I stop him?"

"You really don't know?"

"No."

Moric grunted, either surprised or disbelieving. "Observe." He put his palm against the side of his mule's neck, and said, "Forward, please."

The mule began plodding forward at a slow pace. After a few steps, Moric touched it again. "Stop, please." The mule came to a halt. Moric looked back at Quinn. "Clear enough?"

Smart mules. Alissia would never cease to amaze him. Quinn laid his palm against his mule's neck. "Forward," he said.

Nothing happened. The others laughed.

"You forget your manners, boy," Sella said. "Try it again. Politely, this time."

Quinn tried it again. "Forward, *please*," he said.

His mule hesitated another second, as if making a point, and then started moving.

"Unbelievable," Quinn said.

Tioni mules never seemed to tire. They'd ridden at a good pace for two hours when Moric made an announcement. "I believe we're at our destination. Our protectees should be along in a day or so."

"Why didn't you just bring us here?" Quinn asked.

Moric shrugged. "I brought us to a place that I knew well, where we might expect to have privacy."

"Transportation magic is not for trifling with," Sella said.

"Do you trust Holt?" Quinn asked.

"As much as I trust any politician," Moric said. "Perhaps more than some. He's given us reason to believe that we share similar interests concerning Alissia."

Quinn wanted to ask what that would be, but didn't dare risk seeming too curious. Like everything on this mission, Holt was a subject for a delicate touch.

"I take it you have a strong opinion of our mutual friend," Moric said.

"I've got an opinion about everyone," Quinn said.

"Even of me?"

"I'd rather not say."

"And Sella?"

"I'd *definitely* rather not say."

"Good lad. You're learning after all."

They dismounted and let the mules graze. Sella did something to create a tiny spring that welled up in the middle of camp. Moric and Leward began working on some joint piece of magic: they stood side by side, arms held out so that their fingers and thumbs formed a circle. This they swept back and forth while speaking the incantation. They were looking for something.

"Got them," Moric said. He spread his arms farther apart; an opaque circle flickered into existence between them.

Now Quinn could see it, so he ambled over for a

look while trying not to appear overeager. It was like looking into a circular window that let out into another place. Same sky, same mountains in the background, but they looked much closer. Five figures in the middle of it drew his eyes. They were all mounted, and moving northward at a steady gallop. He recognized Kiara, Logan, and Chaudri, but the other two men were strangers to him. Was one of them Holt? Probably not, seeing as how the Valteroni Prime had still managed to offer the guild contract. The Latino definitely had a military vibe about him.

There was something familiar about the other guy, but Quinn couldn't place him. He edged closer to the window for a better look. Recognition struck him like lightning.

Thorisson.

The guy from the theater back in Vegas who'd given him the jack of spades. *What the hell is he doing here?* Maybe he'd been with CASE Global after all. The thought turned his insides to ice.

How much did I tell him?

On his third day on the island facility, before they'd come through the gateway, Quinn had reached out with the jack of spades. *I might have overreacted a little.* But he'd just learned that his performance would take place in another world entirely, and Logan had gone to great lengths to explain how likely it was he'd die here.

Thorisson had promised to get him out, but then Kiara moved up the mission timetable and it was too late. Now, here he was.

Leward adjusted the window, centering it right on Thorisson. "This one's got his hands tied together."

Moric harrumphed. "The Prime didn't mention a prisoner."

He's not with CASE Global.

Quinn must have made a sound, because Moric glanced back and noticed him.

"Quinn, something wrong?"

"No," Quinn said quickly. "No, nothing. I've never seen that kind of spell before."

"It's called a scrying. Just a window to a distant place, nothing more."

"How far away are they?"

"Not more than an hour's ride. They're behind schedule; they must have encountered some—" He paused, for Leward had tugged urgently on his shoulder. "What?"

"Look at this," Leward said. "About a league north of them." He enlarged his own scrying window so that they all could see. A group of horsemen rode against the same backdrop of mountains, only they were headed in the other direction. They were armed and armored in burnished plate metal, with banners flying from the tips of their striped lances. It was like something right out of Camelot. They rode two abreast in a long column; there had to be sixteen or eighteen men.

"Who are they?" Quinn asked.

Sella, drawn by the tone of Leward's voice, frowned at him. "Strange that you would not recognize your own countrymen. That's a Landorian patrol."

Whoops. He'd failed to notice the colors on the banners. "We didn't get a lot of patrols in my village," he said.

"Nor do most villages, or so I'm told," Moric said. "They rarely come this far, unless they're after smugglers. Unfortunately, our friends are about to ride right into them."

He let the scrying window fade away and led them to where they'd tethered the Tioni mules. They mounted.

"Stay with me," Moric said. He whispered something to his mule that had it take off at a gallop.

"Follow him, please," Quinn said to his mount. The animal took off running. It was all he could do to hang on.

Magic mules! Logan's never going to believe this.

They crossed one ridge, and then another, heading for the mountains. Less than an hour's ride. How far was that? It couldn't be more than ten miles. Maybe even close enough for the link. *I need to find out what the hell is going on.* He let go of the pommel long enough to tap on his comm unit to listen-only mode.

He gasped. God, he could *hear* them.

"It's been a few days since we saw another traveler," Kiara said. "Are you sure this pass is still open?"

"It should be, unless they got an early avalanche."

"There's not much of a road here."

"Smugglers aren't really known for their road-building skills," Logan said. "Draws too much attention."

"I believe Logan's correct on this point," Chaudri said. "Even Dr. Holt said he could never find smugglers here, if they didn't want to be found."

They were trying for one of the *less official* mountain passes that Logan had used on other missions. Smugglers wouldn't look twice at them or their cargo, as long as you greased them a little. Landor and Felara maintained two main travel routes through the mountains that marked their shared border, but taking either of those would be too risky. They might be searched, and they'd certainly have to answer questions about the prisoner. Landorians prided themselves on doing what was right, what was just. Offering one of their officials a bribe was the surest way to get tossed into a dungeon.

"How long ago did you last come this way?" Kiara asked.

"When we were putting relays on the northern coast," Logan said. "Right before Maggie was born, so it had to be two and a half years ago."

"A lot can happen in that time," Kiara said.

"Oh, I'm sure there's been some turnover. But catching smugglers is like swatting flies in a stable. You think you got them all, and the next day there's even more of them."

"And these stable flies are the people you trust to let us pass through the mountains unmolested?"

"No one said anything about trust. We'll pay well and also let them know we're not to be trifled with."

Mendez came into view, returning at a full gallop. "Heads up," he said over the comm unit. He was breathing hard. "Some kind of mounted patrol ahead. Coming right at you."

"So much for a quiet passage," Kiara said.

Logan ignored that. He made a quick scan of the area. "Not much cover around here."

"If it's a Landorian patrol, we don't want to be caught while trying to hide," Chaudri said.

"We'd never keep the horses quiet anyway," Logan said. "Damn." *We just can't catch a break on this mission.*

"Hands off weapons, but keep them ready," Kiara ordered. "We're just Felarans returning home."

Logan eased his mount closer to Thorisson. "I'll have a crossbow ready to shoot you. Don't try anything."

Thorisson glanced at the crossbow, then at Logan. He said nothing, which was worrisome.

Mendez reached them and fell into line beside Logan, so that both of them could keep an eye on the prisoner. A cloud of dust and a thundering of hooves marked the approach of the Landorian patrol. They spotted Kiara's group and lowered their lances, peeling away smoothly into two lines that quickly encircled them. Logan had to admire the clean execution of the maneuver; this was something the patrol had clearly done before.

The riders halted at the same time. Everyone had a lance lowered at them, a spare lashed to the saddle, and a sword at his belt. No crossbows, though, which was curious. Their mounts were warhorses; the large, powerful animals were good for charges but not distance.

One man rode forward and lifted the visor on his helmet; the red-and-white crest on his shoulder marked him as an officer. "State your business in Landor," he said.

Kiara didn't have a chance to speak, because Chaudri—of all people—decided to call an audible.

"State your business in asking, sir," she said. "Who are you to challenge us?"

The officer hesitated. "Fair enough." He removed his helmet, revealing a shock of red hair. He even had the mustache and beard to match. "Staff Sergeant Rupert of the Landorian Royal Corps."

"Lieutenant—" Logan said under his breath.

"Let her roll with it," she muttered back.

Not that he had much of a choice—Chaudri was already in full swing. "Thank you, Staff Sergeant. And I appreciate what you and your men are doing to keep the border safe. You needn't worry about us, however. We're Felarans and on our way home."

"Why not the southern pass?"

"Selfish reasons, really," Chaudri replied. "Eastern Felara is bleak this time of year, but the Landorian forests are truly breathtaking. At least, that's what my husband's favorite aunt used to say, and I'd never hear the end of it if I took the easier route home and missed Landor's finest colors."

The sergeant nodded. "I can understand that," he said. He signaled his men, who raised their lances, but still kept them neatly encircled. "You don't have the look of smugglers, but we've been having problems in this area. Will you consent to a search?"

Logan tensed. A lot of the gear might pass inspection, thanks to the company techs, but the MP5s would almost certainly raise questions. And they definitely couldn't afford to have them confiscated. Yet he was at a loss at how to stop them.

But Chaudri wasn't.

"I'm sure you and your men have more important things to do," Chaudri said. "Perhaps it would be more expedient to provide you a list of our belongings. My secretary keeps one at hand." She gestured vaguely at Kiara.

The lieutenant's eyes widened slightly, and she bit her lip. Logan did, too, but mostly so he wouldn't laugh.

Hell—she said to let Chaudri roll with it.

Kiara removed the parchment from the satchel behind her saddle and handed it to the staff sergeant. The list itself was innocuous; the company linguists prepared a number of such documents for encounters like these. The officer squinted at it. His eyes didn't move across the words, though—he probably couldn't read. It made sense: with the polyglossia, speech made for far easier communication.

And it would be embarrassing for a leader to admit such a deficiency, even if it was fairly common in Alissia.

"I don't see anything of concern," the staff sergeant said.

How could he?

"We'd just as soon be on our way, then," Chaudri said. "I'd like to cover some ground before sunset."

"Very well," the staff sergeant said. He put his helmet back on and signaled to his men. They spurred their mounts and began moving, forming up into two columns once more.

Logan's horse shied at the sound and movement, spinning him half around.

Thorisson saw his chance and took it.

He kicked hard at the side of his horse. The already-frightened animal leaped forward through the widening gap in the line of patrol horses. Logan put a hand to the hilt of his crossbow, but hesitated. He didn't have a clear shot, and one of the patrolmen was likely to skewer him if he raised a weapon.

Mendez managed to nudge his horse clear and went after him. Kiara and Chaudri broke away as well.

"What's happening?" the staff sergeant demanded.

"His horse must have spooked," Logan said.

"His hands were bound. Were you holding him *captive?*"

Logan sawed the reins around so that his mount spun in a half circle. A gap appeared in the cavalry line riding past. "Beg your pardon, Staff Sergeant." He kicked hard and his mount shot forward.

I'll let Chaudri explain that one.

Moric had slowed them to a walk, and now signaled a halt. He dismounted. Quinn did the same, and ran up just as the magician cast his scrying window. He could barely see them beyond the line of surrounding horsemen.

"Where are they?" he asked.

"Just over the next ridge," Moric said.

"Shouldn't we do something?"

"Hush, child!" Sella said. "Intervening now would only get them killed."

He watched as Chaudri did most of the talking; she gestured at Kiara, who handed over some kind of parchment.

"Good, good," Moric said. "Give them a good story, back it up with some papers."

Quinn heard Chaudri doing just that. Gods, but it was good to see her again. She certainly looked convincing. Nothing but confidence on her face. The red-headed officer seemed to be buying it, too.

"Look there," Leward said. "The prisoner is up to something."

Quinn realized he was talking about Thorisson. *Oh, no.*

It looked like the patrol was moving on, but then Thorisson ruined it. He broke away from the group and rode off. Chaos ensued; Kiara and others rode hard after him. The red-haired Felaran officer took command of his patrol again and sent them off in pursuit. They were all riding west, toward the mountains.

"*Now* we can intervene," Moric said. He turned to the two magicians. "Keep it subtle, please. Better not to reveal our involvement."

"Better not to have been involved in the first place," Sella said. She strode off in the direction of the pounding hooves. Leward followed at her heels. Quinn lost sight of them almost immediately; the concealment spell seemed to be working.

"What should I do?" he asked.

"Watch, and stay quiet," Moric said. "I need to concentrate."

Logan ducked under another tree branch, trying to keep Thorisson in view. He swerved left around a dead pine; the Landorian soldiers riding hard behind him didn't see it in time. They crashed heavily into the pine and rolled. Another close call. By rights he should have been captured a dozen times over. Another rider turned up on his six almost immediately. There was no end to the expert horsemen, and he was on *their* turf.

At least the trees are close enough that they can't use their lances.

They had been so close to getting away from the patrol and into Felara. Damn Thorisson for screwing it up. If Logan got the chance to shoot him, he would.

And then he'd probably do it again, just for the hell of it.

Unfortunately, the man seemed to know it. All of that awkward riding and tugging the reins had been for show. He rode perfectly well now that his life depended on it, even with his wrists bound. Was that by chance, or had whoever sent him already known what to expect through the gateway? If he got away, they might never know.

Kiara was somewhere to his left, and Chaudri with her. They were trying more to elude the Landorian patrol than anything. *I guess they didn't even try to talk their way out of it.*

He felt a little bad about just taking off, but he'd be little use to them if he were captured by the Landorians. And Thorisson was now the key to this mission, so letting him escape wasn't an option. Even if it meant leaving Chaudri and the lieutenant in Landorian hands.

Still, that thought tore him up inside.

He cleared his head of regret—*time for that later.* With a quick glance over his shoulder to see where his pursuers were, he focused his attention ahead of him once more.

"Mendez, where are you?" he asked.

"On your three. But I've got a couple of these King Arthur types on my tail."

A crashing noise came from somewhere to Logan's right. A horse screamed.

Hope that wasn't him. "Mendez!"

"Make that one on my tail," he answered.

Thorisson cut right; he'd found a trail heading downhill.

"Bearing right!" Logan said. His mount stumbled over a hidden log, but kept its footing. Another stroke of luck. He pounded on down the trail. There was a creek ahead, swollen nearly to the banks with groundwater from the recent storms. Thorisson plunged into it. The water nearly reached the stirrups. He gained the far bank just as Logan's mare hit the water. Thorisson leaned low against his horse's neck; Logan could have shot the packhorse, but couldn't bring himself to kill it just to recapture the prisoner. He had other problems, too. Muddy water swirled over his boots, halfway up his mount's back. It was rising.

"Watch the creek," Logan told the others. Almost instantly, the water picked up speed, gurgling and swirling around him. *That doesn't seem right.* His horse gained the far side and clambered up. He tugged back on the reins to watch the others cross.

"Keep moving, people," he said. "The water's rising."

"Don't wait for us," Kiara said.

He pretended not to hear. *I abandoned them with the Landorians. I'm not leaving them again.*

Mendez splashed in next. The women were right behind him, but the water was twice as deep now. Twice as fast, too. Kiara's mount balked at the edge and nearly threw her. Chaudri's mare crashed into hers. Both stumbled down into the churning waters.

Shit. Logan jumped out of the saddle and waded in, keeping hold of his reins. Mendez tried to turn back to help, and then *his* mount was slipping.

"Go, go!" Logan shouted. He skirted them and made a grab for Kiara's bridle. Never had cold, wet leather felt so good. "Easy, girl. Easy." He braced himself with his own reins and started backing out. The lieutenant had kept her saddle, and managed to grab hold of Chaudri's mount. Logan was almost to the bank, but the water surged around him. He slipped and would have gone down, but an arm slipped under his shoulder and held him up.

"Gotcha!" Mendez said.

Shouts came from the woods behind; the Landorian patrol had spotted them. There came a rumbling sound from somewhere upstream, too, and it sounded ominous. A wall of churning, muddy water swept around the bend upstream.

"Move!" Mendez shouted. He tugged at the bridle of Chaudri's mare and half dragged them up the bank.

Logan did the same with Kiara's, but the bank was slick with mud. He couldn't get purchase. Then the muddy wave was on them. It swept over the back of the mare, nearly took the lieutenant out of her saddle. She shouted and spurred her mount, hard. Somehow the mare found a grip and surged out, dragging Logan with them.

He dropped the bridle and threw himself back on his own horse. They clattered away as the water surged up over the banks. Four Landorian horsemen appeared on the far side and had to wheel their horses to the side to avoid riding in. That was some good horsemanship. Timber and detritus rushed past in the heavy current. There was no crossing now, and the Landorians knew it. That was one problem solved.

"Time to get our prisoner back," Logan said. "Mendez, with me."

They thundered over the ridge . . . only to find Thorisson right on the other side. He'd ridden right into the drooping branches of a large tree and gotten stuck. The more he struggled, the more the branches clung to him and the packhorse. He was tangled up and cursing mightily. The sight of it made Logan laugh. Thorisson continued to thrash until Logan and Mendez were nearly on top of him. He heard them approach, but couldn't quite turn around for a look.

"Hello again," Logan said.

Thorisson's whole body seemed to slump; though the branches held him mostly upright. The packhorse whinnied in dismay.

"Nice of him to wait for us," Mendez said.

"Wasn't it?"

Kiara and Chaudri rode up next; their horses were still soaked from the creek crossing.

"Wow, a sticky willow!" Chaudri said. "Always wanted to see one of these. From a safe distance, obviously."

It resembled a weeping willow, except that the leaves and whip-like branches were a dusty brown color. They were coated with tiny hooks, almost like Velcro. And they latched on to *anything*—clothing, leather, skin, hair. The limbs were deceptively strong, so even though it was always tempting to try to jerk free, doing so only caused more branches to come down on top of you.

As Thorisson had discovered.

"What do you think, Lieutenant?" Logan asked. "Can we leave him?"

"He *did* cause me to ruin my favorite riding boots," Kiara said. She turned her horse. "Let's go."

Logan and Mendez went to follow. They hadn't gone twenty yards before Thorisson started shouting.

"Don't leave me here!" he cried.

Kiara sighed and reined in. "I suppose I want the packhorse back, at least. We might as well get him out, too."

"How the hell do we do that?" Mendez muttered.

"We'll have to cut the branches," Chaudri said. "As high up as we can reach."

The rescue took the better part of an hour. Logan and Mendez worked methodically under Chaudri's direction, cutting branches and handing them back to the others. Kiara and Chaudri stacked them well away from the tree and the other horses. Eventually they extracted both the horse and rider. Mendez held a crossbow at him while the others removed every twig and leaf that still clung to him or the packhorse. It was tiresome work, but they had to be certain no bits of sticky willow tagged along. Otherwise, the gateway's biological scanners would lock them in Alissia until they were clean. Granted, the company had brought a couple of leaves through for study.

They'd already spawned a new generation of industrial adhesives, the patent revenues for which had underwritten the last few missions in Alissia.

Kiara had them under way soon after, just in case the Landorian patrol had found a way around. Thorisson's escape attempt had brought them right to the base of the mountains. They made camp after a few hours. Tomorrow they'd try to cross via the smuggler's pass.

For a considerable bribe, Landorian smugglers would guide you through narrow mountain passes into Felara. Logan had dealt with them before, but never with a group this large, or a prisoner in tow.

He had told the lieutenant that it would be a piece of cake.

Maybe it actually will be.

> **"Honor among thieves is a romantic notion, one that criminals here have yet to stumble across."**
>
> —R. HOLT, "MY TIME WITH TIONI CUTPURSES"

CHAPTER 23

THE SMUGGLER CODE

By sunset, Moric and the other two magicians were exhausted. Keeping Kiara's team on their horses while they fled, leading them to the cutoff point, and flooding the creek had taken a lot out of them. Moric had retrieved their Tioni mules; that was about all he could manage. Leward had been dozing off while they waited. Sella put her customary wards around their campsite, but even she looked a bit drowsy.

All three would need to sleep soon, and probably for a good day or two. Even so, they monitored the progress of Kiara's group while they rode toward the mountains.

Moric made an unpleasant sound.

"What's wrong?" Quinn asked.

"I thought perhaps they'd take one of the main passes, at which point we'd have some assurance of their safety."

"Maybe they're lost," Quinn said, though he knew that they weren't. The creek crossing seemed to have put the comm units on a bender, but from the bits and pieces he'd picked up, Kiara had a destination in mind. He couldn't share that with Moric, of course.

"They're probably aiming for a smuggler's route through the mountains," Moric said. "It's a quieter way to slip into Felara. Lower profile, which some find appealing."

Low profile. That had to be Logan's idea.

"How far is it from here to the smuggler's pass?" he asked.

"A few hours' ride, no more, if memory serves," Moric said. He yawned and reclined on the grass.

He could probably catch them. Maybe in time to warn them about the danger the smugglers had to offer. Once Kiara got through the gateway, who knew what kind of draconian measures she'd put in place? With Holt in a position of power, she might think it safer to seal the gateway from the other side. No telling how long he could be stuck here. Or what Thorisson might say about him.

Then again, if he went back with them, they might never let him return. *And then I'll never know if I could have learned the magic here.*

"How long will you need to sleep?" he asked.

"At least a full day," Moric said. "I hate to let the Prime down, but we've done all that we can for his friends."

Holt had hired the Enclave to make sure they ended up as far away from Valteron as possible. They were no friends of his. But they'd become something like that for Quinn.

"Let me fulfill the contract," he said.

Sella perked up. "Absolutely not. You're only here to observe. Nothing more."

Damn. He'd thought her asleep already.

"Look, we all know I'm not an ordinary student," Quinn said. "And Moric's in enough trouble with the council. How is a botched job going to look to them?"

"Not well," Moric admitted. "But I'm not sure what you think you can do to help them."

"I can make sure they reach Felara."

"What if there's a problem?" Moric asked.

"I'm a grown man, and I can be resourceful."

Sella shook her head. "This is too dangerous for him."

"And this coming from someone who recently threw me off a waterfall," Quinn said.

"There were safeguards for that," Sella countered. "And I didn't throw you. You fell on your own, probably because you were distracted by that—"

"All right, all right, I fell," Quinn said quickly. No need to bring up *that* subject. "But it didn't work. Nothing has worked. Maybe it takes more to bring the ability out in me."

"Maybe you're not trying hard enough," she said.

"I appreciate everything you've tried to do, Sella," he said. He smiled at her. An earnest smile this time. "But I need more. I think we both know that."

She frowned, as if mulling this over. Leward had closed his eyes and now began to snore.

"Overextended himself again, I'll wager," Moric said. "That leaves just the two of us to decide, and I vote against it. You're too valuable to risk on a contract job. The Prime will understand."

"Well I vote *for* it," Quinn said.

"You don't get a vote," Moric said.

"Why not? I'm part of this mission, too."

He sighed. "Fine. One for, one against."

Sella looked at Quinn for a long time, her face unreadable. "I'm in favor," she said at last.

"Sella!" Moric said.

"The boy wants it bad enough, I'll grant him that. Never thought he'd stick it out in my class in the first place. Let him try playing the hero." She closed her eyes again, and muttered to herself. "If the black hearts of smugglers can't bring a spark out of him, nothing will."

Moric glared at her, but gave over. "Very well, Quinn," he said. "Follow them to Felara. The concealment spell should hold that long. But I don't want you taking any foolish risks. The moment they set foot on Felaran soil, your job is done."

One of his jobs was done, at least. Quinn buckled on his sword and threw his riding cloak over his shoulders. "How will I find you again?" he asked.

"We should be here at least another day. I'll set some wards to protect us, but you'll be able to cross them."

"What if it takes longer?"

"Try not to let that happen."

"It might," Quinn said. "And I don't think I can just wander around asking the way to the Enclave."

Moric yawned. "A fair point. Come over here, lad," he said.

Quinn went and knelt by him. Sella had fallen asleep and began snoring at an ear-shattering volume.

Moric took a leather cord from around his neck. It held a pale white stone, teardrop-shaped and wrapped in wire. "Don't lose this," he said.

Quinn took it, surprised at how light the stone was. "What is it?"

"A wayfinder stone. It points the way to the Enclave."

Quinn put the cord around his neck, and lifted the stone in the palm of his hand. The teardrop quivered and spun, pointing southwest. "Outstanding," he said.

"I get the feeling that you have other business besides our mission," Moric said.

Quinn kept his face neutral, but didn't answer.

Moric stifled another yawn. "Don't stay away too long. I'm not finished with your training."

"Don't worry, Moric," Quinn said. "Neither am I."

There was no formal marking to the smuggler's pass—they certainly didn't want to make it easier for outsiders to find them—but Logan could read the signs. A wagon rut here, some broken reeds there. Rocks arranged a certain way along an embankment to prevent cart wheels from going over the edge. Movement along a ridge to the south only confirmed it; someone was watching them.

They encountered the first checkpoint a quarter mile later. Two men lounged against a boulder, spears propped casually beside them. They wore steel discs over boiled leather. A heavy form of armor, but it came cheap. Neither had shaven in some time, and their hair was matted under dented steel helms.

"Sentries," Logan said over the comm unit.

"They don't look like much," Mendez said. "Should we take them out?"

"Do that and they'll cut us down from the cliffs," Logan said. "I'm sure they have a bowman up there."

"We should try not to pay very heavily at the first touch," Kiara said.

Logan leaned close to Thorisson. "Don't try anything. You'll never get out of these passes without us."

Thorisson shrugged. Not promising anything. Logan was pretty sure he must have something up his sleeve, but couldn't figure out what.

The smuggler's pass comprised a series of narrow trails that wound through gaps in the mountains. There would be more seemingly random encounters, more checkpoints. Logan didn't recognize these two men, and that worried him. They had a bottle of dark stuff with them, probably *jennah*. Maybe they were drunk. That would help.

"Think you must have lost your way, m'lady," one of them called.

"We're headed to Felara," Kiara said.

"Better try one of the passes."

"We'd prefer to get there quietly," she said. "We'll make it worth your while."

The man looked them over, rubbing his beard the whole time. He had the most crooked set of teeth Logan had ever seen on a man. It was hard not to stare. "We might know a quiet way through. Going to cost you, though."

"How much?" Kiara asked.

"Fifteen silvers."

She scoffed at him. "Three coppers."

"Th-three coppers?" he stuttered. He burst into a raucous laugh, elbowing his companion. "She thinks she'll get by with three coppers!"

The other man leaned closer and whispered something.

Snaggletooth grinned wickedly. "What about three coppers, and you do a little something for us? Private, like."

"How about I ask my men not to put a quarrel in each of you?"

The moment she said it, Logan and Mendez raised crossbows, leveling them at the men's chests. At this range, the bolts would cut through the steel and leather like it was plastic. Each of the sentries took a step back, their hands involuntarily reaching for their spears.

"Don't do it," Logan said.

The one who'd spoken put up his hands. He didn't look happy, but he held fast. "Five coppers," he ventured.

"Four coppers," Kiara said. "And only because you have the balls to negotiate with a crossbow on you." She took out a small purse and tossed it to him.

The man caught it, shook it, and stood back so that they had room to ride past. "Right this way, m'lady."

Logan cleared his throat. He wasn't about to let her be the first one to go by these jokers. He nudged his mount past her and trotted ahead to scout. These passes were going to be a tactical nightmare. Narrow trails, blind turns, and gods knew how many smugglers lurking about. The thought of it made his back itch between the shoulder blades. There wasn't an immediate trap here, as far as he could see, though, so he turned and gave the signal for all clear.

One checkpoint down, probably eight or nine to go.

Quinn spotted the two men with spears, and asked his mule to slow. Politely, of course.

They were leaning against a boulder sharing a bottle. They noticed him approaching and put their helms back on. At least they left the spears leaning against the boulder; a lone rider on a mule wasn't much of a threat. *Good, let them think that.* The one had some trouble getting his helmet on. He straightened it with the exaggerated care of a man trying to hide just how drunk he was.

Even better.

Quinn put on his grin and hailed them. "Here's just the two fellows I've been looking for."

The more sober of the two sauntered out from the boulder. "Think you must be lost, fella." He slurred some of the words. Whether it was from the drink or the horrific set of teeth, Quinn couldn't say.

He bowed his head from the saddle. "I don't think so, my good man. I'm trying to catch up with some friends. Did they come this way?"

"Can't say I remember."

"Here, perhaps this will help," Quinn said. He snapped his fingers and held up a fat round coin—he'd lifted Moric's purse before he left. The coin danced across Quinn's fingers. Then he flicked it toward the smuggler. It arced through the air, spinning with that high-pitched ring of metal.

The man caught it in one hand without dropping the bottle. Maybe he was a little more sober than he appeared. He bit the coin between his teeth, then tossed it to the other one, who managed to trip over his spear while trying to catch it. Quinn pretended not to notice.

The sober one shook his head. He looked back at Quinn and crossed his arms. "Might be some folks came through. What's it to you?"

"I'm trying to catch up with them. Can I pass?"

"Sure, for five coppers."

Quinn did a quick calculation, figuring on a few more stops like these. No doubt they'd get more expensive, too. "Tell you what," he said. "How about a little wager? You look like the gambling type."

The man straightened. Apparently he took it as a compliment. "I've been known to make a bet or two. What's the wager?"

Quinn dismounted from his mule and asked it to stay put. "Could I borrow that bottle?" he asked.

The man frowned. "Fine." He took a last pull and tossed the bottle to Quinn. It was a crude glass, but somewhat transparent. The opening was about as wide as his thumb. That would work.

"I've got another copper here," Quinn said. He produced the coin from his sleeve and let it dance across his fingers. "Bet you I can get it into this bottle without breaking it."

"In there? Good luck."

"If I do, you get the bottle back with one copper. If I don't, I'll pay the full five."

The man pondered this a moment, and spat to one side. "If you don't, you pay eight."

"Deal," Quinn said. He hefted the bottle. "What was in here, anyway?"

"Valteroni gold."

He sniffed the lid; it smelled of stronger, coarser stuff. "If you say so."

He laid the coin across the top of it. "Hmm. Doesn't want to fit."

"You don't say," the smuggler said.

Quinn laid his palm across the coin and held it there while he put the bottom of the bottle against his chest. He made a fist with his free hand.

"No breaking it, now," the man said.

"No worries," Quinn said. He pounded his fist against the hand across the bottle. A coin shot into the bottle and rattled around the bottom. "There we are." He tossed the bottle back to the man.

He looked down the opening and shook it, as if to make sure. "Have a look at this, Bert!"

Quinn had his mule's reins and led the animal forward. The drunker one grabbed the bottle and shook it hard, trying to get the coin out.

"Stop, you'll break it!" his companion hissed.

Quinn slid the mule past them. "No breaking it, now," he said.

They were still arguing when he mounted. The boulder was nearly out of view when he heard the tinkle of shattering glass. He chuckled to himself. *Every time.*

Eleven checkpoints later, they were deep into the mountain range. Kiara's purse was getting a bit light. Logan had yet to find a smuggler that he'd met while passing through here two years ago; a friendly face might have gotten them by for cheaper. Every man was new, and none of them were interested in making friends with outsiders.

Mendez rode back from taking a look ahead; his

face was grim. "It gets really narrow up there, almost like a canyon. I saw movement on the cliffs above, too. We should expect some kind of a welcoming committee."

"How much do we have left?" Logan asked Kiara.

She hefted the last of her purses; it clinked with metal and a few synthetic jewels. "It might be enough, so long as this is the last checkpoint."

"No turning back now," Logan said. "You pay in both directions, like a toll road."

"I'm in the wrong business," Chaudri said.

"It's not usually this exorbitant," Logan said. "I've come through with entire cartloads of—"

Kiara gave him a sharp look; he caught himself. "Things," he finished. "Something's obviously changed."

They took it slow approaching the canyon. Logan wished there were another way to go. He could feel eyes on them. There should be another checkpoint around here, but they saw no one.

"What do you think?" Kiara asked.

"You know what I think, Lieutenant," Logan said.

"Let's keep our wits about us," she said.

Logan led them to the mouth of the canyon.

"Here we go," he said. He didn't like that it was so narrow; they had to ride single file. Once more he took the lead, Kiara at his back, then the packhorses, the prisoner, and Chaudri. Mendez had the rear. Pebbles clattered down the canyon wall, once on each side. Smugglers on the high ground.

They got about fifty yards into the canyon before the archers appeared. A grating noise came from behind them. Then a deafening crash.

With all of the horses behind them, Logan couldn't see more than a cloud of dust. "What was that?"

"They've dropped a wagon or something behind us," Chaudri shouted. "Nearly fell on my head!"

Clever. They were boxed in, with only one way to go. It might be a scare tactic, or it might be something worse. The archers were a nice touch. Shooting from an elevated position at a long line of riders, they almost couldn't miss. They could cut down half of Logan's team in seconds. They wouldn't need more than five or six men to pull it off, either. Two to throw the wagon, two with the bows. Another to negotiate.

Right on cue, another man appeared, this one bearded and not wearing a helmet. "Hello down there," he said.

"Have you lost a wagon?" Kiara called.

The man grinned, revealing a mouth without teeth. "Just wanted to get your attention."

"Well, you have it. What do you want?"

"The cost of passage."

"What would that be?"

The man looked them over for a few moments, and conferred with someone they couldn't see. "Thirty silvers," he said. An outrageous sum, even for this.

"A little steep, don't you think?" Kiara asked.

"Hey, it's the end of the season," he said. "And you almost brought the Landorians to our door."

"I'll give you half of that," Kiara said. The archers nocked arrows; she ignored them. She gave Logan a hand signal. *Take cover.*

He eased his mount forward a bit, trying to keep the attention of one of the archers. There had to be a way to get up to that higher position, but he might have to ride a long way to find it. And with at least one bowman trying to shoot him from above.

The negotiator had disappeared; some kind of discussion was taking place. He came back into view. "Show us the money," he said.

Kiara hesitated, then lifted the purse and let some of it spill out into her hand. They'd already burned through the gold and gems; only silver and copper coins remained. A decent sum, but she'd been right. It would be about half of their ask.

"Satisfied?" she asked. She dumped it back into the purse and tied the string.

"Throw it here, m'lady."

Logan gave her the tiniest shake of the head. She should push back on that.

"It'll be yours the moment we're out of this canyon," Kiara said.

"It's already ours. Toss it up."

"No." Kiara nudged her mare forward.

The negotiator made a sign to his archers. They bent their bows.

"Keep moving," Logan whispered. "Spread out a little."

His mare shook her head; she wanted to move

faster. Logan held fast to keep her at a walk; bolting now wouldn't help. Gravel slid down the sides of the canyon. The archers hadn't fully drawn, but they were shadowing him. He came to a hard turn, a natural choke point. The perfect spot to pin them down. The negotiator kept watching them, clearly uneasy. Kiara's refusal to pay had disrupted some plan.

"All right, that's far enough!" he shouted.

They ignored him and kept riding. Then he made a fist and pulled it down, a signal that Logan recognized. Every branch of military Earth-side used that one. The meaning was clear.

Execute.

"Down!" he shouted.

Bows thrummed from above. One arrow shattered on the rocks above Kiara. Another one clipped Logan's shoulder, but glanced off the alusteel.

"Go, go!" Mendez shouted. He and Chaudri were bottled up at the back.

Five seconds until the archers could fire again.

Logan dug his heels into the Arabian mare.

Four...

Three...

Two...

One!

He dropped to the side of his mount. An arrow shot past his ear. Hooves thundered behind him; the others were riding hard. How long was this damn canyon? He should have seen this coming. Should have known from the way they set up over the canyon with archers.

He leaned into the next turn. His shoulder scraped against stone. It was getting narrower.

"Getting tight up here," he said. Much more and his horse wouldn't be able to squeeze through. Then they were all dead for certain.

"Don't stop now!" Chaudri shouted.

Open sky ahead. They were nearly out of the canyon. Just a little bit farther.

He'd forgotten to count. An arrow slammed into his back. It threw him forward against the mare's neck. Hurt like hell, but without the armor he'd have been dead. Someone grunted behind him, another hit for the archers. Logan hoped it wasn't Thorisson. A corpse wouldn't tell them anything.

I won't be torn up if it is, though.

There was no time to look back. Logan charged forward. The negotiator poked his head over the rim. His eyes widened when he saw Logan still mounted. And raising his crossbow. He ducked away; Logan's shot went wide. One of the bowmen returned fire; the arrow whistled past Logan's face.

Jesus!

"Shoot the horses!" a smuggler shouted.

Damn. The horses weren't armored, and they couldn't afford to lose a mount now.

Four. . .

Three. . .

Two. . .

Flame spouted over the top of the canyon. One of the archers fell screaming, his arms aflame. His body slammed into the canyon's floor. Logan's mare jumped over the body. The air smelled of charred flesh. A hooded figure leaped across overhead. The tail of his cloak was on fire.

"Did you see that?" Logan shouted.

"It was a little hard to miss," Chaudri shouted back.

Quinn was out of coins. Even with all the charm and street magic he could muster, this smuggler's pass had emptied his purse with some efficiency. He'd taken to avoiding the checkpoints that he could. The Tioni mule handled uneven terrain well; a few times they managed to climb a rocky slope or slip quietly up a dry creek to get around a few of the less ambitious gate-keepers.

He'd been coming back from one such workaround when he finally caught up to his companions. They were a few hundred feet below, in the bottom of a canyon. Five smugglers stood along the rim in between him and them. They were about a hundred yards below him, down a nasty slope of loose rock and gravel. Two of them had bows. He heard one of them demanding money. Thirty silvers. *God, I hope they have it.*

If the negotiations went sour, Logan and Kiara and the others would be like fish in a barrel.

He stashed his mule in a secluded spot and hurried down the incline. Tried not to dislodge any more gravel than necessary. He picked up snippets of the conversation over the comm unit. The demand for money. Kiara's refusal. Logan and another man shouting. Then they started shooting.

Damn it.

He was fifty yards away now, close enough that they'd hear him if he was careless. He checked to be sure his sword was loose in the scabbard. He crouched low as he moved. The moss-covered stone gave a good, quiet grip. In another minute he was level with the smugglers and running hard.

The nearest bowman had nocked an arrow; he went to draw. Quinn raised an arm when he ran and made a throwing motion. A fireball streaked from his palm. It expanded as it flew, enveloped the archer as he drew again. *God, the gel-fuel is really something.* The man was on fire instantly. He screamed something terrible, took a step, and fell into the canyon.

Two swordsmen were running for the far end of the canyon. Out of reach. The other bowman was the real threat. He was closer, but on the far side of the canyon. Quinn tried to lob another fireball, but the elemental projector was out of juice. It sputtered just enough to catch his own cloak on fire.

Perfect. He kept running.

How far across is that gap? It couldn't be more than five yards. He probably shouldn't think about it too long, so he ran and jumped. His boots caught the rim. He tumbled over, hit the ground hard. The bowman started to turn. *Why didn't I draw my sword first? Damn.* He tried pulling it loose. The man had an arrow nocked. He turned and drew in a single movement.

Quinn fumbled the projector controls but shot a jet of air . . . which is what he wanted. He aimed low. Dirt and pebbles flew up into the archer's face, blinding him. His arrow flew over Quinn's shoulder.

Quinn's sword rasped out of the scabbard. The bowman clearly heard it, as he tried to bring up his longbow to block a downward slash. But Quinn used the sword like a crossbar instead, and shoved the man as hard as he could. He tumbled over the edge.

The other two were nearly to the mouth of the canyon. Quinn ran after them. He closed on one of them, the man who'd been doing the negotiations. They must have taken a lot out of him, because he'd slowed to a walk and was huffing like an asthmatic.

Quinn forced himself to slow. He stilled his breathing and slipped forward, stalking quietly up behind him. Thought he could do it, which is why he wasn't ready when the man suddenly turned and lashed out with his sword. Quinn backpedaled and scrambled back. He barely kept hold of his own blade.

"Going to hit a man in the back?" the smuggler snarled. He had no front teeth, and spoke with a kind of hiss. "Only a fool attacks downwind."

Quinn scrabbled away across the rocks and regained his feet. The man came at him. Logan's warning kept flashing through his mind: *a twelve-year-old with a sword could gut him like a pig in a fair fight.*

This was definitely not a twelve-year-old.

The man jumped forward and slashed at him. Quinn knocked the blow aside, racking his brain for a way to tip the odds in his favor. No magic, no prep, and no plan.

I'm in trouble.

At least this one wasn't as strong as Logan. During all their practice sessions, the man had pounded on him relentlessly. It wasn't just how good he was, but how devastating the blows felt even when Quinn was able to block them. The smuggler seemed less threatening by comparison.

Still, Quinn danced back from his next cut; dodging was easier than parrying—another bit of Logan's wisdom. Then he attacked, though not as fast as he could. No need to give away the sword's advantage just yet. The man parried easily. His counterattack nearly took Quinn's arm off at the shoulder, were it not for the hidden armor.

His arms were starting to feel leaden. And no matter what, he was definitely outmatched. He had to finish this.

He made another slow attack. The smuggler blocked it with contempt, and attacked again. He got a piece of Quinn's side, this time. Hurt like hell, but didn't cut him.

Thank God for alusteel.

Quinn made another attack, the same overhand slash he'd done two times before. The smuggler snickered as he went to block. But Quinn spun it and made a low side-hand slash instead. Both hands, swinging as hard and fast as he could at the knees. The sword shuddered as his blade cut through sinew and bone.

The man cried out and went down, his leg fountaining blood.

Quinn didn't linger to see if he died.

Logan didn't know what had happened to the archers . . . and he didn't really care. All that mattered at the moment was escaping this death trap of a canyon. The lieutenant was nearly caught up to him; behind her came Thorisson—still alive, it seemed—Chaudri, and then Mendez. Thirty yards to the mouth of the canyon. Twenty yards. He pulled gently back on the reins, slowing the mare to a trot. He wouldn't put it past the smugglers to have a few men out here, to mop up anyone who made it through.

He drew his sword, and signaled for the others to do likewise. The hilt felt good in his hands. He wouldn't mind having the crossbow as well. But it was tough to crank from horseback, making it the wrong weapon now. That was a point he'd have to make to the engineers—if they got out of this mess alive. At the mouth of the canyon he spurred his horse so that he came out at a good clip. A harsh landscape greeted the end of the canyon: boulders and piles of dead trees that could hide dozens of enemies. He checked back over his shoulder for movement on the cliffs above the canyon's mouth. Nothing there, but that didn't mean they were clear.

And there was still the matter of a man catching on fire with no explanation. It was helpful, surely, but there was no proof it was *meant* to help them. *Wish I knew what that was about.*

Kiara rode out, her saber at the ready. Thorisson was right on her six. For once, the infuriating calm was gone from his face. He looked haggard. Going through that with your hands bound would have been no picnic. Logan nearly felt sorry for him . . . but not quite. Mendez and Chaudri seemed hale, though Mendez was favoring one shoulder.

Logan brought his mount to a halt, ten yards from the canyon egress. "It almost looks—"

A shrill whistle cut him off. Logan spun about, just in time to see five men with hooked spears emerge from the rocks. They wore brown-and-gray cloaks over ring mail. The pole weapons had a good reach and were specifically designed so that they could stab or pull a rider from a horse with equal ease.

Son of a bitch.

This was the sharp end of the stick—literally—and they'd ridden right into it. Two more swordsmen were climbing down behind them, cutting off any kind of retreat. Not that he'd consider riding back into that death trap.

"Logan, find a weak point," Kiara ordered.

Logan made a quick circle, careful to keep out of range of the hooked spears. Every smuggler was armed and armored. None of them even blinked when he came near. They had the scarred, dead-eyed look of veterans. He rode back to the group.

"Not sure I see one, Lieutenant," he said.

"Suggestions?"

"We could engage them, but I don't like the reach of those spears," Mendez said.

"Give me a weapon," Thorisson whispered.

It reminded Logan that they'd stashed the firearms deep in the saddlebags. Kiara's orders. Seemed foolish now.

Kiara looked to Logan. A security question, so it was his call. Another fighter would be useful, he had to admit that. But only if he could be trusted. Which this Swedish bastard could not.

"Never going to happen," Logan said.

The men with hooked spears approached warily. They were twenty yards out, closing the vise around them. No one spoke. The time for negotiations had ended.

"Let's use the horses," Logan said. "Stick together, try to break through the line somewhere." Knowing that they'd probably lose a couple of people, but what choice did they have?

As he readied himself, though, there came a noise from the cliffs, above and behind them.

"Watch the cliffs!" Logan hissed. Damn. If the archers showed up, that would be that.

Quinn drew his hood and stood on the cliffs above the canyon mouth. Rocks and gravel tumbled down the slope, and alerted Logan to his presence. The smugglers had every route covered, and they weren't screwing around. He maxed out the volume on his voice amplifier.

"Leave them be!" he shouted.

The smugglers hesitated, and looked up at him while his voice echoed down the canyon. He had to show them something. But the elemental projector was empty, and the microfan out of juice. He had nothing. The smugglers started to move again, and he knew he'd failed. That Logan and Kiara and Chaudri would die. *And I probably will, too.*

The defeat was a weight that pressed on him. Something fought it, though. A part of his core that just wouldn't give in. It pushed away the despair. Welled up inside of him. His skin tingled all over. It felt alive, it felt wonderful.

Most of all, it felt powerful.

Logan stared up at the hooded figure. He held a bloody sword in his hand. That wouldn't be enough.

"Last warning," the man thundered. A tempest of wind buffeted all around him, though he seemed not to feel it. He lifted his sword, blade up. "I have the pow-errrrr!"

Blue lightning shot from the tip in four directions, sizzling and crackling in the air. They all flinched away from it: Kiara, the smugglers, everyone.

"A magic user," Mendez whispered. "God help us!"

"*Gods* help us," Chaudri muttered. But she couldn't stop staring at the man above.

Logan shook his head. He couldn't believe it. There was just no way.

Apparently the smugglers couldn't believe it, either. The two closest to them shared a look and backed away. The rest took off running. They melted into the rocks and were gone.

Logan waited until they were well out of earshot before he started laughing.

Kiara looked at him strangely.

"Logan, what the hell?" Mendez demanded.

Logan caught his breath. "Didn't you ever watch *He-Man* as a kid?"

"Never heard of it," Mendez said.

Of course he hadn't. He'd grown up in Cuba. "Chaudri?" Logan asked.

Chaudri just stared at him.

"Lieutenant?"

She shook her head. "*She-Ra*. What's going on? Do you *know* him?"

"We both do," Logan said. He cupped his hands and shouted, "Bradley, get your ass down here!"

"Who is this Bradley you speak of?" the voice shouted down. "He certainly sounds handsome."

"I'll be damned," Chaudri said. "It's Quinn!"

"Sorry I'm late," Bradley said. He had that infectious grin on his face. "Did I miss anything?"

> **"I work on my poker face as much as anything. Magicians can't afford to be surprised."**
>
> —ART OF ILLUSION, MAY 17

CHAPTER 24

HIDDEN THINGS

Quinn was surprised at how happy it made him to see them again. Logan, Chaudri. Even Kiara. Logan introduced their companion—a Latino guy named Mendez—who had the look of a soldier. Quinn offered him a friendly nod. Thorisson was there, too, with his horse lashed to Kiara's.

"Who's that?" Quinn asked. *And how did he get here?*

"Prisoner of war," Logan said. "Don't talk to him."

Quinn might have said more, but Thorisson caught his eye and gave the tiniest shake of the head. It put him off. He felt like he should say something, but how in the hell would he explain it? They'd probably just hog-tie him, too.

"Get down here, Bradley," Kiara said. "We need to clear the area."

He shook his head, trying to clear it. "I have to get my mule. It's stashed on the other side of the canyon."

"Leave it."

"Be there in a minute," Quinn said. He ducked back from the precipice.

"Bradley!" she called.

He ignored her. He wasn't about to leave his mule tied up where it would starve, or be sniffed out by wild dogs. Strange as it was, he cared about it more than a little bit. Spend so much time talking politely to an animal, and you were bound to grow attached.

He found the mule where he'd stashed it, and rode down through the canyon of death they'd created. He tried not to look at the bodies. It was one thing during the heat of battle, but it was quite another thing now that the fighting was over.

I killed people.

The fact that it was him or them didn't matter—the corpse of the archer he'd burned was still smoldering. He nearly vomited when he ran past it. The rest of the way, he held his breath.

He rejoined Kiara and Chaudri on the other side. The lieutenant told him that Logan and Mendez were scouting farther down the trail, to make sure that there weren't any more smugglers.

"Please stop here," Quinn told the mule. He patted its flank as he said it; the animal complied.

"Bradley's deigned to rejoin us," Kiara said over the comm unit. She fixed him with a frown.

Quinn shrugged. It was all he could do not to look at Thorisson.

"We're half a click up," Logan said. Quinn could hear him again; his comm unit must still have some charge left. "Can you ride to meet us?"

"On our way," she said. "Bradley, I want a full debrief once we're out of these mountains."

"Oh, I look forward to it," he said. He had plenty of news, but hadn't yet decided how much to tell her. He'd figure that out when he got a good night's sleep. The day's exertions had taken a toll on him.

And now I know what Moric goes through, I guess.

She prodded Thorisson with the crossbow. "Let's go." She glanced back at Quinn's mule. "I hope that thing can keep up."

"You'd be surprised."

They set out in front; Quinn fell in behind them, beside Chaudri.

"Sweet Gods, is that a Tioni mule?" she asked.

"It is. You really do know everything about this place, don't you?" Quinn patted its neck, feeling a twinge of fondness. Without the sure-footed beast, he'd probably not have made it this far.

"I do my best," Chaudri said. She rushed on. "I've read something about them, and I very much hope that you can confirm it. Is it true about the manners?"

"One hundred percent," Quinn said.

"Ha, ha! I knew it." Chaudri's grin wide, joyous. She looked like a kid opening a birthday present.

"So," Quinn said. "I couldn't help but notice that you don't have Holt. What happened?"

"We met with him in Valteron City," Chaudri said. "It was . . . well, it was quite an experience."

"How was he?" he asked.

"In a word? Sublime."

"I guess he didn't want to leave his new gig to come home, eh?"

"He declined the lieutenant's offer."

God, would I have loved to be a fly on the wall for that meeting. Just to hear someone tell Kiara "no."

Quinn couldn't ignore the underlying tension when Chaudri talked about him. Not just with the scholar, but with the lieutenant as well. She sat stiff-backed on her mount, shoulders almost hunched. It was apparent the failed mission didn't sit well with her. And Chaudri, well, she was a mix of emotions. Half admiration and maybe half chagrin. Holt sure had a polarizing effect on people.

Logan and Mendez trotted into view, signaling the all clear. The mountains were dropping away behind them; only foothills remained. They must have reached the unofficial end of the smuggler's pass. That, or the smugglers had decided not to press them further.

The whole lightning-sword display might have had something to do with that.

Felara's air temperature had dropped another ten

degrees since they'd first come through the gateway. The cold forced them to make camp earlier in
the already-short day. Kiara consulted her map a few
times, then directed Logan down a faded trail off the
smuggler's road. They found a dilapidated log cabin; it
looked to be a hundred years old—and in Alissia, that
meant *rough*.

"We'll camp here," Kiara announced.

"Doesn't look like it'll offer much shelter," Quinn
said. Even so, he was grateful. He'd been dozing off
in the saddle. The sleep was like a gravitational force,
pulling his eyes downward. He wouldn't have lasted
much longer.

"Looks can be deceiving, Mr. Bradley," Kiara said.
"You above all should know that."

Logan kicked aside some old planks and pulled
away some undergrowth. Beneath lay a pair of cellar
doors in near-perfect condition, and a numeric passcode lock. "This is one of our hidey-holes," he said. He
ducked inside. Quinn heard a spark, and soon warm
lantern light glowed from within.

Quinn tied his mule to a cleverly disguised hitching
post. "Stay here, please. Try not to get eaten."

He hurried down the steps to a room below, and
was surprised to find it was quite a bit warmer than
the Felaran outdoors. The cellar was also larger than
Quinn's apartment back in Vegas. Five oil lanterns
hung around the main room, which was twenty by
twenty feet. They stashed Thorisson in a lockable storage closet so they wouldn't have to watch him. Quinn

was still unsure whether or not he should mention knowing him. *How exactly am I supposed to bring that up?*

Storage bins lined one wall, and Chaudri was already raiding these for food. There were medical supplies as well, so Kiara ordered Logan to sit down so that she could examine his back where the arrow had struck him. Chaudri, too. She'd already patched up Mendez's shoulder—he'd wear the arm in a sling for a day or two.

Logan's armor had stopped the arrowhead, but left him a nasty welt the size of a golf ball. That reminded Quinn of his sword fight. He took a deep breath and unfastened the torso piece of his armor. His side was a mottled tapestry of black and blue. He touched it and gasped at how much it hurt. Next thing he knew, Kiara had him sitting right beside Logan in her makeshift infirmary.

"How many of these hidey-holes does the company have?" Quinn asked.

"Not as many as we'd like," Kiara said. "They're nervous about Alissians stumbling across one."

"On a related note, don't punch the wrong code on that pad outside, unless you want to learn how serious they are about it," Logan added.

"What's the correct code?"

"You don't have the clearance for it," Kiara said.

He should have seen that coming. He didn't have the clearance for anything interesting.

"Noticed the blood on your sword," Logan said softly.

"Yeah," Quinn said.

"Not yours, is it?"

"Ah, no. I got into a fight. With someone older than twelve."

Logan examined Quinn's bruise and winced. "Looks like it cost you. Just like I said it would."

"I've gotten worse from you," Quinn said. "Heck, I'm fairly certain I've *given* you worse."

Logan smiled. "You and Mendez are going to get along just fine." He leaned over to Kiara, whispering loud enough that Quinn could hear. "Check for head trauma."

Quinn woke groggily to the unpleasant sensation of Logan shaking him awake. "What?"

"Jesus. I've been trying to wake you up for five minutes."

"I'm tired."

"So it appears. Lieutenant wants us to get a move on. You can sleep when we get back."

Quinn groaned but forced himself to sit up. His whole body felt like it was made of lead. Kiara had wanted to question him after she patched up his wounds, but apparently he had fallen asleep as she talked.

Someone had thrown a blanket over him. Chaudri, probably. It didn't seem like Logan's style.

They left the hidey-hole at dawn, all of them in heavier cloaks thanks to the cellar's wardrobe. Even

Thorisson got an upgrade; it wouldn't do to transport the man this far only to have him freeze to death in the Felaran snows. These ran even deeper as they rode northwest; sometimes the horses were nearly up to their haunches in it. Having lived only in Tion and the Enclave's island—so far as he knew, at least—Quinn's mule had never really seen snow. It balked at the white stuff initially. A long conversation with lots of polite words followed. Nothing doing. Finally, he scooped up a handful and put it in his mouth while the mule watched. The mule tried it after that, and eventually was willing to walk in it.

If the others thought Quinn's dialogue with his mule was odd, they at least kept quiet about it.

It was a cold, quiet ride to the foothills. Kiara was grim, Logan and Mendez serious, and Chaudri just distant. Quiet.

The wyvern didn't seem to be around, thank the gods. But the Alissian wild dogs took to howling as it grew dark. The sound of it ran a shiver down his spine. Quinn reclaimed his bow and quiver. Having them tied to the saddle, right by his hand, offered at least a little comfort.

They also crossed a few deer-like tracks in the snow, some of them fresh, but he felt no burning desire to hunt them. There would be other, less pressing opportunities to hunt someday, and they didn't need the food. Besides, he had enough blood on his hands to last a while. The thought hit him like a punch to the gut. *I think I'm going to throw up again.*

The lieutenant didn't let that bother her when she gave him full license to shoot Thorisson if he tried to escape.

Talk about an awkward situation.

Soon enough they were climbing the slope to the mouth of the gateway cave. Here Logan conferred briefly with Kiara, then went ahead with Mendez to secure the area.

"There's probably a bear hibernating right in front of the gateway," Quinn said. "That's been our luck so far."

"Personally I'd be more concerned about snow tigers," Chaudri said. "They like caves, and they're incredibly territorial."

"Wonderful," Quinn said.

Logan came in over the comm units. "All clear, Lieutenant. Want us to try the gateway?"

"Not until we're all there," she said.

Right, the gateway had been closed from the other side under some security protocol. Christ, what if it still was? Quinn didn't want to cool his heels in another hidey-hole until Kiara figured things out. If it was blocked, then he was leaving and going back to the Enclave. He didn't care what they said. He pressed a palm against his armor's chest plate, felt the teardrop-shaped amulet Moric had given him against his skin.

Even then, though, he hesitated at the thought. Going to the Enclave might finally put it on the company's map, and that was a risk he wasn't prepared to take. Not yet, at least. The longer he'd been in Alissia, the more it had become apparent that the company had a substantial presence here. The communications relays, the hidey-holes, the carefully built false identities. He suspected that the company's presence wasn't quite as benevolent as they claimed.

They were just as much a threat to the Enclave as the magicians were to them.

He mulled this over while they made the last climb to the gateway cave.

"Bradley, take your saddlebags off the mule," Kiara said.

"What for?"

"He's not allowed through the gateway. Or in the cave, technically speaking."

"You're joking, right?" Quinn asked. They were well past company policy enforcement here.

"No fauna. Unless you want him going to the lab for study?"

"No, thanks," Quinn said quickly. They'd probably do a brain autopsy or something.

He dismounted and started undoing the leather straps. He piled the saddlebags by the mouth of the cave while the others rode in. Then he unstrapped the saddle as well.

"Listen," he said. "You can't come with me, where I'm going. But you saved my life, and I won't forget it." He offered a few handfuls of grain, not the high-performance stuff, but stout Alissian feed that the hidey-hole had in dry storage. He patted the mule's flank. "Farewell, my friend."

He picked up his saddlebags and marched into the cave. There it was. The gateway flickered between silver and gray, like a television without a signal. No way to tell if it was open or not. If it was, he had a long-ass debrief waiting for him on the other side. He wasn't looking forward to that one. But there was coffee and maybe a hot shower, too. Those, he wouldn't mind so much.

"Got it all?" Kiara asked.

Quinn patted the saddlebags. "Right here," he said.

"Good." She turned to Mendez and jerked her head toward the cave's opening.

He said nothing, but unstrapped the crossbow from his saddle.

"What are you doing?" Quinn demanded. He dropped the saddlebags and took a step. Huge arms wrapped around him from behind in a bear hug. *Logan.*

"Let me go!" Quinn shouted. "What's he doing?"

"Sorry about this, Bradley," Logan said. "A burden animal wandering around might attract attention to this cave. We can't afford that."

"No!" He squirmed, but Logan had him in an iron grip. Quinn had forgotten just how *strong* he was. He fought against it anyway. He cussed at Logan. He tried to shut his ears, dreading the inevitable *clack-thrum* of the crossbow.

It never came.

Mendez returned and stomped the snow from his boots. He wore a quizzical expression. "The mule's not out there."

"It must have wandered off," Kiara said. "Go track it down."

"There aren't any tracks, Lieutenant. The thing is just *gone*."

Gods be praised. Whether it was some piece of Enclave magic, or just an extra smart mule, Quinn couldn't say. When Logan released him, he threw the big man a dirty look and rubbed his arms.

"What did you do, Bradley?" Kiara asked.

Quinn offered her a little bow. "One last disappearing act for our little journey."

Her face was stormy, but Chaudri laughed. Mendez joined in.

"I did warn you against bringing a magician," Logan said.

> **"The hardest part about our
> work over there is the moment
> we must return home."**
>
> —R. Holt, "A Decade Devoted"

CHAPTER 25

MODERN WARFARE

Logan wanted to be the first through the gateway, but
Kiara had different ideas.

"I'm pulling rank on you, Logan," she said.

Logan planted himself in front of her. "Not this
time, Lieutenant. It's a security matter."

"Command assured us that they have control of the
island facility."

"Those messages could have been faked."

She sighed, but gave in. "Anything looks off, I want
you back here in double time."

"Roger that."

Logan unbelted his sword and handed it to Mendez;

anything larger than a knife triggered knockout gas on the other side while the security protocols were in place. A gear retrieval team would be through later to decontaminate all of their gear and take it back to the armory.

He took a breath and leaped through. Cold washed over him, then darkness. He landed on the stone of the gate room. Spotlights blinded him. He shielded his eyes and looked down. The incoming alarm sounded, a single klaxon. Four neon green dots appeared on his chest and hovered near the solar plexus. Company-issue laser sights. Sweet Jesus, they had the facility back.

He laced his hands behind his head and knelt on the stone floor.

"Sergeant Major Logan, Alpha Team," he said.

The Plexiglas door ahead of him remained shut, but there was a speaker inside. A woman's voice came through it. "Passcode?"

"Echo. Foxtrot. Seven. One. Victor," Logan said.

"What was your first daughter's weight at birth?"

"Five pounds, three ounces," he said. Olivia was a tiny thing; she took after her mother. Thinking of his girls made him smile. He missed the next question. "Say again?"

"How many hostages survived in Beirut?"

His smile fell. "Screw you."

"Answer the question."

"None of them." His last mission for Uncle Sam had been a bloodbath. It made saying yes to Kiara much easier.

The Plexiglas slid aside; four black-clad soldiers lowered their weapons. He stepped out of the airlock. "I've got four more behind me, and one prisoner."

Kiara came through next. She went through the drill while Logan surrendered his knife, comm unit, boots, and armor to a couple of soldiers from the armory. Bradley was next, then Chaudri. The gate room had changed since he last came through; lead panels six feet tall and about half as wide formed a semicircle around the gateway. The men with guns were positioned just beyond. Thorisson stumbled through a moment after, still bound at the wrists. Mendez entered behind him and stepped on his knee, forcing the man down.

Logan picked up a phone that let him talk to the control room. "Gas them."

"Including Mendez?"

"He'll forgive me. Do it."

A white cloud billowed noiselessly in the airlock. Two thuds. The exhaust fan whirred into motion, clearing the knockout gas. The Plexiglas hissed open. Both men were down, and had fallen in a scandalous position.

"Well, look at that," Logan said.

Chaudri laughed softly. "I didn't realize they were so close."

Logan snapped a photo on his wrist-camera. "For posterity."

Four security officers hurried in to check vitals and drag them clear. Kiara took command of things and ordered the gateway lockdown that was standard protocol after a mission returned. Later, a retrieval team would go get the horses and blow artificial snow out of the cave to cover their tracks leading up to it.

Mendez passed both retinal and fingerprint scans; they stripped his knife and boots off him, then lifted him into a cot to recover. Two others searched the prisoner thoroughly, turning up a nylon pouch with a tiny pill capsule inside.

"What is that?" Logan asked. "Looks prescription or something."

The pill went into a tiny, portable mass spectroscopy instrument. They had the readout in just under thirty seconds.

"Hmm," Logan said. "Sodium cyanide."

Kiara pursed her lips; she was impressed. "A suicide pill."

"Nice touch," Logan said. "Very KGB."

As all this happened, both men gradually came around. In about two minutes the effect of the knockout gas wore off.

Mendez sat up and had a coughing fit. "Was that really necessary?" he groused.

"Matter of security," Logan told him.

"Next time, maybe I'll clear the room and you can bring the prisoner."

Thorisson woke to the friendly greeting of guards with machine guns. Logan started to walk over, to offer the man a personal escort down to the brig. Thorisson shook his head. He locked eyes with Logan and slipped out of the flexsteel bindings on his wrists.

How in the hell? He must have dislocated a thumb. Now he used his free hand to press something on the inside of one wrist. What was it, another suicide pill?

"Watch him!" Logan shouted.

No, a faint light glowed there beneath his fingers. Some kind of subdermal electronic device.

Logan darted toward him. "Hold him still!"

The guards grabbed him, but they were too late. There was a soft beep.

Explosions began to rock the complex.

Quinn was still unlacing his boots when Logan shouted. The force of the first two explosions threw him into a wall of the cave. The fluorescent lights went out, replaced by the weak orange glow of emergency backups.

"What the hell was that?" Kiara shouted.

Logan grabbed Thorisson's wrist while the two guards held him down. He jabbed at the light, but couldn't seem to undo whatever the man had done. He reared back and punched Thorisson in the face. Really put his shoulder to it. The man crumpled. He was out cold.

"Take him to holding," Logan growled. "Find a sedative that keeps him out."

Kiara had a radio to her ear; she was getting a report. "It's the goddamn drone!" She had to shout to be heard above the blaring alarm sirens.

Another explosion; this one sounded closer. Quinn

laced his boots back up. "Sorry, I'm going to need these," he told the men from inventory.

Kiara handed out radios. She strode to punch a code into the panel on the wall; the thick steel doors leading out into the complex started to slide open, but halted about a foot apart. "Logan!"

He ran over and threw a shoulder into one of the doors, heaving. Mendez did likewise on the other one. Quinn ran over to help. So did Chaudri. The doors were six inches thick, and some kind of steel alloy. The four of them managed to heave them apart another foot, just enough that everyone could squeeze through.

"Logan, Mendez—you're on tactical support," Kiara said. "I'll be in the control room."

"What about us?" Chaudri asked.

"You're civilians. Find somewhere safe and low until we get the all clear," Kiara said.

She stalked away down the hall; Logan and Mendez had already jogged out of sight.

"What's the safest place on the island?" Quinn asked.

"Theoretically it's the control room where Kiara's headed. I'm more of a mind to try the subbasement, though. When it comes to this sort of thing, I prefer good, solid stone," Chaudri said. "No matter what they claim about the Plexiglas."

That gave him an idea, and it was crazy enough that it might make a difference. "Did you say that we had siege equipment somewhere?"

"On the roof of the armory."

"Come on." Quinn started down the stairs.

"Wait! The roof is the other way," Chaudri said.

"We're headed to the prototyping lab first. I need my team."

Quinn found Julian Miller and most of the techs down in their lab, frantically securing delicate equipment to the walls and floors. Mostly with yards and yards of duct tape. He and Chaudri jumped in to help. There were millions of dollars in this room. The woodworking equipment would hold, but the three-dimensional printer and other delicate robotics teetered precariously.

"Bradley!" Miller called. "I knew you must have gotten back."

"Oh, yeah? How so?"

"Things started blowing up."

"It's the drone," Quinn said. He helped Miller close and lock the materials drawers that were sliding out of the wall. He did a double-take when he saw one of them was filled with *gold* ingots. It took another fifteen minutes before all of the equipment was secure. The lab now looked like a hazmat crime scene.

"The drone, eh?" Miller asked finally. "Damn thing ruined my best argon laser."

"Sorry, chief," Quinn said. "Hey, you built the siege equipment on top of the armory, right? Is it still there?"

"As far as I know."

"What's the range on those?"

"A few hundred yards for the mangonels. But the trebuchets can throw half a mile." Miller frowned. "You'll never get the drone that close, though."

"Let me worry about that. I need to borrow all of the 3-D projectors. And a few of your guys."

"What are you planning?" Chaudri asked.

"A little razzle-dazzle," he said, grinning.

Logan got to the command center just in time to hear Kiara give the launch order. Six missiles, one second apart. They whined as they streaked around the island, a six-fingered claw of airborne destruction. The drone shifted back and forth as they targeted and homed in. Maybe its defenses couldn't handle that many.

The screech was high-pitched and deafening. It came from every speaker, every surveillance system at once.

"What is that?" Kiara shouted.

"Jamming signal!" Logan said. He ran to the window.

Four of the missiles went down like stones. Another one peeled away and diverted back toward the control tower.

Shit.

"Take cover!" he shouted.

He dove behind the console closest to him. The detonation rocked the floor under him. Incredibly, the Plexiglas windows had held. He regained his feet.

Most of the surveillance cameras had gone all snowy on them.

Radar was still up, though, and it tracked the last missile. It was making a wide circuit of the island.

"What's it doing?" Kiara said.

"Looking for a target."

The biggest heat signature came from the cooling units behind the central complex. The missile bore down on these and exploded. A light warhead, but that was sure to have taken out the condensers.

"There goes the A/C," Logan said.

Kiara got on the radio. "Shut down nonessential systems. Everything but the computing cores."

People could sweat. Hard drives could not.

Right around then, Logan looked out the window and saw that the residential building was gone. "What the hell?"

"What now?" Kiara demanded.

"The residential building's gone."

"Flattened?"

He grabbed a pair of binoculars. The area where the building had been was just empty, bare rock face. Like nothing had ever been there at all. "No—just . . . gone." He looked up and then the warehouse was gone, too. "Shit, the warehouse!"

Kiara was at the window, too. "Did you see an impact?"

"No. It just disappeared. Like a . . ." He trailed off, and he figured it out. "Like a goddamn magic trick."

"Bradley," she said.

"Has to be."

The outer buildings went first, then the inner ones. And it worked, too. The drone was almost in rifle range.

"Did they have any luck getting the specs for this bird?" Logan asked.

"Right here," Kiara said. She unfolded a set of blueprints that had probably been acquired at exorbitant expense through company intermediaries. They both pored over them, looking for weak points.

"Here's the comm array," Logan said. But a metal dome housed that, and he doubted they'd be able to punch through.

"What about these?" Kiara asked. She ran a fingernail on the wires beneath it, the ones that ran from the comms to the drone's body.

"Going to be a small target," Logan said.

"It's all we've got."

Logan got on the radio. "Mendez, you raided the armory yet?"

"I'm here now," Mendez said.

"Get a sniper rifle, too," Logan said. "Highest caliber you can find. See you in the bunkers in five."

"Roger that," Mendez said.

"Good hunting," Kiara said.

Logan ran down two flights of stairs and followed the tunnel to the foxholes that peppered the cliffs above the shoreline. Mendez was there with a few men, getting set up. Logan took the sniper rifle. The others had M4s. They opened fire. Not like crazy cowboys, but with each one taking aim, squeezing off a burst. Every shot was plinking off drone metal.

Logan went for the junction, guessing at where those wires would be. *This one's for my girls. . .*

He put his shot right in the tiny gap. The drone lurched sideways for three wonderful seconds. Then it righted itself, and decided then to take them seriously.

One of Mendez's men was on the spotting scope, watching the drone for any sign of damage. "Shit!" he said. "Gun port just opened."

Logan recognized the sound right away. A distant percussion, then the whizz of the incoming round.

"RPG!" he shouted. He and the spotter hit the floor of their foxhole. The first detonation hit the roof, and others rapidly followed. The entire hillside housing their positions erupted in a storm of shrapnel and white smoke.

Mendez had the presence of mind to jump on the fixed-position M2 with hopes of jamming the drone's weapon. Good old Ma Deuce delivered four hundred and fifty rounds per minute of 0.50 caliber armor-piercing bullets.

Rounds that *plink-plinked* off the drone's shielded exterior.

What the hell is that thing made of?

"Gatling—" said the spotter. Then a hail of bullets cut him practically in half. Logan yanked Mendez away from the M2 a second before the Gatling ripped it to shreds.

"Cease fire!" Logan shouted. They needed a new plan.

The radio crackled. "Logan, come in."

What the hell does the magician need now? "Not a good time, Bradley."

"Can you bring the drone a couple hundred yards south?"

"Why would I do that?"

"To put it within range of the mangonels."

The siege machines? He seriously doubted that they'd make a difference, but it was worth a try. They certainly weren't having luck with modern weaponry, and it had been Quinn's trick that had gotten the drone close enough in the first place.

"Give me three minutes," Logan said. He climbed out of the foxhole and took off running before he could really think through what a bad idea it probably was. He still wore the dark fatigues from under his armor. Not a bit of Kevlar on him, and the color would show up clear as day against the sandy hillside. The drone picked him up and began firing. He dove behind a rock at the sound of the Gatling gun. There was another bunker just up the hill, nearly on the south face. One more sprint should do it.

He took off again as the drone switched to RPGs.

Boom!

Ten yards behind him.

Boom!

Another one in front. Probably meant to turn him around, but he kept charging forward. Clouds of sand billowed in his face, and he could barely see, and it didn't take long until he was stumbling. Then his boot caught on something and he fell hard. It was the edge of the bunker. He managed to roll himself in before the next RPG hit.

"Get ready, Bradley," he said over the radio.

He threw open the weapons locker and found an M4 on the rack.

He smiled. "Hello, old friend."

He crawled into a prone position, easing the barrel around the edge of the bunker's window until he could just see the drone's rotor. He started firing at it. *Plink, plink, plink.* The .223 caliber rounds had zero chance of penetrating the drone's armor; at best, he could hope to annoy it.

But annoying gets your attention. Just ask Bradley, he thought to himself.

Plink, plink, plink.

"Come on, you bastard," he said. "Come around for a better shot."

The drone obliged him.

Quinn watched Logan's desperate run with binoculars. He made the bunker by a hair. Then he started shooting back. Rounds sparked off the rotor housing, more annoying to the drone than anything. After a few rounds the drone tilted slightly and glided south. Right into the designated kill zone.

Way to go, Logan. "Here it comes!" Quinn shouted.

Miller himself called out the marks. "Sixteen degrees, range four hundred yards."

The crews made adjustments. "Set!"

"Set!"

The wind died at just the right time.

Chaudri was spotting for them through a pair of binoculars. "Little bit more, little bit more." Then she shouted, "Fire!"

The arms of the mangonels snapped forward; a hail of heavy stones filled the air. Quinn watched them arc through the sky, impossibly slow compared to the bullets slamming into Logan's bunker. But the rocks fell short, and the drone didn't even notice them. *Damn.*

"Fifteen degrees!" the crew chief called.

"Set!"

Chaudri was watching. "Fire!"

The mangonels launched another volley. *Here we go again.* This wasn't going to work. What had he been thinking?

The engineers had the range perfect this time, though. The projectiles rained down on the drone. It shuddered under the impact, losing altitude. Hell, maybe he was right after all. *Time to finish this.*

"Trebuchets," Quinn said over the radio. The engineers signaled that they were ready. He raised his arm, trying to predict where the drone would end up. Its rotors made a horrific noise, like the screech of an old car starting up in cold weather, but so far they'd held. The craft banked just so. He brought his arm down sharply. *"Fire!"*

Counterweights dropped. Two great arms rotated in a great *thwump*, slinging twin seven-hundred-and-fifty-pound stones in high arcs. They flew over the mangonels, over the wall . . .

"Damn, overshot it," Quinn said.

Then the stones hit their apogee and dropped straight down. Slammed right onto the wings of the Raptor Tech drone. It plummeted beneath them and crashed with the horrific screech of wrenching metal.

Quinn pumped his arm in the air. "Yesss!" The engineers saw it and gave a yell of triumph. He hugged Chaudri and slapped the chief engineer on the back. They shook hands, laughing.

Logan's voice crackled on the radio. "Now that, Bradley, was magic."

> **"Magicians don't have to be
> smart. But it sure helps."**
>
> —ART OF ILLUSION, DECEMBER 29

CHAPTER 26

LEVERAGE

The good news was that the drone was down. The bad news was Thorisson had escaped during the chaos. Surveillance footage showed him being escorted down a hallway toward the holding cells. An explosion hit, and the lights went out. When they came back on, both guards were down and Thorisson was no longer in frame.

That was right about when Kiara had ordered the nonessential computing shutdown, and the cameras had stopped recording. A comprehensive search two hours after the drone's destruction turned up only his old clothes and a missing Zodiac raft. There was no water cavalry to call in since they'd kept most of the company boats away while the drone controlled their sea lanes, so pursuit was basically impossible.

Company executives put out a BOLO, leveraging their contacts at the ports and travel centers. Thorisson would turn up soon enough. Or not—the island was pretty far from everything, and the Zodiac wasn't really designed for cross-ocean voyages. Either way, they hoped he wouldn't get a chance to pass along any intel on Project Gateway.

Quinn's own official debriefing with Kiara and the others began the morning after the attack and ran well into the night. He recounted what had happened since Valteron City. The encounter with Moric, the trip to the Enclave's island. His time there, watching, studying, taking classes. The library, the guild contract, even his little performance that allowed him to stay. In one day, he told them far more about Alissian magic and magicians than company researchers had gleaned over fifteen years.

Of course, he didn't tell them *everything*. He left out the part with Jillaine. Nothing really to tell there; she was just another magic user, so no need to single her out. He also kept the Captain Relling encounter in his pocket for the time being. The last thing he wanted was an excuse for the company to lead some kind of military extraction, even though he could guess how much the news would mean to Kiara. *Now's not the time.*

Besides, what he could tell them about the Enclave had everyone riveted enough.

"Hundreds of magicians in one place," Chaudri said, almost to herself. "Our counts were farther off than we knew."

Kiara insisted that he recount every single use of magic that he'd witnessed while on the island or in the company of guild magicians. Quinn did his best, but there was simply too much. For weeks, he'd lived and breathed in a society that lived by magic. Existed *for* magic. Nearly anything she asked about, he'd seen happen once or twice. Teleportation, obviously. Telekinesis. Animal husbandry. All sorts of elemental manipulation. The only category of magic use he didn't really witness was violence. As a whole, magicians in Alissia were reluctant to use their arts against other people.

"That's consistent with our encounters with them," Logan said. "The one that we met outside Valteron City—I had my back to her, and all she did was immobilize me. She could have done a lot worse."

He left one bit of magic out, though. One that he kept playing in his head over and over, to make sure he remembered it right. It happened on that cliff in the smuggler's ambush, when he'd shouted stop and put the sword over his head. He'd been out of tricks and illusions by then. And terrified he was about to watch his friends die. That's when the warmth rose up through him like an electrical current, and bright light crackled all around.

His breakthrough at last.

That's why he was so worried they'd confiscate the

amulet from him; the inspection team had already made a note of it as an "acquired possession." He even admitted that it was a key for finding his way back to the island. No way in hell he was going to let them take it, though, so he hedged a little.

"I wouldn't take it off me, if I were you," he said.

"Why not?" Kiara demanded.

"Moric said I'm the only one who can use it, and if I take it off, it breaks the enchantment," Quinn said. Not exactly truthful, but it was one of his only bits of leverage and he didn't want it to disappear into a company lockbox. *In case that's not convincing enough* . . . "And he also mentioned it wouldn't be pleasant for the one who took it off me. I don't know what he meant, but seeing some of the things I've seen, I don't doubt the creative nature of the magicians' retribution."

Kiara ground her teeth. "You can keep it for now, Bradley, but I want you available to the research teams whenever they want a look at it."

"Fair enough," he said.

Once he'd answered Kiara's questions, she excused herself to confer with her superiors. Logan and Chaudri caught him up on what he'd missed. His heart went cold when he heard about Bravo Team.

I did that, didn't I?

Raptor Tech never would have found the island facility if he hadn't used the jack of spades. They'd played him.

I was just trying to save my own life. I didn't think it would cost others theirs.

The thought made him sick. It was all he could do to keep his face under control.

If the company discovered his role in the breaches, he'd never get off this island alive. That fact was written all over Logan's face, when he talked about Bravo. Maybe it was a good thing Thorisson had escaped. He was the only one who could give Quinn up.

Again, it was a treacherous thought. But hadn't he done what he could to make amends? Hadn't he saved them time and time again?

I'm not sure it'll be enough.

He shoved the thoughts away and turned to Chaudri. "So, are you glad you went?"

"Oh, most definitely. It's given me a great deal of insight into Alissian culture and society. Things I didn't realize until I was there among them." Her eyes were shining.

"Maybe it's time to drop the 'interim' from your title," Quinn said.

Chaudri cleared her throat. "You're probably right. And that means I'm responsible for our research write-ups. I'd better go get started." She nodded to both of them and hurried out of the conference room.

"There's a spring in her step," Quinn said.

"She did pretty well over there," Logan said. "To be honest, I was worried about her."

"You were worried about everyone."

"That's my job. So I'll ask you the same question. Are you glad you went?"

"More than you know," Quinn said. "In fact, I'll bet

you a bottle of Valteroni liquor that I get to go back again."

"Developed a taste for the good stuff, eh? Don't tell me you managed to smuggle a bottle back."

"Sadly, no. But I know a guy."

"Oh, I'm sure. But I'll take that bet," Logan said. "Pretty sure we won't need a magician from this point on."

"There's more to me than just quick fingers."

"That's what I keep hearing." Logan scratched his chin. "I must be missing something."

"You usually are."

Kiara joined them a minute later. Her face was a mask, but Quinn noted the slight hesitance in her movements. That was one of her tells, the one that meant "reluctantly following orders."

"My superiors asked me to convey their gratitude," she said. "You played your part well, and collected some valuable intelligence besides."

"You're welcome," Quinn said. He left it at that and waited. Negotiations 101: let the other party start.

"We agreed to a six-month engagement, and the company believes that contract has been met already. The funds have already been wired to your accounts."

"And the equipment?"

She frowned. "Yours to take, though I'll remind you that almost everything you designed has proprietary technology in it. If anything should fall into the hands of our competitors, you'll be fully responsible."

"Don't worry, I'll take precautions." People were

always coming after his stuff; it was a way of life for the Vegas magician. He waited again.

"Do you think you'd be welcomed back by the Enclave, if you were to return?" she asked.

Ah, here it came at last. "Moric certainly made it sound that way," Quinn said.

"Could you bring a small group posing as magicians, maybe get them in?"

He leaned back in his chair. "Nope."

She blinked. "I'm sorry?"

"It's magicians only in that place. Not even Holt was allowed there, and I think we can agree he's got more influence than any of us."

She tapped her pen against the conference table for a few beats. If the jab about Holt bothered her, she didn't show it. "Moric brought you there as a candidate. You hadn't proven yourself then."

"He brought me there as a criminal." He gave her a little smile. "Funny how all of those mission briefings failed to cover the fact that impersonating a magician is a crime over there."

"You landed on your feet, didn't you? And you've managed to infiltrate one of the most powerful groups in Alissia."

"It almost cost me my life. I still had to win them over, which wasn't easy," Quinn said. "I think it would go badly if I tried to get someone in. That's the honest truth." *Or most of it anyway.*

Her lips twisted downward. Knowing Kiara, though, he wagered she was ready for this possibility.

There would be a backup proposal, and probably another one after that.

"Would you be interested in returning there?" she asked. "Alone?"

More than you can possibly imagine. "What's in it for me?"

Logan snickered. "You can take a magician out of Vegas . . ."

"I don't suppose you'll volunteer as your patriotic duty?" Kiara asked.

"We don't work for the government, last time I checked," Quinn said.

"No, we do not," she said. "We work for an organization that knows the home address of every single living relative you have. Whose subsidiaries employ some of them. Whose financial division holds the mortgage on your friend Rudy's theater."

Quinn felt a chill down his back as she spoke. He didn't let the fear show, only the anger. "That's starting to sound like a threat, Lieutenant."

She put her hands flat on the conference table and exhaled slowly. "It's a *reminder*, Bradley. Don't get cute with us. You have no idea what the company has at stake here."

"Oh, I have a fair idea," Quinn countered. For once, he knew nearly as much as she did about it. "But you don't see me running to any news outlets. I just want a piece of the action."

"How large a piece?" she asked. "Give me a number."

"Ten."

Her eyes widened, which was the Kiara equivalent of shouting. "Ten *million*?"

"Oh, no. I didn't mean money—although that's not a bad starting place. But no, that's what I want my security clearance to be. It puts me two below Chaudri, twelve below Logan, and still a bit more below yourself." Yet it meant he'd finally have access to learn about some of the stuff they'd been keeping from him.

"You're not supposed to know our clearance levels," Logan said. "You don't have the—"

"Clearance," Quinn cut in. "Yes, I'm aware. But I'm about to. If you want my help, you're going to have to read me in. A lot more than you have."

"That may be possible," Kiara said. "What else?"

"I want some time off, to perform back in Vegas. Major casino, on the Strip." The very thing they'd robbed him of months ago, and he hadn't forgotten. He just had to do it at least once. He'd promised his parents that much. Besides, with the new equipment, he could really dazzle a Vegas audience. Get his photo up on the wall, and show them that he belonged there. Even if he might actually belong somewhere else.

"You want the company to *encourage* one of them to hire you?"

"That wouldn't work. I just need some well-connected people who could vouch for me. I'll handle the part of being good enough to perform there."

She shrugged. "If that's what you want."

"Even you can't bully the big casinos into putting my name on the neon sign."

She had no reaction to that. No frown, no scowl. Another one of her tells.

"Unless the company happens to *own* one of the big casinos," Quinn ventured.

Still nothing. Of course. Why hadn't he seen it before?

"Which is it?" he asked. "The Venetian? Treasure Island? No," he said, and he waved her off. "Don't tell me. But that will make this a lot easier."

"We agree on that much," Kiara said.

"I would have made it on my own, you know," Quinn said. "They were almost ready for me. Right when you showed up."

"I'm sure they were. What else?"

"If I agree to this, I'll need more training. From people like him." He gestured at Logan. "And Chaudri, and the other researchers."

"You're smarter than I thought, Bradley," she said.

He gave her a grin. "I'll take that as a compliment."

"Is that the end of your list of demands? No knighthood or mansion or private island?"

"Gods, no," he said. "Hey! I said it right that time." He looked at both of them. "There's just one more request, and I have a feeling it might be the hardest one."

Kiara sat up, as if steeling herself. "Let's hear it."

"I want to meet Richard Holt. Face-to-face."

Her pupils dilated, and she smiled. He couldn't remember ever seeing a smile on her face before. There was something wicked about this one. "Now there's a meeting I'll be happy to arrange in person."

> "The magic of Alissia should not be
> taken lightly. There's an allure to this
> world that we have yet to understand."

—R. HOLT, "ALISSIA RETROSPECTIVE:
FIFTEEN YEARS"

CHAPTER 27

VEGAS DREAMS

Quinn Bradley had finally arrived.

For twenty years, he'd dreamed of seeing his name in the neon lights of the Las Vegas Strip. Of taking the stage at a major casino there, and joining the ranks of magic's elite. Siegfried and Roy, David Copperfield, Penn and Teller. He'd worked his ass off to get here. Designing his own tricks, performing seven nights a week, building his profile online and onstage.

Even so, as he waited in the shadowy alcove backstage, he fingered the stone pendant that hung from a silver chain under his shirt and wished he were more excited about it. Quick fingers and cleverness had taken him a long way, but he couldn't help but wonder if he'd ever have made it happen without help from CASE Global Enterprises. Kiara had made good on her promise, and suddenly Rudy Fortelli called—nearly panting with excitement—to tell him that a major casino had a slot open. Just a three-night engagement, but still a big deal. Quinn hadn't asked what they were offering to pay. He'd just cashed one hell of a big check.

It was The Bellagio, of course. The most iconic casino of them all, the home of Cirque du Soleil and countless other top-notch acts in the entertainment business. He should have known. CASE Global never went in for anything but the best.

That's why they picked me, he thought with a smile.

"Quinn?" a woman asked. Timid and quiet, but he'd know that voice anywhere.

"Veena! I'll be damned."

The newly minted head of research for CASE Global's largest and most secretive research project looked downright uncomfortable in a silver cocktail dress. Never mind that it was Armani, and worth a small fortune.

She probably doesn't even know.

They went to shake hands, but ended up hugging instead. Six months ago, he hadn't even known her. But they'd fled from reptilian predators and been stranded in another world together. She was like the sister he'd never had. "Damn, it's good to see you."

"Likewise. And it looks like you're doing well."

He winked. "I'm a tough negotiator. But I'm glad you came."

"It's on business, I'm afraid."

"Company business?"

"Exactly."

He should have guessed. She wasn't the kind to take a pleasure trip. "I'm not due back for another couple of weeks."

"Yes, well. It's a big crowd out there."

"Is it?" He shook himself and rubbed his arms. "Thank God. I was afraid to look." Afraid he'd see a wide field of empty seats.

"That kind of exposure makes the executives a bit nervous."

"For security reasons?"

"Not exactly. I'm to remind you of the, ah—" she leaned close and lowered her voice "—nondisclosure agreements."

He laughed. "Is that why they sent you? I thought stern intimidation was Kiara's department."

"She wasn't able to come herself."

"Logan, then." The big man could have just said it all with a look.

"He's busy as well, I'm afraid."

"Did they find the Swedish guy?"

"Only his boat. He made the mainland, but Mendez is hot on his trail." She looked away, and grimaced.

I should invite her to play poker sometime. "What's going on, Veena?"

"We're under a lot of scrutiny because of the mission failure. And the news from over there, about my former mentor . . . let's just say it's worrisome."

"Sounds serious."

"You'll be briefed on-site. Kiara wants you there as soon as possible."

"I can fly down in the morning."

He'd have to make some arrangements for an early departure—The Bellagio manager was sure to throw a fit—but that could wait. It surprised him a little how quickly he'd agreed. Normally he didn't like to jump when Kiara said to, but the idea of being near the gateway again excited him. *Maybe even more than what I'm about to do . . . and that's saying something.*

"Oh, that would be wonderful."

A chime sounded, a polite warning from the theater manager.

Chaudri's eyes widened. She looked as nervous as he felt. "I suppose I should give you some time alone. Are you ready for this?"

"To hear my name announced on the Vegas Strip?" He flashed her a grin. "Been ready my whole life."

AUTHOR'S NOTE

Dear Reader,

Thank you for reading my book! I had a lot of fun writing this story, and hope that you found it entertaining. If so, maybe you'd be willing to help spread the word about it. Here are three ways you can do so:

1. Review this book.

Book reviews are incredibly valuable for debut authors like myself. Even a short review would give my book some visibility, and encourage other potential readers to take a chance on a new author.

Leaving a book review is easy and doesn't take a lot of time. For a quick primer on how to write a book review, visit this page on my author website:

http://dankoboldt.com/reviews

You'll also find direct links to Amazon, Barnes & Noble, Goodreads, and other sites where you can review *The Rogue Retrieval*.

2. Join my mailing list.

If you'd like to hear about my future books, blog posts, and author events, please consider joining my e-mail list. This is the best way for us to keep in touch, and I promise not to spam you (or share your information). If you join the "Readers and Fans" list, I'll even throw in some bonus content from the world of *The Rogue Retrieval*. Sign up here:

http://dankoboldt.com/subscribe

3. Tell your friends.

It might seem like a small thing, but recommending my book to a friend or coworker could make a huge difference. Nothing's more powerful than word of mouth.

It means so much to me that you took the time to read my book. Thank you again!

Sincerely,
Dan Koboldt
October 2015

ACKNOWLEDGMENTS

This book would never have been possible without the efforts of many people. I'd like to thank my wife, Christina, for her endless support. She and our little ones (Audrey, Elliott, and Sam) somehow tolerate my writing obsession, which takes me away far too often.

Special thanks to my critique partners—Dannie Morin, Eric Primm, Gina Denny, and Kate Mayrose—who helped me get this book into shape. I'm also lucky to have friends like Diana Urban, Tex Thompson, Shana Silver, and Michelle Hauck, to keep me sane along the way.

I'm grateful to my agent, Jennie Goloboy, for believing in me and serving as my coolheaded career adviser. I'd like to thank my editor, David Pomerico, for acquiring my book and helping it reach its full potential. Rebecca Lucash, Christine Langone, Caroline Perny, and the rest of the team at Harper Voyager have been fantastic. Thank you!

Last but not least, I'm thankful for my writing groups and communities: Codex Writers, The Clubhouse, the Pitch Wars community, WashU Fiction, and Impulse Authors Unite! Writing is a solitary profession, but because of them, I've never felt alone.

ABOUT THE AUTHOR

Dan Koboldt is a genetics researcher and fantasy/science fiction author. He has coauthored more than sixty publications in *Nature*, *Human Mutation*, *Genome Research*, *The New England Journal of Medicine*, *Cell*, and other scientific journals. Dan is also an avid hunter and outdoorsman. He lives with his wife and children in St. Louis, where the deer take their revenge by eating the flowers in his backyard.

The Rogue Retrieval is his first novel. You can find him online at http://dankoboldt.com/ and on Twitter at https://twitter.com/DanKoboldt.

Discover great authors, exclusive offers, and more at hc.com.